DEFIANCE

DATE DUE

MAR 1 5 2007		
APR 3 0 2007		
MAR 0 4 2015		

DEMCO 38-297

Books by Don Brown

The Navy Justice Series
Treason
Hostage
Defiance

BOOK THREE

DON BROWN

THE NAVY
JUSTICE SERIES

DEFIANCE

ZONDERVAN®

ZONDERVAN.com/
AUTHORTRACKER
follow your favorite authors

Three ways to keep up on your favorite
Zondervan books and authors

Sign up for our *Fiction E-Newsletter*. Every month you'll receive sample excerpts from our books, sneak peeks at upcoming books, and chances to win free books autographed by the author.

You can also sign up for our *Breakfast Club*. Every morning in your email, you'll receive a five-minute snippet from a fiction or nonfiction book. A new book will be featured each week, and by the end of the week you will have sampled two to three chapters of the book.

Zondervan *Author Tracker* is the best way to be notified whenever your favorite Zondervan authors write new books, go on tour, or want to tell you about what's happening in their lives.

Visit *www.zondervan.com* and sign up today!

 ZONDERVAN®

Defiance
Copyright © 2007 by Don Brown

Requests for information should be addressed to:
Zondervan, *Grand Rapids, Michigan* 49530

Library of Congress Cataloging-in-Publication Data

Brown, Don, 1960–
    Defiance / Don Brown.
        p. cm. — (Navy justice series ; bk. 3)
    ISBN-10: 0-310-27213-0
    ISBN-13: 978-0-310-27213-7
    1. Brewer, Zack (Ficticious character) 2. United States. Navy—Fiction.
  3. Courts-martial and courts of inquiry — Fiction. 4. Terrorism — Fiction.
  5. Kidnapping victims — Fiction. I. Title.
  PS3602.R6947D44 2006
  813'.6 — dc22

        2006034921

Interior design by Michelle Espinoza

Printed in the United States of America

---

07 08 09 10 11 12 • 23 22 21 20 19 18 17 16 15 14 13 12 11 10 9 8 7 6 5 4 3 2 1

This novel is lovingly dedicated to
Judy and Mark Angel of Charlotte, North Carolina,
and
Crystal and Jeff Lettow of San Diego, California

"There is a friend who sticks closer than a brother."
Proverbs 18:24

From the mission statement of the
Naval Criminal Investigative Service (NCIS):
The Combating Terrorism Directorate directs NCIS support
for efforts aimed at detecting, deterring, and disrupting terrorism
against Department of Navy personnel and assets worldwide.

PROLOGUE

Gobi Desert
Southeast of Ulaanbaatar, Mongolia

The light.

Her eyes followed the light.

If the sun still rose, if it traced its way across the sky, if it forced a small ray through the pinhole in the wall of a tent, across a cold, barren floor in the middle of nowhere, then surely God was still in control.

Wasn't he?

The light, even such a small ray, proved it was so.

She remembered places of bright sunlight—the ports where she once served her country.

Pearl Harbor.

Key West.

San Diego.

Were these great ports of call still in existence?

Did the gray warships of the American fleet still sail from these navy towns? Did cool, salty breezes still roll off the oceans, breathing life into Old Glory?

Did naval officers and enlisted men and women, dressed smartly in white, still stop in their tracks every morning under sun-spangled palm trees to salute as the national anthem echoed all over the bases of the U.S. Navy? Did they stop again at sunset, coming to attention as the flag came down?

Lying in a fetal position on the floor in the corner of the tent, she felt tears slide from her eyes. She was surprised she had any tears left to cry, but here they were, turning into a silent, sob-wracked torrent.

Still curled on her side, she swiped at her wet face with her fingers; her tears dripped from her cheek and chin to the floor, just shy of a small patch of sunlight.

She opened her eyes.

The sunbeam inched closer to the far corner of the tent. When the beam reached the corner of the tent, he would come.

He always came.

Moisture gathered in her palms. Sweat beaded on her forehead.

For months she prayed that he would forget her, that he would leave her alone. Why had God ignored her prayers?

She knew what came next. Her heart jackhammered inside her chest.

She shut her eyes again, squeezed them tight.

Sweet memories of home danced in her mind, memories of the Bible on the coffee table when she was a girl.

Thanks to her mother, she memorized a few verses. Those verses lived somewhere in the shadows of her memory.

She spoke silently.

Perhaps God still listened. Perhaps not. But just in case ...

"Yea, though I walk through the valley of the shadow of death, I will fear no evil ..."

The sound of his footsteps cut through the walls of the tent.

"For thou art with me ..."

"Prepare yourself, my infidel," he called in broken English.

"Thy rod and thy staff ..."

"I come for you."

"They comfort me."

Hyperventilation gripped her body. Her breathing constricted. Her chest thumped violently. Brief, disconnected thoughts whirled through her brain.

The door of the tent flew open. It was him.

"Jesus, help me!"

CHAPTER 1

L'office de droit de Jean-Claude la Trec
56, rue Charles de Gaulle
Paris

10:00 p.m.

The door exploded in a shower of glass.

Three black-masked bandits rushed in from the night.

Slinging their Uzis across his desk, they jammed steel gun barrels into his cheek, grinding his lips into his teeth. Jets of pain shot through his jaw. Violent shaking took possession of his body. Liquid soaked his pants—perhaps spilled pinot noir dripping from the desktop—or a bladder rendered useless by fear. He could not tell.

Jean-Claude la Trec, the great avocat of France, the man whose golden voice enraptured the media and earned him the title "the most magnificent lawyer in all of Europe," cried out in a pitiful, helpless whine.

"*M'aider Dieu.*" God, help me.

"What is this?" A jarring punch bloodied his lip. "The great Jean-Claude la Trec, a self-avowed atheist, cries to God for help? Allah has nothing to do with this." A sharp backhand bashed into his cheek. "We had a deal!"

"Who are you?"

"Does thirty million dollars say who we are?"

"But—"

"You demanded *thirty million* U.S. dollars to defend these pilots. You promised *victoire*, and one of them cuts a deal with the U.S. Navy!"

"That was not my idea—"

"Shut up!" A gun stock smashed his jaw. Sharp pain pounded the back of his skull.

"What information was compromised?"

"None. I assure you."

"Liar!" The accents blended. French and Arabic.

"*S'il vous plâit.*" A slight burst of energy. "Nothing was compromised. *S'il vous plâit.*" Fighting for his life, his great advocacy skills flickered, then flamed. "They murdered one pilot before the trial ended. The other did not receive the death penalty." His voice gained strength. "*S'il vous plâit.*"

"You promised victory!" a third voice cried.

"We did everything!"

"*Victoire!*"

"But the great Wells Levinson lost to Brewer. You never busted into his office with machine guns."

"Silence!" A fist from the dark crushed his lower front teeth. Blood gushed. The overhead chandelier whirled, and he crashed to the floor. "We paid Levinson half what we paid you ..."

A high-pitched band saw hummed in his ears. Voices faded in and out. He reached in his pants pocket, feeling for the number *trois* on his cell phone. The phone slipped out of his pocket and dropped onto the floor.

"... and *at least* Levinson's clients were executed." He referred to a U.S. Navy court-martial that had taken place in San Diego, involving the trial of three navy chaplains for treason. The three had been prosecuted by LCDR Zack Brewer, the famous Navy JAG officer, and defended by Wells Levinson, regarded as America's preeminent defense attorney. All three were convicted and executed by the U.S. military.

Jeanette stood just outside the front of the old stone office building on rue Charles de Gaulle, hailing a taxi, when an electronically synthesized rendition of "La Marseilles" chirped from inside her purse.

Jean-Claude's final overture for the evening.

She smiled at the thought, then waved off a slowing cab and reached for her cellular. The caller ID flashed a picture of her handsome, silver-haired employer.

"Bonsoir," she said in a soft voice.

"Of course they were executed!" An angry voice boomed through her cell phone. "Levinson's clients can no longer talk. But *your* client is in the hands of the Americans. Ready to betray our organization."

Jeanette looked over her shoulder at the light coming from the second-floor office window. From this angle on the street, she could see no one.

"This was not my idea." Jean-Claude's voice trembled. "I urged him not to talk. He was *your* recruit. Perhaps you should have been more selective when you recruited him."

"Shut up!" The sound of shattering glass pierced her eardrums. "Produce the file, and tell us where we can find the witch lawyer."

Mon Dieu.

"Please!" The thud of a punch and more shattering glass. "Lower left drawer ... The file ..."

"Pierre!"

"Bien sûr!"

The sound of rustling papers.

"Where's the witch, L'Enfant?"

"Who?"

A sharp thud was followed by a tortuous grunt. "Where is the traitor to Islam and to France who orchestrated this so-called plea bargain?"

Run, her mind commanded. But her legs froze.

"S'il vous plaît. She is not here. She is not in France."

"Liar!" She heard a thud, fist against flesh. This was followed by a moan, then heavy, desperate breathing. "We saw her enter the building."

"She's gone." Jean-Claude wheezed heavily as if short of air. "Please."

"The file, Ramon! I have it!"

"You have the file. Please," Jean-Claude pleaded.

"Pierre." An Arab-accented voice spoke in French. "Please express the official gratitude of the French government and the Council of Ishmael for Monsieur la Trec's performance in the *Quasay* court-martial."

"Avec plaisir, monsieur."

The burst of machine-gun fire rattled her eardrums. She yanked the phone away.

Dear Jesus. This was her first prayer in years. Her heart hammered. She craned her neck, gazing up at the window. She brought the phone back to her ear. Cars whizzed by just a few meters away.

"Check him!"

"He's dead."

Non. S'il vous plâit.

"Take the file. Find L'Enfant!"

"Abdur."

"What is it?"

"His cell phone!"

The connection dropped.

"Look! Down on the street. It is her!"

Jeannette quickly slipped off her high heels and sprinted down the sidewalk alongside rue Charles De Gaulle, toward the Arc de Triomphe. She ducked into the first dark alleyway and kept running.

CHAPTER 2

B. Dalton Bookseller
Level 4, Horton Plaza
Just outside Gaslamp Quarter
San Diego, California

1:30 p.m. (PST)

Chris Reynolds sat alone at a table in the refreshments section of the B. Dalton Bookseller in downtown San Diego's chic Horton Plaza. His latte had faded to lukewarm more than thirty minutes ago, but he abandoned his position in the refill line when his gaze caught the magazine rack beside the condiments table.

People magazine featured the smiling photo of the naval officer in summer whites. The headline above it asked "Where Is He Now?" with a subtitle that instructed the reader to turn to page 38. He stepped to the magazine rack, snatched a copy, and returned to the table.

He quickly flipped to the page.

More than a year has passed since Lieutenant Commander Zack Brewer, USN, prosecuted Lieutenant Commander Mohammed Quasay, the Islamic U.S. Navy aviator accused of launching a rogue missile attack that destroyed Jerusalem's Dome of the Rock. The court-martial, the third prosecuted by Brewer that garnered international attention, followed the disappearance of Brewer's alleged girlfriend, Lieutenant Diane Colcernian, a Navy JAG officer kidnapped by Islamic extremists. Colcernian is believed to be dead.

The picture of the smiling redheaded woman in her service dress blue uniform was under Brewer's. He swigged cold coffee.

Brewer, who, during the course of his incredible winning streak, surprised many pundits by besting two of the world's best-known defense attorneys, American Wellington Levinson and Frenchman Jean-Claude la Trec, has by all accounts returned to life as a normal naval officer.

Despite his brilliance before the international media, Brewer prefers anonymity. The JAG officer declined an opportunity to resign from the navy and run for a congressional seat in Louisiana. Brewer was the hand-picked candidate of U.S. Senator Roberson Fowler and the strong front runner had he entered the race. Afterward, he refused millions from book contracts, opting to stay in the navy.

After refusing Fowler, Brewer returned to San Diego to finish his tour of duty. The man lauded by the president of the United States and called "America's most eligible bachelor" has refused all press inquiries since the *Quasay* court-martial.

Since Colcernian's disappearance, romantic speculation has linked Brewer to two women. The JAG officer has been spotted at dinner with Shannon McGillvery, the NCIS agent credited with cracking the *Quasay* court-martial. But oddsmakers speculate his new interest may be the lovely Wendy Poole, the blonde JAG officer who represented the navy before the Supreme Court. Poole argued for the execution of the three chaplains Brewer and Colcernian prosecuted for treason.

Chris slammed the magazine closed and stood, leaving it on the table. What a spineless ideological nomad! Brewer had a chance to run for Congress. What an idiot! *Control yourself, Chris.* He got back in the refill line and watched the clerk pour a stream of steaming black replenishment into his cup. More *hot* caffeine. The latte oozed down his throat. *Better.*

A deep breath.

Then another.

He reopened the magazine.

Later, after Colcernian's disappearance, Poole teamed with Brewer in the Quasay prosecution against la Trec. When a navy jury convicted Quasay of murder for launching the missile attack against the Dome, the government sought the death penalty. But in a strange course of events, Quasay announced to the military judge his desire to fire la Trec and hire his associate attorney, Jeanette L'Enfant. The motion was granted, and L'Enfant negotiated a life imprisonment term with Brewer, presumably in exchange for information.

It is unclear what, if any, information the United States gleaned from the last-minute "life-for-information" plea bargain. The Pentagon remains mum on the subject. Just as mysterious—Brewer's self-imposed disappearance from the public limelight. As tabloids drool for information on his personal life, Brewer seems content secluded behind the walls of the 32nd Street Naval Station, where the press can't reach him. Except for occasional forays out to dinner with either Wendy Poole or Shannon McGillvery, Brewer hides from the camera, leaving curiosity seekers to feast on rumor. Speaking of which, the latest Brewer rumor has America's most available naval officer headed to an aircraft carrier next year.

Where better could the publicity-shy Brewer seclude himself from the press? But is this true? Will the hero of the *Olajuwon* and *Quasay* courts-martial soon sail the seven seas? Or will he reconsider Senator Fowler's offer and get involved in the senator's presidential campaign?

With Fowler in a tight race against Vermont Senator Eleanor Claxton for this year's Democrat nomination, rumors are again flying around Washington that Brewer may accept a high-level position in the campaign, where his presence could help Fowler defeat Claxton in several primary battleground states in the South, where moderate and even a few conservative Democrats tend to outnumber liberals in the northeast and western states. Brewer has reiterated his disdain for politics, but the rumored trade-off in this case—a possible nomination as Attorney General of the United States—may be too sweet a carrot to keep Brewer in his beloved United States Navy.

"We'll see about that," Chris mumbled to himself. "If this naval pretty boy thinks he can quit the navy and help swing that Neanderthal oaf Roberson 'Pinkie' Fowler into the White House, he's got another thing coming."

"You said something, sir?" asked the cute brunette working behind the cash register just a few feet away.

"No, nothing—" frowning, he returned to the article. He flipped a few pages, away from the Brewer garbage, and saw her picture. Her photogenic smile electrified him.

Eleanor Claxton would become the first woman president of the United States. And his destiny was to be a part of her election.

He would stand near her at the presidential podium next January for her oath of office. She would raise her right hand, and rather than placing her left hand on the Bible, that antiquated book of bigotry, she would place her hand on the U.S. Constitution and vow to preserve, protect, and defend it.

The thought of it! Eleanor renouncing the Bible for the Constitution, eliminating that offensive phrase at the end of the presidential oath, "so help me God."

During her oath, their eyes would meet as she placed her hand on the Constitution. She would smile at him, acknowledging his vital role in her new administration. This administration would change history. And he would be there with her.

Forget that they had never met.

Soon they would.

He would prove himself to her.

Nothing could stop them.

Not Brewer.

Not anyone.

Rue Charles de Gaulle
Paris

Sometime before midnight

Jeanette ducked into a small alleyway between Votre Jupe, an upscale skirt shop, and La Maison du Vin, a popular wine-tasting hangout. She prayed they hadn't seen her.

The alley was pitch-dark. The odors of fermented wine and rotting garbage hung in the air. She squinted, searching for her bearings. She scurried deeper into the alleyway, away from light cast from the street. Something sliced her foot. She reached down and felt warm blood.

Five minutes passed.

Then ten.

The sound of French police cars—their sirens blaring middle C, then F, then middle C, then F—grew louder. Perhaps someone had heard the burst of machine-gun fire and called. Perhaps she was a suspect in the murder of Jean-Claude.

A scampering across her foot. She reached down. Something furry squealed.

A rat! *Dear God, help me.* A chorus of rodent-like squealing rose from the blackness around her feet. A nest of them! She suppressed the urge to scream. She gritted her teeth. She would live with the rats or die.

Cars zoomed by on rue Charles de Gaulle, their headlights painting bright horizontal streaks in the dark.

The killers would reach her position in a moment, she calculated. Silhouettes of two men jogged past the entrance of the alley. They ran from right to left. From the direction of Jean-Claude's offices.

It was them.

It had to be.

She turned away from the boulevard and crept deeper into the alley, feeling for a way out the back. She paced one foot in front of the other, holding her breath. Ten paces later, she felt the brick wall. There was no way out, except back on the street.

The sounds of the police sirens faded in the distance.

A third black-clad man appeared from the right. He stopped at the entrance of the alleyway. He peered into the alleyway, the whites of his eyes glowing like the full moon.

She felt the cool, aluminum lid of a garbage can just to her left. She reached into the trash can. She felt the glass curvature of an empty bottle.

She slipped down onto the ground, sandwiching herself between the trash can and the brick wall. Curling her body into a ball, she waited, prayed that the rats and the man would disappear into the streets, and clutched the bottle.

A beam from the pursuer's flashlight flooded the alley. Shadows danced across the filthy concrete as his footsteps grew near.

Click, click, click … The sound of his shoes echoed off the brick walls. *Click, click, click.*

Silence. His spotlight flooded the trash can. She froze against the brick wall, hiding in the shadowy eclipse.

Click, click, click. The edge of the flashlight protruded just beyond the trash can, shining light into the back of the closed alley.

Maintenant!

She sprung at him, swinging the bottle at the silhouette of his head. Smashing glass reverberated off the brick walls of the alley. Blood gushed from her hand. The flashlight bounced off the concrete, then went black. His silhouette staggered in the moonlight, first to the left, then to the right, then down to the concrete.

She reached for the flashlight. As she fidgeted with the switch, the beam sputtered, then intensified. The man's features were Arabic. Blood gushed from a cut over his ear. A bruise on his temple protruded just above that. She searched him for identification. Nothing. Only a pistol wedged under his belt.

He moaned and moved.

She thrust the jagged bottleneck into his Adam's apple. He flinched. Blood spewed from his neck. *Mon Dieu, what have I done?*

She had to escape. But the street was too risky. She swirled the flashlight up and around the back of the alley. There was an open window, in the building housing La Maison du Vin.

If she could move the trash can into place below it, then maybe ... just maybe ... She climbed onto the trash can. Reaching for the ledge, she pulled herself through the window and tumbled into darkness.

She landed in some sort of storage room. She killed the flashlight and tiptoed to the closed door. Music, muffled conversation, and the sound of clinking glass flowed from an adjacent room.

She gripped the doorknob, cracking the door into a dimly lit back hallway.

A dozen or so swankily clad couples in the room to the left sipped wine and laughed, paying no attention to the direction of her temporary refuge. The hallway was empty.

Perhaps she could mingle with the crowd as she slipped to the front door. But what if they were still out on the streets? She had no option but to exit from the rear of the building.

She tiptoed into the hallway toward the back exit. A woman's eyes caught hers. She sipped her wine and then turned back to her companions.

Jeanette stepped into the night. No one seemed to notice.

CHAPTER 3

As the sun descended over the aqua waters of San Diego Bay, wavelets reflected its light, sparkling like a thousand multicolored jewels. With the mighty aircraft carrier USS *Dwight D. Eisenhower* moored just across the bay at Naval Air Station North Island, Shannon McGillvery rounded the last bend along southbound North Harbor Drive.

Stretching her legs to a gazelle-like pace for the final two-mile stretch of her late-afternoon waterfront run, she glanced at her stopwatch. She had maintained an eight-minute pace for the first four and a half miles.

Good.

So far.

Now was decision time.

To sprint or not to sprint. That was the question.

She *should* push it for the last couple of miles. After all, San Diego's annual Rock 'n' Roll Marathon was fewer than sixty days away. And Shannon was determined to finish in less than three and a half hours. And in doing so, she would kick the derrieres of a couple of obnoxious, chauvinistic SEAL buddies from Coronado who were giving her some lip.

"Law enforcement is a man's game," they boasted last Saturday night at the North Island Officer's Club. "Plus, women weren't designed for the military."

Of course their ribbing was all in good jest.

When she, in equally good jest, flashed her badge as a special agent of the Naval Criminal Investigative Service and threatened to arrest them for harassing a federal officer, she grinned just enough to make them wonder if she was serious or joking. Then she watched them swig their beers and concede that women make better NCIS agents.

But the SEALs, they boasted, were the world's greatest athletes.

They were probably right about that. But she would *never* concede, at least not publicly, that she agreed with anything they said.

Shannon McGillvery, a good Irish-Catholic girl from Chestnut Hill, Massachusetts—via Boston College—wasn't about to concede that Lieutenants Jeremy Bevins and Brad Miller were athletically superior to anyone—especially not a Boston College coed who had gone to school on a women's field hockey scholarship.

"Your money where your mouth is, guys," she said, folding her badge back into her purse. "The Rock 'n' Roll Marathon. Three months. Be there. Watch this five-foot-five Catholic girl leave both of you buffoons in the dirt."

They cackled and slopped their beer. But their special-warfare, supersized male egos would not allow them to ignore her challenge.

"Fifty bucks says you can't crack four hours, pretty lady," Lieutenant Bevins snarled, then flexed a huge bicep as he curled a bottle of Corona to his lips.

"I don't bet, Lieutenant," she said. "Against navy regs." That brought more guffaws. "But I *do* kick butt. And if I *were* a betting woman—one hundred fifty bucks says that I leave both of you in the afterburners … *and* crack three and a half hours."

"I *love* a pretty lady with a huge ego," Lieutenant Bevins shot back through a thick Texan drawl. "Let's make this *real* interesting—" He snapped his fingers for another Corona.

She drew closer to him and peered into his sparkling bloodshot blue eyes. "Yeah? And how do you propose that, Lieutenant Rawhide?"

"Here's the deal, Special Agent McGillvery." A smile formed on his rugged face. "Unless you beat me in the Rock 'n' Roll"—a gulp from the next Corona bottle—"I get to take you out on a date." Laughter cascaded from the grunting chorus of Bevins's SEAL shipmates now gathering around.

"Don't think I need to worry about that, Tex."

"Ooohhh," jeered half of SEAL platoon Bravo.

"And if you beat me," Bevins said, "you arrest me for harassing a federal agent?"

Howls and the clanking of bottles.

"Deal," she snapped. Then she'd shaken his hand and scooted out into the night.

Why?

Why couldn't she resist the urge to challenge arrogant chauvinism?

Why get roped into this? She raced into the setting sun and crisp breeze, passing the *Star of India*, the clipper ship permanently moored in San Diego Bay, on her right. It wasn't as though she had any particular romantic inclination toward the world's deadliest warriors.

Sporting a fourth-degree black belt herself, the SEALs' Rambo mystique didn't impress her the way it did other women. Sure, Lieutenant Rawhide Bevins was downright handsome. But date him?

Nah.

Her sights were on another naval officer. More of an intellectual type. A JAG officer, in fact.

But whom could she tell of her interest in Zack Brewer? He'd never gotten over Diane Colcernian. Or so she suspected. Besides, she'd rarely seen him in the months that had passed since the *Quasay* prosecution. And despite the talk on the streets, he'd never shown any real interest in her.

Zack was every woman's dream, she decided as she turned left at the base of the Broadway Pier. Leaving the gorgeous San Diego waterfront behind her, she increased her pace. She'd maintain a six-and-a-half-minute pace for the last couple of miles. She had to push it. Anything to whip Lieutenant Rawhide.

Minutes later, panting in a controlled fury, Shannon sprinted past NCIS headquarters at A Street and Sixth Avenue. Slowing her pace to a jog, then a slow walk, Shannon checked the black Olympia Sports stopwatch on her left wrist.

Good. A sub-eight-minute pace for the ten-kilometer jaunt along the waterfront and through the downtown area of "America's finest city," as the locals called San Diego. To finish at less than three and a half hours, and keep Rawhide off her back, she would need to hold an eight-minute pace over the course of the twenty-six-mile run. *Doable,* she thought, hands on hips, elbows akimbo, as she headed toward the shower in the NCIS locker room. *Tough but doable.*

Exhaling, she walked into the entrance of NCIS Southwest Field Office and flashed the ID card that hung around her neck.

"McGillvery!" It was the gruff voice of the special agent in charge — SAC — of NCIS Southwest, Barry MacGregor, booming from just inside the security checkpoint.

The potbellied New Yorker, his federal agent's badge clipped to one side of his belt, wore a nine-millimeter Beretta holstered on the other side. Sporting a white golf shirt with slightly-too-tight khaki slacks, the ruddy-faced MacGregor had that *I've got a job for you* look on his face.

"Why do I get the feeling that I'm not going to just go inside and shower and then drive home for a quiet dinner tonight?"

"Love your instincts, Shannon." He tossed her a towel. "That's why you're my best field agent."

"What's up, Barry?" She swiped the towel across her forehead. "Another drug bust on the Amphib base?"

"It's Brewer."

She choked on her bottled water. "*Zack* Brewer?"

"One and the same," the SAC said.

"So what's up with him?" She tossed the towel back at him.

"NCIS Command thinks there's a heightened threat to his safety. So does the FBI." He waved her past the security checkpoint, then walked with her down the familiar antiseptic hallway toward his office.

"What threat?" She followed him into the office.

"Listen, we're getting intel out of Europe that there's been a shooting. Tied to the *Quasay* court-martial."

"A shooting? Who?"

"That French lawyer, la Trec. Just a few hours ago, according to our intel."

"Not good. Anything else?"

"Yep. More death threats to Zack. Spawned from that *People* magazine article."

"I was afraid of that." She polished off the bottled water. "Suspects?"

"Not yet. Usual crackpot stuff. Probably nothing. But we've gotta respond."

"What can I do?"

"Hit the shower. Then get to the helo pad at North Island. Zack's gonna meet you there. Then don't let him out of your sight until I say so. Got it?"

"Got it."

CHAPTER 4

Pacific Ocean
Two miles east of Point Loma
San Diego County, California

Saturday, 5:30 p.m. (PST)

Lieutenant Commander Zack Brewer, in orange swim trunks and tanned from his recent leave in Hawaii, turned the Sunfish into the breeze. He tugged on the jib line and yelled, "Duck!" The aluminum boom swung around the aft of the boat.

Zack's companion, a well-figured blonde in a royal blue one-piece, dropped down, squealing as the sail swung over. She dove for the tiller as salt water sprayed over the bow. He already had hold of it and laughed as she wrestled him for control.

Zack glanced into her Ray-Bans and saw the reflection of his face. He was surprised, almost stunned, to glimpse his joyful expression mirrored in the glasses. After mourning the loss of Diane for so long, he thought he'd never smile again.

But now this.

Another whitecap drenched them with cool Pacific water, and Wendy shrieked with delight.

"You're going to get us capsized, Wendy!"

"But I'm a sailor!" She laughed again, the tiller still firmly in her hands.

"You're a Navy JAG officer!" He splashed salt water in her face. "You know as much about sailing as I know about flying an F-18."

She pushed him playfully. "Oh? And I'm supposed to trust *your* navigational abilities?" A white smile flashed across her face. "You think you're Popeye the Sailor Man?" She stroked his chin. "How did I talk you into this, anyway?"

Another wave sprayed the boat, sloshing them with cool water. "You talked me into it because you're crazy." He laughed. "We never should've sailed out here in the ocean! We're too far out."

More water sprayed over the gunnels. More laughter. They abandoned their playful fight over the tiller. The rudder could flap in the wind if it wanted.

★

"What's the matter, Zack?"

"Nothing." He released her from his arms. The bulb nose of a *Los Angeles* class submarine broke the surface about a half mile across the rolling swells of the Pacific.

"Don't lie to me." She rested her hand on his shoulder. "I see that faraway look in those eyes."

He looked away. "I'm not ready for a relationship." He met her eyes. "Not yet."

"Zack, it's been almost eighteen months." She combed her fingers through his wet hair. "I know you keep hoping. We all do. But they found her DNA in that cave in Afghanistan. It was *her* hair. There was mortar fire. Nobody could have survived that avalanche."

"But there was no body."

"I know."

He gazed west over the expanse of water. Somewhere beyond the horizon was Hawaii, then the Philippines, then Indonesia, and beyond that, the Indian subcontinent, then Pakistan, then Afghanistan. And maybe . . .

His cell phone chirped.

"Do you have to answer that?"

"Depends." He reached into the gym bag and saw the name Captain Glen Rudy on the digital screen of his cellular. "Sorry. It's the skipper."

"You *promised* we'd sail out of range."

"I tried." He gave her a wink, which brought a smile from her. "Yes, sir, Skipper."

"Zack, sorry to interrupt your Saturday sail," said Captain Glen Rudy, JAGC, USN, the commanding officer of Navy Trial Command San Diego.

"We're coming in anyway, sir."

"Liar." Wendy patted his knee.

"Two things, Zack. First, the SEALs have a speedy trial problem I need you to take care of."

"You're kidding, sir," Zack said. "America's finest special-warfare warriors neglecting the rules and regulations of the military justice system?"

"Who'd have thunk it?" Rudy chuckled.

"How bad?"

"They've had an ensign in confinement for eighty-five days. You know the drill, Zack. Another five days in the brig and he walks."

"Roger, Skipper," Zack said. "And any navy prosecutor who loses a speedy trial case gets treated like a captain who runs an aircraft carrier into a sandbar—a court-martial sandwich for lunch."

"Sorry, Zack," Rudy said, "but you're the only trial counsel I've got who can pull this off. Admiral's on my can."

"Yes, sir. In other words, sail into port on a Saturday, get the file, read the file, find the witnesses, subpoena the witnesses, then go to trial by Monday and hand the SEALs their conviction on a silver platter."

"The SEALs have supreme confidence in you. Besides, this is a cupcake compared to *Olajuwon* and *Quasay*. Not a single reporter should show up. I guarantee that."

"That's a relief," Zack sighed. "So did our boy do it, Skipper?"

"Can't talk about it now. Let's just say the SEALs aren't too happy with this guy."

Zack rolled his eyes. "I'm surprised the SEALs didn't kill him."

"They almost did. That's why we have a speedy trial problem. He's been at Balboa Naval Hospital recovering from a broken arm and collarbone."

Zack snickered. "Why am I not surprised?"

"Anyway," Rudy continued, "Captain Noble called saying they want to prosecute this guy and he's been in solitary confinement at Balboa for eighty-some-odd days."

"Our old friend Captain *Buck* Noble from the *Blount* court-martial?" Zack was referring to the court-martial of *United States v. BT3 (SEAL) Antonio Blount*, a high-profile case Zack had prosecuted involving a Navy SEAL who was accused of raping a young naval officer who happened to be the niece of a powerful United States senator.

"That's him. Now the skipper of SEAL Team 3," Rudy said. The Sunfish dipped in a rolling swell. "He wants you to handle this case."

"And the admiral said yes, of course." Zack smirked at Wendy.

"What can I say? You're a victim of your own popularity, Zack."

"Okay, Skipper. We're getting a little too far out in the ocean for a Sunfish anyway. Wendy can talk me into some crazy things, sir." That comment brought an alluring smile and another splash of cool salt water from Wendy. "Anyway, I'm turning this baby east right now." He wedged his cell phone under his chin. "Raising the jib as we speak, Skipper."

"Forget the jib, Zack. Your ride should be coming in at about ninety degrees right about now. Can you see North Island from where you are?"

Zack looked to the southeast, across a mile of rolling Pacific water and to the right.

Two dragonflies danced in the distance over the middle of the entrance of San Diego Bay. But dragonflies don't spew black smoke from their tails, nor do they emit the cacophonous staccato of rotor blades.

"Skipper, I've got two inbound Seahawks in sight." He was referring to the SR-60B Seahawk helicopters. "They wouldn't be headed this way, would they?"

"Commander, you have a way of running up an expensive cab fare for the government. Get ready to swing through the air on a line at a hundred feet over the ocean."

Great. Zack gulped. The press had described him as a model naval officer and as a fearless, swashbuckling trial lawyer. But when it came to heights, Lieutenant Commander Zack Brewer, JAGC, USN, was anything but swashbuckling. Dangling from a narrow rope over the ocean from the belly of a helicopter? Not what the recruiter promised he'd be doing as a JAG officer.

The dragonflies in the sky became dragonflies in his stomach. The sonorous blips grew into gray-hued navy helicopters, their approaching rotor noise drowning out Rudy's voice.

"We'll be home in a few minutes, Skipper," Zack yelled over the sound of the twin engines now hovering over the boat.

Zack craned his neck back. A rope was being lowered from one of the helicopters, dangling like a long, squirming snake in the Pacific wind.

"Ladies first," he said.

"This is so much fun!" Wendy grinned. The strands of her blonde hair blew back as if she were a model standing in front of a fan.

She started to strap herself into the harness, but stopped when a voice boomed from the hovering helicopter. "Hang on, ma'am. We're coming to help you."

Three rubber-suited frogmen leaped from the helicopter. They dropped feet-first into the ocean on each side of the boat. A moment later they swarmed the Sunfish, barking instructions to Wendy about tightening her harness. Three minutes later, she dangled in the air, giggling and waving, as the chopper hoisted her up and away.

When they pulled her into the chopper, a second rope and harness slinked down through the wind.

"You okay, sir?" One of the frogmen hung on to the gunnels of the Sunfish.

"Great, Petty Officer." *Is it that obvious?*

"Okay, sir," the frogman said. "Just slip your arms through the harness and pull the cord."

"Like that?"

"Looks good, sir. Ready?"

"Ready."

The frogman looked up, gave a big thumbs-up. And then ... *Wooaahhh* ... Zack dangled like a spider from its web over the Pacific. He looked down. The Sunfish and the frogmen were specs in the water, vacillating from left to right.

"Just look up, Commander," one of them yelled. A gust of cool air blew him to the left — "Whoa, Nellie" — and then to the right.

When they had pulled him halfway between the ocean surface and the hovering Seahawk, the winch stopped.

"What's the deal?" he yelled.

"Hang on, Commander." A voice blasted from the Seahawk's loudspeakers. "Little problem here."

"Great."

A minute passed. Then two. *Not good.*

"Commander! The winch is stuck. Hang on, sir!"

Zack swung like a pendulum.

"Gonna fly you over to North Island and set you down real easy, sir. You'll be fine."

The nose of the chopper dipped. Zack careened wildly underneath. The pilot turned toward Point Loma. Zack bobbed and weaved in the wind on the rope about fifty feet below the helicopter.

The rolling waves of the Pacific, bathed in the orange glow of the setting western sun, blurred under his feet. He wanted to vomit, but the cool wind whipping across his face prevented it.

The chopper rushed toward the large, jutting, mountainous land mass that was Point Loma.

The pilot looped to the right. Zack slalomed in the air in a wide loop behind, following the chopper over the magnificent white cross at the tip of Point Loma. A dozen visitors at the observation platform under the cross pointed up. Zack was a bird ... a plane ...

Above the entrance to San Diego Bay, over the bottleneck separating Point Loma from Coronado, he saw a *Ticonderoga* class cruiser split the bay wide open, headed to sea. Sailors on the fantail pointed upward.

He was Superman.

His stomach leaped into his throat as the pilot descended. A moment later he dangled over the helicopter pad, inching down to the concrete.

Then his bare feet touched the warm concrete.

The things I do for God and country.

Three enlisted men, aviation types, rushed to him, unleashing him from his harness. One gave a thumbs-up, and the chopper, with Wendy still aboard, ascended and then flew across the base, disappearing from sight.

A white staff car drove onto the tarmac and stopped just in front of where he stood. Its driver emerged. She smiled, scooted up onto the hood, and crossed her arms. "Your suntan seems to have faded a bit, Zack," Shannon McGillvery teased.

"Shannon! Now I get it. This winch thing was a planned event, right?"

"I'll never tell." She laughed, then hopped off the hood, reached in the car and grabbed a towel, and flipped it to him.

Four more white cars drove out onto the tarmac. Eight hulks, with close-cropped hair and wearing dark blue blazers and reflective sunglasses, emerged. They drew their sidearms and surrounded Zack and Shannon.

"What? I'm being arrested?" Zach wrapped the towel around his waist.

"You're being protected, Zack." Shannon handed him a T-shirt from the backseat of the car. "We're not letting you out of sight until this Jeanette L'Enfant thing gets sorted out."

"What Jeanette L'Enfant thing?"

She explained.

"Come on, Shannon. That's France. We're in America."

"Zack." Her voice hardened. "NCIS thinks that this could be related to the Council of Ishmael and that you and Wendy could be in danger." She paused, meeting his eyes. "Remember, they came to America and grabbed Diane. They could be operating in San Diego."

The reminder of Diane's kidnapping hurt. But Shannon was right.

"So that explains the chopper ride?"

"You got it, hotshot. We wanted to pluck you out of the water before some terrorist in a speedboat got to you. Besides," she continued, "you and I have this speedy trial case to work on for Captain Noble."

"Why do I ever doubt you, Shannon?"

"Need a ride, Commander?"

"I thought you'd never ask."

Gobi Desert
Southeast of Ulaanbaatar, Mongolia

The light was gone.

The darkness had returned.

Her tormentor had left. For now.

He would be back. Perhaps with one of his fellow terrorists.

She closed her eyes and prayed.

About the only semblance of humanity they'd shown her, besides her daily rations of rice, beans, and carrots, was clothing and warm blankets. One of them—the short, fat one—brought the clothing and blankets. When the fat one slipped up and announced in broken English that the clothing had been purchased in Ulaanbaatar, she suspected that they had taken her to Mongolia, probably the Gobi Desert. Of course, that slipup may have been intentional to throw her off. Maybe they were in the Australian outback or something.

"Ahh!" The screaming jolted her senses. The flap flew open. The silhouettes of three monsters stood against the moonlight.

"Out! Out! Out! You infidel dog! Aahhh!"

They rushed into the ger, slinging her to the wooden floor. Pain shot through her knees and jaw. One of them gagged her mouth. The other bound her hands behind her back with coarse rope.

"Up! Up! Up!"

They yanked her hair, jerking her up to her knees. One grabbed the back of her shirt and pulled her to her feet.

"Move, infidel dog! Tonight may be the night!" they yelled in broken English, pushing her out of the tent. She stumbled as her feet hit the ground. One of them snatched her hair again, pulling her back to her feet.

They pushed her across a rocky courtyard of sorts, then forced her to her knees. One of them pushed her face to a cold stump.

"Pray that tonight isn't your night, my beautiful infidel!"

She felt the heavy blade of the cold ax rubbing against her neck. Her heart hammered in her chest. *Please, God. No!*

"Perhaps your phantom God will save you!"

"No, please!"

"Executioner, prepare to decapitate!"

The figure raised the ax high over his head. She caught a glimpse of its blade glistening in the moonlight.

"Now!"

"Nooo!"

CHAPTER 5

Rue Foyatier and plaza Saint-Pierre
Base of Montmartre
Paris

The starry black canopy in the eastern sky disappeared as the morning fog rolled in, leaving an eerie backdrop behind the Basilique du Sacre Coeur. Jeanette gazed through the chilly mist at the great Catholic cathedral standing on the grand hill overlooking Paris's best-known chic artist community, Montmartre.

Her short black dress was rumpled and dirty from hiding all night in the catacombs. She brushed at it absently as she looked over her shoulder at the base of the steps.

Nothing unusual.

Exhausted from the night of sleeplessness, she reached into her purse and pulled out a small bag of almonds for a quick energy boost as the first hunger pang seared her stomach.

The sharp, piercing sensation on the back of her neck triggered an instinctive scream. She pivoted, her heart pounding like a jackhammer as the pigeon darted off, looking for some other tourist willing to share peanuts.

Jeanette caught her breath and scanned the scene at the base of Montmartre. Satisfied that she had not been followed, she scampered as quickly as her worn-down heels would allow up the sea of steps toward the base of the basilica. Stopping again to catch her breath, she looked back over the vista of the city down below, then turned left and into the still-empty cobblestone streets where dozens of artists would soon be peddling their paintings and sketches to hundreds of tourists hoping to come across an original work by the next Toulouse-Lautrec, whose studio remained in Montmartre to this day.

A handful of eccentric-looking artists stirred already under the ghastly glow of predawn. She slowed her pace to a casual walk. A few had lights shining on their canvases, like torches in their little booths. Touching up portraits and impressionist Parisian landscapes, the artists seemed not to notice her as she walked down the center of the streets.

She squinted at the small dark booth at the corner of rue d'Orchampt and rue Giardon.

"Louis!" she called.

No answer.

"Louis!"

A pale incandescent light switched on in the booth. "Do my ears deceive me?" A thin dark-haired man in his thirties, wearing a button-down white shirt and black slacks, rushed out of the booth and wrapped his arms around her. He kissed her on both cheeks, then stepped back and looked at her.

"Oh, you just look like hell," he said. "What *have* you been doing, *ma jolie*?"

"Louis, I need your help."

"What is it, darling? Come sit in my booth." He pointed toward the wood and canvas tent-looking structure. "I'll make café noir, and we can chat."

"*Non*," she said, grabbing his arm, "this is no good. They're trying to kill me."

"Kill you?" A look of astonishment crossed Louis Boulanger's very pale face. "Who?"

"We need privacy." Jeannette thought for a moment. "Perhaps *le cimetière*."

"*Le cimetière? S'il vous plaît.* The dead give me the shivers. Come with me." He took her hand and led her back into the cobblestone streets. "*Venez avec moi.*"

"Where are we going?"

"To a safe place. You'll see."

Council of Ishmael western headquarters
Sahara Desert
Near Zag, Kingdom of Morocco

Three hours later

Hussein al-Akhma donned a pair of designer sunglasses and looked down at the bright, blinding sands of the Moroccan desert. His private multimillion-dollar Citation jet looped low over the deserted airstrip in the desert.

The plane banked again, this time turning Hussein's window at the azure morning sky. One of the two Egyptian fighter jets that had flown cover for this hastily executed flight wagged its wings, then shot off into the east.

Minutes later, the pilot announced in Arabic that the jet was on final approach for landing. Hussein strapped in, adjusted his turban, and sat back. His security detail did the same. Then he closed his eyes.

Hussein felt a sudden drag on the jet's forward thrust, then an elevated whining from its engines. The landing gear had deployed, causing the sudden deceleration in the plane's descent that always made him feel as though the plane were about to drop from the sky. If that ever happened, Allah would take the plane in the palm of his hand and set it down or, even better, bring Hussein into the presence of a thousand beautiful maidens.

Of course, within just a few days, he would have for himself one of the most exotic heathen maidens he had ever laid eyes on. The redhead. Unless, of course, his men had already eliminated her. For this reason alone, he prayed Allah would keep his plane in the sky. The thought of the redheaded JAG officer made him smile.

It was not merely the assassination of Jean-Claude la Trec that had prompted Hussein al-Akhma to emerge from the bowels of his clandestine headquarters in the Saudi desert, board his private jet in Saudi Arabia, then fly east at near supersonic speeds and at low altitudes across the scorching deserts of Egypt, Libya, and Tunisia and finally into Morocco.

La Trec was a capitalist dog who took $30 million of the council's money but failed to gain an acquittal for Lieutenant Commander Mohammed Quasay, a devout Muslim and an American naval fighter pilot who launched an attack on the Dome of the Rock. Quasay was a secret Council operative who was carrying out Operation Islamic Glory. The orchestrated attack was Hussein's secret plan to divide America from the Arab-Islamic world by making it appear that the United States had launched a missile attack on one of Islam's holiest sights in retaliation for 9/11.

And the plan succeeded.

Vehement anti-American protests had raged in Arab-Islamic capitals for the last year, with no end in sight. Splinter Islamic groups launched attacks with increased fervor against American installations around the world. Hussein's prestige skyrocketed as a result.

He commanded no armies. At least, not yet. But the demise of American diplomatic prestige left him as the most powerful Arab alive. He was called the greatest Muslim to walk the face of the earth since the Prophet himself—*peace be upon him*. Even the Russians reached out to him.

By Allah's will, he would soon become the leader of a consolidated Arab superpower stretching from the Arabian Gulf to the Atlantic Ocean. For that to happen, details of Islamic Glory must remain secret.

Above all else.

La Trec's murder was ordered for this reason:

The French lawyer, by brokering a deal for Quasay after his conviction, a deal that allowed Quasay to avoid the death penalty, could not be trusted. La Trec was to win an acquittal or allow his client to be executed. He failed both.

Had top-secret information about Islamic Glory been leaked to the American enemy?

The plane's landing gear bumped against the white concrete runway. Military jeeps, painted the color of sand, sped alongside the plane as it slowed and came to a halt at the end of the deserted Moroccan air base. Arab freedom fighters, wearing turbans and bearing AK47s, jumped out of the jeeps and formed two columns for an impromptu honor guard, as two more Arab workers pushed a mobile aluminum ladder to the base of the plane.

Soon Hussein al-Akhma would have his answers.

Or he would have more blood.

Sunlight streamed through the richly colored stained-glass window in the forth-floor administrative office of the great Sacre Coeur. Boxes stacked on spartan-looking desks and clutter strewn in the far corners of this forgotten enclave of the great cathedral made the room feel more like a prison cell than a church office—if not for the stained-glass window reflecting the image of Jesus cradling a white lamb.

At least she was safe for the moment.

Or was she?

Jeanette checked her watch. Three hours had passed. Where was Louis? He hadn't gone to the authorities, had he?

She could trust Louis. They had been best friends growing up. As a teenage girl, she had posed down by the Mediterranean while he painted her portrait. Then he would touch up her hairstyle, tilt her head, and sketch her from another angle.

Louis would *never* sell her out. No, their bond was deep.

Or was it?

Maybe she should escape by foot while she could. Perhaps just walk to Gar du Nord and purchase a ticket on the Eurostar for London. Britain was still friendly to the United States. She could request asylum at the Court of St. James.

Of course, Gar du Nord, or any other metro station in Paris, would be crawling with *gendarmerie*, all on the lookout for a young blonde woman wearing black, suspected of killing the great Jean-Claude la Trec. And even if she made it to London to request asylum, no one would believe her claim that the French government was involved somehow. How could she even be sure of this? Was the information she heard on her cell phone last night reliable? Would her own government have collaborated with the Council of Ishmael to assassinate Jean-Claude?

She heard what she heard. She could take no chances.

Of this she was certain. They, whoever *they* were, wanted Jean-Claude dead. They wanted her dead too. She knew too much. She knew all about the Council of Ishmael. She knew the details of Operation Islamic Glory.

Louis should have been back by now.

What if they had killed him too?

She had to get out of there and get her hands on the file.

Jingling keys on the outside of the large oak door caused her heart to pump faster. She exhaled when the familiar pale face appeared in the crack of the door.

"Louis!" She wanted to slap him. "You leave me alone here for three hours?"

"Shhh." He brought his index finger across his lips. "I have someone who can help."

Another man stepped into the room.

"I'm Father Robert. I'm a member of the pastoral staff here at Sacre Coeur," the priest said in English. He wore black slacks and a black shirt with white clerical collar. Slender, and with the exception of a small linear scar running diagonally across his left cheek, he resembled the late American actor Christopher Reeves. "I understand you may be in need of sanctuary," Father Robert said.

"Your English is impeccable, Father."

The Catholic flashed a compassionate smile. "I'm American. Grew up in northern Virginia."

She met her friend's eyes.

"It's okay," Louis said. "Father Robert can be trusted. He ministers to the artist community at Montmartre."

"Just because the church has assigned me to the world's most beautiful city, I'm not required to agree with the policies of the French government. Not when I perceive the government is inclined to embrace Islamic fundamentalism," he said, switching to fluent French. "I work for the Holy Father, and my boss detests the type of indiscriminate murder committed by your former client, Commander Quasay. Islamic fundamentalism is an anathema to Christianity and the teachings of the church." His black eyes exuded compassion.

"Besides," he continued, "the church is still a place of holy sanctuary, *non*?" The warm, tender touch of his hand reassured her. The priest sat down and motioned Louis to do the same. "Now, how can I help?"

She thought for a moment. "Two things, Father."

"Name them."

"A legal file. In a safe deposit box at Le Banc de France."

"You want me to take you to the bank?"

"Non!" she snapped. "Sorry, Father. *Non, merci.* I cannot risk being spotted in Paris under the circumstances. I have placed a power of attorney on file with the bank giving Louis access to the vault in my stead."

"You have?" Louis raised an eyebrow.

"Oui." She took her friend's hand. "I anticipated this day. The box is registered in the name of a Swiss corporation, La Montagne Company." She turned again to Father Robert. "I need that file. Father, it contains secrets of international importance concerning the existence of Islamic groups that murdered Jean-Claude and seek to kill me—along with top-secret data about Islamic operatives placed within the U.S. military. I must retrieve the file and take it to America."

CHAPTER 6

Courtroom 1, Building 1
Navy-Marine Corp Trial Judiciary
32nd Street Naval Station
San Diego, California
Court-martial of United States v. Lieutenant Wofford Eckberg, USN

Day 1

It was good to be home.

Zack sat alone, leaning back in the wooden prosecutor's chair in Courtroom 1. Sunlight streamed in from the clear pane windows behind the empty jury box onto the still-empty judge's bench, illuminating the flags of the United States of America and the United States Navy positioned on each side of the bench.

This grand courtroom had been the site of two high-profile trials, both garnering international attention and catapulting him into his status as the world's most recognized JAG officer—a status that was most unwelcome.

Today all vestiges of the national spotlight had faded. Thank God.

A handful of onlookers, including his newly assigned bodyguard turned shadow, Shannon McGillvery, Navy SEAL Captain Buck Noble, and several witnesses, sat behind him. At defense counsel table, Lieutenant Karen Jacoby, fresh from Naval Justice School and trying her first general court-martial, conferred with her client, Ensign Wofford Eckberg.

Both attorneys wore U.S. Navy summer white uniforms with black shoulder boards. Zack's uniform bore the two and a half gold stripes of a navy lieutenant commander. Karen's uniform bore the one and a half stripes of a lieutenant junior grade; it was nearly identical to Zack's, but she wore a white skirt and pumps, and her shirt bore no service medals.

This would be a low-key trial, a case not too many people cared about except the SEALs. The prosecution should win—with one complication: the SEALs had whipped the defendant, who in Zack's opinion was guilty as sin of homosexual assault aboard a U.S. Navy submarine. Such conduct could not be tolerated in the midst of brave fighting forces ready to die for their country. But the broken arm and collarbone had created some big-time legal and logistical problems with this case.

The first problem was the speedy trial issue. Ensign Eckberg had been sitting in the brig nearly ninety days. Under military law, a case not brought to trial within ninety days after an accused is confined will be dismissed.

Eckberg's SEAL team was scheduled to deploy on a top-secret mission to Southeast Asia in two weeks, which would make this case even more difficult to prosecute. Prosecution and defense witnesses scheduled to deploy with a SEAL team on a military mission could not be in two places at the same time. Karen Jacoby was a rookie out of justice school. More experienced defense counsel could tie things up long enough to interfere with the team's deployment. Given the grand scheme of things, this team's orders to slip onto Chinese soil and monitor and photograph the movement of Communist Chinese marines along the Yellow Sea took precedence over the court-martial of Ensign Wofford Eckberg.

As well it should.

The SEALs wanted Eckberg's head on a platter, and they didn't want the case interfering with their deployment. Zack was fighting against the clock.

"All rise!"

"Morning, Commander Brewer." A tall, affable-looking navy captain, wearing a summer white officer's uniform and wire-rimmed glasses, his once-reddish hair now tinged with smatterings of gray, walked into the courtroom and stood behind the judge's bench. Captain Richard Reeves, JAGC, USN, was a sight for sore eyes.

"Morning, Your Honor." Zack stood at attention, waiting for Captain Reeves to be seated.

"And welcome to Courtroom 1, Lieutenant Jacoby." Reeves turned to the defense counsel. "I understand you've just reported from the justice school."

"That's right, Your Honor." Jacoby's voice trembled. Fresh meat for the grinding.

"Be seated." A slight shuffling of chairs. "This is the case of *United States of America versus Ensign Wofford Eckberg, USN*. Is the government ready?"

"We are, Your Honor," Zack said.

"Is the defense ready?"

"Yes, Your Honor." Jacoby's voice still held a tremor.

Zack turned around and saw Shannon sitting just behind counsel table with her attention focused on him. She wore a navy blue women's business suit and a nine-millimeter Beretta, which Zack knew was concealed inside her blouse. All of five feet five inches tall and maybe, just maybe, 110 pounds, Shannon possessed neither the ravishing looks of Diane Colcernian nor the natural beauty of Wendy Poole. But with her strawberry-blonde hair, impish smile, and black belt in karate, she was a tough little stick of dynamite. In fact, she was a magnetic, and attractive, bundle of TNT that Zack wouldn't want to take on in a fight — gun or no gun.

Shannon was the best agent in the NCIS. She had cracked the navy's case against the Islamic navy fighter pilots who attacked the Dome of the Rock. That gave Zack the evidence he needed to knock off the great Jean-Claude la Trec, who before his murder had been called Europe's greatest trial lawyer.

"Will the government make an opening statement, Commander?"

Judge Reeves's question brought a confident *good luck* wink from his dynamo bodyguard, prompting him to whirl around in his seat, then stand and face the venerable military judge. "We will, Your Honor. Very briefly, I might add."

"Very well," Captain Reeves said. "The members are with the government."

Zack stepped from the mahogany counsel table, his white dress shoes clicking across the burnished hardwood floor as he approached the banister rail separating the courtroom well from the military jury.

The military jury — or members, as they are known in the military justice system — resembled a sea of ice-cream white uniforms. Their leader and senior officer, a navy captain, wearing the gold wings of a naval aviator on his chest, sat front and center. He was surrounded by two commanders. One was a SEAL, like the defendant; the other was a surface warfare officer. Flanking the commanders were two lieutenant commanders—one an aviator, the other a navy nurse. The junior officers, four navy lieutenants, sat on the back row.

"Mr. President, distinguished members, this is a very simple case.

"The United States Navy, or any military organization for that matter, cannot function when its members engage in conduct that is prejudicial to good order and discipline.

"When members betray the privacy of others, when members invade the very personal spaces of other members, when sailors let their personal, lustful desires override their duty to country, the basic tenets of military discipline disintegrate."

Zack took two steps back. "When officers"—he pointed to Ensign Eckberg—"engage in conduct unbecoming of an officer and a gentleman"—his finger dropped as his gaze moved back to the members—"the very fabric of the chain of command is mocked."

He stepped into the banister rail, lowering his voice. "I regret to inform you, ladies and gentlemen, that Ensign Wofford Eckberg, a graduate of the United States Naval Academy and a member of the U.S. Navy SEALs, did on various occasions on board the submarine USS *Bremerton* attempt to engage in homosexual activities with various members of his SEAL team while that submarine patrolled off North Korea."

All eyes shifted to Eckberg.

"It is a sad day, ladies and gentleman, when one of our officers has fallen. But the government will prove beyond a reasonable doubt, through the testimony of various witnesses, that one of our officers has engaged in reprehensible conduct—that one of our officers has fallen."

Zack stepped back and paused.

"This we will prove beyond a reasonable doubt. Thank you."

The sound of Zack's shoes clicking against the hardwood floor echoed through the courtroom. His eyes caught Shannon's. She wore a rather curious smile. He nodded to her and then sat down.

Gabriel's Bar
Gaslamp Quarter near Fifth Avenue and Market Street
San Diego, California

Chris Reynolds never understood why they called this joint Gabriel's.

Several theories—all involving the establishment's owner, Michael Mozerelli—had circulated among the all-male clientele of this smoky, off-the-wall bar in San Diego's posh Gaslamp Quarter. One theory held that Mozerelli, once believed to be an accomplished artist, had hoped to go to Paris to unveil a nude painting of the angel Gabriel he had been working on for years. The painting was to launch his career on the international art scene. When it was stolen from his New Jersey studio, Mozerelli plunged into depression, contemplated suicide, and then moved to San Diego to start a new life. The restaurant had seen moderate success through the years, but after a time Mozerelli stopped coming. Now there were no reminders of him except a mysterious photo hanging on the wall, picturing him standing arm in arm with a man in front of the Eiffel Tower.

"May I help you?" The voice ripped Chris's gaze from the photo. A pale, smiling thirty-year-old in a black turtleneck stood at the host's station.

"I'm sorry, you startled me."

The host smiled and inclined his head toward the picture. "Distracting, isn't he?"

Chris stepped closer. He knew how to play the game, and he would play it to the hilt—if it got him the results he needed. "Yes, yes. He certainly is." He paused, smiling at the host. "Actually, yes, there is something you can help me with." Chris lowered his voice to a whisper. "I've heard there's this guy—a directory assistance operator for Pacific Bell—who comes in just before his shift. Is that true?"

The host gave him a knowing smile. "I know exactly who you mean. His name is Brad." He stepped away from his station. "Come on back. He leaves for work in fifteen minutes."

Chris followed the black turtleneck along a dimly lit corridor, dotted on each side with round bar tables where a few patrons were talking, gazing at one another, and sipping beer. They turned left into another dimly lit room. A couple of incandescent spots hung from a cord over the billiards. The four corners of the room were dark. In the back left corner, the intermittent glow of a cigarette cast an orange pall on the round face of a patron sitting on a bar stool.

"Brad, someone wants to meet you."

"Oh, *really*?" The end of the cigarette lit up like a bulb on a Christmas tree. A cloud of rank smoke floated around Chris's face.

"I'm Chris Reynolds." Chris extended his hand. A clammy grip met his palm.

"Nice to meet you, Chris. And what can I do for you?" The handshake continued.

The host softly cleared his voice. "I'll give you two some privacy."

A smile crawled across Brad's face as Bobby, the host, sauntered away. "To what do I owe this pleasure?" Brad slid a stool toward Chris.

"I hear you're with Pac Bell." Chris sat on the stool. "That true?"

"Maybe" — he took another drag from the cigarette — "maybe not." Then he doused the cigarette. "What about it?"

"Two beers, please." Chris held up two fingers in a V as a young man wearing a T-shirt and tight jeans, holding a tray over his shoulder, nodded. "I need to contact this guy." Chris slid the cover of the *People* magazine article across the table.

"Brewer?" A pleased look of recognition crossed Brad's face as he lit another cigarette. "What makes you think I can help?"

The server in tight jeans brought two Coronas and set them on the table. Chris stuck ten dollars in the server's hand, then smiled at Brad.

"Brewer's number is unlisted. So is his address."

"Hmm." Brad swigged his beer. "This could cost me my job. Pay's not great. But the benefits" — a puff — "the *benefits* are fabulous. Why should I risk it?"

"Look." Chris sipped his beer. "I won't tell." He gazed straight into Brad's piercing black eyes. "Please. I give you my word."

"And I'm supposed to believe that?" Another drag. "The *benefits*! I need my medicals. Know what I mean?"

"Of course."

White smoke spewed from his mouth. "Besides, what's in it for me? You haven't even offered to buy me dinner for two." Brad batted his eyelashes.

"Okay, okay." Chris hesitated. "Dinner for two. Anywhere in the city."

"Anywhere?" A mischievous grin inched across Brad's face.

"Anywhere."

Brad hesitated. "I dunno. That's still asking a lot. My benefits." Another puff. "I need my medical."

"Look, Brad," Chris said, "I don't need Brewer's number. How 'bout this." Brad clasped his hands tepee style under his chin and leaned forward. "How 'bout if we still do the dinner for two, and you just slip me his address."

Brad rolled his eyes to the top of his head, threw his hands in the air, and leaned back. "You *do* drive a hard bargain." Looking at the ceiling, he pursed his lips into a circle. Perfectly formed O rings of white smoke wafted into the dark. "How 'bout this?"

"What?"

"We're still in for the dinner for two. Okay?"

"Okay."

"And . . ."

"And what?"

"And I share some very valuable information about Brewer that doesn't get me in trouble with Pac Bell."

"You're playing games." Chris flashed a contrived grin, trying to control his temper. "Why should I trust *you*?"

Brad beamed. "Trust me. If my information doesn't lead you to Brewer within three weeks, then I reimburse you for dinner. And you don't have to take me out again."

Blood boiled in the back of Chris's neck. "Deal." What choice did he have? "Whatcha got?"

Brad leaned forward, his smiling face within inches of Chris's. "I happen to know where Brewer sometimes goes on Saturdays."

Chris's heart pounded. "Tell me." He touched Brad's hand. "Please."

"Old Town."

"Really? Where?"

"Old Town Mexican Café."

"Are you sure?"

"Sure I'm sure. Some of my friends have seen him there. I even saw him once myself. Sometimes has lunch with that McGillvery chick."

"What time?"

"It was about twelve thirty when I saw him."

Chris swallowed hard. "Okay. Okay. I'll try that. Thanks." He drained the Corona. "Here's my card." He slipped a business card across the table. "I know you've gotta get to work. Let me know where you'd like to have dinner."

"But—"

Chris rushed from the dark room, past the host, out the front door of Gabriel's, and onto Fifth Avenue. He gulped in huge breaths of fresh air as if to cleanse himself of the darkness inside.

Then he smiled. What if what Brad said about Zack was true? Then maybe, just maybe, he would get a shot at Zack.

CHAPTER 7

Rue de Clignancourt
Base of Montmartre
Paris

Fadil Abbas aimed his binoculars up the hill and saw orange rays bathing the dome atop Sacre Coeur. Below the dome, the morning sun cast a heavenly glow into the early-morning fog that caressed the base of the cathedral.

Why were such magnificent structures controlled by Catholic infidels who disregarded Mohammed—*peace be upon him*—as the one true prophet? *Perhaps to glorify Islam? Yes, that's it.* France was home to Europe's largest Islamic population. One in ten Frenchmen now embraced Islam. In Paris, the Muslim ratio was even higher. Muslims in Paris would soon outnumber Catholics, who had controlled the city since long before the days of Napoleon.

"Are you sure she is there, Fadil?"

"Yes, Pierre, I saw her go in the side door. I'm sure of it."

"I hope you are right, Fadil."

Fadil felt for the nine-millimeter Beretta jammed in the back of his black jeans. If he was wrong, he would use the Beretta against his own skull to avoid the wrath of Hussein al-Akhma.

Outside Courtroom 1
Navy-Marine Corp Trial Judiciary
32nd Street Naval Station
San Diego, California
Court-martial of United States v. Lieutenant Wofford Eckberg, USN

Day 1

Shannon parked the white Taurus in front of the yellow stucco building that served as the military courthouse at the 32nd Street Naval

Station. She was sandwiched between two other government vehicles, each carrying two NCIS agents, all assigned to guard her passenger, at least until NCIS determined that any immediate danger to Brewer had subsided. As for Zack, he was sitting beside her in his summer white officer's uniform, studying his notes.

Protecting Zack would be the challenge of her life. Could she remain professional in the face of her growing feelings for him? Should she ask to withdraw from this assignment?

Excuse me, Barry, but I don't think I can guard Zack. You see, there are these, well, feelings I can't really explain ...

Imagine that. The top special agent in the NCIS, as Barry had called her, wimping out over something like this. Such a confession would make her the laughingstock of the NCIS.

Besides, a lot of women had a thing for Zack. Even *People* magazine said so, right?

She should sue *People*. The article had linked them together. And Zack had seemed friendlier after the article came out. That was when she noticed her feelings toward him had changed. She blushed like a schoolgirl just thinking about it.

Was her mind playing tricks? What did Zack think?

Get hold of yourself, Shannon!

"We're here, Matlock." She shifted the car into park.

"You're too young to remember Matlock." He looked up from his legal pad and smiled, flashing that irresistible dimple in her direction. He checked his watch. "Fifteen minutes early today. How could I ever question the efficiency of the Naval Criminal Investigative Service?"

"Wal-Mart."

"Excuse me?"

"Wal-Mart. I bought some old *Matlock* DVDs." She scanned the outer area of the courthouse just as NCIS teams Alpha and Charlie, the agents in the cars to her fore and aft, jogged up the steps to make sure everything was okay. In the inconspicuous earpiece tucked in her left ear, the agents gave an "all clear," indicating that the area was safe for "Matlock," the code name that NCIS had—unbeknownst to Zack Brewer—assigned to Zack Brewer. "Any chance this one might settle, Zack?"

"Who knows?" He opened the door but kept his eyes glued on her. It was no wonder he was so deadly in the courtroom. Charisma could take a trial lawyer a long way.

"Wait."

"Can't. Gotta talk to Lieutenant Jacoby about settling. No point pinning a federal conviction on this guy if he's willing to resign."

"You're thinking admin discharge?"

"Why not?"

"Think this guy will admit to homosexual conduct?"

Zack tipped his officer's cap as he stepped out of the car. "Beats a felony on his record, doesn't it?"

"Can you at least wait until we get security in place?"

"No time. Gotta go." He smiled, grabbed his briefcase, and, flanked by two U.S. Marines, strode through the front doors of the military courthouse.

Main gate
32nd Street Naval Station
San Diego, California

The white panel truck with "Aqua Pacific Water Products" painted on the side turned right off Harbor Drive onto 32nd Street.

A U.S. Marine with a black M16 slung over his shoulder gestured for the truck to halt. With his other hand, he pointed to a parking area just to the left of the main gate of the naval station.

"Pull over here, please, sir," the marine ordered.

Mohammed's heart jumped. He had been assured that his paperwork was in order and that he could enter the base unimpeded. A greater cause depended upon the success of his mission.

And now this.

"Identification, please, sir," the marine snapped in a stentorian voice.

With his foot, Mohammed Khadiija shoved the gun under the seat. Without speaking, he handed his identification papers to the marine.

"State your business, Mr.—"

"My company has a contract with the Navy Exchange for beverage deliveries to the exchange and several other buildings around base."

"Nice panel truck you got there, Mr.—"

"Khadiija."

"Khadiija," the marine parroted. "Mind if my buddy and I have a look?"

"Feel free."

"Mind stepping out, Mr. Khadiija?"

"No problem."

Mohammed stepped out of the white panel truck into the warm California morning sunshine. His organization had spent a considerable amount of bribe money to procure for him one of those very rare concealed carry permits issued by the San Diego County Sheriff's Department, but that permit did not extend to federal property. Of course, he was not yet on federal property.

"Want to step around the back and open the back doors, sir?"

"With pleasure."

Mohammed followed the marines around the back of the truck and swung open the back doors. Two rows of crates rose from floor to ceiling, each containing a dozen clear plastic bottles. One of the marines stuck his head in the back of the truck.

"Looks like water to me," the marine said. "Okay, sir, you're free to pass."

Mohammed tried not to look anxious as he got behind the wheel. He pressed the accelerator and waved at the stone-faced marine. Two minutes later, the white panel truck rumbled inside the barbed wires of the naval station.

Courtroom 1, Building 1
Navy-Marine Corp Trial Judiciary
32nd Street Naval Station
San Diego, California
Court-martial of **United States v. Lieutenant Wofford Eckberg, USN**

Day 1

Shannon slipped into the side door of Courtroom 1, just behind the prosecution table. Captain Reeves hadn't yet arrived. Zack, Lieutenant Jacoby, and the defendant, Ensign Eckberg, were decked in their smart-looking summer white uniforms.

Other than a few witnesses and two NCIS agents just behind Zack, the courtroom was empty. Good.

Still, she wanted more agents around covering the perimeter. But conventional NCIS doctrine held that inside the naval station, the threat level was diminished because the whole place was surrounded by barbed wire and water.

And the armed marine sentries posted at the entrances to the courthouse would, at least in *theory*, deter anyone not authorized to enter the building.

She sat behind Zack, then felt for the nine-millimeter Beretta under her blouse.

"All rise!" Legalman Senior Chief Fred Gimler, the military clerk of court, called out. Judge Reeves, wearing the summer white uniform of a U.S. Navy captain, complete with black felt shoulder boards with four gold stripes, walked into the courtroom and sat in the black leather swivel chair behind the bench.

Mohammed turned left for a good show, toward the Navy Exchange. He glanced in the rearview mirror. The reflection showed that the marines had stopped yet another vendor. When they disappeared from view, he turned right, heading straight down to the waterfront where a huge gray ship was moored on a large pier.

Concrete barricades about three feet high were positioned at the end of the pier, blocking vehicular access to the ship. On each side of the barricade, more marines stood guard like stone men.

Behind the marines, blue-dungareed sailors with "Dixie" caps and officers in khaki uniforms moved up and down a ramp from the pier to the ship. On the other side, attached to the railing where the sailors were walking, was a white bunting marked USS *Ticonderoga* (CG 47) in blue lettering.

Anger boiled under his breastbone. This was a navy that stood for discrimination. The likes of Mohammed Khadiija would never be welcome here.

As he turned right on the street paralleling the waterfront, he saw two other mammoth concrete piers jutting into the bay on his left. In the stop-and-go traffic along the busy naval station waterfront, he inched by the massive bows of several other gray warships—sleek, triangular steel wedges hovering out of the water and casting long, triangular shadows over the panel truck.

A group of sailors stepped across the road just in front of him, their sea bags bouncing over their shoulders. Mohammed braked and glanced over his left shoulder. More buntings led upward to more warships, including the USS *Yorktown* (CG 48) and USS *Valley Forge* (CG 50).

The blast of a horn from the Humvee behind him brought Mohammed's foot off the brake. The panel truck rolled forward, turned right at the next stop sign, and eased down a narrow asphalt alleyway between two buildings. The back of Building 1, the military courthouse, was right in front of him.

Two marines guarded the back entrance of the building as Mohammed brought the Aqua Pacific Water Products truck alongside the curb just across the street. He stepped out and, eyeing the marines, walked to the back of the truck and opened the swinging rear doors. He felt for the pistol crammed in his back waistband, then slid a crate of bottled water into his arms. Cradling it, he walked toward the steps leading to the back entrance. He estimated he was about fifty feet away.

He had been told by the regular driver that metal detectors were not used at the entrances of the military courthouse. He needed only to slip past the two marines and reach his target.

CHAPTER 8

Near the west entrance of Basilique du Sacre Coeur
Rue de Chevalier
Montmartre, Paris

Fadil lifted the binoculars to his eyes and studied the movement of people entering and exiting the cathedral. He was seated in a black Renault parked on rue du Mont Cenis just around the corner from the back of Sacre Coeur. Ghazi Jawad, another Council of Ishmael operative, sat beside him in the backseat. The driver, Salah Abdul-Alim, sat in the front alone. All three carried nine-millimeter Glock pistols and Uzi submachine guns.

Fadil considered his predicament. Twice, earlier in the day, he had taken calls from Abdur Rahman, the number two man in the Council of Ishmael. He was also Hussein al-Akhma's most trusted lieutenant. Rahman, considered a genius and the financial mastermind behind the world's foremost terrorist organization, had been diplomatic in his approach.

But the call that had come twenty minutes ago was not so diplomatic. Fadil's stomach had knotted when he was told to hold for a call from the great Hussein al-Akhma himself.

"Can you give *absolute* assurance that L'Enfant is in the building?" the leader had screamed in an angry pitch.

"Yes, Leader, I am sure she is there," Fadil had lied.

"You had better hope that is right, Fadil. Because I hold you responsible for letting her slip away. Produce her within forty-eight hours, or you will be *replaced*"—he drew out the word in a sinister tone—"as ground leader of this operation. Do I make myself clear?"

"Perfectly clear," Fadil had said just as the line went dead. Indeed, al-Akhma's intentions were not ambiguous. The leader of the Council of Ishmael had just signed his death warrant. Within forty-eight hours, COI operatives would track him down, anywhere in the world, with the single-minded purpose of slitting his throat.

Still, Fadil had no option but to wait. He could not storm the building and go looking for L'Enfant. The building was too large. L'Enfant could be anywhere in it. That would alert the gendarmerie, leading to a potential standoff with elements of the French police who were not sympathetic with the council.

Council of Ishmael operatives, under his command, watched Sacre Coeur from every direction. In forty-eight hours they would become his assassins.

Rear entrance of Basilique du Sacre Coeur
Rue de Chevalier
Montmartre, Paris

Jeanette and Father Robert slipped down the narrow, twisting marble stairway in the rear of Sacre Coeur.

Their steps echoed into the heights of the cathedral, startling a nest of pigeons somewhere in the rafters.

When they reached the base, Robert, in black clerical garb, stopped and uttered a prayer of protection for what they were about to do.

"Our Father, who art in heaven, grant your divine protection for the journey we are about to take. Wherever that journey may lead, we beseech your safety in reaching our destination. And for the papers we carry, may they, Father, be given into the proper hands, and may your will, your mercy, and your justice prevail. In the name of our Lord Jesus Christ, who died for us, and whom you resurrected from the grave. Amen."

He made the sign of the cross, then pushed open the large wooden back door. They stepped into the late-afternoon sunlight toward the green Peugeot waiting on rue de Chevalier.

Jeanette felt awkward—almost sacrilegious—wearing the black garb of a Catholic nun. Her life was anything but pure. Yet somehow Sacre Coeur had been a spiritual sanctuary for her. It was as if the Spirit of God himself had been there with her.

The feeling evaporated when Father Robert guided her with his hand on her elbow to the backseat of the Peugeot. He jogged around to the opposite side, opened the door, and tossed his briefcase onto the seat between them.

"Allez! Maintenant!" Go! Now! Robert commanded the driver. The Peugeot lurched forward along rue de Chevalier, passing the green vegetation and white daffodils growing in Parc de la Turlure, just behind the great cathedral. A moment later they made a hard right onto rue Ramey, the centrifugal forces nearly slinging Jeanette from her seat.

By the time she recovered, the Peugeot merged from rue Ramey onto southbound rue de Clignancourt and sped down the hill, away from Sacre Coeur.

Fadil lit another cigarette when his cell phone rang again. His stomach knotted. He flicked the cigarette out the window and silently prayed to Allah that the caller was not Hussein al-Akhma again.

"Abbas here," he said.

"Fadil! Fadil!" The call was from a lookout posted in Parc de la Turlure.

"What is it?"

"A Catholic priest just got into a car and sped off. A woman was with him."

"Her description?"

"Red hair, Fadil. Wearing the dress of a Catholic nun."

"L'Enfant does not have red hair."

"She resembled L'Enfant. Similar facial and body features."

Fadil froze for a split second.

"Tag number?"

"8947747."

"Which way?"

"Right on rue Ramey."

"Stay here," Fadil ordered. "Keep sentries posted around the building in case we are wrong."

"Yes, Fadil," the voice replied.

"Let's go! Now!" Fadil's driver responded to the order. The Renault's tires squealed.

The Renault sped past Parc de la Turlure, swinging to the right on rue Ramey. "We are in pursuit."

Fadil felt under his seat for the submachine gun as the Renault peeled right on rue de Clignancourt. The car accelerated to sixty kilometers per hour.

"I see the Peugeot," the driver said.

"Tag number?"

"8947747."

"Good." Fadil removed his hand from the submachine gun and leaned forward. "Keep the car in sight, but don't get too close." The Peugeot was in traffic, weaving between lanes about two car lengths ahead. A black Mercedes, now flashing its left signal light, separated the two cars. Finding the right opportunity to kill her—or better yet, to capture her—would be a delicate matter.

CHAPTER 9

Courtroom 1, Building 1
Navy-Marine Corp Trial Judiciary
32nd Street Naval Station
San Diego, California
Court-martial of United States v. Ensign Wofford Eckberg, USN

Day 1

Zack stood as Captain Reeves stepped back onto the bench. The military judge was returning from a ten-minute recess in chambers, where Zack surmised he visited the head and made a call to finalize his afternoon golf plans for the North Island Naval Golf Course.

"Evidence for the government, Commander?" Judge Reeves asked.

"The government calls Petty Officer Marvin Williams."

"Petty Officer Williams, please step forward," Judge Reeves said.

A muscular African-American petty officer, wearing a white Cracker Jack uniform, walked down the center aisle from the back of the courtroom. He stepped into the witness box, raised his right hand, and was sworn.

"Commander Brewer, your witness."

"Thank you, Your Honor." Zack stepped to the wooden podium separating the prosecution and defense tables. "State your name, rate, and duty station, please."

"Williams, Marvin. BT3, SEAL. SEAL Team 3, Naval Amphibious Base, Coronado. Sir!"

"Petty Officer Williams, do you know the defendant in this case, Ensign Ekberg?" Zack pointed to the defendant, keeping his eyes on the witness.

"Sir, yes, sir!"

Zack took a sip of water. "I appreciate your enthusiasm, Petty Officer, but just try to relax, okay?"

"Sir, yes, sir!"

Zack turned around. Shannon's right eyebrow was raised. Her eyes sparkled. She mimed the word SEALs, then rolled her blue eyes to the heavens.

Zack pivoted back to the witness. "How is it that you know Lieutenant Eckberg?"

"Lieutenant Eckberg was our assistant platoon leader! Sir!"

"I call your attention to the evening of January eighth."

"Sir, yes, sir!"

"And where were you that evening?"

"Sir, our platoon was stationed aboard the submarine USS Bremerton. We had been on surveillance patrol in the Yellow Sea, off the coast of North Korea."

"What time did you hit the rack that evening?"

"Sir, approximately 2200 hours, sir."

"And where was your platoon berthing that night?"

"The forward torpedo room. My rack was over a Mark-48 torpedo. Torp number two. Sir!"

"Okay, Petty Officer. And did you see the defendant, Ensign Eckberg?"

"Objection!" Lieutenant Karen Jacoby brushed back a strand of blonde hair from her forehead and rose to her feet.

Judge Reeves peered at her over his black reading glasses. "And what are the grounds of your objection, Lieutenant Jacoby?"

"Relevance," Jacoby snapped.

"Relevance?" Judge Reeves's tone signaled that Jacoby should withdraw the objection. "Should Commander Brewer respond before I rule?"

Like so many young JAG officers fresh from justice school, Jacoby had interposed the wrong objection at the wrong time. Plus, she'd blurted out the objection in front of the jury. This was her opportunity to save face.

"Why, yes, Your Honor! If it's relevant, the prosecutor should show why!" She crossed her arms, as if crossing her arms would somehow give legal validity to her objection.

"Commander Brewer." Reeves looked over at Zack, adjusted his glasses, and cleared his throat. "Your response to that?"

Zack swigged ice water from a white Styrofoam cup. When he spoke, he kept his voice calm to show some modicum of respect toward his green but well-meaning opponent. "Your Honor, the government will offer direct testimony from Petty Officer Williams that on the evening in question, Ensign Eckberg, the defendant, sexually assaulted Petty Officer Williams and three other members of the SEAL unit who were sleeping in their bunks over the torpedo tubes."

"Objection!" Jacoby's arms flailed in the air. Her client, Ensign Ekberg, turned a shade that approached the color of his white uniform. Mumbling rose from members of the military jury.

"Order!" Judge Reeves whapped his gavel twice. Silence fell in the jury box and over the courtroom. Reeves's eyes bore into Jacoby. "Lieutenant Jacoby, I have not ruled on your first objection, and now you're raising a second one?"

"Your Honor ... ah ... ah ... This is prejudicial. That's it! Prejudicial."

"Prejudicial?" A tinge of impatience crept into the judge's voice.

"Your Honor," Zack interrupted before Jacoby could respond.

"Commander Brewer?"

"The government requests a recess."

"A recess? Commander, we just finished a recess."

"I'd like to speak with Lieutenant Jacoby outside the presence of the members. Please, sir."

Karen Jacoby was as helpless as an earthworm in the hot Carolina sunshine. Zack could deliver the knockout punch in round one. He knew it. Judge Reeves knew it. Ordinarily, he would never stop a trial with an opponent about to take a fishhook through the midsection.

But Karen Jacoby seemed like a nice young officer who was in way over her head. This might provide an opportunity to discuss a plea bargain.

If Jacoby wanted to be bullheaded after they talked, he would finish her off. If Judge Reeves denied his request for a recess, he would finish her off right now. Problem was, if he didn't shut her up, her greenhorn incompetence would have her stumbling all throughout the weekend, putting the command in the position of dropping charges in order to make their movement.

"Very well, Commander," Judge Reeves sighed. "You've got fifteen minutes."

"Thank you, Your Honor."

"All rise."

Rear entrance, Building 1
Navy-Marine Corp Trial Judiciary
32nd Street Naval Station
San Diego, California

Holding the crate of bottled water in his arms, Mohammed walked up the concrete steps leading to the rear entrance of the courthouse, where two marines, decked out in camouflage battle fatigues and hoisting M16 rifles over their shoulders, stood erect on each side of the door.

"State your business," the marine on the left snapped.

"I'm with Aqua Pacific. Delivering bottled water to the attorneys' lounge," Mohammed said.

"It's okay, Corporal," said the marine on the right. "These guys come by every week."

"Very well, sir. You may pass," said the marine on the left.

"Thank you." Mohammed exhaled and stepped through the back double doors and into the main corridor splitting the first floor of the courthouse.

Courtroom 1, Building 1
Navy-Marine Corp Trial Judiciary
32nd Street Naval Station
San Diego, California

Shannon stood up, and as Captain Reeves stepped off the bench, she held her wrist to her mouth and spoke into the microphone attached to her watch.

"Another recess. Stand by for traffic in the hallway. Stay alert. I've got Matlock with me."

"Alpha team, roger that." Alan Raynor's voice boomed through her earpiece.

"Charlie team, roger that," Mike Wesner chimed in.

Zack grabbed a file and started down the center aisle to exit at the back of the courtroom. "Zack," Shannon barked. He turned, and before he could speak, she said, "Don't get out of my sight, please."

"Yes, ma'am." He rendered a mock salute.

"Where to, Zack?"

An irritated smirk crossed his face. "Up to the second deck to chat with Jacoby in the attorneys' lounge."

Shannon spoke into her wrist mike again. "Raynor."

"Raynor here."

"Belay that last order. Matlock is headed to the second deck to the attorneys' lounge. Cut him off, then meet me here."

"Attorneys' lounge. Second deck. I see Matlock and Jacoby now. Roger that."

Shannon felt again for her pistol, then followed him out into the hallway.

10065 English Ivy Way
Rancho San Diego
Spring Valley, California

The sun was rising above the majestic silhouette of Mount Miguel. Its brilliant rays poured through the back bay window of Chris Reynolds's immaculate townhouse, revealing three thumbprint smudges on the black Formica countertop.

Smudges were *so* unacceptable. Chris reached in a drawer for a neatly folded rag. Grasping the bottle of 409 under the sink, he sprayed the smudges with a vengeance.

There. That was better.

A gold-plated cage hung from a stand just to the left of his gleaming black Yamaha baby grand. Already the sun's rays were bringing the cage's occupant to life.

Chris opened the cage and stuck his finger inside.

"Alvin! Alvin!"

The blue parakeet chirped at the sound of his master's voice. The bird's little three-pronged feet wrapped around Chris's right index finger.

"That's a good Alvin!" Chris said, carefully removing the chirping bird from his cage. Chris brought his right forefinger to his right shoulder. Alvin, his wings clipped, hopped onto his master's shoulder.

A sterling-silver eight-by-ten-inch frame sat atop the baby grand. In it, the cover of *Time* magazine displayed the breathtaking visage of the junior senator from Vermont, the powerful woman who would become the first female president of the United States.

With Alvin still perched on his shoulder, Chris scooted the black leather piano bench from under the baby grand and sat down.

He raised both of his hands in the air, as if surrendering to an armed robber. Stretching his fingers apart as if he were about to make a handprint at Hollywood and Vine, he closed his eyes, inhaled, and then attacked the keyboard with furious passion. Every corner of the townhouse rung with the grand sounds of Ernesto Lecuona's "Malagueña."

Attorneys' lounge
Floor 2, Building 1
Navy-Marine Corp Trial Judiciary
32nd Street Naval Station
San Diego, California

Mohammed had entered the building and, based on directions from the driver who had been paid a handsome sum to take the day off, headed up the stairs to the second floor of the military courthouse.

The third door on the left was marked Attorneys' Lounge, just as he had been told. Three knocks on the door. "Water delivery!" Two more knocks. No response.

He turned the doorknob. A clicking sound followed, and the door opened. The room, a spartan-looking rectangular office with a wooden table in the middle, was empty. He stepped in and began stacking crates of bottled water on the counter just above the refrigerator. One by one, he removed the bottles and lined them in the back of the refrigerator.

If his intelligence reports were correct, the court-martial judge would take recesses about every hour and a half. If he could linger here long enough and remain in the building undetected, he would meet his target.

Patience.

He squatted down by the refrigerator. A click at the door brought him up to his feet.

The door opened. A petite light-haired woman wearing a blue business suit stepped in. She looked to be in her midtwenties. Her attractive green eyes locked in on him like laser beams.

"Is there something I can help you with?" she snapped with an air of authority.

"I work with Aqua Pacific," Mohammed said.

A man in a blue business suit with a squiggly wire running to a small earpiece stepped into the room just behind the woman.

"I am delivering bottled water."

"I'm Special Agent McGillvery. NCIS. This is Special Agent Raynor. You'll have to leave."

"But—"

"Sorry. Leave your water on the counter. We'll take care of it." The woman reached inside her suit, withdrew a pistol, and held it down at her side.

In the name of Allah the munificent! This woman was no-nonsense.

"Any questions?" she asked.

"No, Agent McGillvery."

"Raynor, escort this gentleman to the stairway," the woman ordered.

"Roger, Shannon." The well-chiseled man in the blue suit, who also was holding a gun at his side now, shot him a *let's go out in the hallway* nod. Mohammed complied, and as he stepped through the doorway, two naval officers, a man and a woman, both in summer dress white uniforms, walked toward him. They were engaged in animated conversation.

The woman's shoulder boards bore the one and a half stripes of a lieutenant junior grade, and the man's bore the two and a half stripes of a lieutenant commander.

Mohammed caught the commander's eyes as they passed in the hall.

Brewer! It *was* him. Mohammed recognized his face from the media coverage.

"Move on," the NCIS agent ordered. Mohammed turned around. What to do? The agent's gun was drawn from the body holster, and he was pointing it at the floor. That could change in an instant. And the light-haired woman inside the room had a gun as well.

"Move it!"

"Yes, sir." Mohammed headed down the staircase to the first floor, leaving the NCIS agent on the second. He jogged down the stairs and, checking over his shoulder, discovered that the NCIS agent had not followed him. At least not yet.

He reached the polished hallway of the first floor. The rear entrance was to his left. If the NCIS agent had followed him back down, he could slip out the doors, past the two marine guards, and try again later. But "later" might never come. The trial could end. A number of problems could arise. This was a narrow window of opportunity to advance the cause of his organization. The future of the nation, he knew, rested on his performance.

Mohammed turned right and headed down the hallway toward Courtroom 1.

Two navy petty officers, in white uniforms with black armbands emblazoned with the letters *SP*, walked past him. The two shore patrolmen looked away. Perhaps the light blue Aqua Pacific shirt that he was wearing, complete with the name Mack embroidered in red thread, helped him blend into the woodwork.

Two more shore patrolmen, standing with their legs askance and their fists balled behind their backs, guarded each side of a large mahogany door just down the hallway to the left. Officers and enlisted personnel bustled in both directions.

If his map of the courthouse's layout was correct, this was the entrance to Courtroom 1. Soon Brewer and the female lieutenant would walk back through these doors. Perhaps he should just walk in. But his blue Aqua Pacific shirt wouldn't pass for a navy petty officer's uniform. Of course, loitering was not an option—especially if the fiery-eyed female NCIS agent showed up.

He passed the head—the men's room—and just as he was about to step in, the door of Courtroom 1 opened. A handsome blond officer stepped out between the shore patrolmen. He wore the same ice-cream white summer uniform that Brewer wore, except that his shoulder boards bore a single gold stripe. Over his left chest, the Neptune pitchfork of a Navy SEAL was pinned to the uniform. Over his right chest, a plastic name tag was marked Eckberg.

Mohammed caught the defendant's blue eyes. Their gazes lingered. The defendant smiled, and for a moment, time froze. The sound of footsteps coming down the stairway jolted Mohammed. He reached into his shirt pocket and handed a card to Eckberg.

"Is there anything else we can help you with?" The male NCIS agent from upstairs was rounding the corner of the stairs, his spit-polished leather shoes echoing a Nazi-like *click, click* as he made his way down the hallway toward Mohammed.

"No, sir. I was just on my way out."

Attorneys' lounge
Floor 2, Building 1
Navy-Marine Corp Trial Judiciary
32nd Street Naval Station
San Diego, California

Lieutenant Karen Jacoby kept reminding herself she was not dreaming.

Like every member of her law school class at the University of Maryland — like every law student across the nation — who had prepped for last year's bar examinations, her memory was seared with the images of two separate "trials of the century," both of which happened to be navy courts-martial prosecuted by the very handsome officer who had invited her to the attorneys' lounge.

In two years, Zack Brewer had made the U.S. Navy JAG Corps the most sought-after job for law school grads. For Karen, Zack had become her hero and had influenced her, as he had many others, to apply for a commission in the corps.

And now here she was, in the same courtroom, in the same attorneys' lounge ... Maybe she *was* dreaming!

Focus, Karen. Concentrate. Show no sign of awe or intimidation.

"Have a seat, Karen." His tone was caring. She sat at the conference table as the NCIS agent — Special Agent McGillvery — stood by the door and appeared to be examining the hallway.

"You wanted to discuss the case, sir?"

"Care for coffee?" Zack turned to the coffee mess just to the left of the refrigerator.

"Cream and sugar, please, sir."

"Cream and sugar it is." She watched as he searched for a white mug, poured what looked to be about three tablespoons of sugar into the bottom, doused that with a squirt of milk, and poured steaming black coffee over it all.

"Coffee is served," he said. He poured a cup of straight black for himself, then walked around to the other side of the conference table, sipped his coffee, and seated himself in front of her.

"So you wanted to talk with me?"

"First, I think you're doing a great job for your client."

"Thank you."

"Anyway, although the type of conduct your client engaged in—"

"*Allegedly* engaged in."

"Yes." He took another sip. "*Allegedly* engaged in—although the conduct is prejudicial to the good order and discipline of the armed forces, there are better ways of disposing of this matter than a general court-martial."

"I thought the SEALs demanded a court-martial in this case." Karen stirred her coffee and added another teaspoonful of sugar.

"The SEALs already laid a severe licking on your client. What'd he have? A broken collarbone?"

"Broken collarbone and right forearm."

Zack shook his head. "Look, Eckberg faces six years' confinement—one for conduct unbecoming of an officer and a gentleman and five for the sexual assault. I've seen dozens of these cases handled as administrative discharges coupled with a resignation from the navy."

"An admin discharge?"

"Why not? Saves your boy a federal conviction, *and* he avoids confinement."

"On what grounds?"

"That's the catch. Homosexuality."

"You expect him to admit to that?"

"I don't expect him to do anything. But if he's willing to consider it, I might have enough leverage with the admiral to persuade them to take it."

Karen thought about that for a moment. Why was Brewer being so nice? Was there a catch? "Yeah, but even if my guy gets convicted, you think he'll serve time?" She paused. "Besides, with all due respect, I think I have a defense. After all, it was dark in the berthing area on that sub. You may have a problem identifying my guy. Beyond a reasonable doubt is a high burden."

Zack smiled. "Karen, I quit trying to predict judges and juries a long time ago. Look no further than *The State versus OJ Simpson* or *Bush versus Gore* to see how judges and juries with the same set of facts produce different results."

"Good point."

"But," he added as he rose to refill his coffee mug, "your guy is looking at a maximum sentence of six years." He reached into a cabinet above the coffeemaker, grabbed a glass, and poured water into it out of the tap. "And"—he took a swig of water as he returned to his seat—"if we get a conviction after having gone to all this trouble to bring this case to trial on such short notice ..." The prosecutor's smooth voice shifted to a tone of resolution that reminded Karen of steel. "If we get a conviction, I will ask for maximum confinement."

Karen sat for a moment. Zack smiled, his hazel eyes boring into her like steely darts. He had the right mix of charm, fire, and innuendo to underscore his point. Maybe there was no catch. Maybe this deal was best for Eckberg. Or maybe he had questions about his own case. All she knew for sure was this: she had just been intimidated by the most charming man she had ever met.

"Okay. I guess there are some advantages to your proposal. I can't promise anything. It's my client's decision. But I will recommend that he take it."

"Good choice." Zack's steel-like eyes warmed again. "Let's go talk to Captain Reeves."

CHAPTER 10

Westbound avenue Foch
Isle de la Cité, Paris

By the time the black Renault had tailed the Peugeot down the Champs d'Elysses, around the Arc de Triomphe, and onto westbound avenue Foch, Fadil realized that L'Enfant was probably aboard. Weaving between traffic, running traffic lights, speeding—all pointed to something other than a routine priestly visit to a retirement convent. The Peugeot driver's speed telegraphed a sense of urgency. *Someone* was trying to get somewhere fast.

But where? An escape out of the country through either of Paris's major airports, Orly or Charles de Gaulle, would be too risky. Local police at major airports would identify and question L'Enfant about la Trec's death.

The cars swung around the traffic circle Bois du Boulange—the large, tree-lined park opposite the Arc de Triomphe. The Renault tailed the Peugeot on northbound boulevard Périphérique, racing along the edge of the beautiful park that had been bequeathed by Napoleon III in 1852.

A moment later the lead car headed west on rue Charles de Gaulle. They raced past boulevard du General Koenig, then across the bridge spanning the Seine River.

The Peugeot was headed toward the Normandy coastline, perhaps to take a ferry to England. And from there, a flight to America? Or even an asylum request at the American embassy in London?

From Paris, the realistic destinations along the English Channel were anywhere from 90 to 150 miles away. Close enough that neither car would need to stop for refueling.

Fadil would have to intercept either somewhere along the route or in the channel itself. He picked up his cell phone and punched the speed-dial number for Council of Ishmael headquarters in Morocco. In less than two minutes, Abdur Rahman was on the line.

"What's your status, Fadil?"

"We are pursuing L'Enfant by car."

"Have you made a visual of her?"

"Yes, Abdur," Fadil lied. "She is in the car with a priest and the driver. No indication that they are armed."

Lying to the brain trust of the Council of Ishmael could get Fadil killed; he knew this. But if he was wrong about the identity of the passengers in the car, he was dead anyway.

"Good. I will report this to the leader," Abdur said.

"There is one request, Abdur."

"What is it?"

"I believe that she may be headed to the coast. I request three armed boats stationed in the channel between Granville and Dieppe." There was a moment of silence. Then static. "Are you there, Abdur?"

"I assume you are asking for these boats to evacuate L'Enfant out of France, and not for interception purposes in the channel?"

"Of course, Abdur." *Unless she gets into the channel before I can capture her.*

"Because as you know, using force in the English Channel might bring excessive attention to the situation—a situation that would not please the leader."

"Of course, Abdur."

"You are expected to capture or kill—preferably capture—L'Enfant *before* she leaves France."

Fadil shielded his eyes from the setting sun, now a blinding orange ball just over the wide boulevard leading out of Paris.

"Yes, Abdur. As you say."

CHAPTER 11

Claxton campaign California headquarters
Situation room
Hyatt Regency Hotel
Century City
Los Angeles, California

Jackson Gallopoulous gazed up at the wide-screen TV showing a bright picture of his boss, Vermont Senator Eleanor Claxton, who was downstairs, stepping back to the podium to face a throng of cheering conventioneers. Screams from the crowd rocked the loudspeaker that beamed the speech into the campaign war room.

It was no coincidence that the Claxton presidential campaign California headquarters were at the very same hotel that was hosting the national convention for the National Organization for Women. Already Eleanor's speech had been interrupted four times by standing ovations.

"Elll-a-nor! Elll-a-nor!"

The camera panned the crowd. Hundreds of angry women shook their fists in the air, shouting his boss's name. These women, mobilized into a political army, could prove a valuable force in the upcoming California primary.

"Elll-a-nor! Elll-a-nor!"

Jackson glanced around the long conference table at the young men and women comprising Eleanor's inner circle. Like him, most of the vigorous young staff were in their late twenties and early thirties. Most wore jeans, flip-flops, and sweatshirts.

Like him, most of them were idealistic. Like him, most were tired of the worn-out conservative rhetoric that championed big money and suppressed the rights of gays and other minorities. Like him, they were all sick of the so-called Christian Right, the myopic, ignorant pigs who were disciples of Jerry Falwell and Pat Robertson and had put the likes of George W. Bush and Ronald Reagan in office. Like him, they felt that real religion meant action, and that meant serving the poor by working in soup kitchens and building low-income housing—not kowtowing to big business. Like him, and like his boss, all were graduates of Yale—thus earning their nickname the "Yale mafia."

In this room was the brain trust of the most dynamic presidential campaign in American history, the campaign that would, at long last, put a woman in the White House. If Eleanor pulled this off, the young talent in this room could make up members of America's future cabinet.

Jackson himself dreamed of becoming White House chief of staff.

Or maybe the secretary of state.

Ladies and gentlemen, the Secretary of State of the United States of America, Jackson Kennedy Gallopoulous.

If only Betty and Ray Gallopoulous could see him now. His parents had named him for the great John F. Kennedy for a reason. JFK's immortal words "Ask what you can do for your country" meant one thing, they had said, and that was embodied in one noble concept.

Service.

To serve the poor and to serve government were life's highest callings. And Raymond and Betty Gallopoulous had taught their son well. They had taken him to Africa on summer mission trips where they had served in the Peace Corps. Each Thanksgiving and Christmas for as long as he remembered, the family would forgo their own comforts and spend all day serving the homeless at the Salvation Army's Lexington Avenue Armory in New York City.

The sparkling eyes of homeless children wrapped in blankets; the trembling hands of elderly women sipping hot soup with wrinkled, parched lips; the beaming faces of poor minority parents watching their children open a single present, be it a fire truck or a rag doll, on Christmas morning—all of these images had driven Jackson toward the great Democratic Party of Franklin Roosevelt, which had made a clarion commitment to use public funds to right the wrongs of such social injustices.

He was destined for greatness, Ray and Betty had promised. Now he realized they were right. The thought of it all gave him goose bumps.

Either position—secretary of state or chief of staff—would be an appropriate reward for the whiz kid who was running the campaign of the first female president of the United States.

"Elll-a-nor! Elll-a-nor!"

The women, many with their arms interlocked and swaying to and fro, as if intoxicated with uncontrollable joy, were demanding an encore performance from their heroine.

And they had every right to be angry after all those years of pig-headed conservative politics. Jackson wondered how this scene, at this moment being broadcast live in living rooms across America, was being viewed. Probably not too well in the South. But the general election was months away. Without California, there would be no general election. And Gallopoulous's political instincts told him that this scene was probably playing just fine in San Francisco and Los Angeles.

Inside the situation room, members of the Yale mafia smiled, cackled, and high-fived one another.

"Shhh," shushed Mary-Latham Modlin, the campaign's press secretary. "She's going to speak again."

"Thank you! Thank you!" Eleanor Claxton remounted the podium, her larger-than-life image again beamed into the situation room via the large plasma screen.

"We love you, Eleanor!" a gruff voice shouted. Cheering. Whistling.

"I love you too!" She smiled, her dirty blonde hair chopped off at her collar. More cheering. She threw her arms out, made the V sign like Eisenhower, and shouted, "And I love America!"

That set them off again.

"Elll-a-nor! Elll-a-nor!"

"And the America that I love ..."

"Elll-a-nor! Elll-a-nor!"

"... is an America where there is equal justice for all!"

"Elll-a-nor! Elll-a-nor!"

"We will put an end to discrimination!"

"Elll-a-nor! Elll-a-nor!"

"I call upon this administration to end—once and for all—this anachronistic, outmoded, outdated, discriminatory policy in the military known as 'Don't ask, don't tell.'"

Cheers, catcalls, and whistles sounded from every corner of the auditorium.

"No American fighting for this country should be ashamed of who he or she really is. That's not what this great land of ours is about!"

"Tell 'em, Eleanor!" a solitary voice shouted from the crowd.

"Yes, I'll tell 'em!" The junior senator from Vermont shook her fist to more cheering. "*We* will tell 'em!" The enthusiasm of the feminist crowd reached a fevered pitch. "We will tell this Williams administration to abolish 'Don't ask, don't tell,' or we will come to Washington and do what should have been done long ago.

"We will restore equal rights for *all* Americans. For the gay. For the lesbian! For *all* Americans!" Wild cheering. The camera panned to some women wiping tears from their eyes.

"And one other thing!" Eleanor Claxton shook her fist in the air. "We will *end* the trigger-happy involvement of this administration that has been so anxious to get us into foreign wars!"

Pandemonium erupted.

"At every opportunity, this administration has been too eager and ready to place the brave men and women of our armed forces in harm's way. Who does the president think he is?"

Boos arose with the reference to President Mack Williams.

"John Wayne?" Laughter. "Clint Eastwood?" More laughter. "Dirty Harry?" Still more laughter. Some women could be seen smiling and wiping tears from their eyes. The charisma of this great woman was overwhelming.

"Well, let me tell you something ladies." A pregnant pause. "Soon there will be a new sheriff in town!"

"*Elll-a-nor! Elll-a-nor!*"

"A new sheriff ... Thank you ... Thank you ..." Beaming, Claxton waved down the shouts of admiration. "Soon there will be a new sheriff in town who doesn't have to draw her six-shooters and point them at the world to show the world how tough she is!"

"*Elll-a-nor! Elll-a-nor!*"

"Thank you ... Thank you ..."

"*Elll-a-nor!*"

"God will help us ..."

"*Eelllll-a-nor!*"

"Thank you." The crowd silenced again, and Claxton again shook her fist. Her voice exuded determined anger. "God will help us win California. God will help us win the Democratic nomination. God will help us win this election!" The crowd was on the precipice of a riot. "God will help us. Yes, she will! God will help us. Yes, she will!"

Pandemonium resumed as the crowd picked up the chant. *"God will help us. Yes, she will! God will help us. Yes, she will!"*

Senator Claxton stepped back, again threw her arms out with her fingers forming the V symbol, and shouted, "May God bless us. May she bless us richly. And may God bless America!"

In the situation room, the Yale mafia broke into cheering as their heroine stepped out of view on the plasma screen.

"Heads up, everybody. Get ready," Jackson Gallopoulous shouted. "She'll be here in five minutes. Get on your games. She'll want a report."

Five minutes later, the double doors of the situation room flew open. Two black-suited Secret Service agents burst in, followed in close proximity by Senator Claxton, who was followed by two more agents.

The applause of the starry-eyed Yale mafia was drowned by the profanity-laced tirade of the junior senator from Vermont.

"Who picked out this pantsuit that I had to wear out there?" Her shrill voice matched that of an angry hyena. After spewing a few select curse words, she added, "How many times have I said this beige makes me look too feminine?" Pin-drop silence. Her eyes swept the room. Jackson felt her stare bore into him, then move on to the next staffer. "Who do you people think our constituency is, anyway?" No answer. "The June Cleaver fan clubs of America?" Still no answer. "A bunch of Bible-thumping, anti-choice, what-can-I-do-for-my-man-today Southern belle idiots?"

Silence.

"Do you people realize this is *California*? And we *need* this state for the nomination? And we are in a tight race? And that was the *National Organization for Women* out there? And that some idiot on my campaign staff brings me a feminine, weak-looking, pale beige pantsuit and claims that all my navy blue pantsuits are in the hotel cleaners and then has the audacity to suggest that I wear a *dress*?"

A chirping cell phone broke the tension-filled gap in the tirade.

"This is a *presidential campaign*, people!" Claxton screamed over the sound of the cell phone. "A *presidential campaign!*"

"Please, Senator." Jackson hoped his voice would begin to calm the most recent of a thousand similar tantrums that the press had speculated on but that only the senator's staff had seen.

Her eyes blazed.

"Eleanor." He softened his voice. This time, something seemed to snap in her face; then her twisted, knotted cheek muscles relaxed and she began to mellow. At least to the extent that Eleanor Claxton could mellow.

There, that was it. The face of brilliant reason that the country saw every night on television had returned to the situation room. If Jackson believed in God, he would have thanked him. But Yale had taught him that there is no God. Now he alone would take credit for taming the ferocious temper of the world's most powerful woman.

"What is it, Jackson?" Claxton exhaled. She was not unattractive when she relaxed. In fact, Jackson found her to be appealing at times, a fact that may have led to rumors in the press that the two of them were an item.

And on top of all that, there was the constant media speculation about the senator's mercurial relationship with her estranged husband, former Vice President Fred Claxton, the charismatic Democrat hero who would have been running for president himself had he not been impeached by the U.S. Senate and later convicted of perjury by the Republican-controlled House.

"Senator, I think you knocked it out of the park."

"Hmm." Claxton sighed. "Think so?"

"What do you guys think?" Jackson glanced at the members of the Yale mafia.

Mary-Latham Modlin started with three evenly spaced claps, and in a few seconds, the applause of the mafia sounded like furious raindrops on a tin roof, and the soon-to-be first female president of the United States was smiling again. "You were *great*, Senator," Mary-Latham gushed.

"Yes, you were," agreed the others.

"Okay, okay." Claxton smirked. "Let's all be seated. We need to review poll numbers."

The senator motioned for them to be seated around the long conference table. Jackson caught Mary-Latham's gaze and saw visible relief in her eyes. Mary-Latham had arranged for the beige pantsuit to be brought to the senator's room because of polling data indicating that softer colors would help the senator's widespread appeal.

"Okay, Jackson," Claxton began from her swivel chair at the end of the table. "What's our situation in California?"

"Senator, we're neck and neck with Congressman Warren. It's the same old story. The hometown boy is pulling heavy numbers in the Bay Area. We're way ahead in the rest of the state. Senator Fowler is way, way behind."

The Senator slapped her hand against the table and cursed. "What's wrong with those people in San Francisco? They're *my* kind of people. And they know Warren's got no chance."

"Senator," Mary-Latham spoke up. "Warren's been up there for years, battling for gay rights on the Hill. He's sponsored a federal gay marriage amendment. Our polls show that the Bay Area voters view you as liberal enough, but more determined to get elected than to do anything."

"The idiots!" Claxton fumed. "They're confusing me with my husband again!"

"That's part of the problem, Senator," Jackson added. "We're fighting confusion by association."

"I should've killed Freddie years ago. I should've gotten him before the Republicans did."

"Yeah." Mary-Latham glared at Eleanor. "You should've gotten him after the fortieth time you caught him womanizing."

Five seconds of silence.

"Well." Eleanor turned to Jackson. "How goes this dramatic strategy you've devised to put us over the top?"

"So far, so good, Eleanor."

"Explain."

"Brewer's on the case, just like we hoped. Our guy has infiltrated and made contact. We should know soon if our boy will play ball."

"He'd better." Claxton tapped her pen on the table. "This had better work." An aide poured more coffee. "If I'm going to politically castrate a conservative icon like Brewer, we'd better win California."

"You will, Eleanor," Jackson said. "Trust me."

"I don't trust anybody, Jackson." Eleanor swigged her coffee. "Not after what the Republicans did to Freddie. Somebody got a light?" A Secret Service agent positioned a flaming butane lighter under the end of the senator's cigarette of choice, a long Virginia Slim.

That she could secretly puff like a pre-EPA-era Pittsburgh steel mill, then publicly berate the tobacco lobby, was an example of her great courage. Great leaders must divorce their private beliefs from their public positions. A candidate could *claim*, for example, to personally oppose abortion, as long as she publicly advocated pro-choice positions and policies. Same with cigarettes.

"So anyway," Eleanor said, puffing the Virginia Slim, "what's the deal on our press releases?"

"All done." Mary-Latham spoke with a swaggering, self-assured confidence. "Leaks go to the press tomorrow. We should get a feel for how all this will play by Monday morning."

Eleanor raised an eyebrow and displayed a self-satisfied smirk, which was imitated by Mary-Latham, who shot her brown eyes at Jackson.

"Okay," Eleanor said, "by Monday, we'll see just how brilliant my two top assistants are." Another drag from the cigarette. "Or else maybe we'll see them in the unemployment line."

She blew a cloud of cigarette smoke at Jackson, then laughed.

Courtroom 1, Building 1
Navy-Marine Corp Trial Judiciary
32nd Street Naval Station
San Diego, California
Court-martial of United States v. Lieutenant Wofford Eckberg, USN

Day 1

The military jury was still sequestered in the jury room when Captain Reeves returned to the bench.

"All rise!"

Zack looked across the aisle at the defense table, where Lieutenant Jacoby and Ensign Wofford Eckberg were whispering. Eckberg was nodding his head.

"Very well." Captain Reeves looked over his half-moon wire-rimmed glasses. "Is the government ready to continue its case, Commander Brewer?"

Zack glanced back over at Jacoby and Eckberg. They were still whispering. "Yes, Your Honor. I'm pleased to announce an apparent resolution of this case."

"Very well," Reeves said. "Lieutenant Jacoby?" This brought the lieutenant out of her conversation with her client. "Is this correct?"

"Ahm ... yes, Your Honor," Jacoby affirmed.

"Very well." Reeves shifted back to Zack. "Would you care to state the terms of this resolution for the record, Commander?"

"Your Honor, at this time, the government and the defense will move the court jointly for a continuance, for the purpose of resolving this matter, hopefully, out of court. The continuance would be for a period of two days, or until Monday morning, during which time Ensign Eckberg would tender his resignation from the navy and agree to an administrative discharge from the naval service. All time accrued during the continuance would be chargeable to the defense and not the government for speedy trial purposes. In return, the government would drop all charges and not go forward with this general court-martial for sexual assault."

Reeves took a sip of water, wrote a few notes on his legal pad, then looked over at Jacoby. "Lieutenant Jacoby, does the defense concur?"

"Ahm ..." She glanced at Zack. He nodded. "We concur, Your Honor."

"Ensign Eckberg." Reeves looked at the defendant. "It is my understanding that you wish to tender your resignation from the navy and seek an administrative discharge in return for the government dropping all charges against you. Is this correct?"

Eckberg resembled a deer in the headlights. Karen Jacoby whispered something in his ear. "That is correct, Your Honor."

"And you are asking for a continuance in this trial for the purposes of seeking to start the process of resigning your commission?"

"Yes, sir."

"And this court will be in recess until you have, in fact, resigned?"

"Yes, sir."

"And if you do not resign and go through with the administrative discharge, the government could go forward with its prosecution?"

"Yes, sir."

"Very well. This court is in recess for forty-eight hours, until Monday morning, unless I hear from either counsel before then."

Judge Reeves rapped his gavel on the bench once.

"All rise!"

CHAPTER 12

Expressway E05
Outside Bourneville, France
Near the Normandy coast

Their route into the setting sun had taken them along the modern expressway E05, the toll road following the snaky curvature of the River Seine as it flowed from Paris and pointed northwest to the English Channel, just east of Le Harve.

They had not stopped for petrol. Father Robert had been peering over his shoulder and had seen no evidence that they had been followed. Now that the sun had set, the darkness would provide even greater protection. Perhaps one call of nature could be attended to before they boarded the ferry from Le Harve to Portsmouth.

"Driver, please pull over at the next restaurant."

"Yes, Father." The driver clicked his signal, and moments later the Peugeot headed down the next exit ramp.

"Fadil!" shouted the driver, Salah Abdul-Alim. "They are pulling off the expressway."

Fadil squinted at the Peugeot's taillights. "Stay with him, Salah." Fadil worked the action on the Uzi—a metallic clacking—readying it to fire; then he checked the silencer and flipped on the safety. "Ghazi, arm your weapon, check your silencer, and load Salah's too. This could get bloody. But remember, we want L'Enfant."

"Yes, Fadil," Ghazi said. The Renault swung onto the off-ramp, two cars behind the Peugeot.

"Cut the headlights. Leave the parking lights," Fadil ordered.

"Yes, Fadil." Salah killed the headlights as the cars decelerated to sixty kilometers per hour.

Fadil opened a can of shoe polish and wiped his face jet black. "Here." He passed the can to Ghazi.

Ghazi dipped three fingers into the polish, swirled them, and started masking his face too.

The neon sign just off the off-ramp flashed the name of the establishment: Le Café du Côte Normandie.

"This looks good," Robert said. He looked over his shoulder, satisfied that they had not been followed.

The Peugeot swung right into the parking lot.

"Anyone else need to go?"

"I'm fine," Jeanette replied.

"Stay with her," Robert ordered, eyeing the driver. He was so young, just an intern who had started as a volunteer last summer at Sacre Coeur. "I'll be right back. Take off if you see anything suspicious."

"Yes, Father," the driver said.

Robert stuffed the papers under his shirt, then stepped out the rear driver's-side door and walked toward the café.

"Fadil, someone's getting out of the car," Salah Abdul-Alim said.

"Pull over!" Fadil shouted. Salah stopped the Renault along a grassy bank 150 meters from the Peugeot. "Ghazi and I will approach on foot. Salah, when you see us reach the vehicle, drive up along the left side. Ghazi, you take out the driver. I will deal with the witch. Understood?"

Both men nodded.

"Good. Let's go."

Fadil and Ghazi jumped from the car and, crouching low, moved along in a ditch to avoid detection toward the back of the Peugeot. They approached the vehicle from the driver's side. The Peugeot's motor was running. No other cars were nearby.

Climbing out of the ditch, Fadil crouched onto the asphalt parking lot just a few feet from the Peugeot. The driver's startled eyes locked with his.

The burst of machine-gun fire from Fadil's Uzi sent splattered glass, blood, and brains across the seat. A cry rose from the back of the Peugeot.

Fadil fired into the door, blowing it open and setting off the car alarm. The target was crumpled in the backseat, screaming. Her eyes were fixed on the driver, whose head hung over the seat.

Fadil grabbed her by the collar and yanked her toward the open door. She started to scream again, but Fadil pressed his hand over her mouth. Like a cat, she clawed and scratched. "Over here," he yelled to Ghazi, who ran around the car and helped him pull her through the doorway and onto the asphalt.

The Renault screeched to a stop just behind Fadil. Ghazi opened the back door as Fadil yanked the woman's hair, twisted her arm behind her back, and shoved her into the backseat.

Fadil followed her in and held her down as Ghazi rushed to the other side. "Let's go," Fadil commanded, pulling the car door closed. The Renault shot back into the black night.

Father Robert was still in the restroom when he heard a cacophony of shrill voices in the restaurant on the other side of the door. Hurriedly he headed to the sink, splashed water on his hands, rubbed them together, and grabbed a towel. In less than an hour, they would be on a ferry for England. And from there, they would board a plane from Gatwick back to the States. The noise in the restaurant made him nervous. It also made him realize they needed to be on their way. And fast. He tossed the towel aside and hurried through the door.

Wending his way through the knots of patrons who'd stood to look out the front windows, he jogged to the restaurant's entrance and opened the door. A short distance away, the Peugeot's lights were flashing, its alarm bleating into the night air.

Robert sprinted across the parking lot, then stopped in alarm as he reached the open driver's side door. The driver's head was twisted at an odd angle and now hung over the seat, fresh blood seeping from the cranium. Shattered glass covered the front seat and the floorboard. Robert fought to keep his breakfast down, and lost. He bent over and heaved.

Jeanette.

Where was Jeanette? He stood again and looked into the car. The backseat was empty. The passenger doors were open. A smattering of restaurant patrons were now running toward him.

Robert scanned the dark horizon to the right, then scrutinized the parking lot.

On the EO5 expressway, cars raced in both directions, leaving red and white streaks of light in their wake. Sirens grew louder. The police were close now.

What could he do except pray?

And run.

Eastbound Expressway EO5
Outside Quillebeuf, France

Ten minutes later

Fadil pinned the woman down, one hand pressing her face into the fabric of the seat. He was proud that his sheer brute strength made it impossible for her to move. Her cries were muffled now, and he wondered whether she could breathe.

He yanked her head up by the hair to see.

She unleashed a piercing scream. "Burn in hell!"

He shoved her face back into the upholstery. This time he momentarily lost his grip and she twisted out of his grasp, half falling to the floor. He grabbed for her, but she was faster. She fought him like a cat, scratching, biting, clawing.

"Pull over!" he screamed to the driver.

"Yes, Fadil." Salah turned onto a rapidly approaching off-ramp, then pulled onto the shoulder.

"Salah. The glove compartment. Get the syringe."

"Yes, Fadil."

"Let me out! Now." The woman kicked at him. He lunged and caught her mid-kick around the waist.

"I can't see it, Fadil."

"Turn on the dome light, you moron! But hurry! The police will be on our rear."

"Yes, Fadil." Salah turned on the dome light.

As he wrestled her back onto the seat, the woman continued to kick wildly, crying and biting and scratching.

"Oh! She kicked me!" Ghazi winced, holding his stomach.

"Hurry, Salah!"

"Got it!" A syringe flashed in Salah's hand. He leaned over the seat and jammed the needle through the woman's skirt and into her rump. Her scream turned into a moan, then she went limp.

"Let's get out of here!"

The Renault's tires squealed. A minute later, they sped down the EO5 expressway, headed toward the coast.

Côte d'Albâtre, France
Northeast of Saint-Pierre-en-Port

Two hours, thirty-five minutes later

From the beach near an isolated village on the Normandy coastline, Fadil gazed across the waters of the dark channel toward England. A light breeze blew in from the sea, sloshing gentle swells onto the desolate stretch of beach halfway between the towns of Dieppe and Fécamp. Fadil checked his watch, then looked out at the horizon. The red and green lights of a few seagoing vessels, several miles out to sea, bobbed in and out of view. Other than that—nothing.

One hour had passed since he had called in their position on the handheld GPS. The boat coming from the sea—the boat that Abdur Rahman, the second most powerful man in the Council of Ishmael, had promised—was nowhere to be seen.

Fadil considered his predicament. He congratulated himself as his captive began to moan. Her *live* capture would catapult his status to the top of the council, perhaps making him a candidate for the coveted council status. To become a member of the Council of Ishmael—the most powerful Islamic organization in the world—was more than he could have dreamed of as a boy. But now, with the help of Allah, he would become a council member and sit at the right hand of the great Hussein al-Akhma himself—if he could finish this mission.

His mind turned back to the captive. The last of the sedative was now wearing off. Once she awoke and started to make noise again, they would have to either knock her unconscious or kill her.

So far, no one had passed by on the beach. But the longer they waited, the greater the chance they would encounter someone. They still had enough ammunition to eliminate a few stray bystanders, but the less noise the better.

He wondered about the accuracy of the GPS device, which he had purchased from a hunting goods store in America and shipped to France. Perhaps he should call again. But that would risk detection.

Fadil wanted a cigarette, but igniting his lighter would be a risk as well. Still, the nicotine urge twisted his insides. He retrieved the pack of Camels from his shirt pocket, popped one out, and stuck it in his mouth. Maybe if he lit the end, he could just keep his palm over it.

A silhouette running toward him on the beach to the right brought his Uzi into a firing position. An excited whisper came from the figure. "Fadil! Fadil!"

Salah. Fadil brought the Uzi down.

"This way." Salah motioned for Fadil to follow him back down the beach.

Fadil broke into a jog, and a few seconds later, three more dark silhouettes were visible, wading in the surf.

"Brother Fadil," one of them whispered. "You have a prisoner for us?"

A large rubber raft bobbed in the surf near the men. *Praise be to Allah. Blessed be the prophet. Peace be upon him.* "Salah, go get Ghazi. You two bring L'Enfant!"

"Yes, Fadil."

Two minutes later, Ghazi and Salah jogged back down the beach, carrying the woman. They laid her in the bottom of the boat, then shoved it back into the surf.

All six council commandos—Fadil, Salah, Ghazi, and the three from the sea—piled into the craft. One ripped a cord, cranking the small motor. Soon they snaked across the rolling inbound swells and out into the black night.

Five minutes later, Fadil reached into his pocket, extracted his lighter, lit a cigarette, and dreamed of glory.

CHAPTER 13

10065 English Ivy Way
Rancho San Diego
Spring Valley, California

Chris opened the front door of his townhouse to the spectacular view of the sun rising just over Mount Miguel. He drew the crisp California air into his lungs, threw back his head, and smiled at the blue sky.

Today will be the day! He smiled. *The day I meet Zack! And after I've taken care of Zack, Eleanor will surely call! And after that, my destiny will be assured!* He picked up the *San Diego Union-Tribune* and stepped back into the foyer to the sound of the beeping microwave.

"Green tea's ready," he said to Alvin the parakeet. "Daddy will be right there." The bird chirped as Chris opened the microwave and inhaled the aroma of the green tea that was part of his daily breakfast routine.

Mmm.

He opened the cupboard and retrieved the package of Oreos he had just purchased. The first Oreo went precisely in the middle of an octagonal white ceramic plate. Chris removed the top, exposing the white cream, like a sunny-side-up egg. He reached for a toothpick, then began his morning routine of dissecting the Oreo cream. First he cut a diagonal line through it. Then, crossways to the first cut, he made a second diagonal cut. Repeating the process, he meticulously carved the cream into eight slices.

With the blunt end of the toothpick, he lifted the first wedge of cream from the cookie base and placed it on the center of his tongue. *Oh, so good.* A sip of hot green tea, then another wedge of cream. Two more cookies fell victim to the toothpick turned scalpel, each wedge followed by a glorious sip of green tea.

When the last delectable slice had been consumed, Chris carefully folded the six brown cakes into a napkin and dropped them into the wastebasket.

"Come to Daddy." Chris extended his hand, palm down, into the cage. The parakeet hopped onto the back of his hand, then jumped onto his right shoulder. "That's a good boy."

The bird peeped and pecked at his ear as Chris sipped more herbal tea and glanced at the *Union-Tribune*.

A drop of tea splattered onto his shirt when the headlines jolted his concentration:

NAVY, BREWER PROSECUTE GAY MAN
Claxton Criticizes "Neanderthal" Mentality

By Adrian Branch, Military Affairs Editor

The *Union-Tribune* has learned the navy has filed court-martial charges against a gay naval officer in San Diego for allegedly "sexually assaulting" sailors aboard a U.S. submarine.

The defendant, Ensign Wofford Eckberg, is a U.S. Navy SEAL, who according to court documents filed by COMNAVBASE allegedly committed the sexual assaults while on board a U.S. Navy submarine.

Eckberg himself has been hospitalized for nearly ninety days, having suffered from a broken arm and collarbone at the hands of other Navy SEALs. No charges have been filed against the SEALs who allegedly assaulted Eckberg, according to the source, who spoke on condition of anonymity.

To add even more drama to this developing story, the *Union-Tribune* has learned that the navy has assigned its top prosecutor to the case, Lieutenant Commander Zack Brewer.

Senator Eleanor Claxton was quick to criticize—

No. This could not be true!

Chris's face flushed. He balled the paper into a wad and slung it across the floor. The Oreo-less ceramic plate flew across the room, crashed into the piano, banged against the keyboard, and shattered into a dozen pieces.

He would have to show Zack what he needed to do. With Zack professing a political conversion, publicly supporting Eleanor, Eleanor would certainly take notice of Chris's political talents to bring even pigheaded conservatives into the fold. Of course, that was it. He would find Zack and straighten all this out.

Café Pacifica
2414 San Diego Avenue
Old Town
San Diego, California

Old Town, home of the original Spanish Mission, which later became modern-day San Diego, had been restored as a pristine California State Park. Adjacent to Balboa Park and just a mile or so inland from San Diego Bay, the palm tree–lined oasis in the midst of California's second-largest city brimmed with quaint art shops, museums, and restaurants. It became Zack's favorite weekend off-base hangout when he was first stationed at the 32nd Street Naval Station four years ago.

Then came the case of *United States v. BT3 (SEAL) Antonio Blount*, followed by *United States v. Mohammed Olajuwon et al.* and finally by *United States v. Mohammed Quasay*. Zack had acquired such celebrity status that even a stroll anywhere in the city became a nonstop marathon of autograph seekers, gawkers, well-wishers, and even an occasional heckler or two. As a result, Zack confined his life to either his La Mesa home or inside the barbed-wire fences of the naval station.

But in the last year, with media interest waning, he'd started slipping out in public again, often unnoticed.

With the case of *United States v. Ensign Wofford Eckberg* now about to settle, Zack decided that a Saturday morning foray to Old Town was just what the doctor ordered. Dressed in jeans and a black turtleneck and wearing dark shades to preserve anonymity, he sat on the outdoor patio at Café Pacifica, sipped fresh black coffee, and bathed in the warm morning sunshine.

The waitress, an attractive Hispanic-looking girl who spoke impeccable English, smiled and asked if he was ready to order. Her pretty black eyes showed no sign of recognition.

Good.

"A vegetable omelet with wheat toast," he said.

"Anything else?"

"No, thank you."

The waitress smiled again, nodded, and walked away.

Along the sun-soaked, palm-lined pedestrian street, a dozen or so tourists took in the sights of the old Spanish village. They paid him no attention.

Zack took another sip of coffee, then picked up his copy of the official U.S. Navy newspaper, the *Navy Times*. Today's edition contained the staff corps promotions list, showing the names of all of the officers promoted in the navy's medical, nursing, medical service, dental, chaplain, and JAG corps. While Zack had been deep-selected for lieutenant commander a year ago—one year ahead of his Naval Justice School classmates—he was interested in how his colleagues were doing. He turned to page 44, which contained the names of all those JAG officers across the world who were in his "year group" and thus eligible for promotion at the same time.

PROMOTIONS TO LIEUTENANT COMMANDER
Judge Advocate General's Corps: (2500)

Sarah Jennifer-Abigail Blanzy
Graham Hardison Brown
Kevin Deacon Clark
Martin Somerset Chilton
Diane Jefferson Colcernian (posthumously)

Zack removed his shades, squinted against the bright sunlight, cupped his hand over his eyes, and reread the last name.

Diane Jefferson Colcernian (posthumously)

Dear Lord. How could she still freeze him in his tracks? Every little thing that reminded him of Diane let him know he would never get over her.

Never.

"Sir, your omelet is ready."

They had promoted her posthumously. It was an honor reserved for dead officers.

"Sir."

He looked up. The smiling waitress held a tray with his veggie omelet. He folded the *Navy Times* and laid it on the table.

"Excuse me, but you look familiar. Do I know you?" An inquisitive look crossed her face.

He slipped his shades back on. "No, I don't think we've had the pleasure."

His cell phone rang. He checked the caller ID and saw the name Shannon McGillvery.

He smiled and nodded at the waitress, who took his cue and walked away; then he popped open the chirping cell phone.

"Hi, Shannon."

"Zack, what's the matter?"

"What do you mean, what's the matter? Nothing is the matter."

"Zack, you don't sound right."

"I'm fine."

There was a pause. Shannon spoke again. "You know, Zack, you weren't supposed to leave your house until we got there. You know what Washington said, and you know Captain Rudy's directives."

Zack rolled his eyes. "What are they gonna do? Kick me out of the navy?" He sipped his coffee, waiting for her answer.

"I'll pretend I didn't hear that."

"Good." This time he switched from the black coffee to the ice water. "Maybe it's a male ego thing. You know. The concept of being protected by a five-foot-five redhead."

"I thought you liked redheads."

Zack didn't respond.

"Sorry," she said. "That was insensitive."

Zack forked the omelet. "No problem."

"What did you do, head down to Old Town?"

"Yep. Café Pacifica."

"I had a feeling that's where you'd go."

"Yeah. You had a feeling *and* you had that magnetic GPS transmitter you stuck under the hood of my car." Zack snickered.

"How do you know such things?"

"Maybe I should apply for a job with NCIS."

"I'm almost there, Commander."

"Want me to order for you?"

"Sure. How about coffee and pancakes?"

"Got it." Zack hung up and motioned for the waitress. Though he hated the idea of having a bodyguard, he looked forward to seeing Shannon.

Chris parked his yellow Volkswagen Beetle in the lot just off Juan Street, behind the Alvarado House, one of the better-known landmarks in Old Town. He opened the door and stepped out into the sunshine. A relentless twisting grabbed hold of his stomach.

He sat back down in the car and pulled the dagger from his pocket. Senator Claxton was right. Zack *had* to be persuaded not to endorse hate crimes against gays. He must get out of the national spotlight and not interfere with Eleanor's destiny. This was a family matter. And Eleanor was family. This was for her honor. This was for her historic election.

Two SDPD officers walked across the parking lot, toward the car. Chris shoved the dagger under the bucket seat and held his breath.

They strolled past the car, about twenty feet parallel to the driver's side. Chris watched in the rearview as they disappeared around the Alvarado House and into the park. He blew a sigh of relief.

Shannon swung the white U.S. government Ford Taurus a little too quickly into the parking lot behind the Alvarado House. Her briefcase flew across the backseat, into the passenger's door.

Her job, she had decided, had made her a reckless driver. Guarding Zack Brewer should qualify her for hazardous-duty pay. That he would venture out alone, despite NCIS warnings, made her want to slap him. If he were anyone else, she would complain to his commanding officer. And she might do that yet for his own protection if he didn't get with the program. She was a professional assigned to protect him, yet she felt like a schoolgirl in a stupid, stupid game of he loves me, he loves me not.

She hit the brakes, parked the car, balled her fist, and pounded it against the steering wheel.

Ouch.

She slipped her gun in the holster under her warm-up suit, got out of the car, slammed the door, and started a fast walk—almost a jog— toward the park.

She barely noticed the yellow Volkswagen bug as she walked past it.

The woman who'd just stepped past his car looked familiar, Chris thought. Where had he seen her? *Hmm.* Maybe it was just his imagination.

He reached under the seat and grabbed the dagger.

The stainless-steel blade glistened in the sunlight streaming through the sunroof. Yes, this would be the perfect object lesson, he thought.

He opened the door, stepped out of the car, and scanned the area for any police officers.

All clear.

He locked the door and headed toward the park.

CHAPTER 14

English Channel
25 miles northwest of Dieppe, France
Course 290 degrees

Allah, in all his providence, had supplied the crew of this godforsaken rubber boat with additional syringes and sedatives, which had kept Fadil's prize heavily sedated through the night. Now it was daylight, and the hours crept by while Ghazi and Salah vomited and heaved—fourteen times, Fadil had counted, between the two of them—and Fadil had been sick for the last hour. If only Allah had provided Dramamine for the incessant rocking out in the middle of nowhere.

"There it is," one of them cried.

Fadil rose up from the bottom of the boat.

The ship was off to the left, lying low in the sea. Except for the hideous boxy superstructure that rose from the aft, it was a sleek craft, long and black. An ensign with white, blue, and red horizontal stripes fluttered in the wind off the stern.

The flag of the Russian Republic.

"Are you sure?" another crewman asked. "We cannot afford any unwanted rescues."

"Everyone arm weapons," the coxswain of the boat ordered. All of the crew members except the coxswain, who was navigating the craft, grabbed their guns. "No firing unless on my order."

The craft swung closer around the rear. Now they saw the writing on the stern, but the rolling swells made it difficult to focus on the ship's name. A few sailors armed with rifles stood along the stern.

"Be ready. We're moving in closer," the coxswain announced. A couple of the sailors on the ship brought their rifles down on the boat, which brought the barrels of the Uzis up toward the ship.

"Ahoy, the boat!" shouted one of the sailors in heavily accented English through a bullhorn. "Halt in the water!"

The coxswain ignored the admonition, inching the boat closer toward the stern. Rifle fire rang from the stern of the ship. Bullets whizzed in a perimeter around the boat.

"Get back, you idiot," Fadil yelled at the coxswain. "You will get us all martyred." He looked back up at the stern and saw the Russian lettering on the back of the ship: *Александр Попович.*

"That is it!" the coxswain yelled. "The *Alexander Popovich!*"

"Turn this boat around or I'll shoot." Fadil pointed his Uzi at the coxswain.

"Ahoy, *Alexander Popovich*," the coxswain, ignoring Fadil, yelled back at the sailors through the boat's megaphone. "Black Sea Express! Hold your fire! Repeat! Black Sea Express!"

The firing stopped.

"Drop your weapon," the coxswain snapped at Fadil. "For your own sake I will ignore your stupid stunt this once. Anything else stupid gets reported to the council. Understand?"

"Ahoy, Black Sea Express!" a sailor on the back of the *Alexander Popovich* called out through the bullhorn, still in Russian-accented English but in a friendlier tone. "Bring your craft around to port!"

"Coming to port!"

Fadil put down his weapon and stared up at the ship. The Russian freighter *Alexander Popovich,* its captain and crew available for hire to the highest bidder, would be his ride to glory. Fadil looked to the heavens and mumbled thanks to Allah. He felt like saluting the white, blue, and red flag of the Russian Republic waving from her stern.

Twenty minutes later, he looked up from the rubber boat as an unconscious Jeanette L'Enfant dangled supine in a metal basket halfway between the Atlantic Ocean and the gunwales of the *Alexander Popovich.* The ship's mechanical cranes were hoisting his bounty up gradually. He envisioned the embrace and kisses he would receive from al-Akhma. A minute or so later, they slung her over the top, out of his view.

The sun was setting now, enveloping them in shadows as another basket was lowered. This one was for him.

"I should leave you out here with the sharks," the coxswain snapped through a lit Camel, then blew a blast of smoke in Fadil's face.

"My apologies," Fadil said. "I reacted too rashly."

"Get off my boat." The coxswain pointed Fadil to the hanging basket.

Fadil stepped in, and as he sat down, the basket lifted him out over the water. Five minutes later, they swung him over the gunwale, onto the deck.

A stocky, gruff-looking man with a black beard, wearing a black jacket and smoking a cigarette, greeted him. "I am Captain Yuri Mikalvich Batsakov." The wind was picking up now, blowing the captain's smoke into Fadil's face. "Welcome to *Alexander Popovich*."

The captain disappeared below, and Fadil walked to the port gunwale and, with a steady cool breeze blowing in his face, watched the sun sink into the Atlantic.

CHAPTER 15

Gobi Desert
Southeast of Ulaanbaatar, Mongolia

The darkness.

At first she had been petrified of it.

She had not known what it might bring.

When he had started coming in the afternoons, she had stayed up all night, certain he would reappear through the walls of the tent. It was the same each time. They would yank her outside, force her onto a chopping block as if to behead her, then stop.

Night after night, she had remained awake, shaking, her eyes wide open with fear, not drifting off until dawn's first light.

She had waited for him to come. But it was the light—the sunbeam through the pinhole reaching the far corner—that seemed to trigger their animalistic instincts.

Weeks passed. Then months.

Over time, she became convinced that he would not come in the dark.

The dark became a security blanket of sorts. A blanket of solitude. She sat alone in the corner, absorbing the gentle sound of the wind working the flaps of the tent.

For the moment, there was a peaceful repose. At least another twelve hours would pass before she fought him again.

She closed her eyes and began to pray.

"Dear Lord, without your intervention, my time is short. They keep talking about my death after a certain number of days. I'm afraid and lonely. And if it be your will, please rescue me from this place. Let me see my family again. Let me see him again.

"In Jesus' name. Amen."

She lay on the floor, her mind drifting. He was so handsome in white. In his chokers, at the end of the aisle with his groomsmen ... bearing swords and standing at parade rest.

Claxton campaign California headquarters
Situation room
Hyatt Regency Hotel
Century City
Los Angeles, California

Jackson Gallopoulous sat alone, drinking coffee and perusing the articles in this morning's editions of the *Los Angeles Times*, the *San Francisco Chronicle*, and the *San Diego Union-Tribune*.

California's three major newspapers had run the press releases issued by the campaign, giving front-page coverage to the carefully planted story. Each had, at his personal insistence, included the "Neanderthal mentality" quote within the first six paragraphs.

Fabulous.

Campaign polling showed that among likely voters considered most liberal, tough talk against the military would draw favorable responses. The phrase "Neanderthal mentality" was one of several phrases tried out on a sample test group in San Francisco and had scored higher than "stone-age mentality," "discriminatory mind-set," and "stone-age witch hunt."

The phrase was written into Eleanor's speech, and when she delivered it, she made an on-the-spot change from "Neanderthal mentality" to "Neanderthal witch hunt."

Some papers had picked up on the "Neanderthal witch hunt" comment and quoted her on that. "Neanderthal mentality" was quoted by the big three based on the press release he had issued.

Good.

Preliminary poll numbers should be out soon. And Eleanor should be down for her morning political briefing.

Jackson checked his watch. The double doors swung open. Eleanor, wearing a black pantsuit, was followed by her Secret Service entourage.

"Whatcha got, Jackson?" She pointed to the coffeepot. One of her Secret Service underlings obliged. She sat at the head of the table, beside Jackson, and flicked off two flakes of dandruff.

"Just what the doctor ordered, Eleanor." Jackson slid all three news-papers in front of her. She picked up the *Los Angeles Times* first.

Jackson braced for a curse-laden tirade as her blue eyes scanned from left to right.

The first sip of coffee brought a sly smile from the woman who would be president.

CHAPTER 16

Café Pacifica
2414 San Diego Avenue
Old Town
San Diego, California

The handsome JAG officer was enjoying a mug of black coffee when Shannon approached the table. He looked up at her. His face bore a smile but also a *whatcha gonna do about this?*

"What's up, Fireball?"

"If I were your mother, you'd be in time-out, Commander Brewer." Shannon pulled off her designer shades.

"Just time-out?" He motioned for her to be seated. "I must say I'm a bit disappointed."

"Oh, really?" She sat down. "I'm glad you're okay."

Just then the waitress arrived with an order of pancakes. "Were these for you, ma'am?"

"Those are for her," Zack confirmed as she set the pancakes and coffee in front of Shannon, who nodded and thanked her.

"Reading the *Navy Times*?" Shannon poured cream into her coffee.

"Read all I need to read."

"Then you saw?"

"Yes, I saw."

She squirted syrup on her pancake. "How do you feel about that?" She looked at him. The dimple. It was that slight dimple in his chin that made him so distracting.

"You mean the posthumous promotion?"

"Yes."

"I think it was appropriate." He downed his coffee as she cut her pancake into small portions. "I wish there was some way she could know."

Shannon chewed a very small bite of pancake, then dabbed the cloth napkin against her cheek. "Zack, have you read this morning's *Union-Tribune*?"

"Excuse me, waitress. More water, please?"

"Of course." The waitress poured more ice water into his glass.

"I don't read liberal rags," he said.

"Just what's wrong with liberal? You know, my family is from a long line of Democrats. Jimmy Carter is one of the most decent Christian men in the world."

"I didn't say Democrat rag. I said liberal rag."

"Here." She ignored the comment. "You should read this." She slid the *San Diego Union-Tribune* across the table. "Front page."

Zack picked up the paper.

NAVY, BREWER PROSECUTE GAY OFFICER WHO MAY BE VICTIM OF HATE CRIMES

By Laurie Jane McCaffity, Military Affairs Correspondent

San Diego—The *Union-Tribune* has learned that the navy has begun the general court-martial of a gay naval officer accused of sexual assault on board a *Los Angeles* class attack submarine. The officer, Ensign Wofford Eckberg, is a Naval Academy graduate and a U.S. Navy SEAL.

"What?"

Unnamed sources close to the situation say Eckberg may have been the victim of hate crimes, having suffered a broken collarbone solely because he is gay.

"That's ridiculous! He was assaulting sailors in their bunks!"

"I know that," Shannon said. "And you know that, but—"

"Hang on a second." Zack wagged his index finger in the air.

But the navy has taken no action against the gay officer's attackers. Moreover, the navy's top prosecutor, Lieutenant Commander Zack Brewer, is prosecuting the case.

"Oh, that's just great."

Brewer's presence in the case is viewed as a symbol of the navy's determination to convict Eckberg, and immediate fire has come from Democratic presidential hopeful, Senator Eleanor Claxton —

"Oh, please."

— who criticized the navy and Lieutenant Commander Brewer for his involvement in the case.

"The navy should be ashamed of itself for this homophobic witch hunt," Claxton said. "The American people deserve some answers. Why is the victim of these hate crimes being prosecuted while the perpetrators, thugs who call themselves sailors, are left alone?

"Ensign Eckberg is a Navy SEAL. He is an American hero —

"Please. A hero?"

— and the navy is prosecuting him for one reason alone. He is gay. Commander Brewer, who was viewed as an American hero before all this, is now the chief witch-hunter in this witch hunt. Brewer should be ashamed —"

"That's it," Zack said. "I can't take any more of this garbage." He slid the paper back to Shannon. "And to think this person could become president of the United States."

"That would make her *your* commander in chief."

"I'm going to vomit."

"Hey, I'm just the messenger."

"So much for my return to anonymity." Zack finished his ice water. "Come on. Let's get out of here before I get recognized." He stood, then walked around the table and pulled out her chair. "I'll buy the rest of your breakfast on base."

"I'm with you, sailor."

Old Town
San Diego, California

Chris felt for the dagger in his pants pocket and stepped onto the main pedestrian walkway in Old Town. The dagger was ready for use if Zack wasn't cooperative. The restaurant was about two hundred yards away. He would have been there already, but he couldn't control his breathing.

Control, Chris. Control.

He inhaled, and then his lungs froze.

Zack! Walking toward me. Dear God, help me.

The woman with the strawberry-blonde hair was with him. He'd seen her before. Was she the woman from a moment ago? The one who had walked past his car?

Yes, and before that too. In the magazine article.

McGillvery.

As he mentally prepared to strike, hot jets of blood shot into the back of his head. He felt in his pocket for the cold handle of the dagger. Like a cat, he sprang forward toward Zack and the woman.

A blur of movement caught Zack's attention. The man rushing at them looked like a safety blitzing a quarterback.

"Get back!" He swung Shannon behind him, shielding her.

A wet mass splattered his face. He glanced at Shannon. Saliva dripped down her hair. He sprinted after the man, who had doubled back toward the restaurant.

"Wait!" Shannon called from behind him.

Ignoring her, he threaded his way through pedestrians, closing the distance.

"He could be dangerous!"

Zack leaped forward, bringing the assailant down in a tackle.

"What's the deal with you, man?" Zack grabbed his collar from each side, pinning him to the ground. The man struggled to reach for his pocket. Zack thrust his knee into the man's stomach.

"Stop!" Shannon's voice grew closer.

"I ought to take your head off!"

"No!" Shannon said, now directly behind him.

"Get up!" Zack yanked the assailant by the collar, jerking him off the ground, and jacked his back into a palm tree. "That was a *lady* you spit on back there." He cocked his fist into a striking position. "I should smash your head in."

The man cowered. "No hate crimes!" he screeched. "Don't break my collarbone, Zack!"

"You know my name?"

"Forget Pinkie! Support Eleanor!"

"We'll see if your teeth can support my fist!"

The man's eyes bulged with fear.

"It's okay, Zack." Shannon spoke softly, her hands resting on his biceps. "I'll take care of this."

Zack stared at the man, and strangely, the thought of the one who had died for him—for this wimp in front of him—brought a wave of unexpected compassion. He released the man's collar, and the assailant tumbled to the ground.

Shannon drew her gun. "All right, show me some identification!"

"Don't shoot!" the man pleaded, his eyes filling with tears. "Please."

"Hands up!" Shannon ordered.

Sobbing, the man complied.

"Stand up!"

He stood, his hands on his head. Onlookers gathered, chatting among themselves or on their ubiquitous cell phones.

"Check his wallet, Zack."

The wallet bulged in the back right pocket of the man's jeans. Zack lifted it out and handed it to Shannon.

"Hmm." Shannon pulled out his driver's license, flicked to the man's face, then to the license, then back again. "Normally go around spitting on people, Mr. Reynolds?"

"I ..." He eyed Zack, then Shannon. "I was sending a message to Zack." He looked back at Zack.

"Oh, you were, were you?"

No answer.

"And how do you know who Zack is?"

Reynolds's eyes rolled over to Zack, and his creepy gaze froze into place. A knowing smile crossed his face.

"Not gonna answer? How bout I send *you* a message, Mr. Reynolds?" The *chink-chink* sound of the bolt action on Shannon's pistol yanked Reynolds's attention from Zack.

"Please don't kill me, Shannon." His voice cracked again.

"You know me too, do you?"

"Shannon," Zack said. "Let him go. I don't want to hassle with the police or the press."

She glanced at Zack and then back at Reynolds. "Get out of here, Reynolds, before I blow your head off!"

"Okay," he said, his mouth quivering. "I'm leaving."

"Go!"

Reynolds scampered into the crowd.

"Let's go, Zack."

"I'm with you."

U.S. Navy brig
32nd Street Naval Station
San Diego, California

Karen Jacoby, dressed in a working khaki female officer's skirt and blouse, pulled her Lincoln Navigator into the parking area separating the military courthouse from the navy brig. She grabbed her briefcase, which contained the Eckberg file, and stepped into the warm Southern California morning sunshine.

Stepping across the asphalt parking lot to the front steps of the navy brig, she wondered why the senior defense counsel had ordered her to the brig on a Saturday.

Frowning, she slipped on her sunglasses. Her duty was not to question orders; her duty was to obey orders.

She barely noticed the long, black Lincoln Continental with tinted windows as she walked by.

Two shore patrolmen in white jumper uniforms with Dixie Cup hats guarded the back entrance to the navy brig. They saluted as Karen stepped through the back door of the facility. The chief master at arms, sitting behind a wooden desk, rose as she approached. "May I help you, ma'am?"

"Lieutenant Jacoby for Lieutenant Commander Carpenter."

"Yes, ma'am," the chief said. "The commander's waiting for you. Right this way." The chief led Karen across the antiseptic-smelling tile foyer toward a closed wooden door. He opened the door, and Lieutenant Commander Harvey Carpenter, the senior defense counsel and Karen's immediate boss in her chain of command, stood.

"Karen, welcome," the senior defense counsel said. "That will be all, chief." He dismissed the master-at-arms with a sweep of his hand and motioned Karen into the office.

"You called for me, sir?" She noticed Carpenter was in his summer whites, which seemed a bit formal for a Saturday visit to the brig.

"At ease, Lieutenant," Carpenter said. Karen shifted to parade rest. "Look, we're not that formal around here. Maybe out in public—that's okay. But right now, just relax."

"Yes, sir."

"We have an important visitor here in the brig who wants to meet you."

"We do?"

"Yes. She's in the commanding officer's office. If you'll follow me …" Carpenter headed toward the door. Karen followed.

"May I ask who, sir?" Karen asked a moment later as they waited for the elevator.

"You'll see for yourself in a minute."

Thirty seconds later, the elevator doors parted and they stepped onto the second deck. A few masters-at-arms, in working blue dungaree uniforms, walked back and forth with radios. Two men in black pin-stripe suits stood guard at the closed door of the commanding officer's office. They wore some sort of listening devices in their ears with wires that dangled into their suits.

Commander Carpenter stopped outside the door and spoke to one of them. "Lieutenant Commander Carpenter and Lieutenant JG Jacoby are here." Then he turned to Karen. "Karen, show these gentlemen your military identification."

"Aye, sir."

The men took the cards, examined them, and gave them back. The guard on the left lifted a walkie-talkie to his mouth. "Lieutenant Commander Carpenter and Lieutenant JG Jacoby are here."

"Very well, send them in," a man's voice said through the walkie-talkie. The guard on the right opened the door, and Karen followed Commander Carpenter into the offices of Captain H. G. Brightwell, the commanding officer of the navy brig. Karen noticed that Brightwell, however, was not sitting at his desk. Instead, Brightwell, also dressed in summer whites, stood just to the left of his desk, beside another dark-suited man. Yet another dark-suited man, resembling the other three, stood to the right of the desk.

Behind the desk, a blonde woman sat in a swivel chair with her back to them, facing the window.

"Welcome, Lieutenant Jacoby." The female voice came from the captain's desk. Then the woman rotated the chair around, flashing Karen a devious grin.

Karen's heart pounded with nervous excitement as the woman, dressed in a blue pantsuit, rose and extended her hand. Her handshake was vicelike—similar to a man's—and charisma seemed to exude from every inch of her body.

"Lieutenant, I'm Eleanor Claxton." The great woman flashed the whitest teeth Karen had ever seen. In an instant, Karen felt as if she'd known her forever.

"It's a true honor to meet you, Senator." Karen couldn't help wondering about the turn her life had taken. First she had a case with the great Zack Brewer, and now she was standing in front of the most powerful woman in America, the woman who might become the first female president of the United States. She looked over at Commander Carpenter and Captain Brightwell, expecting them to say something.

Silence.

Claxton released Karen's hand and, pointing to the back of the room, spoke again. "Meet my chief of staff, Jackson Gallopoulous, and my press secretary, Mary-Latham Modlin."

Jackson Gallopoulous appeared to be thirtysomething and had a Greek look about him. He wore blue jeans and a red sweater. A woman about the same age stood next to him. She wore a black skirt and white top. Except for her frizzy brunette hair, Mary-Latham Modlin could have passed for Claxton's younger sister.

"Nice to meet you, Karen," Gallopoulous said.

"You too," Karen replied.

The senator flashed her a smile. "I suppose you must be wondering what this is all about."

"Yes, ma'am."

"This," Claxton said, pointing behind Karen, "is my legal counsel, Webster Wallace."

Karen turned. A distinguished-looking silver-haired gentleman smiled and nodded at her.

"Lieutenant," Claxton continued, "we'd like to speak with your client."

"My client?"

"Ensign Eckberg."

"Well ..." She looked to Commander Carpenter for assistance. Again there was none. "Well, Senator, I'd be happy to accommodate you. But right now we have a court-martial going on, and my concern is maintaining the attorney-client privilege."

Commander Carpenter winced.

"That's good lawyering, Lieutenant," boomed Wallace's voice from behind her. He walked up and stood beside Karen, making her feel uncomfortable. "What the lieutenant is saying, Senator"—Wallace spoke in low, smooth tones—"is that anything Ensign Eckberg says to you, or to me, or anyone else not his attorney, could be used against him as long as this court-martial continues."

"Mr. Wallace is right, Senator. That's my concern. Otherwise, I would be happy to have you speak with him."

"I'm impressed, Lieutenant," the senator said. "But there are two things you may want to know." A brief pause. Claxton's eyes shot toward Wallace, then back to Karen. "First, your client has called and asked to speak with Mr. Wallace here."

The senator's assertion took Karen aback. How would Eckberg have known Wallace's number? And why wouldn't she have known about it? She looked at Wallace, who gave her a single nod, affirming what Claxton had just said. "Plus, there's nothing we want to do that would compromise any privileged communication. But we feel that your case is of paramount importance to the national interests."

"I don't understand."

"You understand that I sit on the Senate Armed Services Committee and am a Democratic candidate for president of the United States?"

How am I supposed to react to that?

"Senator," Carpenter said, "as Lieutenant Jacoby's immediate superior in her chain of command, she *does* understand and very much respects your position and your work on the Armed Services Committee. We are very happy to arrange a meeting with Ensign Eckberg."

"That's right, Senator," Captain Brightwell added. "As commanding officer of the navy brig, we can escort your party—along with Lieutenant Jacoby, of course—upstairs for a meeting with the ensign right now."

"Well then," the senator said, nodding at Carpenter, "I guess it's settled. If you would lead the way, Captain?"

"By all means." Brightwell motioned for the senator and Wallace to follow him.

"You can come too, Lieutenant. He's *your* client."

Karen filed out of the office behind Senator Claxton, Wallace, Captain Brightwell, and Commander Carpenter.

CHAPTER 17

"Flight attendants, prepare for departure." The male British accent boomed over the plane's loudspeaker.

"Excuse me, Father, but could you bring your seat to the upright position?"

A single electronic tone beeped overhead.

"Of course." Robert looked up at the rosy-cheeked British Airways flight attendant and pressed the button to bring his seat forward. He silently prayed they would soon be airborne.

He'd escaped France last night on the cross-channel ferry, before anyone could connect him with his dead driver. And now if he could just get out of England, the chances of their turning this bird around over the Atlantic were remote. Of course, they could always arrest him when he changed planes at JFK . . .

"Ladies and gentleman, this is the first officer. We are number one for takeoff. We should be in the air and on our way to the colonies in approximately one minute."

The engines' whine turned to a high-pitched roar as the giant airliner rolled, gaining speed, down the runway. He felt the nose tip upward, then felt the wheels break contact with the runway.

Heavenly Father, grant thy servant safe passage to America. And may these papers be delivered into the right hands. And may thy hand

of protection be upon thy child Jeanette L'Enfant, wherever she is at
this hour. Protect her from all harm, and may justice be accomplished
by my mission. In the name of thy only begotten Son, Jesus Christ, I
pray. Amen.

Robert made the sign of the cross as the plane rolled to the right.
He knew the route. They would fly north over England, then Scotland,
and then roll to the east, flying over Northern Ireland and then across
the Atlantic.

He reached into the back flap of the seat just in front of him and
extracted the report that Jeannette had given him, aware that this was
probably the only such copy now in the free world. He had made the
extra copy and crammed it against his chest, under his clerical collar.
Now if he could just get the report into Commander Brewer's hands. He
made another sign of the cross, wrapped his arms around the report,
and closed his eyes.

CHAPTER 18

Bridge
Russian freighter Alexander Popovich
Course 15 degrees
Southeastern entrance to the Bosporus
Sea of Marmara

It is a beautiful sight, is it not?" Captain Yuri Mikalvich Batsakov smiled at the sight outside the bridge. They had reached the entrance to the Bosporus, the narrow strait of water that split Istanbul in half and connected the Sea of Marmara and the Black Sea. Beyond that, the great Muslim city Istanbul waited in all its glory on both sides of the narrow, twenty-mile strait.

Sailing through the Bosporus at night was like sailing through a sparkling jeweled necklace. This was the Bosporus that he, along with so many fellow Russian and Ukrainian sailors, had come to know and love. When he passed through this multicolored gem, its lights blinking along the hills to the entrance of the Black Sea, he would soon be home.

Batsakov brought a glass of vodka to his lips as two other ships—a freighter flying the horizontally striped azure and gold ensign of the Ukraine, and a cargo ship flying the horizontally striped white, blue, and red flag of Russia—moved in front of the *Alexander Popovich*. Both ships sputtered black smoke into a fading orange sky.

The Ukrainian ship was now edging its way into the Bosporus.

"Yes, beautiful indeed, my capitan." Fadil extracted a cigarette and a lighter.

"Soon we will be in the Black Sea. The territorial waters of the old Soviet Union." The captain inhaled a drag from his cigarette and followed that with a swig of vodka. "The finest waters in the entire world." Another drag. The Russian skipper unleashed three perfectly formed smoke rings. "I trust you will find our sailing there most hospitable."

"And I trust, my capitan, that Allah will bless this ship as we sail past the beautiful mosques and minarets of Istanbul and along the Turkish countryside." Fadil took a satisfying puff.

"You sound like a man who has sailed the Bosporus?"

"No, capitan. Only a man who has worshiped Allah in the greatest city of the old Ottoman Empire."

"Engines ahead one-third." Batsakov poured more vodka.

"Ahead one-third, Capitan," the helmsman parroted.

"So then," Batsakov continued as the engines of the *Alexander Popovich* revved, vibrating the ship, "perhaps your Allah will make an exception to his boring rules on alcohol and permit you to share vodka with an old sea dog?"

"Perhaps Allah will forgive me if I make this one exception?"

"Now that's my man." Batsakov chuckled. "Of course Allah will forgive you." The captain snapped his fingers. "Vitaly!" A scruffy-faced Russian sailor came running to attention.

"Dah, Capitan," the sailor said.

"Bring another bottle from my stateroom, for me and our guest, in honor of our passage through the Bosporus."

"Dah, of course, Capitan!"

"Steady as she goes," the captain bellowed. The *Alexander Popovich* edged into the entrance to the Bosporus. On the sides of the entrance, two ancient forts—the Fort at Anadolu on the Asian side and the Fort at Rumeli on the European side—stood as relics of the Crimean War.

"Vas vodka, Capitan," the steward returned.

"*Spaceeba.*" The captain raised his hand. "Pour some for our friend."

"Dah."

There was a clanking of glass, and within seconds, Fadil held a glass of clear vodka in his hand. Alcohol was against the strict teachings of Mohammed and the Koran. On the other hand, the Council of Ishmael was based upon and prided itself on the premise that its operatives could blend into any culture in the world for the advancement of the cause. For the advancement of the council and world domination of Islam, any ends would justify the means. Allah would understand. Allah willed it.

"To friendship." The captain raised his glass.

"To friendship." The vodka burned the back of Fadil's throat.

The captain drained his glass with one gulp and then poured another. "You know," he said, "they used to string a huge chain between these two forts to block ships from passing through."

"So I have heard, Capitan." Batsakov topped off Fadil's glass again. "During the Crimean War, as I understand it."

"Yes," Batsakov said, draining yet a second glass in a single gulp. "And speaking of chains, what is the status of our star passenger?"

"How kind of you to ask, Capitan. Perhaps you could spare another cigarette?" The captain produced a lighter and a cigarette, then lit the cigarette as Fadil sucked in.

"I ask from the goodness of my heart," the captain said. Another swig followed by a deep guffaw.

"And I suppose, Capitan, your interest has nothing to do with the $50,000 bonus you are promised by the council if our star passenger is delivered to the shores of Russia."

"Fadil," the captain laughed, "you make me sound like a capitalist pig. You know all old Russians are communists at heart." Another swig and a smile. "We are idealistic. Not so consumed with the mighty dollar."

"Of course." Fadil tried matching the captain's sips. "Just as we Muslims are all teetotalers, not tempted by the satanic alcoholic drinks of the West."

More laughter. More clanking of glasses.

"And not tempted by the non-satanic beverages of the east, such as pure vodka." Batsakov chuckled.

"But of course not!" Fadil faked a sip. "Anyway, all this talk of friendship and of our star passenger is tugging on the emotional strings of my compassionate heart, Capitan." Fadil mimicked the Russian, raised his glass to his lips, and, with a wobbly hand, downed the rest of his vodka. All in the name of international relations, of course. The bridge seemed to spin, and for a moment, the only sound Fadil could hear was laughter.

Russian laughter.

Lots of it.

And then the bridge stabilized. "My capitan, perhaps I will pay a visit to our star passenger. You know, to ensure our cargo is still seaworthy."

The captain grinned, revealing a yellowish smile in much need of dental work. Some teeth were capped. Others were chipped. A few were missing. "Vitaly!"

"Dah, Capitan."

"Accompany our friend here down to Guspyadeen L'Enfant's state-room. No need to accompany him inside. Just make sure he gets there. Do you understand, Vitaly?"

"Dah, Capitan. Completely."

Fadil felt the captain's aide lead him off the bridge onto the catwalk, where the cool sea breeze invigorated the blood rushing to his head. In a moment, he would rouse the woman who would catapult his status to the stars.

Conference room 1
U.S. Navy brig
32nd Street Naval Station
San Diego, California

Let me make this clear, Ensign Eckberg. We contacted you because we do not think you should plea."

Wofford Eckberg couldn't believe his eyes. Standing before him was the woman he admired most in the world. The woman who would be president. She stood beside his attorney, Lieutenant Jacoby, along with two other naval officers, the commanding officer of the brig and a lieutenant commander JAG type.

But for the time being, the naval officers barely held his attention. The woman who had stood for gay rights more than any other in the world was in a conference room in the navy brig. With him. How was this possible? When he dialed the number the man gave him at the courthouse, he had no idea it would lead to this.

"Senator, this is an honor indeed. I'm overwhelmed by your interest."

"Ensign Eckberg, why don't you have a seat and relax." The senator waved him from a parade rest position.

"Thank you, Senator." Wofford pulled up a chair and sat at the conference table. Claxton sat down just opposite him across the table. "Anyway, Senator, Lieutenant JG Jacoby has already worked out a deal with Lieutenant Commander Brewer. Under the agreement, I wouldn't have to plea at all. I would just resign from the navy. That way, I would avoid any possibility of a conviction on my record."

Claxton exhaled, almost in a sigh, then glanced in the direction of the distinguished-looking man whose name Wofford could not remember at the moment.

"Look, Ensign, do you mind if I call you Wofford?"

"That would be fine, Senator."

"Good. And by the same token, all my staff and close friends call me Eleanor. And I'd like you to do the same."

During his four years of intensive training at the Naval Academy, he had been drilled on the formalities of the chain of command, which placed members of Congress on a higher pedestal than even navy admirals—and made him uncomfortable to even consider addressing the most powerful woman ever to serve in Congress by her first name. On the other hand, if the ranking minority member of the Senate Armed Services Committee insisted that he call her Eleanor, then as far as he was concerned, it was tantamount to a direct order.

"Yes, ma'am ... uh ... Eleanor."

"Now that's better." She mustered a fleeting smile that for an instant cast a soft, pretty look across her face. She reached across the table and patted his hand; her touch electrified his body as if an invisible magnetic field flowed from her. Whatever she wanted didn't matter. What did matter struck him to the core: he wanted to please this great woman. "Wofford, there's somebody I want you to meet." She raised her hand, and Jackson Gallopoulous opened the door behind her.

It was him—the stranger from the courthouse. The Islamic man who had given him the note.

"Wofford, I'd like you to meet Mohammed. Mohammed, this is Wofford."

"Nice to meet you in a more relaxed setting." Mohammed smiled and extended his hand across the table for a shake. Something about this Muslim was very odd. If Wofford didn't know better ...

"You're Muslim?"

"I *was* Muslim, Wofford." He released Wofford's hand and pulled up a chair next to the senator. "Now I work for a greater cause. I kept the name to underscore a point."

"I don't understand."

"Wofford," Claxton said, "we live in a world of constant change. Change is either progressive or regressive. If elected president, I want to be an agent of change. You see, many institutions have been guilty of homophobic bigotry. Religious institutions have led the way. Christians have been the biggest offenders. But Muslims, who also trample on the rights of women, have been complicit in this bigotry.

"Institutions that oppose gay rights, whether religious institutions like Christianity or Islam, or military institutions like the U.S. Navy, must be brought down. Mohammed here had the courage to stand against part of his heritage that is anachronistic and oppressive. He's like Martin Luther King and Rosa Parks. He's a pioneer in civil rights. And you, Wofford"—Claxton reached out and put her hand on his—"*you* also have a unique opportunity, as fate would have it, to become a hero for millions who follow you."

Wofford scanned the room. The Claxton party nodded in agreement. Captain Brightwell, the brig CO, seemed stolid, while Lieutenant JG Jacoby was wincing.

"I don't understand, Senator. What do you want me to do?"

Claxton poured a glass of water from the pitcher in the center of the table, then took a sip. "We are concerned about the hate crimes committed against you, Wofford. We know Lieutenant Jacoby has done a good job for you, but if this is swept under the rug, how will this kind of reprehensible conduct be deterred in the future?"

"I see your point."

"If you stand and fight these charges in a court-martial, we will make the crimes committed against you a public issue. You will have the best legal defense money can buy. If fact, Web Wallace here will step in and defend you—or assist Lieutenant Jacoby in defending you—at no cost. And even if you are convicted, Wofford—and I don't think that's likely—but even if you are, I guarantee there will be book deals, interview opportunities, and a job on my staff when I am elected president of the United States." The senator's eyes narrowed into a piercing gaze. "And, Wofford, I *will* be elected." A feminine smile returned to her face.

"Wofford." This was Mohammed. "What they did to you was *wrong*. They beat you up, and now they're prosecuting *you*. Don't sweep this under the rug."

Wofford glanced at Karen Jacoby. She was looking the other way.

"We'll stick by you," Mohammed continued. "Look. I'll stick by you."

The senator nodded her head in approval, again smiling.

"Okay, Senator. Okay. Whatever you need, I'll do it."

CHAPTER 19

Amidships
Russian freighter Alexander Popovich
Somewhere along the Bosporus

Dusk

They embraced on the rocky beach by the blue waters of the Mediter-ranean. He was stunning in his white shirt and khakis. She looked up into his face as a breeze off the sea blew a shock of silver hair across his tanned forehead.

She had worn a white sundress just for the occasion.

Tonight would be the night.

A woman always had intuition about these things. Or so she had been told.

Tonight he would propose.

She was sure of it.

And then they would drive through the dark the short distance east to Monaco to announce their decision to her parents. Soon Jeanette L'Enfant would no longer be only the associate of Europe's greatest avocat.

She would be his wife.

His arms caressed her waist. His hands moved up her arms. And then he held her shoulders. A fire ignited in his eyes.

"What's the matter, Jean-Claude? Why are you shaking me?" Pain shot through her arms. "Jean-Claude, please. You are hurting me!"

Her vision blurred. The Mediterranean morphed into a fog. A white fog. And then the repulsive grin of a bearded Middle Easterner came into view. His face was menacing, but his eyes were anxious.

Then it hit her. Her dream was shattered. Jean-Claude was dead.

"Wake up, my princess!"

"Robert? Where's Father Robert?" A dull pain throbbed in her head. "Water. Please."

The scruffy-bearded man snapped his fingers and another man, a scrawny European-looking man stepped over her head. Scruffy Beard pulled her up by the shoulders to a sitting position while the other man poured water on her lips. Most of it spilled down her dress. A few drops seeped into her esophagus, reawakening some of her senses.

She heard a humming sound. Perhaps the sound of generators. And when she blinked again, regaining more of her vision, she felt shackles on her hands and feet.

"Where am I? Where is Robert?"

"Come, we'll go for a walk."

They guided her off the single bed and helped her shuffle, chains clanging, across a Formica floor. The steel door was oval-shaped with something that looked like a steering wheel in the middle.

The man with the European features steered the wheel to the left and the door opened. He and Scruffy Beard led her outside into the salty-smelling breeze, which brought her senses back to life. Then she realized she was on the deck of a ship.

The sun had set, and they appeared to be sailing down something that looked like a river, past a well-lit city.

"Where are we?"

"This is the Panama Canal," Scruffy Beard said through a cloud of suffocating cigarette smoke. "That is Panama City. Soon we will be in the Pacific."

Panama City. Of course. She had every reason not to trust these two. They murdered Jean-Claude. And now probably Father Robert. Wherever they were, the writing on the neon signs was not Spanish. And the illuminated mosques dotting the landscape of the city meant one thing.

The Middle East.

That had to be it. Where else would they be taking her? This was all connected to the *Quasay* case. She had angered the wrong people by allowing the plea that saved Quasay's life.

She looked across the waterway to the shoreline, searching for a national flag of some sort to help determine their whereabouts.

"Keep walking. Forward," Scruffy Beard ordered. "Have to keep our star passenger healthy." She felt his slimy hand touch her back between her shoulder blades.

She stepped forward, walking cautiously to avoid falling. Her mind strained for the mental image of a map of the Middle East. Where, where could this be?

Then it hit her.

The Suez Canal.

That had to be it. Yes, what else would account for the narrow waterway and the mosques dotting the landscape? But were there cities along the Suez? Except for her trip to Jerusalem to defend Lieutenant Commander Quasay last year, she hadn't paid much attention to Middle Eastern geography. That meant this had to be Egypt. She just wasn't sure what city.

Think, Jeanette. Think. What are the cities and towns along the Suez? I should know this. After all, the canal was designed and developed by a Frenchman.

Port Said was at the mouth, near the Mediterranean. Could she be there? And didn't the Suez run near Cairo?

No, not Cairo. What is the town midway down the canal? Think. Ismailia. Yes that's it.

And if this is the Suez and I remember my geography correctly, then it flows south into the Gulf of Suez and then into the Red Sea, which borders Saudi Arabia.

Not Saudi Arabia. Saudi Arabia is home of the Council of Ishmael. Dear Jesus, help me!

This was the second prayer she had uttered—albeit silently—in the last two days. A strange tingling fluttered in her chest, as if someone, or something, deep in her soul prayed for her. It brought her a moment of peace.

The feeling disappeared as quickly as it had come. She was in the Middle East, where women were treated like animals. She had seen the broadcasts. She knew what she might face. They would shove her to her knees and force her neck onto a block as the Al Jazeer cameras captured the image of the stainless-steel blade of the executioner's ax, then they would broadcast the footage around the world.

Jesus, help me. There it was again. That strange sense of peace.

"Move along!"

She would die now or die later.

But with shackles on? How could she survive in the water? The shackles weren't very tight. The chains gave her about twelve inches of leeway between her feet and maybe six inches between her wrists.

Maybe that was enough.

The side of the ship was about five feet away. Her chances if she jumped overboard were one in a million. Maybe a fisherman, maybe a boater, maybe *someone* would pull her out of the water. If she waited until they were in the Red Sea, jumping would mean automatic suicide.

And in Saudi, if that's where they were taking her, her chances for survival dropped to one in a billion. *Be decapitated by an ax—or get mangled by a ship's massive propeller in a canal built by a Frenchman.* That was her choice. If she died, at least dying in the Suez Canal would give her death a semblance of dignity.

She would take her chances with the propeller.

"Stop stalling." The Middle Easterner gave her a hard shove in the back, nearly knocking her off her feet. She caught her balance. She brought her hands together in front of her stomach, interlocking her fingers and thumbs, each hand squeezing the other.

"La Salle de Bains," she said. "I must go now." She turned quickly, bringing her face so close to his that she felt his breath. *"Vive la France!"*

She unleashed a sharp two-handed karate chop, striking the European man's groin area. Then her clasped hands clubbed the Middle Easterner's temple.

The man fell back, and she lurched on the steel deck toward the side of the ship. But her leg shackles sent her tumbling to the deck. On her hands and knees, she pushed forward, forward. Her face was now over the side of the ship.

Just a little farther.

She looked down and saw water rushing by. She pushed a little farther. Now her shoulders were over the side.

A hand gripped her hair, jerking her back to the deck. Two other hands grasped her ankles. They rolled her over on her back. The Middle Easterner stood over her again.

"Trying to misbehave, are you?" A clenched fist flew from the starry skies, smashing against her temple. She felt a warm trickle of blood as the stars above began to spin.

And then darkness.

CHAPTER 20

Office of Lieutenant Commander Zack Brewer
Building 73
Navy Trial Command
32nd Street Naval Station

Zack turned his back to the panoramic view outside his office window. Behind him, San Diego Bay's blue waters rippled in the sunlight. He leaned back in his chair and propped his feet on his desk. His spunky ever-present shadow sat in the corner of the office, her legs crossed. She sipped on a bottle of Dasani.

"That guy didn't look like a terrorist." He finished his coffee, then cradled his hands behind his head and yawned.

"Hardly," Shannon said. "But you never know." She placed the bottle on the corner of his desk. "I'm running a check on him just to be safe. Meantime, you stay out of public until we get a better read on all this."

"Too bad. I was going to take you to dinner to thank you for saving my life."

She smiled, and for a moment her face flushed a mild crimson. "We'll have to settle for steaks on the grill," she said, looking down and fumbling through papers.

The buzz of his office telephone broke the silence. "Excuse me, Commander Brewer." Legalman First Class Pete Peterson, Zack's military paralegal, was on the speakerphone.

"Yes, Pete?"

"Lieutenant Commander Poole is on the line."

He picked up the line.

"Hi, Wendy. What's up?"

"How's the case going?"

"Think we've got it settled."

"And they plucked us out of the ocean for that?"

"Tell me about it."

"So when do we finish our sailing trip?"

Zack hesitated. Why did it seem as though Shannon could hear everything she was saying? "We'll see."

Another slight pause. "Okay," she said. "Since it sounds like I might have to wait awhile, how about dinner at my place tonight? I make an awesome shrimp pasta, and I've got two bottles of vintage merlot, 1968. What do you say?"

"Dinner? Ahm." Shannon looked up from her paperwork. Her green eyes narrowed. There was a rapping on the door.

"Wendy, can you hang on for a second?"

"Sure."

"Come in."

The door opened and in stepped a slightly potbellied petty officer with a graying mustache, wearing the dark blue working uniform of a navy enlisted man with red chevrons on his left sleeve. "Sorry to interrupt you, sir, but Lieutenant JG Jacoby is on the line," Peterson said. "She said it was urgent, and your line was busy."

"What line?"

"Line four, sir."

"Thanks, Pete," Zack said. "Wendy, I've gotta take this call. Can I call you back?"

"Sure, Zack." A hint of disappointment tinged her voice. "Just don't forget, okay?"

"Okay."

He hung up and punched line four. "Hi, Karen. What's up?"

"Sorry to interrupt you, Commander, but there's a problem with our plea agreement."

"A problem? What problem?"

"I can't talk about it over the phone. But I can tell you this. None of this was my idea, and I'm opposed to it." Karen's voice wavered as if it were about to crack.

"Okay. Okay. It's going to be all right, Karen. Where do you want to meet?"

"Balboa Park, sir."

"Balboa Park?"

Shannon shook her head and mouthed, "No way."

"Two hours give you enough time, Karen?"

That sent Shannon's palms flying horizontally, like a baseball umpire signaling *safe* at a runner stealing second.

"Two hours will be fine, sir."

"Two hours would be fine, Karen." Shannon's pretty face contorted. "Ahm ..."

"No way," Shannon protested in a loud whisper.

"Where did you want to meet in the park, Karen?"

"Do you know where the Japanese Friendship Garden is?"

"Yes, I do. Good suggestion. That's not too crowded."

"All right. How about by the Buddhist temple?"

"The Buddhist temple it is," Zack said. "See you in a couple of hours."

"Oh, Zack?"

"Yes."

"I think it would be best if you came alone. I don't want to attract any attention."

"Okay, I'll be there." He hung up the phone.

"Excuse me, Zack?"

Shannon's eyes pierced through him. "Shannon, something's wrong."

"I don't have a background report on Reynolds yet. There's no reason you have to go to the park. Why can't Jacoby just come here to the office?"

"I don't know, Shannon, but she sounded spooked about something. Look, I have to go."

"I'm coming."

"No. You can guard me later in the day if you want, but she thought it would be best if I came alone."

"Zack, she's just a greenhorn JG out of justice school. What does she know?"

"She's got enough savvy to know something's wrong. Look, I've gotta go." He stood, gave her an affectionate pat on the shoulder, and walked out of his office.

CHAPTER 21

Gobi Desert
Southeast of Ulaanbaatar, Mongolia

lap, flap. Flap, flap.

F She opened her eyes, then realized that the wind blowing against the outside of her tent had awakened her from a shallow sleep. Sometimes a strong gust of wind meant a sharp drop in temperature would follow. Sometimes snow or ice pellets came after the wind.

At first, the sound of the wind in the darkness of the night was frightening to her. But after a few weeks of being awakened by it, she became accustomed to praying silently as the wind blew. Flitting at the edges of her mind was the memory of something she had read about the wind. It took her weeks to realize it was something about the Day of Pentecost in the book of Acts—the Holy Spirit rushing in the form of the wind. The image brought her peace.

She so longed to have a Bible with her. The wind was just one of the images she had tucked away in her memory. She tried to recall verses from the Psalms her mother had read aloud to her at bedtime when she was a child. Soon snatches of words and phrases came to her: *The Lord is my Shepherd ... He is my rock, my fortress, my refuge ... my place of safety ... Do not be afraid of the terrors of the night nor fear the dangers of the day ... I will rescue those who love me ... I will protect those who trust in my name ...* They became her lifeline at night.

She closed her eyes and listened. *Flap, flap. Flap, flap.*

When she prayed for comfort, the wind blew. And the wind reminded her of the Holy Spirit. The beatings and mock executions happened in the day. The sound of the wind brought her comfort at night.

And when the wind howled furiously and suddenly stopped, its power contrasted with peaceful silence, it was as if a lion had been roaring and had given way to a lamb.

That reminded her of something she remembered from the Bible: one day, the lion will lie down with the lamb.

She also remembered that Jesus was described as both a lion and a lamb. *Flap, flap. Flap, flap.* The thought of Jesus gave her a supernatural peace she could not understand.

The flapping stopped. Eerie silence, and then a warm peace descended inside the tent.

"Lord, I am a walking dead woman. They take me out and threaten to kill me. But they've not killed me yet. If you're there, give me comfort. Give me protection ... as you have promised," she said into the dark. "Lord, in this forsaken place, send me a friend. Help me escape."

The wind blew again, whistling through the top of her tent. She lay back down, closed her eyes, and prayed herself to sleep.

CHAPTER 22

Balboa Park
Park Boulevard entrance
San Diego, California

The silver Mercedes 320 entered Balboa Park on northbound Park Boulevard, then swung left onto Presidente Way, just in front of the Veterans Memorial Center Museum. The driver glanced in his rearview to see if he had been followed.

Nothing.

At least not yet.

A few yards down on the right of Presidente Way was one of several parking lots in the park. But this parking lot was one that Zack Brewer remembered well. The last time Zack had wheeled the Mercedes into this parking lot, Diane was with him. They were about to leave for their trip to Washington to meet the president. It was the last time he had been with her in San Diego.

As he parked under a tall palm tree in the sun-drenched lot, he thought about that Sunday afternoon just a few weeks before Easter. The great organist Vickie McKibben was performing the "Widor Toccata" at the outdoor Spreckels Organ Pavilion that afternoon. Diane saw the notice in the *San Diego Union-Tribune* and remembered the "Widor" being played on the large pipe organ at the church she attended when she was growing up in Norfolk.

Zack's mother had been a church organist in his hometown of Plymouth, North Carolina, and had herself tackled a watered-down version of the grand toccata—at the close of Easter Sunday services at the First Christian Church—and done a decent job with it.

Zack stepped out of the car and walked across the parking lot, his thoughts turning briefly to his meeting with Karen and the nagging sense that something had gone wrong in the Eckberg court-martial.

But his memories pushed even that worry from his mind. Eckberg. Karen. Shannon. All were a million miles away.

They first held hands in public that day. And as they walked into the large outdoor amphitheater, the rapid flurry of thirty-second notes, like a furious musical butterfly dancing through the palm trees and echoing off the pavilion itself, signified that McKibben had launched into the most majestic organ overture known to man.

He had sat with Diane on an aluminum bleacher at the end of one of the back rows, still holding her hand, overwhelmed at the musical glory of the moment.

The grand pavilion was empty now, he saw, as he walked along the sun-bathed path leading to the Friendship Garden. But the stillness, the emptiness, the memories—they all beckoned him.

He walked into the grand pavilion and took a seat on the same bleacher. He closed his eyes, felt her hand, heard the music ...

Gobi Desert
Southeast of Ulaanbaatar, Mongolia

lap, flap. Flap, flap.

The wind was picking up again. She opened her eyes and wondered how long she had been asleep.

But it wasn't the wind that had awakened her. Not this time anyway.

The mighty sound of the pipe organ's bass pedals roared across her consciousness.

Half note, half note, half note, half note, eight beats ... Driving, driving toward the powerful climax of the toccata ... Half note, half note, half note, half note, eight beats ...

Like furious wind chimes, dancing up and down the scale, thirty-second notes trumpeted over the top of the pulsating resonance of the mighty bass pedals.

Glorious.

Furious.

Exhilarating.

These emotions rushed through the air as the organist brought all the power of the organ's pipes to bear in a worshipful climax.

He had grabbed her hand once more as the standing ovation began. She saw tears in his eyes, then realized the same emotion had overcome her too.

They had slipped out the back as the ovation continued. They didn't say a word—neither could speak—as they walked, hand in hand, to the Japanese Friendship Garden.

The garden was quiet. And empty. It was as if everyone else in the park had been drawn like magnets to the nearby organ pavilion, where sustained applause and cheering carried across the park. Then the accolades quieted, and the pipes in the distance rose once more, this time with McKibben's brilliant encore performance of Andrew Lloyd Webber's theme to *Phantom of the Opera*.

She and Zack had stopped at the edge of the koi pond. The distant strains of the theme to the *Phantom* mixed with the musical chirp of songbirds darting among the fronds of sun-bathed palm trees.

The brilliant sunlight illuminated the fiery-colored fish as if they were electric. She had not known until that day that koi swim in pairs. Always. That fact, and the magnificent colors of the koi, was engraved in her memory.

The koi pond that day was a fountain of magic.

That day, at that moment, she knew she was falling in love.

Russian freighter Alexander Popovich
Entrance to the Black Sea
20 miles north of Istanbul

As the narrow straits of the Bosporus relinquished their tight watch over his ship, an unsuppressed grin crossed Captain Batsakov's face as the bow of his ship plowed into the limitless expanse of water. The moon-draped swells served as a glorious calling, almost an invitation to the *Alexander Popovich* to dance with the sea.

"*Chourney Morryeh*," he said with satisfaction, Russian for "Black Sea." Then he said, seemingly to no one, "*Doma*. The gates to the heart of the Russian sailor." He imbibed another gratifying sip of vodka. "Helmsman, all ahead half."

"All ahead half, Capitan," the helmsman parroted in Russian.

"Set course for Sochi. You know the coordinates."

"With *pleasure*," the helmsman said. "Set course for Sochi. Aye, Capitan."

"In just a few more days," he said, turning to the Arab, "I will be frolicking on the most beautiful beaches in all of Russia. The beaches visited by the czars and the presidents of the Russian Republic, and full of beautiful Russian women, who, as you know, are the most beautiful in the world. And you—"

"I," Fadil said, "will have just begun my work."

"Well, whatever your work is, my friend, I will drink to it," the captain said.

"To Russia." Fadil raised his glass.

"To the Council of"—the captain could not remember the rest—"to the Council of *whoever* you are and to your green American money."

That brought an obligatory laugh, a clanking of glasses, and more swigs of vodka. The ship's engines revved to a whine, carrying the celebrants and their ship back into the rolling swells of the open sea.

CHAPTER 23

Balboa Park
Spreckels Organ Pavilion
San Diego, California

The grand strains of the "Widor" were coming to an end, at least in his mind, and cold reality, even in the warmth of the Southern California sunshine, was setting back in.

Zack opened his eyes to the empty seats of the vast pavilion. Then, realizing that he couldn't be paralyzed by the sweet memories of days gone by — of days that might never be again — he remembered his task at hand. Karen Jacoby was waiting for him, and he was still a naval officer.

He strode out of the pavilion, turned right, and followed the curved path toward the Friendship Garden. Before him rose the pagoda, a three-tiered Buddhist temple where he was to meet Karen, and in the distance was the koi pond, another place that brought back memories of Diane.

He checked his watch. Karen was five minutes late.

He walked around the pagoda. Five more minutes passed. Still no Karen.

He tried her cell phone. No answer.

He approached the koi pond, then stopped in stunned disbelief, almost afraid to walk closer. For a moment, he fought the sudden urge to vomit.

Floating just below the surface, facedown, was a woman wearing the khaki uniform of a female naval officer. Blood bubbled up from her neck, leaving a red cloud in the clear water that mixed with her stringy blonde hair. Her legs, performing a hideous slow-motion ballet just under the surface, attracted a curious nibbling from several orange koi fish.

"Dear Jesus!"

Zack reached into the water and turned over the body. Her eyes and mouth were frozen in a wide-open position, her skin as pale as a full moon against the cloud of crimson blood around her.

On her chest was a name tag issued by the Naval Legal Service Office Defense Command. Even before he read the name, he knew it was Karen. "Dear God, no!"

Reaching his arms under her shoulders, Zack heaved her body out of the bloody water and pulled her onto the edge of the cement pond.

"Zack! Zack!"

Zack looked over his shoulder.

A strawberry blonde wearing white shorts and a Boston College T-shirt sprinted across the grass toward him.

"Shannon! Thank God you're here!"

CHAPTER 24

Claxton campaign California headquarters
Situation room
Hyatt Regency Hotel
Century City
Los Angeles, California

Twenty-four hours later

Jackson Gallopoulous sat alone at the long mahogany table, waiting for the arrival of the first female president of the United States and her entourage.

This morning's polls showed Eleanor within three points—a statistical dead heat—of San Francisco congressman William Warren. To break the heat, the campaign banked on the court-martial of the gay naval officer Wofford Eckberg, scheduled to resume tomorrow in San Diego, to attack the navy's Neanderthal mentality toward gay Americans. The fact that Web Wallace was stepping in as defense counsel would give them an extra boost.

The Eckberg trial was the sole matter on this morning's agenda. The strong comments Eleanor had made yesterday to the media had already bolstered polling numbers in the Bay Area and Hollywood.

But an unexpected wrinkle held Jackson's attention. The *San Francisco Chronicle*, the *Los Angeles Times*, and the *San Diego Union-Tribune* had been delivered, and he found his attention riveted to the front page of the *Union-Tribune*.

U. S. NAVY JAG OFFICER
FOUND MURDERED IN BALBOA PARK

Body of LTJG Karen Jacoby Found by LCDR Zack Brewer

By Adrian Branch, Military Affairs Editor

The body of a U.S. Navy JAG officer was discovered Saturday in San Diego's Balboa Park.

Lieutenant JG Karen Jacoby's body was found floating in the koi pond at the Japanese Friendship Garden by Lieutenant Commander Zack Brewer, the well-known JAG officer who first made international headlines for serving as lead prosecutor against three Islamic U.S. Navy chaplains being prosecuted for treason.

Brewer found Jacoby's body floating in the pond. Her throat had been slit and she had been shot in the head with a small-caliber weapon, reportedly a .22 caliber pistol.

NCIS Special Agent Shannon McGillvery was the first to arrive on the scene and helped Brewer pull Jacoby from the pond. Jacoby was declared dead on the scene when paramedics and officers from the San Diego police arrived minutes later.

Jacoby graduated from the University of Texas and the University of Maryland School of Law. A recent graduate of the Naval Justice School, Jacoby reported for duty in San Diego only last month. She was military defense counsel in the court-martial of *United States v. Ensign Wofford Eckberg*.

The Eckberg case gained publicity this weekend when U.S. Senator Eleanor Claxton attacked the navy for its "Neanderthal" policies against gays, citing the Eckberg prosecution as an example of the military's outmoded thinking. Claxton also criticized Brewer for his role in prosecuting Eckberg.

A police spokesman declined to say whether any suspects had been identified, and when asked if Brewer was a suspect, department spokesman Andy Meredith said, "Commander Brewer will be questioned. But we have no comment on whether anyone is a suspect.

"This investigation is ongoing, and we will be working with the NCIS and all appropriate state and federal law enforcement agencies to solve this crime as soon as possible."

The large mahogany door swung open, and Mary-Latham held it open for Eleanor's entrance.

"Good morning, Jackson." Eleanor's smile seemed forced as Mary-Latham and then Web Wallace followed her in.

"Where are Billy Bob and Bob Jack?" Billy Bob and Bob Jack were the names the Yale mafia called Eleanor's two principal Secret Service agents behind their backs.

"Out in the hallway with the other agents," Eleanor said. "They don't need to be in on everything."

"You're the boss."

"Let's get to it," she said. "Poll numbers?"

"Still a dead heat," Jackson said, "but favorable data out of the Bay Area as a follow-up to yesterday's statements."

"Yeah? What?"

"A one-point movement in our favor, in fact. You've touched a cord, and we haven't started yet."

"Fabulous." She turned to Web. "What's our game plan for tomorrow?"

"I've spoken to Lieutenant Commander Carpenter, who as you know is the senior defense counsel—"

"Excuse me," Jackson said. "Sorry for interrupting, Web, but you guys have heard about *this*, haven't you?" He slid the San Diego paper in front of Web and the Los Angeles paper in front of Eleanor.

Eleanor glanced down at the paper and then back to Jackson. "What a shame," she said, then turned to Mary-Latham. "Draft a sympathy statement laced with rage at this criminal act and a God-and-country tinge of some sort. You know, Lieutenant what's-her-name—"

"Jacoby," Jackson said.

"Right. Jacoby was a credit to her country, blah blah blah. We condemn this murder, blah blah blah. Something along those lines."

"Got it," Mary-Latham said.

"But in a sense," Eleanor continued, "this may help us. I never got the warm fuzzies from Jacoby." She glanced over her right shoulder at her legal advisor, as if to punt the whole issue to him. "Web?"

"Right, Eleanor." Wallace looked across the table at Jackson. "I've been practicing law a long time, and I have a sense about these things. Jacoby wasn't with us. She wanted to deal this thing from the beginning. I'm not sure she could have been trusted. Anyway"—he swilled steaming black coffee from a mug featuring the words *Gore-Edwards '04*—"the senior defense counsel is in our camp. We've run a background on him, and get this—he was a registered Democrat before entering the military. He's *stayed* registered that way. That's a real rarity these days. So Commander Carpenter will sit with me at counsel table, announce that I'm taking over, and we'll take it from there."

"Why was she with Brewer in the park? Don't you think that's strange?"

"Jackson, whatever happened between Jacoby and Brewer isn't our problem." Eleanor's eyes grew icy, her voice determined. "Forget Jacoby. Our mission is to change this country for the better. Our campaign's involvement with the Wofford Eckberg trial gives us that opportunity."

Jackson held on to the silence for a moment. "Of course, Eleanor. You're the boss."

CHAPTER 25

Outside LCDR Zack Brewer's residence
4935 Mills Street
La Mesa, California

Sunday, 6:15 p.m. (PST)

It wasn't supposed to be this way. Shannon McGillvery sat in the driver's seat of the government-issued Ford Taurus, looking out at the night sky.

In the last year, she'd solved a terrorist plot to use U.S. Navy jets to attack Jerusalem's Dome of the Rock and then helped Zack Brewer bring the lone surviving pilot to justice.

But a murder?

They sometimes happened in the military. But usually in barroom fights between drunken sailors over sleeping with someone else's girlfriend or something.

Officers didn't get murdered. Not JAG officers. JAG officers work more closely with NCIS than any other group in the navy.

If they could kill a JAG officer, then they could kill an NCIS agent. She had been trained to accept this. But none of that training had prepared her for the startling sight of the pale, lifeless body of Lieutenant Karen Jacoby sprawled beside the bloody koi pond.

She'd held her cool at the scene, her nerves seemingly made of steel while in front of Zack and SDPD crime-scene investigators.

But after her initial interview by the detectives, she'd retreated to the women's restroom and cried. And then vomited. When she emerged, she had been greeted by Barry MacGregor, the NCIS special agent in charge, who had already opened the NCIS investigation into Jacoby's murder.

Barry ordered stepped-up protection for Zack Brewer on a twenty-four-hour basis, assigned three additional agents to security detail, and offered to give Shannon a few days off. She refused and insisted on remaining in charge of the security detail.

She wasn't about to lose another JAG officer, especially not Zack.

She had parked the Taurus across the street and cattycorner from Zack's modest stucco home near downtown La Mesa, the bedroom community just east of San Diego. From here she commanded a clear view of the front door, and though others were posted nearby, she was the closest NCIS agent to the home.

Shannon did a quick radio check.

The static bursts from all NCIS radios reported that no suspicious activity had been noted in the corridors leading to Zack's house.

Still tense, she settled back behind the steering wheel of the Taurus. Who murdered Karen Jacoby? And why? And did Karen's murderer pose an immediate threat to Zack?

Did Chris Reynolds have anything to do with all this? Had he been stalking Zack, seen that Zack was meeting Karen in the park, and somehow perceived Karen as a romantic threat?

She glanced at the report on Reynolds that she had received earlier in the day. For the fourth time, she started reading the FBI's dossier on Chris Reynolds:

Subject is a twenty-seven-year-old Caucasian male, diagnosed as delusional and manic depressive. History of confinement at various mental institutions on the east coast after numerous misdemeanor arrests for stalking and trespass. Subject tends to stalk male attorneys, military personnel and politicians. Neither extensive treatment nor medication has resolved the issue.

Spent over one year at the Northern Virginia Mental Health Institute (NVMHI) in Falls Church, Virginia, for harassment, annoying telephone calls and stalking of an Assistant Commonwealth's Attorney.

A vocational nomad, subject has worked as a florist and as a waiter at several upscale restaurants upon his release from NVMHI to Southern California.

Because of delusional disorder and manic swings, subject is considered dangerous. Caution is advised when dealing with him.

Father Robert walked north along Spring Street, crossed the busy intersection at University Boulevard, then turned right off Spring Street onto Mills Street. The small green stucco house was on the corner of Mills Street and Orchard Avenue. A silver Mercedes 320 sat parked in the driveway.

He double-checked the address on the mailbox, then stepped on the front porch of the house. Something yanked him back, and his head crashed onto the ground.

"On your stomach," an angry female voice shouted. He was face-down in the grass, a pistol barrel jammed into his temple. "One move and I'll blow your head off," the voice snarled. A knee pressed into his spine. His arm was twisted behind his back.

"Identify yourself," the female voice snapped.

"Please. I'm a priest."

"Right! And I'm Mother Teresa!"

"Please! My collar is in my hotel room at Harbor Town."

"Agent McGillvery, what's the problem?" This from a male voice.

"About time you boys got here. He claims he's a priest."

"What's going on?" Another male voice.

"Okay, *Father* ..." the woman said.

"Robert."

"Robert. What priestly duty brings you this way?"

"I have some important papers for Commander Brewer."

"Oh, you *do*, do you?" The woman twisted his arm harder. "What papers? And from whom?"

"I'm a priest at Sacre Coeur in Paris. The papers are from an attorney named Jeanette L'Enfant. They contain important information about the Council of Ishmael."

At that instant, the woman released his arm, but the gun remained pressed hard against his head. "They murdered Jean-Claude la Trec because of the plea agreement. They tried to kill Jeanette too. She said her only chance for survival was to go to the Americans with sensitive information about the council and seek our protection."

"Our?"

"Yes. I'm an American priest, assigned by the Holy Father to Sacre Coeur because of the large number of U.S. citizens in Paris."

"Father, I'm a Catholic girl myself, and so I hope you'll understand when I tell you that there are five federal agents surrounding you right now with their guns trained on your head. So *if* I decide to remove my gun from your temple—and that's a big *if*—then it would not behoove you to try something the Holy Father wouldn't approve of. Do you understand?"

"Perfectly."

"And do you understand you do not move unless and until I give you the go-ahead?"

"Yes, my daughter."

Robert felt the gun barrel withdraw from his head.

"Now I want you to just lie there very still, and out of an abundance of precaution, I'm going to have these gentlemen pat you down for weapons."

"Certainly."

"Arms straight out! Spread eagle!" a man's voice commanded. Robert complied. Hands patted down his legs, his buttocks, his waist, and his back. They pulled off his shoes and checked those too. "Roll over," one of them ordered, and then Robert was looking up at the starry, twinkling sky, which provided a backdrop to a couple of palm trees and the silhouettes of people hovering over him.

"What's this?" An agent pulled the envelope from under his shirt. A flashlight blinded him.

"Those are the papers I'm supposed to deliver to Commander Brewer."

"Give me those," the woman's voice boomed over the blinding light. Someone cut the light. But his pupils were so dilated that everything appeared black. "Okay. Let him up."

Robert pushed against the grass and stood, thanking God that he was alive. He blinked about ten times. The tough-talking woman who'd nearly taken his head off, visible in the soft glow of Brewer's front porch light, was a slim, young, attractive strawberry blonde about six inches shorter than he.

"Wesner. Raynor. Stay here and take the point at Zack's house until I return," the feisty woman said.

"Yes, Shannon," one of them responded.

"Frymier and Carraway, you take a ride with me and Father Robert here."

"Where to, Shannon?" one of them asked.

"To Father Robert's hotel room. We'll find out if I need to go to confessional for roughing him up like I just did, or for killing him if I find out he's lying to me."

Robert suppressed the urge to grin.

"So if you gentlemen would accompany him to my car, I'd be grateful."

"With pleasure," one of them said, then grabbed Robert by his left arm. The other grabbed his right arm. "This way, sir." They led him to the back of a white Ford Taurus, where they sandwiched him between the two of them. The woman they called Shannon slipped into the driver's seat.

"Okay, Father," she said. "Where are you staying?"

"Hilton at Harbor Island."

"The Hilton at Harbor Island, it is." She hit the accelerator, squealing the tires and thrusting Robert back in his seat. He hoped this Shannon would be on the right side in this fight.

Babcock & Story Bar
Hotel del Coronado
1500 Orange Avenue
Coronado, California

8:30 p.m. (PST)

The ornate Babcock & Story Bar, on the ground floor of San Diego's internationally renowned Hotel del Coronado, was named for the hotel's founders, Elisha Babcock and H. L. Story. The original mahogany bar, which stretched forty-six feet in length, had been carried by ships around Cape Horn from Philadelphia in 1888.

None of this was lost on Jackson Gallopoulous, who was just as much a history buff as a liberal activist. Nursing a glass of Scotch, alone with the exception of the smooching couple at the other end of the bar, Jackson contemplated the seaside resort's history of hosting the rich and famous, which included not only movie stars and foreign heads of states, but also fourteen presidents of the United States. Nixon had once hosted the Mexican president for a summit and state dinner here. Clinton, Reagan, Kennedy, and FDR had all been guests at the Del.

It was natural, therefore, that the Claxton campaign would reserve a suite of rooms and establish a temporary San Diego beachhead in preparation for tomorrow's court-martial.

Of course, this was primarily a political stunt designed to push Eleanor Claxton over the top in the California primary. Everybody in the campaign knew this. If Web Wallace could somehow get Wofford Eckberg off the hook, so much the better. If not, poor Wofford would still get a book contract; at least, that was Eleanor's prediction. After a few years in a navy brig.

He swigged his Scotch and smiled.

The risk in all this was Brewer. The naval officer had become a national hero, especially among conservatives.

Two years ago, the powerful Southern Democrat senator Roberson "Pinkie" Fowler of Louisiana tried coaxing Brewer out of the navy to run for a congressional seat in Louisiana, his election "guaranteed" by Fowler. And Fowler, Eleanor's rival and a candidate for the presidency himself, was powerful enough to have pulled it off. The only hitch— Brewer would've had to switch to the Democratic Party to take the seat.

Inside-the-beltway rumors had Brewer seriously considering the proposition before turning it down.

What worried Jackson about this stunt wasn't California but rather the red states that had been Republican in the last few presidential elections. Would Brewer's presence harm Eleanor in these states, some of which she needed to win? That he would consider switching to the Democratic Party suggested he might not say anything that would hurt Eleanor.

All in all, the plan to commandeer this court-martial was a good one, Jackson thought. Well worth the risk.

"Bartender, another Scotch, please."

"Yes, sir."

It was Eleanor's reaction to Karen Jacoby's murder that wasn't sitting so well with Jackson.

"Your drink, sir," the bartender said.

"Thanks." Jackson handed him a ten-dollar bill. "Keep a running tab."

"Yes, sir."

She seemed so ... so nonchalant. Anyway, maybe that was just his excuse for inviting Mary-Latham down to join him. He took another nip of his drink. Maybe he was having a little problem keeping his relationship with Mary-Latham professional.

Another swig followed that thought.

She was smart, attractive, witty, earthy. But she spent so much time with Eleanor. Jackson checked his watch.

Of course, everybody in her inner circle wants to spend time with Eleanor. Maybe it's just political ambition. Heck. I, Jackson Kennedy Gallopoulous, am more guilty of political ambition than anybody on Eleanor's staff save Eleanor herself.

Jackson trimmed a Dominican-brand Macanudo cigar, then lit it.

"Mind if I smoke too?" He felt a soft hand on his shoulder and swung around on the bar stool.

Mary-Latham Modlin wore a black turtleneck, designer blue jeans, and black boots. Her brunette hair wasn't quite so frizzy tonight and had a certain luster about it, its wavy curls resting nicely on her shoulders.

"Anybody ever tell you that you look fabulous in jeans?"

She smiled. "Drinking already?"

"Yes, but I'm quite coherent." He laid the cigar in an ashtray and stood. "Please, have a seat."

"Ever the gentlemen," she said.

He helped her onto the bar stool. "What's this? A feminist relishing chivalry?"

"Quiet. You'll ruin my reputation." She sat down. "Corona, please."

"Yes, ma'am," the bartender said.

"So" — Jackson snuffed out the cigar — "where's the boss tonight?"

The bartender slid Mary-Latham's beer across the counter. She turned to Jackson. "Up in the suite with Web. They're planning the big splash at the court-martial tomorrow."

"Hmm." Jackson stirred his drink.

"So do you have the press ready?"

"Stoked and ready to go," he said. "We've got a surprise at the naval station gate in the morning. I hope tomorrow's a good day for us in the polls."

"Anything to put Eleanor in a better mood." Mary-Latham sipped her long-necked Corona.

"Speaking of Eleanor, did anything about her bother you today?"

"What do you mean?"

Jackson hesitated. Maybe he shouldn't mention it. Another sip of Scotch soothed his hesitation. "What I mean is Karen Jacoby."

"That's a shame."

"Precisely."

"And your point?"

"My point is, did you find Eleanor's reaction—or lack thereof—rather odd?"

Mary-Latham did not respond.

"For that matter," Jackson continued, "Web wasn't fazed by it either."

"Look, Jackson." Mary-Latham touched his hand. "Eleanor ... Web ... We've *all* got a campaign to run. Eleanor ordered me to prep a sympathy statement for release tomorrow. Remember?"

"That's standard stuff. I'm sure the White House will issue a sympathy statement."

"Maybe," she said, "but we'll beat that moron Williams to the punch. Besides, it wasn't as if Eleanor and Karen Jacoby were personal friends. She barely knew her. And with the unfortunate rash of deaths that Eleanor and Freddie have endured, it's no wonder she'd suppress her emotions. Eh?"

She flashed him a stunning smile. But not stunning enough to shake her last statement from his mind. *With the unfortunate rash of deaths that Eleanor and Freddie have endured ...*

Something still wasn't quite right. But as Mary-Latham said, for now, they had a campaign to run. Whatever was wrong, Jackson would worry about it later.

"Hey," he said, downing the last of his Scotch, "wanna take an evening stroll on the beach?"

Her smile washed away all worries of Eleanor and Karen Jacoby. "I thought you'd never ask."

She took his hand, and they walked out of the hotel toward the surf.

Room 301, Hilton Hotel
880 Harbor Island Drive
San Diego, California

9:00 p.m. (PST)

From the hotel suite that had indeed been registered to the Reverend Robert Moore of Paris, France, Shannon gazed at the magnificent panorama of lights reflecting vibrantly on the black waters of San Diego Bay. Straight in front of her, maybe two miles by the flight of the gull, downtown San Diego's skyline rose over the bay and into the California night.

Just across the bay to her right, much closer to Harbor Island, the lights of Naval Air Station North Island provided a sparkling backdrop to the nuclear-powered aircraft carrier USS *Dwight D. Eisenhower*. *Ike*'s hull number, 69, painted on the tower above the flight deck, was grandly illuminated by powerful spotlights.

Three knocks on the hotel room door interrupted the conversation between Father Robert and the two NCIS agents. Shannon went to the door and checked the peephole. A ruddy-faced man stood in the hallway, his potbelly protruding over his khakis.

She opened the door. "About time you got here."

"What's all the hoopla about?" asked Barry MacGregor, the NCIS SAC.

Before she showed him the folder, Shannon made the introductions, then waited impatiently as a few pleasantries were exchanged.

"What the hoopla is about is this." Shannon pointed to a legal-sized folder on a round coffee table in the corner of the room. "You've gotta see it."

MacGregor seated himself at the table, then picked up the file. "French?"

"Look at tab B. There's an English translation. Jeanette L'Enfant had the file translated before she brought it to Father Robert."

"You're talking about the missing French attorney who helped defend those pilots? That Jeanette L'Enfant?"

"One and the same," Robert said.

"The file," Shannon said, "contains sensitive information about Council of Ishmael operations, Barry. It includes names, locations, and secret bank accounts for al-Akhma and all his top lieutenants. And get this—we've got proof, finally, that the attack on the Dome of the Rock was a coordinated conspiracy, planned and executed by the Council of Ishmael, carried out by Islamic U.S. Navy pilots, all as part of a plan to do two things. One, incite the Islamic world against the U.S., and two, divide the U.S. and Israel—"

"Okay, okay." Barry cut her off. "How do we know this is legitimate? And no offense to you, Father," he said, turning to Robert, "but how do I know who you are?"

"Barry," Shannon said, "I've already made contacts through the Catholic Diocese of San Diego. I shot his picture with my cell phone and sent it over by email. They've been on the phone with Sacre Coeur in Paris. Father Robert is who he says he is. Besides, I've threatened to kill him if he's a fake."

That comment brought an impish smile from Robert, who looked down at his feet.

"Let me see that file." Barry flipped to tab B. "Operation Islamic Glory. Plan was to attack Israel's Dome of the Rock, then fly northeast and bail out over Syria. Pilots to be rescued by Council of Ishmael operatives and flown to Saudi Arabia."

"And they *almost* pulled it off, Barry," Shannon said. "Except the Israelis crossed the border and plucked them out of Syria before the Arabs could."

"Interesting."

"Yes. Interesting indeed. Do you see the significance of this, Barry?"

He stared a bit longer at the file. "A wonderful public relations opportunity for the United States."

"Precisely," Shannon said. "This is a smoking gun disproving those crazy theories that the U.S. attacked the Dome in retaliation for 9/11." She thought for a moment. "Maybe the president goes before the United Nations or something with evidence pointing the blame at radical Islam for the destruction of their own so-called holy site. And exposes the real culprit—the Council of Ishmael—the terrorist organization that's responsible."

"If anybody believes it," Barry said.

"It's up to the administration to figure that out. Take a look at the last document at the end of this section." She leaned over her boss's shoulder as he flipped through the file. "One more page over," she said as Barry reached the file.

To: Lieutenant Commander Mohammed Quasay, USN
From: Abdur Rahman
Subj: Reassignment Following Extrication

Upon your extrication from Syria, you will be transported to COI headquarters in Saudi Arabia, where you will brief the council on the success of your mission. You will then be assigned as the leader's liaison to Gobi Desert Detainee Camp Mongolia.

As such, you will assume operation command of camp and shall be responsible for its security.

Our leader, Hussein al-Akhma, has expressed supreme confidence in you for this invaluable assignment to the cause of Islam not only because of your impeccable knowledge of English and your leadership skills, but also because of your intimate knowledge of the U.S. military. This knowledge will become relevant because detainee targets are high-profile members of the U.S. military.

Attached hereto as Exhibit A is a partial list of U.S. military personnel the council is targeting for capture and transportation to Gobi Desert Detainee Camp. As discussed, Plan 547 will be in effect.

On behalf of our great leader, Hussein al-Akhma, the great servant of Allah and his prophet Mohammed, peace be upon him, thank you for your service to the Council of Ishmael and to the great cause of Islam.

In the name of Allah the Merciful,
Abdur Rahman

"Now flip over to the next page," Shannon said.

EXHIBIT A
U.S. Military Officers Targeted for Extrication

Anderson, Joseph, MAJGEN, USMC
Allen, Arthur R., BGEN, USA
Bailey, William, LTGEN, USA
Brewer, Zachary, LCDR, USN
Brown, Graham, RADM, USN
Carrington, James, GEN, USAF
Casey, Jeannette, RADM, USN
Colcernian, Diane, LT, USN
DeAngelo, David, COL, USMC

At least fifty other names were on the list. But before Barry could finish reading, Shannon interrupted him. "Seen enough?"

"Yeah," Barry wheeled around and made eye contact with her. "I've seen enough to know that if this is legitimate, we've got at least fifty officers, including your friend Brewer, who are going to need round-the-clock protection." He paused for a moment, then narrowed his eyes. "Meaning Congress will have to increase its funding for NCIS and the Army's CID if we're going to provide the protection for these officers."

Shannon walked over to the small refrigerator and, feeling the eyes of the four men in the room on her, bent to extract a bottled water. She opened it and took a sip, then turned toward the men. "If my hunch is right, money for bodyguard duty won't be the only extra congressional expenditure required here."

"I don't follow you," Barry said.

"What I'm talking about"—she took another gulp of the cold water—"rather, *who* I'm talking about—is Colcernian."

"Lieutenant Colcernian is dead," one of the NCIS agents said. "She's the one that won't need protection."

"Is she?" Shannon asked.

"Is she what?" Barry said.

"Is she dead?" Shannon set the bottle down, then walked across the room and pulled up a chair beside Barry at the round coffee table. "I mean, who's seen her body?"

"I need a beer." Barry rubbed his eyes as if hoping the question wasn't leading where he thought it was. "You sound like one of those conspiracy theorists who believed Hitler escaped to Argentina just because his body wasn't found. Besides, Shannon, if I recall, the navy declared Colcernian killed in action based on *your* assessment of the evidence and based on *your* recommendation. If memory serves me, *you* were the one who took it upon yourself to convince Brewer the love of his life was dead. Now the navy has promoted her to lieutenant commander—*posthumously*, I might add—based on *your* recommendation."

Shannon walked back over to the window and again looked out into the night, her gaze taking in the dazzling San Diego skyline. "Guilty on all charges," she said. "Based on the evidence we had before us at the time—the collapsed cave, the hair strands, the DNA match with Colcernian's—I stand by the call I made *at the time*." She turned back to Barry. "But this," she said, picking up the file, "this brings a new dynamic into the equation."

"A new dynamic?" Barry folded his arms. "Here's my read—again *assuming* this is legit: Colcernian was on a list with fifty other officers, and she was on that list because she helped prosecute the Muslim chaplains. She was killed before she was captured."

"Think about what you just said, Barry." Shannon held her index finger in the air. "We don't *know* that she was killed. But here's what we do know. We *know* that she was captured. And we know that was part of the plan as set forth in this mem—"

"Come on, Shannon," Barry interrupted. "Colcernian's last known whereabouts was Afghanistan. How far is that, anyway? That's got to be at least a thousand miles from Mongolia. And remember, we know there was a whole ton of mortar rounds shot at the cave where we found the hair strand. What you have here is still wildly speculative."

"What we have here is a stated plan to capture American officers, a missing officer whose name is on that list, no body, and a location."

"A location? The Gobi Desert in Mongolia? That's like looking for a needle in a haystack."

"At least maybe we've got the right haystack."

His eyes drilled her. "Maybe. Maybe not."

"That's it? Maybe? Maybe not?"

"What do you want me to do?"

"I want to go look for her, Barry."

"You can't just go look for her, Shannon. I mean, come on."

"I don't just mean me. This country has to do something." Shannon felt her Irish temper flaring. "Some sort of coordinated intelligence effort to check this out."

"Okay, okay." He scratched his chin. "You know, Quasay was supposed to cooperate with the government in return for our not seeking the death penalty. Has he ever mentioned this?"

"No," Shannon said. "He's given us names of Council of Ishmael operatives, but that's about it."

"Just enough to save his lousy hide from the firing squad."

"You said it."

"We'll run this up the chain. But the call will have to be made at the highest levels." His eyes softened. "I'll see what I can do."

"Thanks, Barry." She gave him a hug.

"Look," he said, "we need to check this out with Quasay. But first, we know Brewer is on the list. We know we've got a dead JAG officer, and we know we've got Brewer in court in the morning. So let's do everything we can to reinforce our protection of him."

"With pleasure," Shannon said. "I'm headed back to La Mesa right now."

LCDR Zack Brewer's residence
4935 Mills Street
La Mesa, California

Forty-five minutes later

The glow of the waxing moon cast a ghastly canopy over the small stucco house. The images of two apparitions, Special Agents Wesner and Raynor, roved about on foot patrol in Zack's driveway, guarding the front entrance to the house. Shannon stepped out of the car.

"Status?" she asked.

"All quiet," boomed Mike Wesner's voice through the night. "La Mesa PD has been by a couple of times, giving us some backup. Matlock's inside prepping for trial."

"Anybody with him?"

"That's a negative, Shannon."

"I'm going inside. Don't look for me until the morning."

The orange glow from Alan Raynor's cigarette revealed a raised eyebrow.

"Don't look at me that way, Raynor! We've lost one JAG officer today. Whoever killed her is still on the loose. We'll lose another one over my cold, dead body."

"Yes, ma'am."

"Besides, if it's any of your business, I'll be on the sofa."

"Yes, ma'am."

"You're to notify me if even one unauthorized mosquito flies within one mile of this house."

"I don't think we have mosquitoes in Southern California," Raynor said.

"Is there any ambiguity about my instructions?" Shannon snapped.

"None."

"Good. Agent Wesner? Bring me an Uzi, please."

"You bet." Wesner popped open the trunk of one of the NCIS staff cars parked out front and brought Shannon a compact black submachine gun. "Safety's on," he said. "Be careful."

"Thanks, Mike."

She stepped to the front door and knocked. The door opened. A dim incandescent glow from two living room lamps flowed onto the porch. Looking weary but otherwise quite fit in a light blue North Carolina Tar Heels T-shirt and navy blue shorts, Zack rubbed his eyes. "Care for some company tonight?" she asked.

She saw his eyes lock on to the Uzi and widen. "Do I have a choice?"

"Not to be pushy, but no, you don't."

"How could I say no to a woman with a machine gun?" he joked. "Okay. Come on in. The coffee's on."

She stepped into the living room, and Zack closed the door.

CHAPTER 26

Inside a wooden coffin

Time and location unknown

It was dark inside the coffin. Her stomach was queasy from the way they were slinging it about.

The motion made her want to throw up, but the tight gag in her mouth would send the vomit sliding back into her stomach and perhaps her lungs as well. The coffin tilted, and she bumped her head against the wooden interior.

Jeanette felt the descent now.

This was it.

They were lowering her down, down into her grave. Was this the price she would pay for neglecting God all of her life?

To be buried alive?

A moist warmth enveloped the interior of the coffin. Perhaps from the coals of hell smoldering nearby.

Why had she believed such idiots as Freud, Neitzsche, and Sartre— all self-avowed atheists who claimed there was no God?

Had she ingested their rubbish because it was the chic thing to do? To sip wine with her young friends and embrace a speculative and unproven philosophy? To take pride in being a self-proclaimed atheist?

Oh, how intellectually superior she had felt, with her legal training, immersed in the grand philosophy of humanism, to hold on to the notion that God is dead, and indeed to propagate such a philosophy to others.

And now this.

What a fool Freud had been. What a fool she had been!

Now this was her lot for denouncing the living God. To be buried alive, descending into the pits of hell!

M'aider Dieu! God, help me!

Russian freighter Alexander Popovich
Seaport of Sochi, Russia
Eastern coast of the Black Sea

8:00 a.m. (GMT); 12:00 p.m. (local time)

From the bridge of the *Alexander Popovich*, Captain Batsakov watched as the port crane swung the wooden crate out over the dock. It dangled in the air, swaying to and fro in the Black Sea breeze. Then the sound of clanking chains commenced, and the crate started its descent toward the soil of the great Motherland.

Russian stevedores, wearing white T-shirts and black caps and working under the midday sun, scurried under the crate and guided it down, down to the concrete dock.

"So, my friend"—the captain drew a puff from his Cuban cigar—"I trust that your star passenger can survive in that wooden box down there?"

"She is well drugged, Capitan," Fadil said. "There are holes in the crate for ventilation."

"Holes in the crate?" The captain chuckled. "I saw no such holes during my inspection."

"Before she awakens, we will be three hundred kilometers east of here. Past the border of Kazakhstan. She can hold her breath until then." Fadil cackled. "Besides, wood is naturally porous, Capitan. The stevedores handling the crate are well aware of the situation and, more importantly, well compensated."

"I am sure"—Batsakov took another puff—"they are most eager to be cooperative."

"Indeed," Fadil said. "I have come to the conclusion that you Russians like the American dollar far more than the Americans do."

"Communist philosophy," Batsakov sneered, drawing a final satisfying drag from the stogie. "Equality for the masses. Dollars for the elite!"

"Your Karl Marx couldn't have said it better, comrade!" Fadil snickered.

"It has been a pleasure doing business with you, my friend. Please call on us should you be in need of our services in the future."

"With pleasure, Capitan. But now I must ask your permission to go ashore. My duties are calling. And a certain wooden box may need a few holes drilled in it for the long journey ahead of us."

"Permission granted." Batsakov slapped the Arab on the back. "And good luck to you, whatever you are up to."

"Thank you, Capitan," Fadil said, then walked off the bridge.

LCDR Zack Brewer's residence
4935 Mills Street
La Mesa, California

Monday, 6:00 a.m. (PST)

The small motorcade formed at Zack's house.

It consisted of a La Mesa PD squad car, a Taurus driven by Special Agent Raynor, Zack's Mercedes driven by Shannon, and a Crown Victoria driven by Special Agent Wesner.

They drove straight through town, south along Spring Street toward California Highway 94, where the La Mesa Squad car dropped off. A San Diego County Sheriff's Department squad car, driven by Deputy Barney Oldham, then moved to the front of the motorcade.

To avoid attention, neither squad car had employed sirens or flashing lights. Unless someone knew that the small caravan was a protective motorcade, it could've passed for four cars blending in with traffic.

Shannon hadn't dropped this bombshell on Zack yet, but protecting him inside the confines of a military installation would be far better than guarding a residence in a civilian neighborhood, having to involve local police departments, and worrying about snipers behind every palm tree.

Sometime before this day was over, she would request that Captain Rudy order Zack on base. The captain wasn't obligated to comply, but she would go over his head if he didn't.

That would chap Zack's ego.

Too bad.

He'd never know that she was behind it. And if he found out, that was still too bad. Better to have a chapped Zack than a dead Zack.

She hadn't told him about Father Robert or the contents of the communiqué from the Quasay file. Not yet.

The navy didn't need its star prosecutor dwelling on the possibility that Diane might be alive. Not now. Besides, statistically, Barry was probably right. Diane Colcernian was likely dead. Shannon probably had it right the first time.

Still, her gut told her otherwise. And so did the hellish nightmare that had scared the living life out of her last night. It was as if Diane Colcernian had risen from the dead out of Karen Jacoby's watery grave. Her face was so real, her voice so desperate.

A cold chill shivered down her neck and goose bumps prickled her arms as they drove west, past the I-805 Interchange.

"Are you about ready for this?"

"We'll see."

"What do you think Judge Reeves will do?"

"No clue."

"Think he might continue the case because of Karen's death?"

But Zack wasn't listening. He was reading through his notes on the legal pad in his lap, oblivious to her question.

Zack was a steel machine when it came to trial preparation. This she knew. She'd hoped a little small talk would extinguish the memory of the nightmare. No such luck.

Naval Station San Diego was just a few miles away now. The car passed under Interstate 5, just a few blocks from the "dry side" of the naval station. They slowed, and shore patrolmen waved them onto the base. Her cell phone rang. It was Deputy Sheriff Barney Oldham in the lead car.

"Yes, Barney?"

"Trouble."

"Talk to me."

"The main entrance to the wet side on Harbor Drive and 32nd Street. Protestors. Hundreds of them."

Oldham referred to the portion of the base where most of the ships of the Pacific fleet were moored. This was also where the military courthouse was located. To get to it, they would have to cross Harbor Drive, the north-south public boulevard that split the naval station down the middle.

"Great," she said as they merged onto the westbound section of 32nd Street that ran through the dry side. "Let me guess. Gay rights?"

That question brought Zack's eyes off his legal pad.

"You guessed it."

"What's our security situation crossing Harbor?"

"SDPD has three black-and-whites at the intersection. They'll stop traffic when we come through. That's six officers on the ground. Should be enough unless somebody's armed."

"Great."

The brake lights of Alan Raynor's Taurus flashed just in front of them. Shannon hit the brakes. She saw Mike Wesner's Crown Victoria close the distance in her rearview. They were inching along now, about to cross Harbor Drive. About a half dozen marines, in battle fatigues and carrying M16s, flanked the cars. Shannon reached inside her sweats, pulled out her nine-millimeter Beretta, and laid it on the seat.

"Zack, you may want to duck down as we cross Harbor Drive."

"What for?"

"We're getting ready to cross through protestors." They moved forward six inches, then stopped again. "Some of them could be armed."

"I'm not ducking." Zack was defiant. "You duck."

"Look, Zack, it's not me they want. We've already lost one JAG officer this weekend."

"I'm not ducking."

They inched forward a few feet.

"All right, macho man," she said in a more feminine, pleading tone, "if you won't duck, would you at least take your officer's cover off and put on some shades?" A pause. She turned and gazed into his hazel eyes. "For me?"

Zack rolled his eyes, shook his head, smirked, and tossed his naval officer's hat into the backseat. Then he slipped on a pair of Oakley sunglasses. "Satisfied?" he asked, still shaking his head.

"Thank you, Commander."

"Anything you say."

The cars rolled a few feet closer to Harbor Drive. Twenty feet in front of them, Shannon saw a flashing blue light.

A voice blared over a loudspeaker from one of the police squad cars on Harbor Drive just ahead. "Stand back. Please stand back."

Now they came into view. Hundreds, maybe thousands.

The angry sea of humanity clogged all of Harbor Drive, blocking the entrances between the wet and dry sides of the naval station. The crowd's attire ranged from bikinis to skin-tight jeans and T-shirts, though some protesters wore the opposite of what gender dictated, with makeup on men, crew cuts on women. Some had donned costumes aimed to offend—and offend they did as they flaunted body parts and lifestyle. They shook their fists, yelling and screaming, jabbing the air with signs and banners.

ANCHORS AWAY WITH NEANDERTHAL POLICIES!

ELEANOR FOR PRESIDENT!

GAY PRIDE!

FREE ENSIGN ECKBERG!

PUNISH HATE CRIMES, NOT HEROES!

ENSIGN ECKBERG—A NATIONAL HERO!

"Oh, please," Zack said. "Can you believe this?"

"I think I'm going to throw up."

"Stand back!" a stern voice blared over a police loudspeaker. "Please stand back, or you will be arrested."

"No! No! We won't go!" A unified chorus arose from the crowd.

The chorus crescendoed to shrill screams, drowning out police instructions—"Stand back! You are blocking the entrance to a United States Navy base. Please stand back!"

Blasts from sirens arose from Barney's sheriff's car and also from several SDPD squad cars along Harbor Drive.

"Shannon, Barney ..." The deputy sheriff was now on the NCIS frequency.

"Go ahead, Barney."

"We're gonna roll right through these suckers. If they get run over, that's their problem. Stay close behind Raynor. Okay?"

"Is that a good idea?" Zack asked.

"Do you have any other suggestions?" she shot back.

"Do you copy, Shannon?"

Shannon picked up the microphone. "Copy that, Barney."

"Raynor, Wesner. Do you copy?"

"Copy that," Wesner and Raynor's voices came over the radio.

"Okay, here we go."

The sheriff's deputy sounded his siren. The tight motorcade began moving. They entered Harbor Drive. Protestors immediately pressed against the Mercedes, surrounding it, faces pushed against the windows, fists pounding, hands rocking the vehicle.

"It's Zack!" a voice cried. "Zack Brewer's in there." Men in bikinis crawled up on the hood, sprawling onto the windshield.

"He's the prosecutor! He's the one prosecuting Wofford Eckberg!"

"Homophobe!" someone shouted.

"Let's get him!"

"Stand back, or you will be fired upon!"

"We want Brewer! We want Brewer!"

Shannon reached for her pistol. "Zack, there's an Uzi in the backseat. Get it."

"Got it."

"Give me the Uzi. You take the pistol."

He complied.

The protesters crawled up on the trunk, beating the back windshield, blocking the light of morning as the car rocked and shook.

"What's your situation, Shannon?" Wesner shouted through the radio.

"Bad, Mike. They're all over the car."

Gunshots rang out. Screams joined the cacophony of shouts and jeers.

"He's dead!" someone cried.

"Run!" another shouted.

The mob scrambled off the Mercedes like rats in the face of a flashlight. They ran in both directions down Harbor Drive.

"Move!" Barney's voice came back over the radio.

Shannon punched the accelerator. Within seconds the motorcade was inside. Shannon checked the rearview. U.S. Marines were closing the front gate, barricading it from the outside.

Claxton campaign San Diego County headquarters
Hotel del Coronado
1500 Orange Avenue
Coronado, California

Eleanor, you've got to see this!" Jackson Gallopoulous called out to the senator, who was in an adjoining room meeting with Mary-Latham.

"What is it, Jackson?"

"Something's going on at the Naval Station. Come check this out."

Eleanor walked into the room, followed by Mary-Latham, just as the distinguished-looking, bespectacled image of CNN's venerable Tom Miller appeared on the plasma television screen.

"This is Tom Miller at CNN Headquarters. Breaking news live from San Diego. A shooting has taken place outside the U.S. Naval Station on 32nd Street, which is the main U.S. Naval facility in San Diego. Someone, local police, U.S. Marines, or someone else, fired into a crowd of protestors who were clogging the entrance of the facility. CNN's Laurie McCaffity is on the scene in San Diego. Laurie?"

"Tom, I'm standing outside the entrance to the U.S. Naval Station on 32nd Street in San Diego, where chaos still reigns outside the massive naval facility after shots were fired into a crowd that was gathered outside the main gates of the facility. Preliminary reports have at least one death and several injuries as a result of the shooting. The crowd, which according to some estimates had swollen to nearly a thousand, had gathered to protest the navy's prosecution of Ensign Wofford Eckberg, a gay naval officer whom the navy is prosecuting for an *alleged* charge of homosexual assault aboard a U.S. Navy submarine.

"We're here with Jamie Bonita, one of the protestors." The camera panned back. The attractive, dark-complexioned reporter stood beside a skinny young man sporting a crew cut and wearing a white ribbed tank top. "Jamie, I understand you were part of the crowd here. What happened, and why was this crowd gathered here?"

"Yes, Laurie. We're here to protest discrimination. We're here to protest hypocrisy. The navy is prosecuting this wonderful man, Wofford Eckberg, *only* because he is a gay man. And, Laurie, they're making a real statement here. They've assigned their top prosecutor to the case, Commander Zack Brewer. But what they won't tell you, Laurie Jane, is that Ensign Eckberg was beaten up by a group of thugs in the navy. His collarbone was broken and he was put in the hospital. And what they also won't tell you is that they're prosecuting Eckberg for something he didn't do, but letting these thugs go free."

"The shooting," McCaffity interrupted. "What did you see?"

"We were demonstrating peacefully. We were threatening no one. We were *outside* the naval base. We weren't harming anyone and we weren't threatening anyone either. And the next thing I know, someone comes over a loudspeaker and says move or we're going to be shot.

And before you know it"—his hands flailed in the air—"they just start shooting. They just fire into an innocent crowd!"

"Who shot? Do you know?"

"The marines. It had to be the marines."

"Are you sure about that? Did you see the marines fire?"

"I'm pretty sure."

"But did you see them shooting?"

"Not exactly, but the shots came from their direction. No doubt about it."

"There you have it, Tom. Chaos reigns in the streets of San Diego, where government officials, either local police or U.S. Marines, are accused of firing into an innocent crowd of U.S. citizens, with at least one death reported so far. From San Diego, this is Laurie McCaffity reporting."

"Laurie Jane, are you still there?" The screen split vertically, showing Tom Miller in Atlanta and Laurie McCaffity fidgeting with her earpiece. She was standing on a sun-bathed street with paramedics and police officers rushing to and fro in the background.

"Still here, Tom."

"Did these protestors have a permit to be on the streets?"

"Tom, I asked that question to a local San Diego police officer, and as far as we can tell, there's no evidence that these citizens were able to get a permit. Tom, I would point out that there were women and even some children out here as well."

"Do you know if they had applied for a permit?"

"We still don't have that information, Tom."

"Do you have any information on how this rally was organized?" The veteran anchor sported a concerned look on his face. "I mean, you don't just have a thousand people show up spontaneously unless somebody is behind it."

The question from the veteran CNN anchor brought a scowl to Senator Claxton's face. "Miller used to work for Fox, you know. Rumor has it he's a closet conservative."

"Tom, there's no real indication that this was something other than a spontaneous rally by concerned citizens, at least not at this point. It's a good question, though, and we will be looking into that question as this story unfolds."

"Laurie, one other thing. We've gotten some reports that this was some sort of gay rights rally. Have you been able to confirm that?"

The attractive brunette nodded her head and paused for a moment, then fidgeted with her earpiece again. "Tom, there were citizens from all walks of life here. As we mentioned, women and children were here. Working people were here today. Now were some of them gay? Yes. Some were. But we don't know that all were. And those here today are saying this was not a gay rights rally, but rather a rally for civil rights."

"Laurie McCaffity in San Diego, thank you for that report." Miller turned to the screen. "We're going to take a break now, and I'll be back with more from San Diego ... right after this."

Jackson Gallopoulous sat back with a loud sigh. "Wow."

"What do you make of that?" Mary-Latham asked.

"Mary-Latham." Eleanor's tone indicated that her mental gears were beginning to churn. "Draw up a statement condemning the violence, supporting the right of free speech, and attacking the navy's anti-gay policy as the root of this."

"Jackson."

"Yes, Eleanor."

"Can you put together a presser in fifteen minutes in front of the Del?"

"Tough but doable. Your press corps is already here."

"Good. Do it. I want to be out front on this."

"Yes, Eleanor."

"And one other thing."

"What's that?" Jackson asked.

"Where's Mohammed?"

"Down by the naval station ... somewhere."

"Get him on the line. I want him here in my suite for a briefing ASAP."

"Consider it done."

Courtroom 1, Building 1
Navy-Marine Corp Trial Judiciary
32nd Street Naval Station
San Diego, California
Court-martial of United States v. Lieutenant Wofford Eckberg, USN

Day 2

As the motorcade passed through the main gate of the naval station and turned right, Zack saw the circus of media trucks congregated outside Building 1.

This was supposed to be a low-key trial. In fact, it wasn't supposed to be a trial at all. Not after the deal he'd worked out with Karen Jacoby. But after Karen's murder, and now after the near-ambush by a mob outside the naval station only moments ago, nothing was surprising.

He glanced over at Shannon. Her cheeks, normally a healthy pink, had gone pale. "You okay?"

"I'm fine." She shot him a forced smile. The Mercedes was now stopped right in front of the courthouse door. "Zack, do me a favor and wait for Raynor and Wesner before you step out the door. Okay?"

"No problem." Zack regretted the hard time he'd given her as they crossed Harbor Drive.

"Thanks."

He looked out the passenger window. Another mob was stampeding toward the car. This mob was armed with microphones and cameras and bright lights.

"Not again."

"Something's not right about all this," Shannon said.

"No joke," Zack replied. "I smell a rat."

"Commander Brewer! Commander Brewer!" they yelled through the glass. Their blinding strobes, now aimed at the car, outshone the morning sun.

"Step aside! Move that camera!" Zack looked over and saw the mob of reporters parting like the waters of the Red Sea. Like Moses and Aaron leading the troops, Wesner and Raynor were charging down the middle, gesticulating with their hands against the cameras and lights and leading a small platoon of armed marines behind them.

The marines, in battle fatigues, formed two walls of six, making a corridor from the car to the front door of the courthouse. Mike Wesner opened the door for Zack. "Ready when you are, Commander."

"Thank God for the NCIS and for the United States Marine Corps," Zack muttered, then stepped out onto the asphalt.

"Commander Brewer!"

"Commander Brewer!"

Zack stepped into the tunnel of exploding flashbulbs and strode through the press hounds, determined to ignore their questions.

"Is this case about the navy's antiquated policies against gay Americans?"

He smiled, nodded, and held up his palm. "No comment."

"Shouldn't the navy prosecute those sailors who broke Eckberg's collarbone?"

He smiled again, nodded again, and said once more, "No comment."

The next question, just as he stepped into the entryway of the court-house, stopped him in his tracks. "Commander Brewer, what do you think of Web Wallace stepping in as defense counsel in this case?"

Web Wallace? Longtime Democratic strategist and counsel to the Claxton campaign? That Web Wallace? Wallace was no Wells Levin-son. He *had* to say something. Either that or look like a deer in the headlights.

"My time is limited right now, so I say only this. It doesn't matter *who* represents the defendant. If that's Mr. Wallace, fine. He has a repu-tation for excellence in his field. If someone else, so be it. Regardless, I expect justice to prevail."

"But, Commander ... Commander!"

Zack stepped into the entryway of the military courthouse, turned to the reporters, and, like a president about to board Air Force One, gave a sweeping half-moon wave to the clamoring mob.

A minute later, he entered the courtroom, its galleries jam-packed by members of the press. He strode down the center aisle and opened the swinging wooden gate that separated the gallery from the counsel area. The senior defense counsel, Lieutenant Commander Harvey Car-penter, in his summer white uniform, sat where Karen Jacoby had sat just two days ago—in the lead counsel's spot closest to the prosecu-tion table. The accused, Ensign Eckberg, also decked in summer whites, sat just to Carpenter's right at the defense counsel table. To Eckberg's right, sitting on the right side of the defense counsel table in the chair farthest from the jury box, was a distinguished-looking man with silver hair, his face deeply tanned with few wrinkles, the apparent product of multiple Botox injections.

Both the silver-haired man and Commander Carpenter nodded as Zack laid his briefcase on the prosecution table. Eckberg stared straight ahead.

So it was true.

Web Wallace had wormed his way into a military courtroom and into this case.

The reporters. The mob scene at the entrance of the naval station. The Neanderthal witch hunt comments.

There *was* a rat behind all this—a stench-laden political rat lurk-ing in the shadows named Eleanor Claxton. Rage boiled. He wanted to slam his fist on the table.

Love one another. The words percolated in his mind from his morning study of First John. *Anyone who hates his brother is a murderer.*

A deep exhale. The words from the Holy Book, yet again, calmed his anger.

He sat, alone for the moment, at the prosecution table and extracted a small photo from his wallet. She had been the focus of his most daring prosecution to date. A wave of emotion swept over him at the image of the smiling little Jewish girl with curly locks who had died at the Wailing Wall over a year ago in a terrorist attack. He'd gone to war for her in a courtroom in Jerusalem. The trial had nearly cost him his life when a bomb exploded in the courtroom. *God bless Anna Kweskin. God bless her family here on earth.*

He pulled a second picture from his shirt pocket. This photo he handled as a precious, fragile ornament. He placed it on the table next to Anna Kweskin's image.

The second photo showed a stunning redheaded woman wearing the white uniform of a navy lieutenant with the insignia of a member of the Judge Advocate General's Corps. "All rise!"

There was a clomping and shuffling of feet at the bailiff's cry. Zack rose to his feet. But his eyes did not search for the tall military judge, who could be heard walking across the hardwood floor to the bench. The image of Diane Colcernian kept Zack's eyes glued to the counsel table.

"Please be seated," Judge Reeves said.

"I don't know what's about to happen, but this is for you, baby," he whispered. "For you."

"We're back on the record in the case of *United States versus Ensign Wofford Eckberg, USN.*" Captain Reeves wore an uncharacteristic worried look on his face. "The record should reflect that the accused is present in the courtroom, along with trial counsel, Lieutenant Commander Brewer. The record should also reflect that detailed defense counsel" — Reeves's voice shook, then cracked — "Lieutenant Karen Jacoby is *not* present."

The courtroom was pin-drop silent. The judge's hand trembled as he brought a glass of water to his lips, and the water shook even as he tried to sip it.

Lord, give him strength.

Even as he breathed the prayer, the affable North Dakotan's eyes took on the glaze of tears.

Zack stood quickly. "Your Honor, the government requests a thirty-minute recess."

"Granted." Captain Reeves gave Zack a quick nod of appreciation.

"All rise!"

Reeves moved his gaze away from the gallery, and at a pace more rapid than Zack had ever witnessed in his dozens of appearances before the military judge, Reeves hurried from the courtroom and into the judge's chambers, almost slamming the door behind him.

First whispers, then a roar of commotion morphed into a cacophonous chorus of voices from behind.

"Commander Brewer ..."

"Commander Brewer ..."

Strobes flashed as the press hounds snapped.

"Lieutenant Commander Brewer, has Judge Reeves broken down like this before?" a loud voice called out over the roar.

"Stand back!" ordered NCIS Special Agent Mike Wesner.

"Ladies and gentlemen, you'll have to stand back, please." A shore patrolmen on the courtroom security detail stepped in beside Wesner.

"Commander Brewer ..."

Zack waved off the questioner.

"Mr. Wallace ..."

Their questions faded into the background. The overwhelming reality of the weekend was sinking in now. Karen Jacoby, a young naval JAG officer, a young woman with a mother and a father, had a family that loved her more than life back in — he didn't even know where she was from. First Diane. Then Anna Kweskin. And now Karen.

Death.

Why so much so close to his heart in such a short time? Was he so callous that he was losing the sensitivity that even a senior naval officer like Captain Reeves was showing in public over Karen's murder?

He closed his eyes and saw the sparkling look in Karen's eyes just two days ago. It was a look he'd seen many times over the last five years. The bewildered yet excited look of a brand-new JAG officer fresh out of justice school and about to try her first case. Now it was all gone.

Like a river overflowing its banks after a rainstorm, brokenness welled in his chest, boiling to his neck and throat.

Zack swiped at the water that filled his eyes.

★

Shannon picked up her cell phone and dialed the preprogrammed number of Special Agent Wesner. A moment later he was on the line.

"Mike, what's the situation at the courthouse?"

"On a break right now. Zack just arrived in the attorneys' lounge. Everything's under control."

"Listen, Mike, I've got to drive downtown to headquarters to meet Barry. I've called in for more backup, but I want you to stay on Zack like white on rice. Got it?"

"Understood."

"We've got something hot cooking. I don't know when I'll be back. But if I'm not back at the close of court, tell Zack that Captain Rudy is ordering him to the Navy Lodge at North Island tonight. One of the legalmen will bring over written orders from Navy Trial Command. The orders will be delivered to you. But don't give them to Zack until you break for the day. We don't want him distracted. Are you with me?"

"Loud and clear."

"When we take Zack out of here tonight, I want you to arrange for an unmarked, windowless panel truck to drive him over to North Island. We'll leave the Mercedes here on base. Got it?"

"Roger that."

"Call me if even a seagull flies within a mile of our guy. Got it?"

"Don't worry, Shannon."

"I'm not worried," Shannon lied, then turned left onto Harbor Drive, unnoticed by the police, protestors, and reporters lingering outside the gate of the naval station.

NCIS Southwest Field Office
A Street and Sixth Avenue
San Diego, California

Fifteen minutes later

Thick gray cigar smoke hung in the room, making Barry barely visible as Shannon stepped into his office. He leaned back in his black chair, his feet propped on his big desk, with a phone cradled under his neck. The fat cigar was a source of contention with some of the health-conscious Southern Californian career bureaucrats working in administrative roles around the offices. Barry was one of those who could get away with flaunting certain government rules, knowing full well the bureaucratic power structure in Washington would do nothing about it. He knew it; career bureaucrats knew it.

For his part, Barry had showed his "sensitivity" to his nonsmoking coworkers by opening his office window and spending his own money at Target for an exhaust fan in the window. It was about as effective as a Band-Aid on a gushing artery.

Shannon never complained about the smoke. Women who wanted to advance in NCIS couldn't afford to complain about things sacred to the good ol' boys' network. Besides, Barry's habit could have been worse. Cigarettes were much nastier.

Barry waved her in, then covered the phone and whispered, "I've got the director on the line." He was referring to the new national director of the NCIS, Dr. Graham Jones.

An ex-naval officer with a PHD in criminal psychology, Jones had spent time with the FBI before becoming the agent in charge of NCIS agents all over the world. Little was known about Jones, except that he had a reputation as a "tough investigator." At least that's what the Williams administration claimed when he was appointed as director one month ago.

The private scuttlebutt on Jones, at least among NCIS agents, said that he was a political appointee—his uncle was Raymond Jones of Oklahoma, a powerful member of the House Ways and Means Committee—and that the director himself, at the young age of thirty, harbored his own political aspirations within the Republican Party.

"Excuse me, Mr. Director"—Barry motioned for Shannon to sit in one of the two wooden chairs in front of his desk—"Special Agent McGillvery just walked in."

Shannon sat, fanning the smoke with her hands.

"Yes, sir ... Yes, sir. By all means, sir." Barry hit a button and the line switched over to speakerphone. "Okay, Mr. Director, you're on the speakerphone now. Special Agent McGillvery is the only one here."

"Good morning, Shannon. Graham Jones here." The director's voice was Southern, friendly, and distinctively political.

"Good morning, Mr. Director. It's an honor, sir."

"From what I've heard of your work during the *Quasay* case, the honor is mine."

"Thank you, sir."

"First, let me compliment you in your work in providing protection to Commander Brewer ..."

Cut the bull and get to the point, Mr. Director.

"... and in your fine work in getting this report from this Father Robert."

"Thank you, sir."

"I wanted to discuss this report in a little more detail with you."

"Yes, sir."

"As soon as Barry forwarded this report to Washington last night, our intelligence people commenced our analysis, and we've forwarded it up the chain of command."

"May I ask how far up the chain of command, sir?"

"Sure. The secretary of the navy has been briefed, and the report has been forwarded to the secretary of defense's office, to the Joint Chiefs of Staff, and to the National Security Council."

"Is the president aware of it?"

"I don't know. Possibly, but right now the memo is being worked at the SECNAV level." The director pronounced the abbreviation as "Seck Nav," referring to the secretary of the navy.

In other words, SECNAV is sitting on this and doesn't see enough political value to push it up the chain of command.

"Mr. Secretary, is there anything at all I can do to assist SECNAV's office in their work on the memo?"

"Frankly, SECNAV is concerned about authenticity."

"Authenticity?"

"I'm sure you understand that, politically, the secretary of the navy cannot stake his reputation on a piece of paper that was intercepted under questionable circumstances. As director of NCIS, I must know that we've got something credible before I stake my reputation on pushing this thing up the chain of command."

Bureaucrats.

"I mean, we've got a JAG officer murdered, for which I have no answers. And now we've got this shooting in a mob scene out in San Diego with claims the marines are involved in firing into a crowd. As you might imagine, the secretary wants answers about all this. I mean, this shooting into a crowd of civilians, if the marines are involved, is a real powder keg for the administration.

"We've got Eleanor Claxton raising Cain. The administration is fighting a public relations war, and SECNAV wants answers. Shannon, these are delicate times. I'm sure you will understand my position. We must be careful, from a political standpoint, about how we focus our fire."

A moment of silence.

Shannon glanced at Barry, who at that moment was firing up another Monte Cristo. He took a drag, then gave her a *what can I say?* shrug.

"Mr. Director," Shannon said, "we've got officers on a potential kidnap list. We're already missing one officer. What if Lieutenant Commander Colcernian is still alive out there somewhere? Can't we run this up the chain a little more aggressively, sir?"

"Shannon," the director replied, his voice turning authoritative, "the navy *posthumously* promoted Diane Colcernian to lieutenant commander. In the eyes of the navy, she is dead. In scanning her file this morning, I see that that determination was based on the analysis of one Shannon McGillvery."

"I could have been wrong, sir."

"Shannon, what do you want me to do? Ask the secretary of the navy to ask the secretary of defense to ask the president to send the navy looking for her somewhere?"

That's exactly what I want you to do.

"Shannon, I know you're a great agent, but we have limited resources. Even if these papers are legitimate, the whole notion that Colcernian may be alive out there somewhere just because she was on a kidnap list is one in a billion, in my opinion."

"But we don't have a body."

"And we don't have bodies for those who died in the World Trade Center either. But we had a mortar attack directed at the cave where we think she was, and we had hair samples showing her DNA. Besides, if this memo is legit, then why wasn't it found on Commander Quasay when Israeli Special Forces pulled him out of Syria after he used U.S. Navy jets to attack the Dome of the Rock?"

"Sir, that's an excellent question."

"Wasn't Quasay supposed to cooperate with us in return for Commander Brewer not seeking the death penalty?"

"That's right, Mr. Director."

"Has he mentioned any of this?"

"He's confirmed that Islamic Glory was part of a coordinated plot by the Council of Ishmael to attack the Dome of the Rock as a means of driving a wedge between the U.S., Israel, and moderate Arab states."

"We've known that for months," the director said. "But nothing about this hostage list?"

"No, sir. Not yet."

Barry doused the Monte Cristo, folded his arms over his basketball belly, and shook his head.

"Well then, you can understand why I'm reluctant to light a fire under this thing, can't you?"

"Of course, Mr. Director."

"Okay. I thought you would understand. Look, Shannon, I'm not saying this isn't legitimate. What I *am* saying is that I need more, and our intel people are working on this."

Bureaucrat. "Yes, I understand, Mr. Director." *I understand that you're content not to rock the boat if it might damage your fledgling political career.*

"Anyway, we appreciate your good work, and we'll be on top of this here in Washington."

"Sure you will," Shannon whispered.

"What was that?"

"I said that I'm sure the service will do all it can."

"Very well. Barry, Shannon. Good to talk with you both. We'll be in touch if we know anything."

Barry unfolded his arms. "Good-bye, Mr. Director."

The line went dead.

"You look like the bloody ghost of Christmas past," Barry said.

"We may have a JAG officer still alive out there. And this guy ..." She could not finish the thought.

"Irish-Catholic temper flaring, is it?"

"Sorry, Barry. That was a bunch of typical political jive talk. Five years from now, you and I will still be with the fleet, busting drug pushers, rapists, or anyone else undermining good order and discipline in the navy. That guy will be in Congress or licking his lollypop in some other political appointment. He's just punching his ticket, and you know it."

Barry held his palms upward. "Hey, I'm on your side."

Shannon rose from her chair and walked over to the window. "Barry, what are you doing tonight?"

"Is that a dinner invitation?" The senior agent raised his eyebrow. "Heck with departmental regulations about dating subordinates. I thought you'd never ask."

"Better than dinner. How 'bout a road trip?"

"Really?" A cheesy grin crossed his face. "What'd you have in mind? La Jolla? The Del?"

"Better than that," she said. "What I had in mind . . . is Kansas."

"Kansas?"

"Sure. We catch a flight this afternoon, chat with our friend tonight, and be back by noon tomorrow."

"Ahh. You know, that might not be a bad idea."

"Then we're good to go?"

"I'll call for our tickets. If you say Kansas, then Kansas it is."

Courtroom 1, Building 1
Navy-Marine Corp Trial Judiciary
32nd Street Naval Station
San Diego, California
Court-martial of United States v. Ensign Wofford Eckberg, USN

Day 2

All rise!"

Zack stood once again. Judge Reeves strode with confidence out the chamber doors and up the steps leading to the bench, then stood waiting for the bailiff's announcement.

"This general court-martial of *United States of America versus Ensign Wofford Eckberg, United States Navy,* is now in session. The Honorable Captain Richard Reeves, United States Navy, presiding. God save the United States and God save this honorable court."

When Captain Reeves said, "Please be seated," Zack was relieved that authority and confidence had returned to the senior military judge's voice.

"Very well. We are back on the record after a thirty-minute recess," Judge Reeves began. "The record should reflect that all parties and counsel are present with the exception of Lieutenant Jacoby. Lieutenant Commander Harvey Carpenter, the senior defense counsel at the Naval Legal Service Defense Command, is present with the accused, along with civilian counsel, whom the court recognizes from his distinguished career in public service, but I will allow you to introduce yourself momentarily, sir."

Web Wallace nodded, then smiled.

"Now then." Reeves looked toward Zack. "At our last session, the government, along with Lieutenant Jacoby, announced that an agreement had been reached whereby the government would accept Ensign Eckberg's resignation and then drop all charges. Now, as I mentioned earlier, the detailed defense counsel, Lieutenant JG Jacoby, is no longer present in court, and the court with great sadness takes judicial notice of the lieutenant's sudden death over the weekend. The court, at this time, will observe a moment of silence for a period of one minute on behalf of Lieutenant JG Karen Jacoby. I will ask that we all stand silently on her behalf at this time. Bailiff?"

"All rise!"

As sunlight streamed through the glass pane windows just behind the empty jury box, silence permeated every corner of the courtroom. Judge Reeves bowed his head, as if praying. Zack kept his eyes glued on Diane Colcernian's picture and prayed that he would not publicly break down.

"Please be seated," Judge Reeves said after one minute had passed. "Now then, Lieutenant Commander Brewer."

"Yes, Your Honor." Zack rose to address the court.

"Has there been a change in the agreement?"

"Your Honor," Zack said, "that's unclear at this time. As the court mentioned, Lieutenant Jacoby died on Saturday. She had asked for a meeting with me that day to discuss this case. I'm sad to say that she died before we could discuss it. To my knowledge, unless Commander Carpenter knows otherwise, we have not received the accused's resignation. Although I can say from the government's perspective that this plea offer is still open."

"Very well. You may be seated, Commander Brewer." Captain Reeves looked at the senior defense counsel. "Commander Carpenter, you've just heard Commander Brewer state that the government will abide by the plea offer that was read into the record Friday. Does the defense still plan to honor this agreement?"

Looking uncomfortable, Lieutenant Commander Harvey Carpenter, who had been a classmate of both Zack and Diane at the Naval Justice School, rose to his feet.

"As you might imagine, Your Honor, the tragic events of this weekend have rocked the Navy Defense Command."

"And the court extends its sympathies to your command, Commander."

"Thank you, Your Honor. After Lieutenant Jacoby's tragic death, Mr. Webster Wallace, distinguished counsel for U.S. Senator Eleanor

Claxton, has volunteered to step in and offer his services to Ensign Eckberg as civilian defense counsel."

"Ensign Eckberg, as we discussed prior to Lieutenant Jacoby's death, you have a right to a detailed military defense counsel or to retain civilian counsel. Do you wish to retain Mr. Wallace as your counsel?"

"Yes, Your Honor."

"Very well. Mr. Wallace, are you making an appearance now on behalf of Ensign Eckberg?"

Web Wallace rose slowly as if he owned the courtroom. He was wearing a gray suit, white shirt, gold tie, and matching gold handkerchief in his jacket pocket.

"I am most honored," he said, his voice dripping with charisma, "to represent this fine young officer, Your Honor."

"Very well, Mr. Wallace. And have you had a chance to discuss with your client the plea agreement that was announced in court on Friday?"

"I have, Your Honor. And I've advised my client that it is in his best interest to reconsider his position." Wallace cut his gaze toward Zack and smirked. "We feel ... I feel, based on my many years in both the legal and political arenas, that, unfortunately, this prosecution is politically driven and is being driven not by what my client allegedly did, but rather by who he is. And in this case—"

"Mr. Wallace," Judge Reeves interrupted. "Does your client wish to *withdraw* from the plea agreement?"

"Your Honor." Wallace rocked back and forth, then, turning around, addressed the reporters in the back of the courtroom. "I am reminded of the words that were spoken by the Reverend Dr. Martin Luther King Jr."—he turned again to address the court—"that we long for the day when men shall be judged not by the color of their skin, but by the content of their character.

"Today the indomitable spirit of Dr. King lives on—in that a man should be judged not by how God created him—either straight or gay—but by his acts of bravery and heroism and commitment to God and country. And so, Your Honor—"

"Your Honor." Zack sprang to his feet, unable to take any more of Wallace's political grandstanding. "With all due respect, you asked Mr. Wallace a simple question—namely, whether we still have a deal—and he goes into an irrelevant spiel about Dr. Martin Luther King—"

"With due respect," Wallace interrupted in a shocked tone, "Dr. King stood for civil rights. This case is about civil rights."

"This case," Zack shot back, "is about homosexual assault aboard a U.S. Navy submarine. Nothing more. Nothing less. Conduct which, by the way, Dr. King would disapprove of. And I still haven't heard an answer to your question, Your Honor."

"Gentlemen, that's enough," Judge Reeves snapped. "I'm not going to have sniping in my courtroom. Is that clear?"

"Yes, sir," Zack said.

"My apologies, Your Honor," Wallace said.

"Now." Judge Reeves looked at Wallace. "Mr. Wallace, Commander Brewer was right about one thing. You haven't answered my question. I'll pose it to you once more, and if I don't get an answer, I'll order Commander Rouse to answer. Now I ask again, is your client withdrawing from the previously announced plea agreement?"

Wallace turned to the gallery again and gave them a smirk that said, *Can you believe this?* Then he turned to look Captain Reeves in the eye.

"Yes, Your Honor. That is my recommendation."

"Very well," Judge Reeves said. "Ensign Eckberg."

"Yes, Your Honor." Harvey Carpenter whispered something to Eckberg, who then rose. "Yes, Your Honor. I apologize for not standing. That is my desire. To withdraw from the agreement."

"And you wish to retain Mr. Wallace as civilian counsel?"

Wallace patted Eckberg on the back, nodding his head as if he were Eckberg's approving grandfather.

"Yes, Your Honor," Eckberg said. "Yes, I do."

"Very well. Having exercised your rights under the Uniform Code of Military Justice to retain civilian counsel, the court approves and accepts Mr. Wallace as civilian counsel. Now then, the accused"—Reeves looked into the gallery—"having withdrawn from the agreement, reenters his plea of not guilty. The court accepts that plea and we will proceed at this time. Commander Brewer, before we broke, I believe the government was in the process of the direct examination of Petty Officer Marvin Williams?"

"We were, Your Honor."

"Do you wish to resume with Petty Officer Williams' examination at this time?"

"Yes, Your Honor," Zack said.

"Your Honor, we object!" Wallace had switched seats with Eckberg. He was now sitting at the center of counsel table, beside Harvey Carpenter.

"Please stand when you address the court, Mr. Wallace."

"My apologies." Wallace stood.

"Let me get this straight, Mr. Wallace. You advise your client to withdraw from the plea agreement, he changes his plea to not guilty, and now you're objecting to the government resuming its case?"

"That's correct, Your Honor."

"All right. On what grounds are you objecting?"

"Your Honor ..." Zack stood, holding his palms upward.

"Hang on, Commander Brewer," Reeves said, still staring at Wallace. "Your grounds for objecting, sir?"

"We have a motion to dismiss, Your Honor."

"A motion to dismiss? All right. On what grounds?"

"Uh ... We move to dismiss on the grounds that my client's civil rights have been violated because of wrongful command tampering."

A quizzical look crossed the senior military judge's face. "*Wrongful command tampering?* That's the basis of your motion?"

Lieutenant Commander Carpenter leaned over and whispered something to Wallace.

"Uh ... perhaps a slip of tongue. What I meant to say is *unlawful command influence.* My friend Commander Carpenter here has just informed me that I misspoke. I believe that's the military term of art. Yes. That's it. Unlawful command influence. Not being a military man myself—I spent my formative years in the Peace Corps—I am not all that familiar with the military terms of art. I am, however familiar, with all those terms of art as they apply to civil rights. And in this case—"

"Hold on, Mr. Wallace." Judge Reeves whapped the gavel once on the bench—something he rarely did. The sound reverberated through the courtroom, halting Wallace's pontification midstream. "I did not understand wrongful command tampering. I do understand the concept of unlawful command influence. Do you wish to be heard on that motion at this time?"

Zack shot to his feet. "I object, Your Honor!"

"To what, Commander Brewer?"

"To the timing here. This is the type of motion that should have been brought before trial. Not in the middle of it. We've received no notice of this. And now in the middle of the trial this happens? After last Friday, when the accused agreed to resign and avoid prosecution altogether? I know some defense lawyers engage in the practice of trial by ambush, but this is unacceptable."

"Commander, I'll take your objection under advisement *after* Mr. Wallace states his position on the record. Now I ask you again, sir" — he turned to the venerable defense counsel — "do you wish to argue your position at this time?"

Wallace and Lieutenant Commander Carpenter conferred in whispered tones. "Your Honor, the defense requests a continuance at this time."

"A continuance?"

"Yes, Your Honor. I've just been retained as counsel. I need more time to investigate the case background. Plus, we are concerned about not only the decision to prosecute, but the policy behind it, and the commanding admiral's conduct in this case."

"The commanding admiral?"

"Your Honor," Zack said, rising from his seat. "There was no admiral on board that submarine." He threw his hands in the air. "Only a perpetrator — Ensign Eckberg — and half a dozen victims."

"Save that for the jury, Commander Brewer."

"Mr. Wallace, how much of a continuance are you asking for?"

"Oh, I don't know ..." He conferred again with Carpenter. "At this time, perhaps a week."

"You realize your client is in confinement, and if I grant this continuance, the defense will not be allowed to count it against the government for speedy trial purposes?"

"That's fine, Your Honor."

"Lieutenant Commander Brewer, what is the government's position on this continuance request?"

"Your Honor, SEAL Team 3, the unit where Petty Officer Williams and most of our witnesses are stationed, is an operational unit. While I can't comment on the unit's operational plans, the navy has an interest in having that unit operationally ready. Leaving the unit on standby while Mr. Wallace prepares for this case is not in the navy's best interest. And so, yes, we do oppose this request."

"Your Honor, if I may address that —," Lieutenant Commander Carpenter began.

Judge Reeves held up his hand, palm out. "That won't be necessary," he said. "I am going to grant the continuance request. This court will be in recess for one week."

"All rise!"

CHAPTER 27

Jackson Gallopoulous marched into the suite of the junior senator from Vermont, checking his watch as he stepped in.

"Eleanor," he said, "the press is waiting downstairs."

Eleanor was sitting on a loveseat, her attention riveted to the television's live coverage of the events at the naval station. CNN reporter Laurie Jane McCaffity had been on the scene all morning, interviewing various eyewitnesses.

Mary-Latham Modlin stood behind her, also watching the coverage. Two Secret Service agents were stationed in the room—one guarding the door and the other looking out the window.

"Any other comments on this yet, Jackson?"

"Not even from the White House."

"Where's Mohammed?"

Odd that she would ask about Mohammed at a time like this. "Back here at the hotel. I'd recommend that you wait to see him after the presser if you want to beat the White House to the punch on this."

"Right. Let's go." Eleanor stood and followed Jackson, Mary-Latham, and the Secret Service agents into the hallway and then into the secured elevator.

★

Five minutes later Jackson stepped through a door leading onto the stage in the Coronado Room, a banquet hall the Del used for conferences and appearances by public officials. Under the glare of bright lights, he folded his arms and stood near the podium. The whir of cameras and the explosion of flashbulbs accompanied Eleanor's entrance onto the stage. As the senator stepped forward, Mary-Latham and Jackson stepped into place at each side of the podium. Mary-Latham, wearing a tailored black pantsuit, looked over and gave Jackson a heart-melting smile.

"Good morning." Eleanor nodded to the press corps, then unfolded the statement Mary-Latham had prepared.

"Some thirty minutes ago, here in San Diego, innocent protestors—American citizens, exercising their most fundamental rights—the right of the people to assemble peaceably, the right to protest the actions of government—were gunned down in cold blood. Innocent blood has been shed by peace-loving Americans.

"We begin by offering our sincere condolences to the families of all who lost their lives.

"While the facts are not yet all in, it appears that shots may have been fired by governmental authorities—perhaps even by United States Marines.

"Until all the facts are in, I urge restraint in rushing to judgment about who fired into the unarmed crowd.

"While the identity of the perpetrators may not yet be totally clear, what is clear is this.

"The policies of the Williams administration—in perpetrating a long-standing policy of discriminating against gay Americans in the U.S. military—have fostered the deadly and heavy-handed atmosphere under which these Americans were gunned down today.

"These Americans had gathered to express their concern about the navy's policy.

"Even as we speak, against the backdrop of this morning's senseless killings, here in San Diego, the navy is involved in a general court-martial against a young officer—Ensign Wofford Eckberg—a Naval Academy graduate—only because he is a gay American. By all accounts, this young officer was beaten by naval personnel, but the navy has turned a deaf ear and has taken no action against the sailors who broke the collarbone of this young officer.

"Nothing." Claxton chopped her hand in the air.

"Just two days ago, the Navy JAG officer who had been assigned to defend this young man, Lieutenant Karen Jacoby, was murdered in cold blood under suspicious circumstances.

"It appears that Lieutenant Jacoby, who fought so hard to represent Ensign Eckberg and to protect his civil rights, may also be the victim of hate.

"I've asked my counsel, Mr. Webster Wallace, to lend a hand and do everything he can to help this fine young man.

"But from a larger perspective, I call on this administration to stop turning a blind eye to discrimination not only in the navy, but in all branches of the armed services.

"Act now, Mr. President, in the name of those whose lives have been lost today, and so that their lives will not have been lost in vain. Act now to end discrimination against patriotic Americans like Ensign Eckberg.

"And, Mr. President, for the sake of Ensign Eckberg and so many other brave Americans in the armed forces who are like him, and in memory of Lieutenant Karen Jacoby, who lost her life because of who and what she represented, I call upon you now, Mr. President"— Eleanor stared into the cameras and pointed on cue, just as she had been instructed—"to make hate crimes punishable under the Uniform Code of Military Justice.

"Act now, Mr. President, to end once and for all discrimination in the military, before there is more loss of innocent blood.

"Thank you."

"Senator Claxton!"

"Senator Claxton!"

Mary-Latham stepped to the podium as Eleanor exited through the backstage door. "Ladies and gentlemen, the senator will not take questions at this time. We need to await more information, and at that time the senator will be available for a press conference.

"Mary-Latham . . ."

"Thank you." Mary-Latham turned, motioned for Jackson to follow her, and left the stage. They stepped through the exit door into a smaller room, where Eleanor, eyes narrowed, was waiting for them.

"Great job," Jackson said.

Mary-Latham stepped up behind him. "Agreed."

"Where's Mohammed?" Eleanor demanded.

"In the bar," Jackson said.

"Get him up to my suite. I want him alone. Is that clear?"

"Mary-Latham," Jackson said, "why don't you accompany Eleanor back to the suite? I'll get Mohammed and bring him upstairs."

"Make it fast," Eleanor snapped.

"Yes, Senator."

Attorneys' lounge
Floor 2, Building 1
Navy-Marine Corp Trial Judiciary
32nd Street Naval Station
San Diego, California

Zack Brewer was not in a good mood.

He'd just been handed an order from his commanding officer, Captain Alan Rudy, instructing him to move into a room in the Navy Lodge at Naval Air Station North Island until further notice.

On top of that, his brand-new silver Mercedes, the only worldly possession that he halfway cared about, would be impounded at the 32nd Street Naval Station until further notice.

And on top of that, he was to be transported around the city of San Diego—to the extent that it was necessary to set foot off a U.S. Naval facility—only by NCIS in a windowless panel truck until further notice.

He wanted to take the Styrofoam cup he was holding in his hand, with its battery-acid excuse for coffee, and hurl it against the wall of the attorneys' lounge. Sure, the navy had every right to order him around. He was a naval officer, subject to the orders of his superiors. But that wasn't the point. The point was that by hiding him inside the naval station and behind windowless panel trucks as if he were some sort of frail petunia, the navy was capitulating to terrorists. When freedoms are curtailed in the wake of terrorism, as with the passage of the so-called Patriot Act in the name of antiterrorism after 9/11, the terrorists win.

He knew he was overreacting, but he couldn't help himself.

Now he was about to get his first chauffeured ride in the windowless panel truck. He was due at COMNAVBASE headquarters in downtown San Diego in thirty minutes for a meeting with Rear Admiral Charles F. Scott. Admiral Scott was the convening authority for the court-martial against Ensign Eckberg, which meant that the admiral had the power to bring the case or drop it—or take some other action as he saw fit.

Zack checked his watch. "Guys, is my paddy wagon in place yet?"

Special Agent Wesner chuckled. "Yes, sir, Commander, they're bringing it over right now. It will be out front."

"You know, if you're going to make me ride in a windowless paddy wagon, at least you could send Shannon back over here to babysit me. She's"—Zack cleared his throat—"shall we say, a bit easier on the eyes."

"Can't argue with that, Commander." Wesner chuckled. "She's down at NCIS headquarters. She'll be back soon."

"Speaking of headquarters," Zack said, "we've gotta roll if I'm going to make that appointment with Admiral Scott."

"Right about that, Commander," Wesner said. "Let's rock 'n' roll."

Wesner, Raynor, Zack, and Peterson all stepped into the hallway on the second deck of the military courthouse building and headed toward the stairway that would take them down to the first floor, out the front door, and to the waiting vehicle for Zack's ride downtown.

"What about these press vultures?" Zack asked.

"Still a few down there, Zack," Raynor answered. "They're camped out, waiting for you."

"Great," Zack muttered. "Any more word on the shootings?"

"Two confirmed dead. Some of 'em are trying to blame the marines," Wesner said. "I don't believe it."

"Don't believe anything you read in the papers," Zack said. "It's all about who can out-sensationalize the other. Ratings and money. That's what the press has gotten to."

They hustled down the steps to the first deck and past Courtroom 1, the now-vacant site of the latest public saga to take over Zack's life.

Mike Wesner stepped out ahead of the quartet, walking to the exit door. He turned and looked at Zack. "Sorry, Commander, we've still got company."

"How much company?"

"Looks like they all stayed for the party."

"Great."

"Panel truck's at the bottom of the steps. Good news is we've still got our marine platoon down there. Just ignore the press if you want, sir. It's up to you."

"Maybe," Zack said. "Let's go."

Wesner flung open the door to the worn-out sight of a press circus.

They barked Zack's name like hungry puppies yelping in a dog pound. He started down the steps toward the panel truck through the cordon of marines.

Raynor had already reached the panel truck, its engine running, and opened its back doors.

"Senator Claxton just finished a press conference, Commander. She criticized U.S. Marines for firing into the peace-loving crowd this morning, saying they had assembled spontaneously to assert their right of free speech."

Zack initially decided to ignore the reporter's comment. But as he put one foot into the panel truck, the thought of U.S. Marines sacrificing their bodies for this country in hellholes like Guadalcanal, Iwo Jima, and Okinawa overtook him. He could've ignored anything, he decided in the heat of the moment, except potshots against God, country, Diane Colcernian, or the United States Marine Corps. Boiling rage rose inside him. He turned and pointed at the reporter who had made the statement.

"Peace-loving, you say? If Senator Claxton had been in the car with me when we tried driving to work this morning, she would have seen how *peace-loving* this *spontaneous* crowd of protestors *really* was." He made quotation marks with his fingers as he uttered the words *peace-loving* and *spontaneous*. "Look, as we tried crossing Harbor Drive to enter the naval station, the senator's *peace-loving* crowd clogged the public streets to the point that no one could go anywhere. And I guess it would have been okay if it had stopped there. But, ladies and gentlemen, it did not.

"I tell you now—" Zack paused and surveyed the quizzical looks on their faces. Several scribbled notes on legal pads. "When our car rolled into the intersection, we were swarmed by an angry mob. They surrounded us, climbed on the trunk, climbed on the hood, on the roof, beat against the glass, and shook and rocked the car as if they were trying to flip it over.

"I don't condone firing into a crowd of civilians. In fact, I condemn it. But I also condemn mob violence. If somebody hadn't done something, I'd be in a morgue right now.

"I didn't care as much about my own life as I did about that of the NCIS agent who was in the car with me. And there were NCIS agents in the cars in front of and behind us. And two cars ahead, there was a San

Diego County deputy sheriff who happens to be a good friend of mine. If anything had happened to them because of that out-of-control mob, I would have cared, believe me."

"But, Commander," said an attractive, young blonde reporter, "what about some lesser means of dispersing the crowd? Don't you think the marines should have used tear gas?"

"The marines? For Senator Claxton, or anyone else for that matter, to take a potshot at the nation's finest fighting force, the United States Marine Corps, without having all the facts at her disposal is irresponsibility at its highest form.

"All members of Congress should, before they are sworn in, go through boot camp at Paris Island."

That comment brought furious scribbling.

"How do you respond to comments made by Mr. Webster and also by Senator Claxton that this court-martial is a political prosecution and is all about keeping gay Americans out of the military?" This came from Zane Jones, anchor for the local NBC affiliate, KSDO Television.

"Ridiculous," Zack said. "Gay Americans already serve in the military."

A young African-American reporter stepped forward. "But doesn't 'Don't ask, don't tell' intimidate many from serving their country?"

"That's a question for the politicians. I'm no politician. I'm just a naval officer trying to serve my country. But if you think for one minute this is a politically driven trial, I can assure you it isn't. It may be politically driven by the defense—which has another agenda—but it is insulting to suggest the prosecution is politically driven.

"As I said in court just an hour ago, this case is about a single act of homosexual assault aboard a U.S. Navy submarine. Nothing more. Nothing less.

"Such conduct undermines good order and discipline in the U.S. military, which in turn, undermines the security of the United States. Even if 'Don't ask, don't tell' were abolished, such conduct will be dealt with severely as long as there is a military justice system.

"For someone to come in now and make a sick attempt to construe this trial into something it's not—that's despicable."

"Commander! Commander!" The pretty blonde had her microphone in his face again. "Are you suggesting that Senator Claxton is despicable?"

Watch your tongue, Zack. Or at least quit while you're ahead. "I made no such suggestion about the senator or anyone else. What I meant was that the act of casting unfounded and unsubstantiated aspersions against United States Marines, or trying to co-opt the defense of a court-martial for political gain—when the purpose of the court-martial is to preserve good order and discipline in the military—now *that's* despicable."

"But, Commander, weren't your comments in fact *aimed* at Senator Claxton, even if you did not use her name?"

"I've just explained that in my previous answer. Thank you all for coming today. Now if you'll excuse me, I have an appointment off base."

Zack stepped into the van and took a seat in back. Mike Wesner closed the door, and in thirty seconds, the yipping cacophony of reporters faded.

CHAPTER 28

Senator Claxton's suite
Claxton campaign San Diego County headquarters
Hotel del Coronado
1500 Orange Avenue
Coronado, California

The junior senator from Vermont sat at the small breakfast table in the corner of her suite, nursing a Bloody Mary. Her press secretary, Mary-Latham, had just seated herself across from her when the intercom buzzed.

"Excuse me, Senator." It was the new Secret Service agent, whose name she could not recall, assigned to her detail. "Mr. Gallopoulous and Mr. Khadiija are here."

"Send Mr. Khadiija in alone, please. Tell Mr. Gallopoulous I'll talk to him later."

"Yes, Senator."

Eleanor took another nip of the Bloody Mary, then said to Mary-Latham, "I need to speak with Mohammed in private. I hope you understand. I'll call you when I need you."

"Sure thing, Eleanor."

Mary-Latham stood and walked out, passing Mohammed Khadiija as he walked in.

"Too bad she's not my type," Mohammed said in a mock-sultry tone.

"What the heck happened out there?" Eleanor demanded, then launched into a profanity-laced tirade.

"Eleanor, please calm down. Mind if I order a drink?"

"I don't care what you order—*after* you tell me what happened this morning."

"I haven't the foggiest, my dear," Mohammed responded through a devilish grin.

"I thought we had a *peaceful* protest planned." She glared at him. "You said your people would stay up on the sidewalks."

"Emotions runneth high. This is a topic near and dear to the hearts of many. Of course, you've fanned those emotions with all your 'Neanderthal mentality' comments. You're building quite a fan base in California from what I'm hearing on the streets. Bravo, my dear!"

Eleanor stood, turned her back on him, and downed the rest of her Bloody Mary. "You know, this thing could have turned sour if something had happened to Brewer. He's a conservative icon, and I need to polarize liberals here in California against him. That would be kind of hard to do if he ... were suddenly unavailable."

"But things turned out okay, did they not? I mean, you got to make a wonderful speech at a press conference. You beat President Williams to the punch. By the way, I just heard on NPR that he's gong to address the country in thirty minutes. And ... *and* you'll get major league coverage tonight in LA and San Francisco, the cities you'll need to spring the upset in this state against that native son Congressman Warren. All in all, I'd say a good day."

"Look, Mohammed, I appreciate everything you do." She turned around and saw that he had helped himself to a glass of Scotch from the wet bar. "But we *must* maintain control of this campaign. Things turned out well this morning, but this could have blown up in our faces. If Brewer dies prematurely, especially in a street riot, then we lose control of the media direction, and I've got a wave of conservative sympathy sweeping the nation.

"We got lucky. But we've got to maintain control to make sure nothing blows up. The protests alone as the backdrop to our coordinated defense against the prosecution would have been enough to get us where we need to be in LA and Frisco. Stick with the plan, please. A bloodbath was just too risky."

Mohammed stood, sipped his Scotch, and walked across the plush carpet to the windows. In front of him spread the expansive view of the Pacific. "Do my ears deceive me? The most ruthless woman in the world, the first woman president of the United States, worried about death and bloodbaths?"

"Who fired the shots, Mohammed?"

That brought a chuckle from the scruffy-faced Middle Easterner. "Why, the marines did. You said so yourself. No?"

"Who fired the shots, Mohammed?"

"And how should I know? What's important is that the voters in the Bay Area *think* it was the marines. By the time all this is sorted out, you will be the Democratic presidential nominee! And then"—he took a triumphant sip of Scotch—"the first woman president of the United States."

"And what do voters in the Bay Area think about Karen Jacoby?"

"Eleanor, relax. This was a vigilante murder. Everybody knows it. No one knows she was a potential problem for us. No one will know, except those of us in the closest circle. That's the way it will remain. Trust me."

"Okay, okay. But listen, Mohammed—no more deviations from the script. Got it?"

"Eleanor, where is your sense of adventure?"

She slammed her empty glass on the tabletop and glared at him. "I don't know if you've considered this, Mohammed, but I've been around politics a long time. A whole lot longer than your so-called conversion from Islam to homosexuality to Democratic activism." She leaned toward him. "Let me tell you what that means, Mohammed. Politics is a dirty business."

"Dirty?"

"Dirtier than you can imagine. You think radical Islam is dirty? You haven't seen anything. What goes on out of the public's eye makes 9/11 look like a picnic in the park. Get my drift? This was a dirty business before you came along, and if there are any more surprises, you are gone."

"Why, Senator"—Mohammed poured another drink, forcing a smile over a twisted expression—"if I didn't know better, I would think you are threatening me."

"Let me put it this way, Mohammed. You aren't the first individual to work for me or my husband and carry out the duties that you do. Now, some of them are still around. Some aren't. The ones who aren't deviated from the script. Some decided to take inside information from our campaigns and use it for political or monetary gain. Some tried blackmailing by threatening to go to the authorities or the press.

"But now they are gone, Mohammed. Every one of them.

"Those who are still around showed unfailing loyalty. And the ones who are ..." She walked to the wet bar and poured herself a Scotch, then turned and glared into his black eyes. "Those who are still around will do *absolutely anything* I ask them to do."

She sat down in a rocking chair across the room from him. "They will do what I've asked you to do—and *more*."

His contrived smile vanished. His eyebrows furrowed. His lips and cheeks contorted.

"Ever read for pleasure, Mohammed?"

"I used to read the Koran. Since I abandoned the faith, I don't read it anymore. Now sometimes I read magazines about politics and other things."

"Ever heard of Machiavelli?"

"Who?"

"That's what I thought. Go find him and read him. When you do, you'll know who you're dealing with."

"Yes, of course, Eleanor."

"From now on, you clear everything with me, understand?"

"Yes."

She sighed. "Mohammed, look. I don't mean to be hard on you. This little talk we've had—you're not the first I've had to give it to. Some listened. Some didn't. Look. You've got a chance to go a long way in our organization. The first Muslim of significance to denounce a faith oppressive to women and children and to embrace gay rights. You, my friend, are that man.

"But you must do three simple things. One, keep your mouth shut. Two, stay loyal to me above all. And three, do whatever I tell you without any deviation. Do these things and you'll go places. Fail to do them, and you'll become a forgotten footnote on the ash heap of history.

"Have I made myself clear, Mohammed?"

"Perfectly clear, Senator."

"So are we now of one accord?"

"We are. You have my loyalty, my obedience, and my unfailing dedication."

"Good. Now get out of my sight."

Somewhere near the Colorado-Kansas border
United Flight 882
Altitude 32,000 feet

As they flew east, away from the setting sun, the wind whipping across the endless carpet of wheat below gave the plains the look of an orange ocean. It had been this way since they passed over the snow-capped Rockies a half hour ago.

When the pilot announced they had crossed over the Kansas border and would soon begin their descent for Kansas City, Shannon's mind turned to Zack. She'd been with him enough to know that he watched no television except college basketball. And next to his beloved Tar Heels, the Kansas Jayhawks were his second favorite team.

Shannon hated basketball.

She'd grown up as a hockey fan and had nearly married the guy who was the trainer for the Boston Bruins. They broke up when she joined the NCIS. But of course she'd never told Zack about her weight-training, hockey-playing ex-boyfriend or her dislike for basketball.

She'd watched a dozen games with Zack at his home in the last year. When Carolina played, he always crowed about Jordan, Worthy, Perkins, Ford, Felton, May, and McCants. And when they watched Kansas, he talked about players named Chamberlain, Manning, Hinrich, and Collison.

Frankly, the only player she'd ever heard of was Michael Jordan. Although the name Wilt Chamberlain sounded familiar.

Something about watching all those games with him had made her jealous.

It was the picture.

The eight-by-ten color photo of Diane Colcernian, wearing the summer white uniform of a female U.S. Naval officer, was hauntingly beautiful sitting atop his television set.

Sometimes when Zack stood up to yell at the television set and pump his fist in the air because some Tar Heel player air-dunked the ball, Shannon locked eyes with Diane's picture.

Maybe deep down she should have known it even then, by the way Diane's eyes seemed to follow her across the room, that she had been wrong. Despite all the evidence that Diane was dead, despite all the mathematical odds against her survival, and despite all of Director Jones's political bull, Shannon knew. Deep down, she knew.

"Ladies and gentlemen, this is your captain speaking. In a few minutes, we will begin our final approach for Kansas City. Please return to your seats and fasten your seat belts. Weather on the ground in Kansas City is partly cloudy, a little windy, and a nippy forty-five degrees. We should be on the ground in about twelve minutes. We do hope your trip from San Diego has been an enjoyable one. Thank you for flying United."

Shannon looked over at Barry, slouched in the middle seat just beside her. His eyes were closed and his mouth agape, and a sporadic snore rattled from his big nose. She reached over and strapped his seat belt across his belly, then strapped herself in.

She closed her eyes and did something that she had not done a lot of lately.

She prayed.

What irony, she thought, that she could pray for something like this. Where was such ability coming from?

Wherever, or from whomever, it didn't matter. She turned her face toward the window, looked down at the great plains of Kansas, and prayed some more.

CHAPTER 29

Jackson Gallopoulous's suite
Claxton campaign San Diego County headquarters
Hotel del Coronado
1500 Orange Avenue
Coronado, California

Fear. Confusion. Disgust.

The three emotions twisted and choked Jackson Gallopoulous's very soul as he sat alone on the sofa in his hotel suite. Sweat soaked his forehead. His hands shook.

He had to regain his composure, and fast. But for the moment, there was nothing he could do to slow the physical reaction. What to do? Call Eleanor and tell her he couldn't come to work because he was sick? She'd seen him less than an hour ago. Would she fall for that? Even so, how would he know he would be able to recover from this?

He sipped a glass of ice water, hoping it would soothe his stomach, and thought about his college days as a political science major at Yale. It was the most idealistic and noble calling, they had told him, those former high-ranking officials from Democratic administrations who had taken professorships at one of the two most academically prestigious institutions in America.

"Only in politics do you have a chance to stamp out poverty," one professor had told him.

"In politics, you can right the criminal injustices imposed on the masses by the satanic greed of evil corporations," another had said.

And then there were the words of his mentor, former Democrat secretary of state turned Yale professor Edmund Gansky, who closed each and every class with the same statement: "Since the days of Nixon, the Republicans have always been known for their dirty tricks. By contrast, the Democratic Party has been the conscience of America. Remain true to the polar star of virtue, young people, and it shall carry you far."

These words were the idealistic gospel to which young Jackson Gallopoulous had dedicated his life. He fumbled for his wallet, found the business card, and looked at the words he had scribbled on the back of it.

Remain true to the polar star of virtue, and it shall carry you far.

He read the words again, then went into the bathroom and vomited.

Headquarters of the Commander
Naval Base San Diego
937 North Harbor Drive
San Diego, California

Zack had been waiting only a minute or so in the receptionist's area when Lieutenant Kurt Kenkel, wearing the gold cord of an admiral's aide looped under his arm and attached just under the shoulder board of his summer white uniform, opened the door.

"Commander Brewer, the admiral will see you now, sir."

"Thanks, Kurt." Zack stepped smartly into the office of Rear Admiral Charles F. Scott Jr. and came to attention. "Lieutenant Commander Brewer reporting, sir." He focused his eyes over the admiral's head, on a plaque that had commemorated Admiral Scott's stint as captain of the aircraft carrier USS *Abraham Lincoln.*

From the corner of his eye, however, he could see various other officers waiting in the room. These included Commander Bob Awe, the senior trial counsel and Zack's immediate boss; Captain Bill Foster, the admiral's personal JAG officer; and Zack's old friend Captain Buck Noble, Commander of Seal Team 3.

Zack's commanding officer, Captain Glen Rudy, JAGC, USN, was not present. All of the officers except Zack were in their working khaki uniforms, with their respective ranks pinned to their collars.

"Zack, Zack, at ease and sit the heck down." The admiral deflated the formal deference that would otherwise be due him.

"Thanks, Admiral." Zack loosened up, then shook hands with a smiling Captain Noble and a widely grinning Captain Foster. When he saw the admiral leaning back in his chair, also smiling, he muttered, "Did I miss out on the joke?"

"Sit, Zack," Admiral Scott ordered again.

Zack complied.

"So is it true?" the admiral asked.

"Sir?"

"We just heard on the radio that you think Eleanor Claxton ought to join the marines and go through boot camp."

"Sir ..."

Captain Foster, a tall, lanky officer who had played point guard at Carson-Newman College in Tennessee before joining the navy, doubled over laughing. "Zack, you know you're going to catch the devil for that comment. But that's the funniest thing I've heard in a long time."

"But, sir, I—"

"That's why we made him an honorary SEAL." The stocky, muscular Captain Noble chuckled. "With his tongue and our laser-guided weapons, we can take out any enemy in the world—military or political."

"But the press—"

"Save it, Zack," the admiral said. "It doesn't matter how they twisted it. You'll be hearing from plenty of friends in Washington by this time tomorrow."

Great.

At this point, Commander Awe, the only officer not smiling, spoke up. "That's why Captain Rudy isn't here. JAG's already heard about this. We're prepping for damage control before the morning. Admiral LeGrand"—he was referring to Rear Admiral W. T. "Biff" LeGrand, the judge advocate general of the navy and top lawyer in all the naval service—"will insist that you make some sort of public statement at a press conference clarifying what you said. Captain Rudy says to remind you that whether we like it or not, Senator Claxton just might be our next commander in chief."

"The day that happens is the day I submit my resignation," Captain Noble said defiantly.

"I'm following you out the door," Captain Foster added.

"I knew I should have kept my mouth shut," Zack said.

Admiral Scott leaned forward slightly. "Don't worry about it, Zack. I admire your guts. If they kick you out of the navy, you can get a job in a private law firm making more than all of us here combined." When he spoke again, his demeanor had changed, and his tone was serious. "It's been a rough weekend for the navy, and we've gotta somehow deal with that dadgum court-marital mess going on down there."

"Agreed, Admiral."

"What's the deal with this defense continuance?" The admiral took a sip of coffee. "I thought they were all up in a wad because Captain Foster's boys over here roughed the ensign up and were threatening a speedy trial violation if we didn't get him prosecuted."

"Want my honest opinion, sir?"

"That's why I've got you here, son. Ain't no reporters within earshot of anything you say right now. Shoot 'er straight with me."

"Could I have a cup of coffee, please, sir?"

"Kurt," the admiral boomed, calling for his aide-de-camp, "rustle up some fresh black coffee for my star prosecutor here. And while you're at it, warm up mine and these other gentlemen's."

"Aye, aye, Admiral," the aide said.

"Now you were saying, Commander?"

"The continuance is a stall tactic."

"A stall tactic?"

"Yes, sir."

"Go on."

"A resignation, a plea, or a trial would be over quickly. All of those options make this go away quickly. But a continuance—well, that keeps the issue in the limelight that much longer. Claxton and her cronies—and that includes this Web Wallace—can call press conferences, express shock and dismay, and keep this in the public eye longer. My guess—and I'm no politician—is that this is a play for San Francisco, where she's neck and neck with that Warren guy. Carry San Francisco and you win California. Win California, and only my ol' pal Senator Roberson Fowler stands in Eleanor's way of the Democratic nomination."

"You still seeing his niece—Ensign ... What was her name?"

"She was Ensign Marianne Landrieu. She's now Lieutenant Landrieu, and no, sir, I'm not seeing her and never did. She's like Senator Fowler's only daughter. He wanted us to hook up and move to Washington and live happily ever after. It was tempting at the time, but I've decided I want no part of Washington, D.C."

"After what you said this morning, you don't have to be worried about being invited to Washington anytime soon," Noble joked.

"Gentlemen, let's get back on point," the admiral said. "Okay, what about the unlawful command influence thing. What's that all about?"

"I think it's a bunch of horse manure, Admiral."

"So is it something I need to be worried about or not?"

"They'll bring the motion, and I imagine they'll do it on the theory that no one was disciplined for breaking Eckberg's collarbone."

"What's that got to do with unlawful command influence?" the admiral demanded. "I didn't have anything to do with that."

"Understood, sir. The unlawful command influence motion could be directed either at you, sir—that is, at COMNAVBASE, the convening authority for the general court-marital—or at Captain Noble here." Zack looked over at Captain Noble, whose left fist was balled in his right hand, an action that flexed his well-defined biceps. "But to answer your question, Admiral, in my judgment, the decision to prosecute or not prosecute anyone else is a red herring. The motion should be dismissed by Judge Reeves. It's just that we have a public relations embarrassment on our hands."

"Thank you, Kurt," the admiral said as Lieutenant Kurt Kenkel returned to the office carrying a silver tray with a silver pitcher and five cups of steaming black coffee. The admiral was served first, then the other officers were served in descending order of rank. As Zack was being served, the admiral asked, "What recommendations do you have for me, Counselor?"

Zack sipped his coffee, contemplating his answer. The admiral might not like what he had to say. Captain Noble certainly wouldn't. He set his coffee mug down on the table between his chair and the chair occupied by Commander Awe.

"The senator and her legal minions—the whining Mr. Wallace—*do* have a point about one thing."

"Go on." An anxious look crossed the admiral's face.

"It looks bad—I mean, *bad*—that Eckberg's collarbone was broken and nothing was done about it."

"A broken collarbone?" Captain Noble roared from his chair. "He's darn lucky my men didn't nail him upside down to the bulkhead of that submarine and then shoot him out the torpedo tube."

The captain's voice resonated through the room, unmet by a response from any of the other officers.

"Yes, sir, Captain, I know how you feel," Zack said after a moment, sipping his coffee to slow the pace of his comments. "What Eckberg did was inexcusable. And you and I both know that the only reason a plea bargain was put on the table to begin with is because the SEAL team is on classified standby deployment orders. Your men could be called out of here by midnight."

That brought a grunt from the peeved SEAL commander.

"But, Captain, no matter what Eckberg did, who am I to remind you, sir, that there are certain principles and ideals that your men — the finest fighting men in the world — are trained to give their lives for. And one of those principles is that in America, we don't resort to vigilante justice, no matter what offense has been committed against us."

That brought another grunt, along with a reluctant, "I suppose you're right."

"Admiral" — Zack turned to the two-star officer — "this is an issue that, at least from a public relations standpoint, they've already bloodied their nose with, and if we don't do something fast, it's going to snowball into an avalanche by the media."

"So what you're saying, Commander," Noble spoke up again, "is that I've got to sacrifice one of my SEAL commandos for the sake of feeding this communist, yellow-bellied politician named Eleanor Claxton."

Zack did not respond.

At this point, Commander Bob Awe spoke up. "Captains, Admiral, Zack and I haven't had a chance to discuss this. We normally have a discussion about things of this nature, but as you know, we've had quite a weekend, and Zack was just whisked down here from the courthouse. But on this point, I happen to agree with him." Zack gave his boss a nod of thanks.

Awe continued, "Unlike the *Olajuwon* and *Quasay* cases, this isn't a case involving national security. This is sheer politics. We are in a public relations war with these people. They will harp on this hate crimes thing until someone in Congress forces our hand and makes us prosecute whoever broke Eckberg's collarbone. I know we spend a lot of time, money, and effort training your men, Captain." Awe looked over at Noble. "And I know your men are the cream of the crop, but if Claxton keeps spouting about this, then the handwriting's on the wall. You'll be hearing about this on the talk shows tomorrow morning, the network news tomorrow night, and on and on. Better sooner than later."

Noble squirmed in his seat. His face turned red.

Admiral Scott nodded at his personal JAG officer, Captain Bill Foster. "Bill, you're legal advisor to this command. What do you say?"

"I agree, sir. Zack and Bob are right. Charges should be referred against whoever attacked Eckberg."

"Also," Commander Awe added, "whoever did this may have a defense. So it isn't likely that the defendant would be automatically sacrificed. You could bring it at a special court-martial instead of a general court-martial. If there's a defense, it's possible that your subordinate might not even be discharged."

That comment was followed by yet another moment of silence. The admiral turned to Captain Noble. "Buck, this is your call and yours alone. I can't tell you what to do on this one, or that *would* be unlawful command influence. Right, gentlemen?"

The three JAG officers in the room nodded their heads.

"It's in your hands, my friend," the admiral said.

"Give me twenty-four hours," Noble snarled. "I'll find a sacrificial lamb."

CHAPTER 30

United States Disciplinary Barracks
U.S. Army Base
Fort Leavenworth, Kansas

9:00 p.m. (CST)

The sun had already set by the time the United airplane from San Diego touched down at Kansas City International Airport. Shannon and Barry picked up their baggage and signed for the rental car, then began the short drive up the Kansas side of the Missouri River to Leavenworth, Kansas, in the dark. Shannon was disappointed not to see Kansas in the daytime, but sightseeing was not part of their agenda.

They pulled off the interstate and drove through the gates of Fort Leavenworth in less than ten minutes. Barry parked the Chrysler LeBaron near the United States Disciplinary Barracks, where the U.S. military housed many of its long-term prisoners from all five branches of the armed services. It was also the site of the execution of the three Islamic navy chaplains Diane Colcernian and Zack had prosecuted.

That execution, which was the first by the U.S. Navy in over 150 years, had been covered by the international press. It had set off wild riots in the Arab world and remained an international flash point even today. Zack, along with several high-ranking navy officials, had been ordered to witness the execution.

Shannon and Barry were met at the entrance of the mammoth barracks by the on-duty army warrant officer.

Shannon flashed her NCIS badge. "I'm McGillvery. This is my boss, Special Agent Barry MacGregor."

"You guys are here to see Commander Quasay, right?"

"You nailed it," Shannon said.

"Sign here." He pointed to a visitor's log. "Attach the plastic visitor tags to your lapels, please." The warrant officer picked up the telephone. "Sergeant Hansbrough, the NCIS agents from San Diego are here. They'll need an escort up to see Quasay."

A moment later a powerful buzz was followed by a loud clanging like hammers striking steel bars. Then two steel doors down the hallway swung open slowly to the sound of another electronic buzz. A U.S. Army enlisted man, a military policeman, approached the warrant officer's desk.

"Ready, sir," the MP said.

"Sergeant Hansbrough, these are Special Agents McGillvery and MacGregor of NCIS. Would you accompany them to their prisoner, please?"

"With pleasure, sir." The MP turned to Shannon and Barry. "Follow me."

They walked through more than a dozen steel security doors and down tile hallways reeking of ammonia, rubbing alcohol, and other chemical smells, which Shannon guessed were cleaning solvents of some sort.

They turned right down yet another fluorescent-lit hallway, walked a few feet, and reached a room with a chicken-wired glass window in the steel door. Above the door was a sign marked Inmate Visiting Area.

The MP opened the door. "Wait here, please. Commander Quasay will be here in a moment."

They sat on one side of the rectangular steel table. Shannon checked her watch. By now, it was almost 10:00 p.m. local time. She and Barry said nothing during this interlude, and a moment later the door swung open and a thin dark-haired man wearing a bright orange jumpsuit, his arms and legs bound, came shuffling into the room.

"Special Agent McGillvery," the MP said, addressing Shannon as if she were in charge of the McGillvery-MacGregor duo, "I can remain in here with you if you'd like."

"Thank you, Sergeant. That's not necessary."

"We'll be right outside if you need us, ma'am."

The sergeant stepped outside and closed the door.

"Well, well, Commander Quasay, so good to see you again."

"Special Agent McGillvery." The former navy pilot's voice was pleasant, almost as if he were happy to see the woman who was responsible for his prosecution. "It's been a long time since I've had visitors."

"This is my boss, Special Agent Barry MacGregor."

"Agent MacGregor."

"Please be seated, Commander," Barry said.

Quasay complied and seated himself across the table from Barry and Shannon.

"Commander Quasay," Barry said, "let me get to the point. We don't think you've been forthcoming in giving us all the information you promised when you plea-bargained."

"I am insulted, Mr. MacGregor."

"I'm the one who is insulted, Commander," Barry roared.

"Look, Mr. MacGregor, my life was on the line. We had a deal. I cooperated with the navy. I verified the existence of the Council of Ishmael. I gave you information about sleeper cells in the navy. I gave you a statement that the council planned the attack on the Dome of the Rock by U.S. Navy fighter planes—flown by Islamic U.S. Navy pilots—to make it appear that the U.S. was striking back at Islam's third holiest sight in retaliation for 9/11.

"Since I made that statement, my life has been threatened several times, even here in prison. I've gotten death threats in the mail. There have been attempts on my life. I've had other Islamic prisoners in here tell me that when the MPs aren't looking, they're going to cut out my heart.

"It's not my fault that none of the Islamic nations believe what really happened, or that many millions of Islamic people throughout the world believe the Council of Ishmael's version. I've given you all I can. I have nothing else to give."

Barry flew to his feet and leaned over the table. "I think you're lying, Commander!"

"I don't care what you think!" Quasay also stood.

"Hold on, gentlemen," Shannon said. "Commander, you've been cooperative, that's true. Barry didn't work your case. I did. So please just have a seat."

Both men sat.

"Look, Mohammed," Shannon said, "some new information has surfaced that has a lot of people upset. People think you withheld some important stuff from us. I, on the other hand, know how easy it is to forget some things. The problem is that there are forces out there who would advocate withdrawing your deal and seeking the death penalty, even now, if they think you withheld something."

"They can't do that."

"I don't know what they can do. I'm not a lawyer. But do you want to take that chance, Mohammed? You want to hack off Commander Brewer? He stuck out his neck for you, and he's angry about what's going on here."

"I told you, I know nothing else." He spoke with reinvigorated resolve.

"All right, I believe you," she said. "But remember, I have no control over Commander Brewer. If he thinks you withheld anything, and if you know anything at all about Lieutenant Diane Colcernian that we don't know, and if we find out about that, you'll be in the execution chair faster than I can say *un hum del Allah.*

"Come on, Barry, let's go." Shannon stood, and Barry did the same. They knocked on the door, and the MP opened it. Shannon turned and glared at Quasay before they walked out. "Just remember one thing, Commander." A pause. "Plan 547 is now in effect."

Quasay's face twisted. "What did you say?"

"I said" — she slowed the pace of her words — "I said that Plan 547 is now in effect."

"How do you know about that?"

Bingo.

"Never mind how. The point is we know all about Plan 547," she bluffed. "That's what has Commander Brewer upset. That's why there's going to be such an outcry to withdraw your life sentence and put you to death. The only thing that stands between you and that ... is me," she bluffed again. "But like you said, you've already told us everything you know. Come on, Barry. Let's get out of here."

"Wait!"

"Commander, we've got a 1:00 a.m. flight to catch to San Diego. I'd be glad to wait, but it had better be worth waiting for."

"Please come back. Now that you mention Plan 547, that *does* remind me of some details I may have forgotten. All in innocence, of course."

"You've got one shot to come clean, Commander," Shannon shot back. "One shot. And then that's it. Unless you tell us everything, there's nothing else I can do for you. It will be between you and Commander Brewer. Understand?"

"Okay, okay. Please sit. I'll tell you everything."

Jackson Gallopoulous's suite
Claxton campaign San Diego County headquarters
Hotel del Coronado
1500 Orange Avenue
Coronado, California

7:15 p.m. (PST)

Jackson had showered, bought himself an extra thirty minutes by feigning to have a stomach ailment, then managed to remain poker-faced at dinner with Eleanor, Mary-Latham, and several other members of the Yale mafia. The shower had not washed away the slimy feeling of what he had done, or what he had learned. After dinner, he excused himself on the grounds that he needed to prepare for the next morning's political briefings.

He needed to check on poll numbers around California, he had told Eleanor, so he could report what effect the campaign's strategy to co-opt the Eckberg defense was having on liberal voters in the Golden State. What he had not told Eleanor was what he had done that afternoon, or what else he would be researching—besides poll numbers—when he returned to his room.

Remain true to the polar star of virtue, and it shall carry you far.

The polar star of virtue.

Please.

Jackson ran to the commode again and heaved.

What would Edmund Gansky think if he knew his star student had slipped a bug into the private suite of his employer, the woman who could become the first female president of the United States? What would Professor Gansky think if he knew his star student had tape-recorded a private conversation between the most powerful woman in the Democratic Party and one of her closest advisors?

Jackson flushed the toilet and walked from the bathroom to the kitchenette, where he swigged more ice water.

On the other hand, what would the professor think if he heard the surreptitious recording that Jackson now had in his possession? Did Eleanor mean what he thought she could have meant? Was politics a corrupt business full of thieves and murderers? Was idealism a false utopia? Was Eleanor crooked? Was Professor Gansky one of them too? Or was all this Jackson's imagination?

What if the small recording device that he'd purchased from Radio Shack was discovered? Should he resign?

The phone rang.

"Gallopoulous."

"Jackson?" Eleanor was on the other end.

"Hi, Eleanor." *Stay calm.*

"Any poll numbers yet?"

"Not yet, boss. It'll be the morning before we can establish any solid trends."

"Raymond is coming in tomorrow morning, isn't he?" She was referring to Raymond Everton, the campaign's private pollster.

"Yes, Eleanor. I've spoken to him. He's in LA tonight watching all the data. He and I will be in touch tonight, and he'll be in first thing in the morning."

"Good. I want to know just as soon as you've got anything."

"Got it."

The line went dead.

He rewound the recording.

"You think radical Islam is dirty? You haven't seen anything. What goes on out of the public's eye makes 9/11 look like a picnic in the park. Get my drift?"

Okay, so maybe her speech was just figurative. He rewound the tape just a bit.

"And what do the voters in the Bay Area think about Karen Jacoby?"

"Eleanor, relax. This was a vigilante murder. Everybody knows it. No one knows she was a potential problem for us. No one will know, except those of us in the closest circle. That's the way it will remain. Trust me."

"Okay, okay. But listen, Mohammed—no more deviations from the script. Got it?"

Dear Jesus, Jackson found himself praying. *What is she talking about?*

He'd heard the rumors all those years. The rumors about people dying who had been associated with the campaigns of Vice President Claxton and Senator Claxton. But all that was just envious Republican mudslinging. Wasn't it? Of course. It had do be.

Jackson fast-forwarded the tape.

"Let me put it this way, Mohammed. You aren't the first individual to work for me or my husband and carry out the duties that you do.

Now, some of those people are still around. Some aren't. The ones who aren't deviated from the script. Some decided to take inside information from our campaigns and use it for political or monetary gain. Some tried blackmailing by threatening to go to the authorities or the press.

"But now they are gone, Mohammed. Every one of them."

Jackson punched off the tape, put the recorder in a drawer under his clothing, and walked across the room. By "gone," Eleanor meant "fired." Right? Of course. People get fired every day for disloyalty in politics. That was it.

He felt better.

But if he felt better about it all, then why was he reaching for his laptop? Why was he tapping into the hotel's wireless services? What was compelling him to do what he was about to do?

The welcome page for the Del popped up as soon as Jackson clicked on Internet Explorer. And after another click agreeing to the Del's boilerplate "terms of service" found on its home page, Jackson typed in a search engine address.

He took a deep breath. "Dear Lord, forgive me if I'm wrong," he prayed, then closed his eyes and typed his query: *Deaths associated with Vice President and Senator Claxton.*

The search yielded about 97,000 hits. He scanned the list.

Scholarly articles for **Deaths associated with Vice President and Senator Claxton**

> Traumatic brain injury in the United States: a public ... - Thurman
> - Cited by 112

> National vehicle emissions policies and practices and ... - Mott
> - Cited by 8

> Is daily mortality associated specifically with fine ... - Klemm -
> Cited by 25

The **Claxton** Body Count

> These men and eight others **associated with CLAXTON**'s visit
> to the Roosevelt all died within four ... He had information on the
> **deaths** of James, Stack and Blanzy ...

> www.jeoffmetcalf.net/397.html - 20k - Cached - Similar pages

The **Claxton** Body Count

> These men and eight others **associated with** former **Vice President Fred Claxton**'s visit to the Roosevelt ... At his **death**, he was the national finance co-chairman of the **Claxton** for ...

> www.theforbiddenknowledge.net/hardtruth/**claxton**bodycount. htm - 33k - Cached - Similar pages

Enigma Journal Issue 19: **Claxton Deaths**

> **Claxton Deaths** by Jack Tigay | Winter 2007/2008 ... there are 58 reported **deaths** of people closely **associated** with the **Claxton**s ...

> www.cropcircleresearch.org/enigma/issue19/**claxton**.html - 13k - Similar pages

QCTimes.com — The Quad-County Times Newspaper

> Published daily for **Claxton**, Muscatine, Scott and Rock Island Counties. National and local news, sports, columnists, entertainment, classifieds and ...

> www.qctimes.net/ - 40k - Cached - Similar pages

Earl's Hideaway

> Dr. Malak has been involved in numerous **Claxton**-**associated** questionable activities and activities surrounding autopsies. * Henry and Ives **deaths**: Keith Koney ...

> groups.msn.com/EarlsHideaway/**claxton**ampstrange**deaths**. msnw - 33k - Cached - Similar pages

KoiVet.com — Dead folks **associated** with the **Claxton** administration

> KoiVet.com Jokes and Humor — Dead folks **associated** with **Vice President** Fred **Claxton** and **Senator** Eleanor **Claxton** ... Richard Summers — Was a suspect in the Ives and Henry **deaths**. Was ...

> www.olivet.com/html/coolstuff/jokes_details.php?joke_id=45 - 40k - Cached - Similar pages

Claxton Body Count

> Sudden **Death** Syndrome. A number of persons **associated** with former **Vice President** Fred **Claxton** and **Senator** Eleanor

Claxton or Mississippi politics in some way have died of unnatural causes over the past six years ...

www.xpub.com/un/un-bc-body.html - 16k - Cached - Similar pages

WorldNetDaily: The **Claxton** Body Count

In recent months, a list of more than 80 **deaths associated** directly or indirectly with **Claxton** has been the buzz of the new media. In the last week alone ...

www.worldnetdaily.uk/news/article.asp?ARTICLE_ID=14583 - 33k - Cached - Similar pages

Claxton Casualties

The **Associated** Press: Vincent Lester: the **death** investigation that hasn't ended ... These men and eight others **associated with Claxton**'s visit to the Roosevelt ...

www.jeremiahproject.org/prophecy/claxtbodycnt.html - 48k - Cached - Similar pages

Urban Legends Reference Pages: Inboxer Rebellions (The **Claxton** ...

Origins: A new version of a lengthy list of **deaths associated** with Fred and Eleanor **Claxton** began circulating on the Internet in August 2006 ...

www.snopes.com/inboxer/outrage/**claxton**.htm - 13k - Similar pages

Jackson tried soaking it all in. Could all this be political dirty tricks? He'd heard about the suicide of Eleanor's good friend Samuel Lester, who had been found with a gunshot wound to the head near an old Civil War cannon in a Washington D.C. park.

Jackson clicked one of the links.

Lester, the link claimed, who had been one of Eleanor's law partners when they practiced together at a large law firm in Jackson, Mississippi, was found dead—shot in the back of the head—only weeks before he had been subpoenaed to testify before a special prosecutor investigating the law firm's billing practices.

One report said the authorities had ruled Lester's death a suicide. A more recent report claimed that the investigation had been reopened by the Metropolitan Police Department and that the bullet that killed Lester had never been found.

He clicked another link. This link claimed that more than fifty-eight people had either died or been found dead in association with Vice President and/or Senator Claxton. Some of the deaths occurred, the links claimed, when the former vice president had been governor of Mississippi, and included even Mississippi state troopers and body-guards assigned to then Governor Claxton.

Jackson clicked again. The next link listed the dead.

Terry McDonald—Key witness in Special Prosecutor Bob Moon's investigation of illegal contributions to the former vice president. Died of an apparent heart attack while in solitary confinement.

Sally Felton—Former intern to the vice president. Murdered in July 2006 at a coffee shop in Alexandria, Virginia. The murder occurred just after Felton was to go public with her story of sexual harassment in the vice president's office.

Samuel Lester—Former counselor to the vice president and colleague of Eleanor Claxton at Jackson's Randell law firm. Died from a gunshot wound to the head, ruled a suicide.

Jack Blue—Secretary of Interior and former DNC chairman. Reportedly died in a plane crash. A pathologist close to the investigation reported that there was a hole in the top of Blue's skull resembling a gunshot wound. At the time of his death Blue was being investigated and spoke of his willingness to cut a deal with prosecutors.

W. Douglas Conner II—Jackson fundraiser and major player in the Claxton fundraising organization. Died in a private plane crash.

Alton Bunn—Democratic National Committee political director. Found dead in a hotel room in Jackson. Described by Vice President Claxton as a "dear friend and trusted advisor."

Joe Washington—Claxton fundraiser. Found dead from a gunshot wound to the head deep in the woods in Virginia. Ruled a suicide. Died the same day his wife, Susan Washington, claimed Fred Claxton groped her at the Naval Observatory, the official residence of the vice president.

Jimmy Matthews—Head of Claxton's gubernatorial security team in Jackson. Gunned down in his car at a deserted intersection outside

Jackson. Matthews' son said his father was building a dossier of Claxton. He allegedly threatened to reveal this information. After he died the files were mysteriously removed from his house.

James Jones—Died from a gunshot wound, ruled a suicide. Jones reportedly had a "black book" containing names of influential people who visited prostitutes in Mississippi and Louisiana.

One associate had been decapitated.

Another jumped from a tall building to his death.

One woman's bruised body was found in her Department of Interior office.

Another slit her wrists. Several died in car accidents. A gunshot wound to the back of the head, later ruled a suicide, was the predominant cause of death. One theme held the reports together: many of the associates were prepared to come forth with information damaging to Claxton.

Jackson closed the search-engine window. He felt as if a bag of crushed ice had been dumped on him.

Could all of this be coincidental—107 deaths over the course of less than ten years?

Of course, Jackson tried to reassure himself, most of the dead were allegedly about to come forth with information about the former vice president, not the senator.

But then there was Samuel Lester, who was about to testify about billing practices at the former law firm where he and the senator had worked. Rumor had it that he and the senator had been romantically involved back when then-Governor Claxton was having his own flings.

Maybe Lester killed himself because he loved Eleanor and didn't want to embarrass or humiliate her.

Then the words came back to him ...

"Let me put it this way, Mohammed. You aren't the first individual to work for me or my husband and carry out the duties that you do."

The modicum of reassurance vanished.

Had Karen Jacoby been murdered because she opposed Eleanor's plan to co-opt Eckberg's court-martial for political gain? Was Mohammed Eleanor's henchman? What if Eleanor knew or even suspected that someone so close to her had bugged her room?

Fear encompassed him, rolling up into his throat, suffocating him. His chest, arms, and legs felt heavy. His teeth chattered uncontrollably.

Straining with all his might, he pushed the words out of his mouth. "Dear God—if there is a God in heaven—" He paused and craned his neck, looking up at the ornate chandelier hanging from the ceiling of his plush suite. "If you're up there, you know I don't do this sort of thing. Pray, I mean." The chattering slowed. "At Yale, they say you aren't real.

"I don't know about all that. But I know this: I'm scared to death, God. If you're there, if you're real, you know that." His nerves calmed slightly.

"As for me, I just don't know what to do. I'm desperate. I entered politics to help people. Not to kill people. Help me, God. If you're there, please help me."

CHAPTER 31

Inmate interrogation room 4
United States Disciplinary Barracks
U.S. Army Base
Fort Leavenworth, Kansas

10:00 p.m. (CST)

So what do you know about Plan 547?" Quasay asked.

The trio was again sitting at the steel table. Shannon leaned forward. "What don't you understand about what I just said, Commander? I told you we know *all* about Plan 547. But there are certain ground rules you will have to follow if you don't want me to walk right out that door and tell Commander Brewer you weren't cooperative. And the first is that you don't get to ask the questions. *I* get to ask the questions. Do you understand?"

"Perfectly," he said. "My apologies."

"Now let me ask you—what do *you* understand about Plan 547?"

Quasay's black eyes shifted back and forth between Shannon and Barry. "Plan 547, I'm ashamed to say, was my plan. I suggested it through back channels to the council even before I was selected to fly the mission. Al-Akhma liked it, and I suppose he still does."

Tell us what the plan is, or I'll kill you myself. "Well, it's fascinating, to say the least. How'd you come up with it?"

"There are two periods of maximum publicity surrounding the capture of a hostage. First, shortly after the capture, the Western press will cover events for a maximum of maybe two months, depending, of course, on the detainee. The more famous, obviously the longer the coverage, which is good for our organization. Groups like the council depend, frankly, on the Western press for survival. Once press coverage dies, so does the organization's ability to raise money and incite fear among the population.

"This being the case, a second event surrounding the detainee can be useful in prolonging press coverage, which produces the same outcome—fear and money. That second event, of course, is the threat of public execution and then the execution itself, usually a beheading.

"The challenge, if I must say so, is *timing*. Act too quickly, and the execution blurs into the hoopla surrounding the original abduction. Wait too long, and the public has forgotten who the detainee is."

"Brilliant, if I must say so myself, Commander," Shannon said. "Dastardly but brilliant." *Tell me what it means.*

"Thank you. As I said, timing is the key. So we decided that the perfect amount of time is eighteen months."

"Eighteen months," Barry said. Shannon gave him a hand signal under the table to leave the talking to her.

"Yes, exactly." Quasay beamed with satisfaction. "Or 547 days."

"I see—547 days."

"Yes. Between date of capture and date of execution—547 days."

Shannon's mind raced. The eighteen-month anniversary of Diane Colcernian's capture—if her math was right—would be coming up in ... about two weeks!

"I take it they've already made a public demand?" Quasay asked.

A public demand. He has to be referring to Colcernian.

"Remember, Commander, I get to ask the questions."

"As you wish."

"Let me show you something your lawyer gave us." She extracted the list from her briefcase and slid it across the table.

"Ah, yes." His face held a look of recognition. "The list."

"We know all about the list," Shannon lied. "What I want you to tell me"—she leaned over the table, eyeing him intently—"is why you didn't have a copy of the list on your person in Syria or on the carrier."

"In the name of Allah the munificent," he said. "Keeping a hard copy of this anywhere"—he waved the paper in the air—"would have been most dangerous, potentially compromising our mission."

"Then how did la Trec have a copy in his file?"

"Because as I explained to Mr. la Trec, I received my instructions from the council through a highly secure website. Mr. la Trec had access to the website and obviously printed the list from his files. That's how we communicated. Nothing would be written down until after I had taken my rightful place on the council."

"And how do we access this website?"

"I can give you the address, and then you'll have to key in a series of five different pass codes. But I'm sure the council has shut it down by now."

She pulled a pen and a legal pad from her briefcase and slid them across the table.

"Write it down," she ordered. "Everything."

Quasay brought his chained hands to the table. The chains rattled against the steel surface. He took the pen and complied. He pushed the pad back.

She studied it.

www.plan547.uk
Code 1: 9863829
Code 2: 76304923
Code 3: 53080294
Code 4: 79709039
Code 5: 14965804

"Thank you, Commander," she said. "I just have a few more questions."

"But of course."

"Why Mongolia?"

"Ah," he said, half smiling. "A very good question, Shannon McGill-very. And the answer is simple if you understand the doctrinal basis for what we were trying—and are still trying—to accomplish."

"The *doctrinal basis?*"

"Yes. Al-Akhma wanted to use this attack on the Dome of the Rock, and the great uproar that it would cause, as a catalyst for forming one Islamic superpower in the Middle East, of which he would be the leader.

"For al-Akhma's dream of a new Islamic superpower to come to pass, we would need weapons. Lots of weapons. We knew we couldn't get them from America. America is the great Satan, as you know." He paused, his black eyes gleaming. "Could I please have a drink of water?"

Shannon nodded, then went to the door, knocked, and asked the MP for water for them all. When the MP closed the door, Shannon returned to the interrogation table.

"Go ahead," she ordered Quasay.

"As I was saying, a new Islamic superpower, to hold its own against America, would need weapons. Not just old throwaway hardware like World War II – era tanks and MiG-21s. In other words, the antiquated weapons like Sadaam had would not be acceptable. To stand up to America, we would need nukes. The best possible sources, of course, were Russia and China."

The MP knocked and brought in a pitcher and three Styrofoam cups. Barry poured water for Quasay, who, because of his bound wrists, held his hands together as he took a sip.

"What made you think Russia and China would cooperate?"

"We did not know so much about China. But the Russians have always wanted two things that our new nation would have. First, they are cash-strapped. We would control the oil fields, and thus the cash pipeline to turn Moscow into an economic Shanghai. Second, the Russians have always dreamed of a warm-water port in our region. We felt that after the attack on the Dome, we could consolidate all the nations on the Arabian peninsula, plus Syria, Iraq, Afghanistan, and possibly Egypt. We would offer a naval alliance with the Russians for one-hundred-year leasing rights where they could bring their ships in — much like the U.S. Navy once had at Subic Bay in the Philippines."

Quasay took another sip.

"Russia was a bit of a gamble, because clearly, there are now pro-Western elements there, even in the government. But there are also many old-time hard-liners in the military and the Kremlin who hate Gorbachev and Yeltsin and who want to return to the glory days of the old Soviet Union. Cash from Middle Eastern oil reserves would allow Russia to modernize its military and get its warm-water port to boot."

"Fascinating," Barry said.

"Fascinating, indeed, Mr. MacGregor," Quasay replied.

"Which leads back to my original question," Shannon said. "Why Mongolia?"

"First, Mongolia is landlocked. The council recognizes that the United States Navy is America's greatest weapon in the world. United States Marines cannot reach Mongolia, at least not by amphibious assault. It has no shoreline. It cannot be invaded by amphibious ships like the shores of Lebanon or Iraq or most other nations around the world with coastlines. Second, the government of Mongolia is weak, easily manipulated, and influenced by Russia and China. It has little means to prevent most of the activities that occur there, even if it were aware of them. The Mongolian government does not know about our camp in the Gobi. Third, any attempt to invade Mongolia by air or land would mean crossing Russian and Chinese airspace.

"We assumed that after we attacked the Dome, the Russians and the Chinese would ally with the moderate Islamic states against America. Especially after al-Akhma approached the Russians with his proposed exchange of a warm-water port and cash for diplomatic recognition and nuclear weapons.

"I felt—and the council agreed—that the U.S. would not risk a war against either of these superpowers by invading their territorial airspace. That's why."

How perceptive. This guy has been incarcerated, out of touch with international events, and he's reading the Russian and Chinese positions as if he were sitting in the White House. Plus, the CIA has reported that secret talks have gone on between al-Akhma and the Russian president.

All of this, Shannon knew, had been a huge concern for the Williams administration, which had been criticized by the Democrats for returning the United States to a cold war status.

"Can you tell me where in Mongolia this camp is located?"

"No, except somewhere in the Gobi. You see, that is also part of Council of Ishmael doctrine. The camp, just like field headquarters for the Council of Ishmael, was to be mobile. The use of tents, barbed wire, and armed guards would allow it to be located in various places. And the plan was to move it from time to time to make it more difficult for U.S. satellites to find it."

"Under Plan 547, can we expect an announcement prior to Colcernian's execution?"

"I can't say."

"Why?"

"First, I don't know if they got her there. I was captured by the Israelis while she was being transported. Second, there was an ongoing argument about whether to announce the execution before or after it actually happened. Some in the council felt that announcing it beforehand would give us more publicity. The problem with that was that the U.S. would immediately launch an all-out search for the camp. Then there was the school of thought that we simply videotape the execution and present the tape to Al Jazeer and other television networks—

after we had pulled up stakes and relocated the camp. Al-Akhma hadn't decided which route to take. The mission was in the planning stages.

"Thank you, Commander," Shannon said. "I'm inclined to plead for leniency in your case in light of your cooperation tonight. But there's one other thing I need."

He nodded as she pulled a tape recorder from her briefcase.

"I want you to repeat everything you just told me as I roll the tape."

"Of course."

CHAPTER 32

Russian-Kazakhstan border checkpoint
Between Krasny Yar, Russia, and Ganyushkino, Kazakhstan

Tuesday, 11:30 a.m. (local time)

Traveling east through the lowlands of the Caspian Depression, they crossed the great Volga River. Soon after, Fadil fell asleep in the passenger's seat of the panel truck.

He wasn't sure how long he had been dozing when the bumping and slowing of the truck wakened him. He rubbed his eyes and saw a checkpoint in the middle of the road. A flagpole stood on each side. The flag on the left had white, blue, and red stripes, just like the flag that had flown on the *Alexander Popovich*. The flag of the Russian Republic.

The flagpole on the right bore a flag that Fadil was not familiar with. It was light blue with the image of a golden sun in the middle and a golden eagle below.

Under each flagpole, to the left and the right of the road, stood guard shacks. Soldiers wore camouflage uniforms, black combat boots, and AK-47 assault rifles slung over their necks. They milled about under the flags, stopping traffic in both directions.

"Where are we?" he asked Sergey, his driver.

"Kazakhstan border," Sergey said in English, their bridge language.

A stone-faced, cigarette-smoking border guard held out his hand, motioning for them to halt.

Fadil reached down for the Uzi as the olive-drab windowless panel truck slowly approached the border checkpoint.

"You not need that," Sergey said.

"What about our passengers in the back? Will they not look inside?"

"Relax," Sergey said. "I cross border many times. Usually no problems. Sometimes find guard with ... uh ... attitude. With hope, we be fine."

Fadil lit his cigarette. He slid the Uzi under the seat. "Just get us across the border and get us to the plane," he said.

"*Zdratsvoitsyeh. Gde vwee preyearhit, moi droog?*" the guard asked in Russian.

"*Ganyushkino,*" Sergey said. "*Ya magu dat vam pyet sto dollaryes yeslee mwee mozhetzyeh piedyume seachess.*"

A grin crossed the guard's face. "*Pravda?*"

"*Dah. Pravda,*" Sergey replied.

"*Harashoa!*"

"*Padazhdeetsyeh admu minuto.*"

"What's going on?" Fadil demanded.

Sergey looked at Fadil. "Five hundred U.S. dollars gets us across the border."

"That's it?" Fadil took a cautious drag from his American cigarette.

"If you want no problems and no questions, that's it."

Fadil reached into his wallet and handed Sergey five crisp one-hundred-dollar bills. Sergey folded the bills into a tight wad and passed them to the chisel-chinned guard, whose smile widened. The guard motioned for two other guards to come over, and when he held up the bills, their stone faces melted too. Fadil heard the words *banya, vodka,* and *zhunski.*

"What are they saying?"

"Tonight they buy banya, vodka, and women."

"Godless communists," Fadil said in Arabic as he waved and smiled at the guards.

"*Da bro pazhalawitz v. Kazakhstan!*" The first guard motioned the truck across the international border. Sergey increased the vehicle's speed, and within a matter of minutes they were speeding down the straight two-lane highway at one hundred kilometers per hour, headed for the airstrip near Ganyushkino.

Claxton campaign San Diego County headquarters
Hotel del Coronado
1500 Orange Avenue
Coronado, California

Tuesday, 8:45 a.m. (PST)

Eleanor hadn't taken Jackson's call this morning. Why? It had happened a few times during the course of the campaign, but he was her *campaign manager*, for heaven's sake. Certainly she would want to chat with him prior to a meeting on poll numbers, wouldn't she?

Had she found out about the bug? Or maybe she had found out about the Internet search he had run last night.

He waited outside the front entrance of the Del for Raymond Everton, the campaign's pollster, who had flown in early this morning from LA. According to Everton's analysis, preliminary numbers looked good; that should make Eleanor happy, at least if she wasn't already planning to kill him.

A black Lincoln continental pulled up in front of the main entrance to the Del. The bellman opened the back door for a bald, potbellied, suspender-wearing, cigar-chewing man about six feet two inches tall.

Ray Everton was a whale of a fellow, a rotund man whose reputation as a slob was exceeded only by his reputation as a political genius for the Democratic Party. He had never been a campaign manager for a major campaign, though it wasn't because he hadn't been given the opportunity.

Everton had turned down senators, congresspersons, and even the two major presidential candidates in this case, Senator Roberson Fowler and Eleanor. His reasoning—running a campaign required too much "bull," in his opinion, and would take time from his idolatrous obsession—polling.

Everton had a reputation for being the most brilliant pollster in modern political history. He could read the mind of the public on an issue months before the issue became newsworthy.

There had been a battle for Everton's services when this presidential election season started. Because he was a Southerner—he had grown up in Valdosta, Georgia, and was a Georgia Bulldog through and through—the media speculated he might wind up working with the campaign of fellow Southerner Roberson Fowler of Louisiana.

Jackson knew the inside scoop on Everton. He liked Fowler. Privately, Everton had once confessed to Jackson over beer that he didn't care for Eleanor, whom he regarded to be a brash, harsh-talking, power-hungry Yankee.

But Everton was also hunting buddies with the former vice president, "Fast" Freddie Claxton, the Mississippian, and that relationship, plus Everton's desire to be a part of history by putting a woman in the White House, where the challenges to his professional expertise as a pollster would be greatest, had swung him over to Claxton.

Thus, politics had again made strange bedfellows, and the Claxton campaign had won a major tactical victory by securing Ray Everton's services. If Eleanor lost, Everton and everyone else knew that he would jump right over to Fowler for the fall campaign against President Williams and then, by sheer force of talent and reputation, become chief pollster for that campaign.

"Jumpin' Jackson Gallopoulous!" Everton bellowed through a wide grin. "The boss ready for some great results?"

"That good, Raymond?"

"We're gonna win California, Jackson."

"Great." Forty-eight hours ago, Jackson would have meant that.

"That's the good news." Ray slapped Jackson's back so hard he nearly knocked him over as they walked through the lobby of the Del.

"That must mean there's bad news."

"Relax, my boy." Ray Everton chuckled and slapped Jackson's back again. "We've got plenty of time before the general election. You'll see the problem in my briefing."

Jackson swiped the card for the secure floor where Eleanor's suite was located, and a minute later, he and Everton were walking past Secret Service agents and into the conference room where this morning's briefing was to be held.

Mary-Latham and Web Wallace had already arrived and were sitting at the table drinking coffee, waiting for Eleanor. Both wore pleasant expressions. If they knew anything, they weren't telegraphing it. Of course, there was no way Mary-Latham could know. Or was there? Eleanor had been careful to keep Mary-Latham out of her meeting with Mohammed.

She wasn't going to share certain information, even with her closest advisors.

The door swung open at the hand of a Secret Service agent. With a lit Virginia Slim in one hand, a steaming cup of black coffee in the other, Eleanor strode in with a smile.

"Good morning, everybody." She set the coffee on the table and reached for Everton's hand. "Ray, thanks so much for coming down. I'm looking forward to your report."

The end of her cigarette glowed. Her red lips formed a perfect O through which smoke drifted to the ceiling.

"Sorry I didn't get a chance to chat with you this morning, Jackson. My husband, the former vice president"—she rolled her eyes to the ceiling—"seems to have long-winded opinions on everything."

She seated herself, then said, "Let's get started. How are we looking, Ray?"

"How 'bout a cigarette, Eleanor?"

"Virginia Slim okay?"

"I ain't picky, Senator."

An irritated look crossed Eleanor's face. She slid the packet across the table, along with a lighter. "Somebody get Ray an ashtray." A Secret Service agent complied. "All right," she said as Ray Everton lit up, "let's have the good news."

The corpulent pollster took a drag. "Well, thanks to you, Senator, and to Mr. Wallace over here"—the pollster nodded to the silver-haired lawyer—"we've got a real good shot at winning the California primary."

That brought another puff of smoke and a wide grin from Eleanor. "Talk to me."

"You've pulled ten points ahead of Congressman Warren in San Francisco, and the trend is still up. The news is even better in LA, where you have a fifteen-point lead over Warren."

"And this is related to the Eckberg court-martial?" Eleanor asked.

"Yes, and the very strong stand you've taken on gays in the military. My polls show we've touched a raw nerve with gay voters concentrated in heavy numbers in San Francisco. Here's the difference, Senator." The Southern-talking political aficionado took a draw from the cigarette, then blurted a curse word. "This cigarette is awful."

"Bring your own next time," Eleanor snapped. "The difference, you were saying, Ray?"

"The difference, Senator, is this. Before this trial, these voters viewed you in the mold of that husband of yours. A lot of liberal talk, but too moderate when it came to action. Now, our polls show that these voters see you as a politician willing to risk your neck for them. They love the Neanderthal comment, and they love the fact that you're lending your personal attorney to this case. Also, because you beat Williams to the punch yesterday after that mob shooting, they now see you as a leader who can make the right decisions in the spur of the moment."

A devious grin crossed Eleanor's face.

"Question, Ray," Mary-Latham spoke up.

"Sure, honey."

Anger flashed in Mary-Latham's eyes, but her voice remained calm. "Aren't these numbers premature?" she asked.

"Yeah, they're premature in one sense, but we've polled the intensity level of these numbers, and unless we screw up, we've touched on a hot button that can carry this state for us."

"All right," Eleanor said. "Three weeks to go until the primary. What do we need to avoid screwing up?"

"Just what we're doing. Drag this thing out. We should introduce a bill in the Congress on the hate crimes in the military thing. Eleanor, you should stay here in San Diego through this trial. Maybe shuttle to and from San Francisco some. Do that, and we take California in three weeks."

"Jackson, work out the details." *Good. If I'm working out details, maybe she thinks I'll be alive for a few more weeks.*

"We've got another problem to watch, Senator." Everton stamped out the cigarette he had complained about.

"I don't see any problems if we win California," Eleanor said. "What problem are you talking about?"

Please don't say it's your campaign manager.

"The problem, Eleanor, is if you win California but get creamed in the general election."

"Go on."

"The problem, right now, is Brewer."

"Brewer. How is he a problem?"

"He's a catch-22 for you right now, Eleanor. Because he's loved by the conservatives, he's hated by your natural constituency out here on the *left* coast."

"Watch your mouth," Eleanor snapped. "You sound like a right-wing radio-talk-show fascist."

Ray Everton laughed. "Your natural constituency hates him out here because they think he's a young, successful, good-looking conservative."

"He's not bad-looking," Mary-Latham agreed.

That brought a glare from Eleanor and ignited a flash of jealousy in Jackson.

"So ..." Ray continued, "your numbers are shooting up here because your constituency is pleased that you are taking on this young, conservative naval officer. Or so that's how they see it. Another cigarette?"

"Just take the pack." Eleanor slid the pack across the table.

"In places like Texas, Florida, Georgia, and the Carolinas, and even the rustbelt—Michigan, Ohio, and Pennsylvania—states you must win to become the first lady president, Brewer's presence in the case may very well backfire. At least that's what our numbers are beginning to show."

"Talk to me, Ray," Eleanor said.

"A lot of people remember Brewer quite well from those big ol' courts-martial he tried against the Muslim chaplains and the Muslim pilots. Remember, your ol' buddy Roberson Fowler tried recruiting him to run for Congress in Louisiana. Roberson's pollsters picked up on what we've picked up on. The kid's got flash, wit, and charisma. Now there's something I want you to check out."

Everton lit another cigarette, exhaled a cloud of smoke, then opened his briefcase and laid out several national newspapers on the table.

"These, ladies and gentlemen, are a sampling of newspapers from this morning in states we have to win. We have the *Dallas Morning News*, the *Atlanta Constitution*, the *Tallahassee Democrat*, the *Charlotte Observer*, and the *Chicago Sun-Times*, just to name a few. Now check out some of these headlines."

He started reading from the different papers.

"Brewer to Congress: Join the Marine Corps!"

"Brewer Blisters Claxton. Democrats in Arms."

"Brewer Suggests Democrats Are Undermining Military Discipline."

"Who does that guy think he is?" Eleanor snorted. "He should be court-martialed for making comments like that about a U.S. senator."

"That's the last thing you want to say in public, Senator," Everton said. "Besides, Brewer didn't say all that. He sort of said that. You're just reading the press twist on his comments."

"Okay, so how much of a problem do you think this is, Ray?"

"Potentially huge. Our polls in Texas, Florida, North Carolina, Pennsylvania, and Illinois are showing a five-point drop for you as of this morning, and we're tracking that to the media's coverage of Brewer's comments last night. The key for us here is to manage this as a gay rights issue with our campaign out front, but we've got to keep Brewer out of the limelight, at least outside of California. His presence could wind up finishing us off in some of these red states that we're hoping to turn blue."

"How do you suggest keeping him out of the limelight?" Mary-Latham asked.

"The continuance was a good move, Web." Everton and Web Wallace exchanged nods. "We can do daily press conferences over the next week, reporting on the progress of the trial and our proposed hate crimes legislation.

"Brewer's camera shy, from what we know. Oh, he's devastating when he gets on stage and his hand is forced, but there's no reason to believe he's gonna go seeking out any press conferences. At least not over the next week."

"Okay," Eleanor said. "Anything else?"

"No. Just keep on this strategy, and keep an eye on Brewer."

Eleanor shot a look at Jackson, a cold glare that made a shiver of fear travel down his spine. And then, with a more pleasant smile adorning her face, she looked around at the group. "Popeye the Sailor Man won't keep me from becoming president of the United States."

10065 English Ivy Way
Rancho San Diego
Spring Valley, California

Tuesday, 9:30 a.m. (PST)

Chris Reynolds sat at his small breakfast nook, carving the cream filling of an Oreo into eight pie-shaped slices with a toothpick. He placed one of the miniature sweet wedges on his tongue and glared at the front page of the *San Diego Union-Tribune*.

Oh, great! roared a voice in Chris Reynolds's head. *That's all I need. And after we had made so much progress after our last meeting at Old Towne.*

He read more of the article.

"Oh, Zack. Zack!" Chris spoke aloud now, his brain seething. "How could you say such a thing? Dr. King would too disapprove, Zack! And those remarks you made about Eleanor? I know what you're doing. You're using the press to gain political leverage to help Fowler beat Eleanor. We'll see about that. Come here, Alvin!" The parakeet landed on Chris's finger. "Don't worry, pretty boy," Chris cooed at the bird. "Zack will *never* be attorney general, and Fowler will *never* be president. You and I are going to Washington. We'll get a beautiful townhouse in Alexandria, and I'll bring you a treat every day on my way home from the White House." He kissed the bird on the head. It chirped, filling him with delight. "Yes, we will."

He tossed the paper on the table, picked up his cell phone, and dialed 411.

"Verizon Wireless Direct Connect. What city and state, please?"

"Las Vegas, Nevada. Business."

"For what listing?"

"Rex's Gun Shop, please."

"Hold, please, for the number . . ."

"Yes, is this Rex's? I'd like to purchase a weapon ... Something small and powerful ... Yes, a handgun of some type ... Okay, how much does that cost? ... Do you take cash? ... Okay. How late are you open? ... And where are you located? ... Okay, thank you very much."

Chris hung up the phone. He kissed Alvin on the head again, put the bird in his cage, grabbed his car keys, and walked out the door.

CHAPTER 33

Office of the Commanding Officer
Building 71, Navy Trial Command
32nd Street Naval Station
San Diego, California

Tuesday, 10:00 a.m. (PST)

About the only thing comfortable about this meeting, Zack decided when Commander Bob Awe told him that the skipper wanted to see him at 9:30 a.m., was his uniform. Working khakis were far more agreeable than either whites or blues. At least Web Wallace's continuance request had allowed him to change into something more comfortable.

"Come on in, Zack," Captain Glen Rudy said. He was the commanding officer of the Navy Trial Command. Commander Bob Awe, senior trial counsel, was in the office as well.

"Morning, sir."

"How'd you sleep last night?"

"Sir?"

"At the BOQ?"

"Oh. Fine, sir. The BOQ at North Island is one of the very first places I stayed when I first moved to San Diego."

"NCIS treating you right?"

"They're like white on rice. Carry me all around in my windowless paddy wagon. Can't seem to shake them, sir."

"Look, Zack. Two things. You know I've got to talk to you about your comments to the press yesterday."

"Yes, sir. I figured that, sir."

"But before I do, I want you to know, also, that when this court-martial fires back up, Trial Judiciary Command is ordering it moved to the courthouse over at Naval Air Station North Island. I know it's a little tight over there space-wise, but they just feel better about it from a security standpoint."

"Fine with me, sir. Doesn't matter where we try it."

"The other thing, Zack, is that I'm going to assign you to our detachment office over at North Island too. No reason to have you coming over here and exposing you to publicity or whatever else."

Great. Imprisonment at North Island. "In other words, sir, am I to assume that since my living quarters are now at North Island, my office is now at North Island, and this court-martial is at North Island, the navy wants me confined to North Island for the time being?"

"With a few exceptions"—Rudy took a sip of coffee—"yes. But there is one exception that we need to talk about."

"Yes, sir?"

"As you might imagine, a lot of liberals back in Washington are raising Cain about your comments to the press yesterday."

"So I've heard."

"Personally, I agree with everything you say—150 percent. But we've got some top navy brass, including the secretary of the navy, who are worried that Claxton might win the fall election. Off the record, SECNAV and CNO"—he was referring to the chief of naval operations—"and every officer on the Joint Chiefs of Staff are hoping like heck that won't happen. But what if it does?"

"If it does, sir, then I resign my commission."

"That's fine, Zack, but you've got all these guys approaching retirement who can't just resign. And if Eleanor comes in as president and the navy hasn't done anything to clear up your comments—and I know they were misconstrued—then some heads may roll up top, and SEC-NAV is worried that his might be one of 'em."

"Sorry for my big mouth."

"Don't worry about it, son. That big mouth of yours has helped put terrorists behind bars and made you a folk hero. But now I need you to use it for a little political damage control."

"Anything you say, Skipper."

"SECNAV wants you to hold a brief press conference and read a statement of clarification. We'll set you up for tomorrow afternoon at 1200 hours at COMNAVBASE. NCIS wanted it done inside, but public affairs and SECNAV's office wanted it scheduled outside, again for political reasons that I don't understand. PAO"—he was referring to the local navy public affairs office—"will prep a statement for you. All you have to do is read."

Zack looked out the windows of his commanding officer's office. The sleek gray hull of a guided missile frigate, the USS *Rentz*, bearing hull number 46, was cutting through the aqua waters of San Diego Bay from left to right. It was approaching the winding, looping edifice that was the Coronado Bay Bridge.

That was the real navy. Men breathing salt air, sailing to ports unknown, to missions that could arise unexpectedly. He felt an urging for the sea. To sail west, to find whatever he might find on the other side of the Pacific ...

"Yes, sir. Understood. Whatever the needs of the navy require of me, sir."

"Very well, Commander," the captain said, "you are dismissed."

"Aye, sir."

"And, Zack?" Rudy's eyes projected sympathy and concern.

"Yes, sir?"

"Be careful out there, okay?"

"Aye, aye, Captain."

"Now get out of here."

"Yes, sir."

NCIS regional headquarters
A Street and Sixth Avenue
San Diego, California

Tuesday, 10:30 a.m. (PST)

Shannon sat at her desk, reviewing her notes on the *Quasay* case. Official records showed that Lieutenant Commander Diane Colcernian had been captured in Wilmington, North Carolina, in the spring almost eighteen months ago. She had last been seen alive attending the funeral of Maggie Jefferies, a University of North Carolina coed who was shot while exiting a UNC basketball game against Duke University.

FBI and NCIS reports concluded that Jefferies's death was the result of mistaken identity, and the bullet was intended for Diane, who had gone to the game with Zack Brewer.

Colcernian was last spotted standing in a Wilmington cemetery in the midst of a driving thunderstorm while Maggie Jefferies was being buried.

Shannon rechecked the date and recalculated the math.

Two weeks from today. That's all we have to work with, assuming that (a) Colcernian is still alive and under the control of the Council of Ishmael and (b) Plan 547 is still in effect.

"Dear Lord, please help me somehow. If she's alive, help me save her," she prayed aloud as she closed the file and headed down the hall toward Barry's office.

A choking cloud of smoke greeted her, as usual, as she walked in and sat down. With a wave of his hand, Barry acknowledged her presence but did not make eye contact. He was poring over some papers on his desk.

"Okay." Barry looked across the desk at Shannon. "I've got everything forwarded up the chain of command. Transcripts of Quasay's comments, our report, everything. I'm awaiting the director's call at any time."

"Barry, I checked my file. We've got two weeks. Two weeks! That's when day 547 falls. Two weeks before they kill her."

"We've done everything we can do, Shannon. If this doesn't light a fire under the chain of command, I don't know what will. By the way, I've just received word that Zack's making a statement to the press tomorrow afternoon at COMNAVBASE." He looked at her and took a drag from his fat stogie. "Outside."

"Those idiots!" Shannon said. "They want us to protect him, but they parade him out in broad daylight."

"We argued our position. Public affairs thinks it scores more feel-good points in natural light." He grunted. "Politicians."

The phone rang.

"Mr. MacGregor, the director of NCIS is on the line for your conference call."

"Put him through."

"Hi, Barry." The voice of the NCIS director, Dr. Graham Jones, came over the line.

"Mr. Director," Barry said.

"Shannon, are you there?"

"Yes, sir."

"Well, let's get started then. It sounds like you guys have been pretty darn busy over the last twenty-four hours."

"Yes, sir," Barry said.

"We got your reports. This is impressive work. It's clear that Quasay was withholding some very important information."

Yes.

"Yes, sir," Barry said.

"This gives me more to work with."

Thank you.

"Mr. Director," Shannon said, "I've run the math under this Plan 547. Dating back to Colcernian's capture in Wilmington, North Carolina, day 547 falls two weeks from today."

"I hadn't run the math," the director said, "but I figured it had to be pretty quick."

"So if we're going to have any chance to save her—"

"That's the problem I'm running into."

"Sir?"

"Well, first off, your report does lend credibility to the papers Father Robert brought to you. That gives me the ammunition to go in and talk with SECNAV, and the reports are now in the hands of the secretary of defense, the chairman of the National Security Council, and the chairman of the Joint Chiefs. This is good detective work by NCIS, and I'm pleased to stand behind this work."

"Thank you, sir." *I think.*

"Here's the feedback I'm getting. While this evidence is being viewed by the powers above me as credible, there still is no proof here that Colcernian is alive. They keep pointing out, and they're right, that Quasay was captured before we found that collapsed cave with Colcernian's hair strand in it."

"But, sir, we did not find a body. This evidence has led me to rethink our position. She was on their hostages list, for heaven's sake."

"You may be right, Shannon, and I've pointed that out to the secretary of the navy. But as he says, if this camp is in existence, Mongolia is a big, big place. SECNAV is going to suggest stepped-up satellite surveillance, but that's still like looking for a needle in a haystack, unless we know where to look. Here's the bottom line. Your report now has more credibility, but without more evidence showing that Colcernian is alive and her location, not much can be done. And even if we did have all that information, I don't know that the president would risk World War III to capture one officer."

Shannon stared at Barry in disbelief. He shook his head and shrugged his shoulders.

"Still there?"

"Yes, sir, Mr. Director," Barry said.

"Well then, good work. I'll see that both of you are put in for commendations for this."

The line went dead.

"Barry, this isn't over. I can promise you that."

"Whatever you've got up your sleeve, I don't want to hear about it."

Northbound Interstate 15
One hour north of San Diego

Tuesday, 12:00 p.m.

The drive along Interstate 15, splitting through the canyons of North San Diego County, with its natural hills, brown rocks, and bright sunshine, always seemed to instill a yearning for classical music. Chris had set the radio to 89.5 AM and was listening to the rippling strains of the climax of a piano concerto by Sergey Vasil'yevich Rachmaninov when the calm, monotone voice of the news director came over the air.

"This just in from the Commander, U.S. Naval Base San Diego.

"Lieutenant Commander Zack Brewer, whose comments at a San Diego court-martial yesterday angered various Democrats on Capitol Hill and a number of gay rights groups, will address the media tomorrow at noon to clarify any misunderstandings his comments may have caused, navy officials said.

"Brewer, who is expected to read a statement, will address the media at noon tomorrow outside the headquarters of the mammoth naval base.

"No reaction to the announcement yet from the campaign of U.S. Senator Eleanor Claxton, whose campaign's attorney, Webster Wallace, is now defending the naval officer being charged with assault by the navy.

"Claxton's polling numbers are up in California this morning, largely due to her support from gay rights groups in San Francisco and Los Angeles. It is unclear how her campaign's involvement with this case will affect her against her principal Democrat opponent for the nomination, Senator Roberson Fowler, or should she defeat Fowler, against President Williams in the fall election.

"Stay tuned to KPBS for the latest updates on this developing story.

"And now, back to the piano music of Sergey Vasil'yevich Rachmaninov."

That's perfect! roared an excited voice inside Chris's head. *Another four hours to Vegas! Then another five hours back! Plenty of time for Zack's conference. And then, once Zack changes, maybe we can have lunch with Eleanor. She will be so grateful for how Zack will be changed. I just love Eleanor. She's going to love Zack!*

Chris pumped the accelerator of his beloved yellow Volkswagen.

Sixty-five miles per hour ... Seventy-five ... Eighty-five ...

Room 207, Navy Lodge
Rogers Road
Naval Air Station North Island
Coronado, California

Tuesday, 8:00 p.m. (PST)

Night was setting in, and the streetlights along the roads of the massive naval air station cast a glow that blanketed the base with an orange hue. As she pulled her car into the parking lot of the Bachelor Officers' Quarters at Naval Air Station North Island, the sounds of jet aircraft, mostly carrier-based on the USS *Eisenhower*, could be heard doing "touch and goes" on the asphalt runway less than a half mile away.

Shannon knew Zack was on base, at least according to Mike Wesner, who had told her that he and Raynor had dropped Zack off in front of the BOQ about two hours ago.

So unless Zack had violated the orders of his commanding officer and slipped off base and into downtown San Diego—which wouldn't surprise her—or unless he was still in the Officer's Club having dinner, Shannon figured her chances of finding him in his room at this time of the evening were good.

She walked across the wind-swept front yard of the Navy Lodge and stepped through the front doors, then presented her NCIS badge to the desk attendant.

"Agent McGillvery. NCIS. I'm here for Lieutenant Commander Brewer, please."

"Yes, ma'am," the petty officer said. "Room 207. But I don't know if he's up there."

She ascended the steps, turned left down the hallway, and within minutes was standing in front of room 207.

After three raps on the door, it swung open. The man standing in the doorway was about six feet tall with an athletic build and a smidgen of salt in his brown hair. The sight of Zack Brewer in a fitted white turtleneck and blue jeans took her breath away.

"Shannon!" His smile and sparkling hazel eyes nearly finished the job.

"Mind if I come in?"

"I thought you'd forgotten about me!"

"Not hardly, Matlock. But we need to talk."

"Let me guess — I've been sentenced to this, the most beautiful air station in the naval service, for a period of ... one year."

"Zack, it's about Diane."

"Diane?" His countenance changed in an instant. The smile was gone, and concern filled his face. "Please come in."

Shannon sat down in a chair in the corner of the room, while Zack seated himself on the end of the bed. "What about Diane?"

"Zack, this may be a long shot, I know. But I think she may still be alive."

"Don't mess with me about this."

"I'm not. I wouldn't. It's a long shot that we'll find her. And I don't want you to get your hopes up. But as of this moment, I believe that she's alive somewhere in Mongolia."

He slumped forward, burying his face in his hands. He just sat there a moment, then Shannon noticed his chest was shaking. He had covered his face, she realized, so that she wouldn't see him sobbing. She stood up, walked over to him, and perched on the bed beside him.

"Sorry," he mumbled.

She massaged his shoulders. "It's okay, Zack. It's okay. Let me get you a Kleenex." She got up, stepped into the bathroom, and retrieved a cold washcloth and the box of tissue that was on the counter.

She sat back down beside him and handed him the washcloth.

"I feel like such an idiot." He took the washcloth and wiped his face. "Grown men aren't supposed to cry."

"If a man isn't sensitive enough to cry once in a while, he isn't much of a man." She took his hand. "Besides, I know how much it hurts to want to be with someone and you can't."

He stood up, walked across the room, and looked out the window. "So why do you think she's alive? And what do I have to do to go get her?"

She explained everything that had happened: Father Robert, the reports showing the hostages list, the strange reference to Plan 547, the trip to Kansas, Quasay's confirmation of Plan 547, the two weeks remaining until the plan would be implemented.

"The problem, Zack, is that I can't get anyone to take any action."

"Unbelievable." He crossed his arms and paced the floor. "Unbelievable."

"I know you're busy with this trial. I wasn't going to bother you with this, Zack."

"Bother me?" He threw his arms in the air. "Bother me?" A pause. "She was . . ."

"I understand, Zack." She went over to him and gently caressed his shoulders. "I do understand."

"How am I going to handle all this?"

"We'll get through it. Listen, Zack," she said as he looked into her eyes, "I need your help."

"You've got me pinned up on this base. How am I supposed to do anything?" he snapped. Then he sighed and said, "Sorry, Shannon. What did you have in mind?"

"Zack, we need contacts in Washington."

He nodded. "Let me grab my wallet." He reached over to the drawer beside his bed, pulled out his wallet, and started thumbing through some business cards. "Got it!"

"What is it?"

"I know it's been a year and a half, but when Diane and I were invited to the White House to meet President Williams, I seemed to hit it off pretty well with his appointments secretary. Her name is Gale Staff. She gave me her card. Even gave me her personal cell phone number."

"Ever used the number?"

"Nah. I figured she was just being nice."

"Think she could get us in to see the president?"

"Who knows? The president said to call if I ever needed him. And he liked Diane. We might have been just another photo op. Besides, talk's cheap. Plus, the president didn't give me *his* number. His appointments secretary gave me hers. And even if we got in, talk about the flack I'd get for jumping over the chain of command." He stared up. Helplessness froze on his face.

"Zack," she snapped. "Are you willing to jump the chain of command for Diane?"

That question brought a flush of color to his cheeks and fire to his eyes. "Shannon, I'd jump off the Coronado Bay Bridge for Diane, or any other bridge or building or mountain."

"Good," she said, touching his shoulder. "Then call Gale Staff. Now."

He looked at his watch.

"I know what you're thinking. It's after eleven back east. Jump off the bridge, Zack. Do it now. For Diane."

He flipped open his cell phone, then dialed the number. A moment later he rolled his eyes to the ceiling. "Voice mail."

Another second or two passed. "Hi, Gale. This is Lieutenant Commander Zack Brewer with the navy. I saw the president about eighteen months ago. Maybe you remember me as Lieutenant Brewer, because I was a lieutenant back then. I was there with Lieutenant Diane Colcernian, and the president had invited us up to meet with him right after a court-martial that we prosecuted in San Diego.

"Anyway, I'm sure you don't remember this, but you gave me your card with your number and said it was all right to call. Sorry for calling so late, but we have an emergency situation here. If you could call me back at your earliest convenience, I would appreciate it. My number is 619-555-3320. Thanks, Gale. Good-bye."

Zack exhaled.

"Okay, you did the right thing. Okay?"

"Okay."

"If you don't hear from her by lunchtime tomorrow, I want you to try again. Okay?"

"Okay."

"Now listen, about tomorrow, have you gotten your statement from PAO yet?"

"Got it right here."

"How long is it?"

"Maybe five minutes max."

"Listen, Zack, there's been a struggle between NCIS and the navy PAO over this security policy. It's asinine of them to make you read this thing out in public, so I'm pleading with you. Read it as fast as you can, then get the heck off stage, okay? We'll have the panel truck ready to take you back to North Island."

"Yeah, yeah." Irritation crossed his face.

"And, Zack, please." She looked into his eyes. "No matter what they ask, don't answer. Okay?"

"Don't worry."

"See you in the morning." She gave him a quick peck on the cheek and left the room.

6817 English Ivy Court
Springfield, Virginia

Tuesday, 11:15 p.m. (EST)

One of the things Gale Staff loved most about being appointments secretary to the president of the United States was that she got to work around the most powerful people in the world. Then in the evenings, she could stop by the Ukrop's grocery store on Old Keene Mill Road in the D.C. suburb of Springfield, Virginia, shop for whatever she wanted for her evening meal, then cross the road to her townhouse and at least try to relax until the next day.

Just before eleven o'clock in the evening, she had stepped out of the shower, sprinkled herself with baby powder, and slipped under the satin sheets. She had just turned off the lamp and put her arm around the pillow next to her head when her cell phone rang.

Only a handful of people had her personal cell number, including the president of the United States and the White House chief of staff. The incoming calls caller ID showed a message received from someone with a 619 area code.

"Who could that be?" she murmured aloud. "A wrong number?" When she punched in the code to check the voice mail, her heart nearly stopped.

"Of course I remember who you are," she said to the recording. "Do you think I just hand out my personal number like popcorn or something?" She punched the redial button. The line rang. *Please answer.*

"Lieutenant Commander Brewer."

"Zack, this is Gale Staff."

"Hi, Gale!"

"You really didn't know if I'd remember you?"

"I figured the president's appointments secretary would have a photographic memory. But I didn't want to assume."

"It didn't take a photographic memory in your case, Zack."

"A scarecrow is that memorable, eh?"

"You're funny." She laughed. "I see you've been making the evening news again."

"That's on TV back in Washington?"

"The boss joked about it today. He's upset about the shootings and Claxton's involvement, but he thinks you should keep up the good work."

"Great, Gale. Just what I want. More publicity."

"You're great in front of the cameras. Anyway, to what do I owe this surprise?"

"Sorry for calling so late, but this is a potential emergency."

"What's going on?"

He went on to explain everything—the message from Father Robert, the hostages list, the reference to Plan 547, the Quasay interview, and the ticking clock.

"Anyway," Zack continued, "I know this is a huge favor to ask, and if it weren't potentially a matter of life and death, I wouldn't. But, Gale, can you help me get this information to the president?"

"Do you want to meet with the president, Zack?"

"I want to save Diane's life, if she's still alive, and if that's possible. If that means meeting with the president, then yes. If there's some other way of getting action short of meeting with him, then I don't want to bother him."

"You want me to call him tonight?"

"Tonight?"

"I will if you want me to."

There was a pause on the line.

"Zack, are you still there?"

"Still here, Gale. I don't know what to say. I just told someone that I'd jump off a bridge to save Diane's life. But asking you to wake up the president ..."

"He's probably awake. The man goes to bed at midnight and gets up at four thirty. It's like he needs no sleep. I've never seen anything like it."

A moment passed. "You know," Zack said, "I don't know what to say. You know him much better than I do. Just do what you think is best. I'll leave that up to you."

"Okay, Zack, I'll see what I can do."

"God bless you, Gale."

"Zack, you know if I pull this off, you owe me lunch."

"Breakfast, lunch, dinner—you name it, you got it."

"I'll hold you to that."

The line went dead. Gale felt herself smiling. She picked up her phone and dialed the private line of the president of the United States.

CHAPTER 34

20 kilometers east of Ganyushkino, Kazakhstan

Wednesday, 9:00 a.m. (local time)

Traveling fifty miles from the Russian border to the small Kazakh town of Ganyushkino, near the northern shore of the Caspian Sea, had taken more than twelve hours. The delay had been caused by engine trouble, and Sergey had gone to find tools on two separate occasions. Both times, they had managed to get the olive-drab panel truck going again after leaving it on the road for a four-hour stretch. After the first breakdown, they had moved the prisoner to an abandoned barn, several hundred meters off the road, where they gave her water, allowed her to relieve herself, and then sedated her. After the second breakdown, they weren't so lucky.

A local police official, curious about the truck sitting on the side of the road, had stopped to ask questions. Vitaly, who waited behind while Sergey went to look for a wrench that he needed, had engaged the officer in Russian. Two hundred U.S. dollars later, the officer disappeared for good, having asked no questions and having not looked in the back of the truck where the woman was sedated on a cot.

They found the remote airstrip twenty miles east of Ganyushkino just off the main road at about 4:00 a.m. It was in the back of a field, not visible from the sparsely traveled main road.

The twin-engine Russian passenger plane sat silently on the airstrip. No one was anywhere in sight.

Sergey made a few calls and learned that the pilot, who lived in Atryau, about 140 miles to the east, had come during the day but had gotten disgusted and left when no one showed up.

"He will be back by nine in morning," Sergey said.

"He had better." Fadil stepped into the cool, dark pre-morning air and lit a cigarette. Sergey and Vitaly joined him, sipping vodka with their cigarettes.

By 8:30 a.m. a white Volga automobile was making its way up the road leading to the airstrip. Two men got out of the car. They walked toward the panel truck. Sergey and Vitaly walked toward them, meeting them about fifteen feet from the front of the truck. Fadil heard them speaking in animated Russian.

A moment later Sergey walked over to Fadil. "He mad because no one show. Say will cost more because he could have flown load yesterday."

"How much?"

Sergey turned to Vitaly and the other two men. *"Skoika?"* There was a response in Russian. "He say depend on where you want go."

"Can he cross the border over into Mongolia?"

Sergey turned and yelled the question in Russian. This time, the man who was speaking started walking toward Fadil and Sergey. He was gesticulating with his hands and chattering in Russian. The man bored his black eyes into Fadil as Sergey translated.

"He say yes but dangerous mission. Must fly low over mountains to avoid Russian and Chinese radar, which he say not good. Also must stop several times for fuel."

If he can fly us across into Mongolia . . .

"Can he cross the country and fly into Eastern Mongolia?"

Sergey translated the question.

"Dah, dah, dah," came the answer from the man's nodding head. *"No ochen doraguyah."*

"What's that mean?"

"He can fly, though very expensive and dangerous. Must fly low whole way to where you want go. Must stop for fuel many time."

"How much?"

"Skoika?"

More Russian from the man.

"He say five thousand dollars."

That is a fair price. "Tell him I want to think about it."

Sergey translated, and the man nodded. Fadil walked around to the back of the truck, opened the door, and told the two Arab commandos, Ghazi Jawad and Salah Abdul-Alim, to be on standby. They nodded, then he walked back to the front of the truck. "Tell him he has a deal!"

Sergey translated, which brought a smile to the man's face. The other man now joined the conversation. Their hands flew in the air. The first man said something to Sergey, who responded in an argumentative tone. This continued for a couple of minutes. Finally, Sergey turned to Fadil.

"They say they reconsider. They want ten thousand dollar."

"Tell them I have to think about it."

As Sergey translated, Fadil turned, walked to the truck, and said, "Now!" in Arabic. He grabbed an Uzi.

Fadil and his two commandos rushed to the front of their truck, their Uzis trained on the Kazakhs. The men's eyeballs widened like full moons.

"*Pazhalsta! Pazhalsta!*" The men threw their arms up in the air. "*Pazhalsta!*"

"Tell these gentlemen that where we come from, a deal is a deal. I am prepared to pay five thousand U.S. dollars in advance, right now, as they agreed, or we will mow them down and dump their double-crossing bodies in the Caspian Sea. Then we will commandeer their aircraft and hire someone who will fly this mission for twenty-five hundred U.S. dollars."

Sergey translated. The Kazakhs nodded their heads. "*Congyeshna! Sudavolstrien!*"

"They say we have deal."

"I thought they would come to their senses," Fadil said.

Twenty minutes later, the twin props of the plane revved, lifting them into the morning sky and taking them across the deep blue waters of the northern Caspian Sea. From there the plane turned and set a course due east, into the bright rising sun.

CHAPTER 35

Headquarters of the Commander
Naval Base San Diego
937 North Harbor Drive
San Diego, California

11:45 a.m. (PST)

Just inside the two front doors of the COMNAVBASE building, Shannon donned a set of dark shades and looked at Wesner and Raynor. They both wore dark pinstripe suits and had microphones in their ears.

"Let's go," she said. They stepped outside into the bright sunshine onto the makeshift podium that some bureaucrat up the chain of command had concocted.

Ten minutes to twelve. At least four or five hundred people had gathered outside, and the SDPD was cordoning off the crowd. The problem, though, was that the roped-off area came up to the stage. Thus, the edge of the crowd was right on top of the stage, almost like a boxing ring being surrounded close-up by spectators.

Too close for comfort.

"Keep your eyes peeled, guys. Big time. Watch the roped-off area down by the podium."

"Got it."

"Roger that."

Shannon stood on the platform a few steps behind the podium and surveyed the crowd. A small army of reporters was gathered close to the roped-off area; beyond them were several hundred curiosity seekers who had come to catch a glimpse of the world's most famous JAG officer.

She checked her watch. Five minutes. Time to go get Zack.

"Wesner, Raynor. Stay posted at each outside corner of the platform. Keep your eyes peeled. I'm going for Matlock."

"Roger that, Shannon."

"Will do."

She stepped back inside the double doors. Zack was looking trim and tanned in his summer dress white uniform. He was standing with Captain Bob Debardelaben of navy public affairs. *Probably the idiot who concocted this lunacy.*

Zack flashed a confident smile as she flicked a piece of lint off one of his black-and-gold shoulder boards.

"Captain. Commander. We're ready."

The captain nodded his head.

"Let's do it," Zack said.

Shannon opened the doors, and Captain Debardelaben stepped on stage, followed by Zack and then Shannon.

They were met under deep blue skies with a warm, sustained round of applause.

Chris had just reached the outer edge of the crowd when he heard the applause begin. He looked up and saw two naval officers, both dressed sharply in their summer dress whites, step onto the stage. *Oh, a man in uniform!* Then he realized that one of the two was Zack! His blood ran so hot with excitement at that moment that he wanted to scream. But then the first officer stepped to the podium.

"Good day, ladies and gentlemen.

"I am Captain Bob Debardelaben, U.S. Navy, and I work for Rear Admiral Simon McClean, who is the chief of information for your United States Navy. The office of the chief of information, or CHINFO, is often referred to as the navy public affairs office. One of our missions is to work with national and international media, and community relations on a national level, to keep the public informed about the missions and operations of your navy."

Hurry up, old geezer! I want Zack!

"In keeping with that mission, today we are pleased to introduce an officer who, no doubt, many of you are already familiar with."

More applause rose from the crowd.

Yes!

"And I can see from your reaction you know who I'm talking about."

The level of applause rose several decibels.

"Yesss!" Chris shouted. "Woo hoo!" Chris wanted to cry. Zack would see the gun and would learn his lesson.

The captain waited for the applause to subside.

"Ladies and gentlemen, it is my pleasure to introduce to you ..." Shrill whistles and shouts of "Zack" rang out during the pregnant pause. "Lieutenant Commander Zack Brewer, United States Navy!"

More whistles and ear-splitting applause broke out.

It's like being at a rock concert. Shannon surveyed the wild-eyed crowd of admirers, many of them young and female. Unbelievable. No, believable. But she'd never get him off the stage if they didn't shut up.

She glanced at Zack, who was sheepishly staring at his feet.

"Zack!" She tried to get his attention. They needed to get this show on the road so she could get him back across the bay to North Island. But her efforts were drowned out when the crowd began shouting, "We want Zack! We want Zack! We want Zack!"

At least that prompted him to get his eyes off his shoes. He gave her a quick wink and then stepped to the podium.

"Thank you. Thank you." He waited as the crowd quieted. Finally, he said, "I have a brief statement I would like to read.

"Regrettably, some confusion has ensued as a result of comments I made to various members of the media earlier this week at a general court-martial here in San Diego.

"Let me say first that the United States Navy recognizes the concept of civilian control over the military, and that I personally recognize the authority of the president of the United States and the United States Congress in their joint exercise of control over the United States military.

"The comments that I made Monday, concerning those in public service joining the United States Marine Corps, were directed at no one in particular and cast no aspersions on any member of the United States Congress. To those members of Congress who have served in the other outstanding branches of the armed services, including the navy, army, coast guard, and air force, I salute you. And to those members of the

Congress whose paths to public service were taken through the civilian sector, I salute you and offer my greatest measure of respect to you.

"I trust that my comments have cast no aspersions on the United States Congress, the United States Navy, or the United States of America.

"To the extent that my comments may have been construed in any other way, I offer to you my apologies.

"Thank you very much, and may God bless America."

The applause erupted again. "Let's go, Zack," Shannon said. But he stood there, waving and thanking those who had come. "Come on, Commander."

"Zack!" A scream sounded above the roar. Everything shifted to slow motion.

A gun flashed in the sunlight. In the middle of the crowd. Shannon reached for her nine-millimeter. The air cracked with the noise of gunfire.

Wesner and Raynor dove at Zack. Shannon aimed at the gunman and squeezed off three rounds.

Pandemonium broke out among the crowd.

"Call an ambulance!"

CHAPTER 36

Kharakhorum, Mongolia
On the northern edge of the Gobi Desert

Willie Mangum opened his eyes when the ferocious arctic blast rippled the felt walls of the Mongolian tent—or *ger*, as the Mongolians called it—that had become his home. The faint glow from the woodburning stove revealed that Pam had rolled away from him, her body in a snuggly cocoon of covers. Her breathing was slow and rhythmic, pulsating the three quilts on top of her.

At least somebody can sleep around here.

The forty-year-old Baptist missionary smiled at the sight of his sleeping wife, checked his watch—5:00 a.m.—and then pushed up on his elbows and squinted at the portable black stove in the middle of the ger.

It was still burning.

Barely.

Willie pondered the situation. The stove *could* use a little more wood. And he *did* need to answer the call of nature. He swung his longjohn sheathed legs out from under the quilts and dropped his feet onto the makeshift wooden floor of the one-room ger. He stood and crossed the creaking two-by-fours to the center of the tent. The chill permeated his slippers and seeped into the balls of his feet, making the need to answer the call of nature even more urgent.

Squinting, he reached down for one of the dry split logs on the floor just beside the stove and tossed it in. The log blazed from the hot embers left from last night's fire, slightly brightening the otherwise dim glow in the ger. Willie tossed in a second small log, and another burst of flame leaped in the stove. He closed the door.

A second arctic blast flapped the ger, assaulting the exterior with salvos of ice pellets that sounded like machine-gun fire.

The blast persuaded him that it was too early, too cold, and too dark to venture out into the freezing snowstorm. Nature could wait until the sun came up.

He hoped.

He slipped back under the sheets, pulled up the quilts, and wrapped his arms around Pam, scrunching up beside her like the perfect-fitting piece of a jigsaw puzzle. The crackling of the fire and the natural body heat trapped beneath the covers lulled his mind back into the shadow lands.

"Willie!"

Dreams sometimes sound so real.

"Willie!"

The squeaky-sounding Mongolian brought Willie back up on his elbows.

"Willie!"

"Okay! Hold on!" he called out in a forced whisper, speaking Mongolian, hoping not to wake Pam. He threw on a robe and trudged across the floor, past the stove, to the door flap. He reached down for the zipper that sealed the inner flap door, then unzipped the inner flap from bottom to top. When he repeated the procedure for the outer flap, cold air rushed in like a freezing wind tunnel.

"Jagtai, it's 6:00 a.m.," Willie protested, waving the short, thirty-year-old Mongolian man into the ger, then zipping both flaps tight.

"Willie, what's going on?" Pam rubbed her eyes, squinting in the direction of her husband and the visitor.

"Nothing, sweetie. Go back to sleep." Willie looked at Jagtai, one of the deacons in the small local fellowship of believers that Willie had started since his arrival two months ago in this forgotten country in the middle of nowhere. Something was definitely wrong. Perhaps one of the believers in their fellowship had been arrested or, even worse, killed. He ushered Jagtai Tsedenbal to the two small chairs opposite the tent from his wife, motioned him into one of the chairs, and asked in whispered Mongol, "Is everything okay?"

"There's a white woman," Jagtai said, gasping for breath, as if he had been running.

"A white woman?"

"American or maybe European. They couldn't tell."

"Jagtai, what are you talking about?"

"In the Gobi! About two hundred miles southeast of here." Jagtai's black eyes danced with fear and excitement. "One of the nomad groups just got back this morning. They are reforming with guns and are going back out for her. It will take several days to get back out to her."

"Wait a minute." Willie was confused. "I don't understand. Is this woman lost out there or something?"

"No. They saw her walk out of a ger, and then she was walking around outside it for a while. I hear that there were three or four gers in a camp. Surrounded by barbed wire. Men with guns. Surrounding her!"

Willie glanced over at Pam. She was sleeping. Good. "It's below zero out there, Jagtai." Another glance at Pam. "Who's going out there with guns? And why would anybody be stupid enough to traipse a hundred miles through a blizzard through some of the most desolate terrain in the world?"

"Kublai's group is going," Jagtai said, referring to Kublai Sühbaatar.

The very name made Willie cringe. Kublai Sühbaatar, a forty-five-year-old Lamaist Buddhist, had been a thorn in the Mangums' side ever since they arrived from America. With the fall of the Soviet Union, religion had again become legal in Mongolia, and the most prominent religion was Lamaist Buddhism. Kublai Sühbaatar made no secret of his worship and admiration of His Holiness the Dalai Lama himself, living reincarnation of the Buddha on earth today.

Kublai, a local member of the ruling council in Kharakhorum, had made it known that non-Buddhists, including Christians and the growing infiltration of Muslims flowing across Mongolia's sparsely guarded borders, were not welcome in his country. The missionary family that preceded the Mangums in Kharakhorum, Bob and Betty Blanzy, had been stabbed to death and found in their ger by a handful of Christians who had come for Bible study. There were no arrests, because there was no organized police force in this desolate country of nomads; more than half the population still lived in gers. But the local believers had warned the Mangums about Kublai and his group and suspected his involvement in the murders.

"What's in this for Kublai?" Willie mustered.

"Reward money," Jagtai responded. "And his hatred for Islam. Word is that Kublai thinks Muslims are holding the woman. He wants to kill them and then kidnap her for himself, then demand a huge reward from the West."

"Okay." Willie pondered Jagtai's cleft chin. "So why are you telling me this at six in the morning?"

Their eyes met. "Willie, we must find her before Kublai does. Whoever she his, she needs our help. If we can locate her before Kublai, maybe we can help her."

"You're not going!" Pam sat up in bed. Her big green eyes, expressing stern disapproval, darted back and forth between Willie and Jagtai. "Willie," she spoke in Mongolian, "we were called here to be missionaries. Not to play Rambo. It's cold out there!" The look of disapproval became one of pleading, as if she knew what he was about to do. "You could freeze to death." A slight quiver in her voice. "Please."

"It's okay, Pam." Willie walked over and sat beside her on the bed. "The weather will be clearing soon. This storm will pass. The days are already getting longer."

"Willie, please!"

Their eyes met. "Pam, we're missionaries. If Jagtai's right, there could be an American or a European out there who needs our help."

"Willie." She caressed his face with her hand. "You're a Bible teacher. Not a cross-country hiker. You went to seminary, Willie. You're not a Navy SEAL. This is suicide!"

He smiled at her. "I love you, honey." He reached over and gave her a kiss. "Do you remember the threshold question we promised to ask if we were faced with danger?"

"But this—," she protested.

"This is just such a situation to apply the question."

She looked down as if she knew he was right.

"Well?"

She looked up. "Jesus would go."

"Of course he would. And so must I." He hugged her. "But I'm not leaving you here in this tent alone." He looked at Jagtai. "I know Kublai's out of town, but I can't just leave her here in a blizzard." He glanced at Pam again, then turned back to his friend. "When the storm clears, can you have Anna come over and help her get to the airport in Ulaanbaatar?" His eyes met Pam's. "Honey, I know you've been homesick. This might be a good time for a sabbatical in the States."

"Forget it," Pam snapped. "I'm a missionary too. Where you go, I go!"

"No way!"

"Why not?"

"It's freezing out there, Pam."

Her eyes blazed with anger. "And if Jesus would go plowing through the snow for someone he doesn't even know ..."

"Jesus *does* know her. And he loves her," Willie interrupted.

"Don't get theological on me, Willie Mangum." She often called him by his first and last name when she was irritated. This he knew all too well. "You know what I mean. I've often heard you say what a privilege it would be to die the death of a martyr for the gospel."

Willie tried to speak but felt his vocal chords paralyzed.

"Willie, I already packed for you," Jagtai said. "Clothes. Everything. Can you come?"

He looked at Pam. Tears had already started forming in her eyes.

"I know," she said. "Let me help you get some of your things together."

He leaned over and kissed her on the cheek.

CHAPTER 37

Alvarado Hospital Medical Center
6655 Alvarado Road
San Diego, California

Wednesday, 8:00 p.m. (PST)

Barry had been sitting in the waiting area now for the better part of two hours, awaiting word on two of the victims of today's shooting at COMNAVBASE. Shannon had been right all along. It *was* an idiotic stunt on the part of the public affairs office to stage Brewer's so-called apology outside in a public place. That was the problem with PAO and half the other commands in the navy. They never took the NCIS seriously.

He'd warned Captain Debardelaben about security risks and had also called COMNAVBASE. But NCIS had always been the redheaded stepchild of the navy.

Now if it had been the blasted FBI warning them, they'd have listened.

Barry cursed under his breath. He needed a smoke.

He fumbled for his cigarettes, then stepped into the hallway, headed outside, when a slim man in his forties, wearing surgical scrubs, walked out of the intensive care area. Barry recognized Dr. Gary Blake as the doctor who had been performing surgery on the shooting victims.

"Doctor, excuse me. I'm Special Agent Barry MacGregor with NCIS."

"You're with who?" A puzzled look crossed the doctor's face, confirming Barry's notion that the NCIS didn't get the respect it deserved.

"NCIS. Haven't you seen the show on television?"

"Sorry, no time for TV."

"Look, you've been operating on one of my agents in there. And also the guy that opened fire on everybody. How are they doing, Doc?"

"Are you family?"

"No. I'm Wesner's boss."

"Sorry, friend, but HIPPA"—he was referring to the federal Health Care Privacy Act—"won't allow me to give out that information."

"To heck with HIPPA!" Barry practically screamed. "I'm a federal agent, buster!" He whipped out his NCIS badge and shoved it under the doctor's nose. "We're in the process of a federal investigation here. HIPPA doesn't apply to block the investigation of federal law enforcement!"

"Okay, okay," the doctor replied in a soft voice. "Why don't we step right in here?" They walked into a dark room, and when the doctor flipped on the light, Barry saw an examination table in the center of the room, a round swivel chair, a counter with rubber gloves, and a lavatory.

"Okay, Agent—"

"MacGregor."

"MacGregor. Your employee, Agent Wesner, took a bullet to the shoulder. He's lost a lot of blood, but I think he's past the worst part."

"You think he'll make it?"

"We're still holding him in intensive care, but yes, I think he will."

"Thank God. What about the other guy?"

"The other gentleman who was brought in, a Mr. Reynolds, took three bullets to the chest. Whoever fired that gun knew what they were doing."

"That was one of our special agents—Special Agent McGillvery."

"Well, Special Agent McGillvery put two bullets within a centimeter of this man's heart, and a third in his left lung. We've got him stabilized for the moment, but his prognosis is weak. Very weak."

"Think he'll make it, Doc?"

The doctor hesitated. "If he has any next of kin, they should be called in. But to answer your question, no, I don't expect him to make it through the night."

"Thanks, Doc. Keep me posted, will ya?"

"You bet."

Barry walked out of the room and outside into the courtyard and lit a cigarette.

Navy Lodge
Rogers Road
Naval Air Station North Island
Coronado, California

Wednesday, 8:30 p.m. (PST)

Shannon found it impossible to believe that twenty-four hours had passed since she was last here. She flashed her NCIS badge as she walked by the navy petty officer at the front gate, but she didn't bother stopping. She was still operating on adrenaline and felt numb.

People took bullets today. Blood was shed. Some would die. And she was in the middle of it. A gunfight in the midst of a public square in one of America's largest cities.

What could she expect when she reached room 207? Would Zack's belongings still be there? Deep down, she hoped somehow, some way, he would be there.

She knocked on the door.

He was sitting in the only chair in the room, watching a recap of the local news, when the raps came on the door. He opened it to find Shannon in the hallway.

"Zack."

"You okay?" He opened his arms. She stood still for a moment, just looking at him. Finally, she moved closer to him, and he wrapped her in his embrace.

"It's okay," he said. "It's going to be all right." He patted her back. They stood there a few minutes, neither one speaking. When a group of people walked by in the hallway, he pushed the door closed.

"Barry called," she said.

"Yeah? Wesner gonna be okay?"

"Wesner took one in the shoulder. He'll be fine."

"What about the gunman?"

"The same stalker that we ran into in Old Town. Chris Reynolds. I put two bullets in his heart, Zack. He's going to die. Oh dear God, I've never killed anyone. I've roughed a few people up, but I've never ..." Her voice trailed off.

"Shannon, you saved my life." She shook her head. "Look at me!" Her eyes met his. "You saved my life."

The phone rang. "Have a seat." He patted the end of the bed. "I need to grab this." Zack picked up the phone as Shannon sat.

"Lieutenant Commander Brewer speaking."

"Lieutenant Commander Brewer, this is the White House calling."

He held his hand over the receiver and whispered to Shannon. "I think it's Gale Staff."

"Commander Brewer, are you there?"

"I'm sorry, still here."

"Could you hold for the president, please?"

"The president?"

Shannon's eyes locked on his.

"Yes, sir."

"Well ... of course."

"Zack, you okay?" The familiar nasal twang of the most famous man in the world was suddenly on the line.

"This is an honor, sir."

"Aw, cut the honor stuff, Zack. I told you to call if you ever needed anything, and I meant it. Now I saw the news today, and it looks like you had a close call. You okay?"

"Yes, sir. I'm fine. Thank you, sir."

"Gale said you called and wanted to see me. How's Friday look?"

"I serve at your pleasure, Mr. President."

"Okay, I'll have the secretary of the navy arrange to get you here."

"Sir, would it be an imposition if I brought Special Agent Shannon McGillvery along?"

"I remember that name," the president said. "Wasn't she the agent who busted open the *Quasay* case?"

"One and the same, sir."

"Sure, bring her along. I'll give the orders."

"Thank you, sir."

"And, Zack?"

"Yes, sir?"

"You're doing a whale of a job."

"Thank you, sir."

"And for the record, I think you're right on the mark. Every one of those suckers up on Capitol Hill ought to have to go through Marine Corps boot camp at Paris Island." He paused. "Three or four times, if you ask me." The president let out a long laugh. "And, Zack?"

"Yes, sir?"

"Don't you worry about Eleanor Claxton. Everybody in middle America sees what she's trying to do. She'll never become president."

"Yes, sir."

"Have a good evening, son. See you Friday."

"Thank you, Mr. President."

The line went dead.

"Can you believe that?" Zack asked. "Gale Staff is amazing."

"God is amazing."

"Amen to that."

CHAPTER 38

At least Eleanor had taken his call this morning. Jackson was starting to believe that maybe no one had discovered the recording device he had slipped under the table in the kitchenette. Nothing of significance had been said the last couple of days. But Jackson was concerned about Eleanor's growing obsession with Brewer.

"Let's get down to business," Eleanor said, calling the morning briefing to order. She turned to him. "Jackson, what do we have on the shooting downtown yesterday?"

"Media reports and also reports that I've gotten from San Diego PD indicate that the gunman was a thirty-year-old single man named Chris Reynolds. He has a psychotic history, having been arrested several times back east for stalking male attorneys and local politicians. Reports that I have are that the guy is or was delusional. He'd been in a mental hospital in northern Virginia for over a year.

"Reynolds got off one shot in Brewer's direction—from a gun he bought the day before yesterday from a gun shop in Vegas—and hit one of the NCIS agents on the stage. One of the NCIS agents, Shannon McGillvery, pumped three rounds into his chest. They don't expect him to live."

"Okay." Eleanor turned to Mary-Latham. "Draw up a statement expressing gratitude that Commander Brewer was not hurt and saying

that our prayers are with the agent"—she waved her hand in the air—
"whatever his name is, for a speedy recovery. Cite this as an example
of the need for *total* handgun control and point out that the administration has opposed gun control on every front. Renew my call for
the National Handgun Prohibition Act, which would ban all handguns
except for handguns carried by law enforcement officers and federal
agents in the official course of their duties. Understand?"

"Got it, Eleanor."

"And I want to move out on this fast."

"Will do," Mary-Latham said.

"And one other thing." Eleanor took a drag from her cigarette,
then blew a cloud of smoke into the room. "Seems to me this is a good
opportunity to make us look tough on crime by commending SDPD
and NCIS for saving Brewer's life and for apprehending the shooter. So
..." She paused. "So why not something to the effect that while we hope
the shooter survives to face trial, it appears that NCIS and SDPD have
worked together to apprehend the deranged gunman who may have
been responsible for the killing of Lieutenant Jacoby as well."

"You think this guy shot Jacoby too?" Mary-Latham asked.

"Yes, I do. He was some psycho intent on murdering every attorney
involved in this court-martial. In fact, why don't you spin it that way
and bring it back to the need for passage of my National Handgun Act
to keep guns out of the hands of mentally disturbed people who would
follow a sick pattern of wanting to kill officials involved in the judicial
process."

"Whatever you say, Eleanor."

Jackson caught a raised eyebrow from Mary-Latham.

"Ray." Eleanor turned to her pollster. "Where are we in the polls
today?"

"Depends on where you're polling."

"Explain."

"You're widening your lead over Warren in San Francisco and Los
Angeles. Overnight, you've jumped from twelve to fifteen points in San
Francisco and from fifteen to eighteen in Los Angeles. Your call for
a Military Hate Crimes Act is the reason cited. But elsewhere in the
country, you're dropping like a rock, especially in the South. Our polls
attribute that to one reason."

"Let me guess." She took a puff of the Virginia Slim, all the while squinting her eyes, which made her look, for the moment, like a salamander.

"I'm guessing you're guessing right," Ray Everton said. "Unfortunately, the navy's attempt to have him apologize yesterday, coupled with the attempt on his life, has generated more sympathy toward him. This is the type of headline we're seeing this morning." He slid the *Miami Herald* on the conference table for all to see.

DERANGED GUNMAN TRIES KILLING BREWER
Zack to Eleanor: "Just Kidding!"

"How bad is it out there?" Eleanor asked.

"Bad."

Jackson saw them lock eyes.

"Let me put it this way," Ray Everton continued. "Forget President Williams for the moment. For you to whip Roberson Fowler for the nomination, you need to win California plus at least four southern states on Super Tuesday.

"We've got New Hampshire first, and it's tight there. Next week, California. Right now, we're getting into real good shape. Win here, and at least we take some momentum into Super Tuesday in the South. You don't help yourself being from Vermont. So our strategy has been to counter Fowler there by the fact that your estranged husband is the former governor of Mississippi.

"Here's the problem. Since we took over this court-martial, you've slipped more than five points behind Fowler in Florida, Georgia, North Carolina, and Texas, and he's near dead even with you even in Mississippi.

"Now these are Democrats who call themselves moderates. They're the swing vote that put the last Democratic ticket in power, and that ticket had Freddie Claxton on it. My polls show it ain't the gay rights thing that's causing you to slip. It's Brewer.

"The boy's got what Reagan had and what your estranged husband has — God-given charisma in front of the camera."

"Tell me about it," Eleanor huffed.

"Anyway, we've gotta find a way to keep that boy out of the limelight, or we're going to be toast. Soon."

"What do you mean by toast, Ray?"

"I mean past the point of no return. The man's not even a politician. And he says things subtly. But he talks in a way that charges conservatives and makes moderates fall in love with him. If he keeps popping up on TV, frankly, as the polls are now showing, we've got a lot of trouble. We have to keep pushing this gay rights issue but get Brewer off this case."

Eleanor's icy stare sent shivers down Jackson's spine. She lit another cigarette. "Perhaps that can be arranged."

SEAL Team 3 headquarters
United States Naval Amphibious Base
Coronado, California

Thursday, 9:30 a.m. (PST)

Captain Buck Noble was finishing his review of the morning's muster report when his command master chief, BTMC Matthew Cantor, arrived at the door of his office.

"Come in, Master Chief."

"Thank you, sir," the thirty-year navy veteran said. As command master chief, Cantor was the highest-ranking enlisted man in the unit.

"So what did you want to see me about?"

"Sir, I understand NCIS has been poking around the command, looking for someone to fess up to breaking Ensign Eckberg's collarbone."

Noble felt anger flare up in his chest at the thought of it. "All in the interest of political correctness. We've got to sacrifice a good man to keep Eleanor Claxton happy. Thing is, every one of our men would give their lives to protect Claxton's right to run her mouth, and she runs her mouth to her liberal colleagues on Capitol Hill and demands that a good man—or good men—sacrifice their careers *even after* a homosexual assault."

He looked up. Master Chief Cantor, his salad row showing three Purple Hearts, a Navy Cross, and a host of other service ribbons for bravery, was standing at attention. His eyes were weather worn. His face, tanned with a few wrinkles, was proud. If there was any one man anywhere in the U.S. Navy whom Captain Noble would want covering his back, it was Command Master Chief Matthew Cantor.

"Have a seat."

"Thank you, sir."

"Coffee?"

"No, sir."

"So what did you want to see me about?"

"Sir, I want to volunteer."

"Volunteer? For what? We don't have our deployment orders."

"I want to volunteer to plead to the assault on Ensign Eckberg."

Noble adjusted his glasses and looked up. "You?"

"Yes, sir."

Noble studied the face of the proud warrior. He was a man who had survived behind enemy lines for months at a time, who had gone into the Middle East and into China undercover, who had been shot out of the torpedo tubes of submarines, then rafted twenty miles through the ocean to hostile shores under the cover of darkness.

"Master Chief, you've been in the navy a long time. You've been under fire, you've saved shipmates, you've faced adversity far more severe than a homosexual ensign. Now forgive me, Master Chief, but what's the deal?"

"Sir, I wish to plead to the assault of Ensign Eckberg, sir."

Noble crossed his arms, leaned back in his chair, and rocked a few times. "Look me in the eye, Master Chief." The old sea dog complied. "Now tell me, off the record, man to man, did you ever lay a finger on the ensign?"

"Sir, I wish to plead to the assault of Ensign Eckberg, sir."

"You dodged my question. Did you lay a finger on the ensign?"

"Sir, I wish to plead to the assault of Ensign Eckberg, sir."

"That's what I thought." Noble stood, walked to his window, and crossed his arms. Another master chief, a Navy SEAL, was down on the beach barking his head off at a newly indoctrinated Hell Week class, screaming and yelling as the potential SEALs, wearing white T-shirts and combat pants, waded in the surf with a log over their shoulders.

"It's about them, isn't it, Master Chief?" Noble nodded out the window to the new SEAL trainees. "This is about watching your men's backsides. About giving your life, or in this case, your career as a Navy SEAL for your shipmates. For the men you lead." He stared at Cantor, whose eyes were now following the recruits, who had just fallen, collectively, in the surf.

"Master Chief, forget the fact that I'm your commanding officer. Talk to me man to man, SEAL to SEAL." Cantor's black eyes shifted to him. "I'm right, aren't I?"

There was a moment of silence. "Captain, I'm retirement-eligible. I've given everything I have to the navy. I've given it all for my country, and I'd willingly die for it. I've had a rich career, and I've gone places and done things that are so classified, not even an international spy novelist could dream them up."

He looked outside again at the trainees.

"But these young men under my command—they've only just begun. There was more than one of them, Captain; there were about three of them."

Noble's eyes locked on Cantor's. "Out with it, Master Chief. Which three?"

Cantor looked away. "The three who were victimized by Eckberg, sir."

"Does that include Petty Officer Williams?"

Cantor hesitated. "Yes, sir, it does."

"Hmph. Go on, Master Chief."

"Yes, sir. They worked over Eckberg all right. But after I walked into the spaces and ordered them to lay off, they did. But, Skipper, honestly, after what the ensign did to them, he's lucky to be alive. I mean, we just can't have that sort of thing going on in a submarine."

He looked again at Noble. "Captain, I love these men. I love my country. I may have another year to serve if I'm lucky, and that's it. And this country is better off parting ways with an old geezer like me than ruining the promising careers of these brave young men. Me and the men have already talked about it. Sir, let me take the rap for this. The way I figure it, maybe I get a nonjudicial punishment and get busted down to chief or maybe petty officer first class. But under these circumstances to punish these young men? I can't see the justice there."

Noble eyed his command master chief. The epitome of America's finest was standing before him at this very moment.

"Master Chief, I admire your honor. That's what makes you the man that you are. But your request is denied."

"But, sir—"

Noble raised his hand. "The fact that the attackers were the ones assaulted changes the facts in my judgment. Granted, vigilantism is never justified. But these men were victims first. They were violated under circumstances that are inexcusable—while serving this country on duty on board a United States Navy submarine. I'm going to call the admiral and inform him of my intention to take these men to captain's mast—*after* a verdict is rendered in the Eckberg prosecution. I will mete out a punishment that is appropriate to the offense." Their eyes met. "Trust me on this." Noble walked over and put his hand on Cantor's shoulder. "You're a good man, Master Chief. The best man I've ever known."

CHAPTER 39

Eastern Kazakhstan
Over the Altay Mountains
Near the Kazakhstan-Russian border

Thursday, 11:50 p.m. (local time)

Flying in the moonlight, between the shadows of large mountain peaks, the twin-engine Russian plane was bouncing like a soccer ball. Fadil was about to vomit. He looked back and saw that the prisoner was heaving convulsively.

"Get a towel for her," he instructed one of his men. He moved forward and stuck his head between the Kazakh pilots. "Why all the bouncing?"

Sergey translated for him. One of the pilots responded in Russian, then Sergey explained to Fadil, "We near Russian border. Must fly low through mountains to hide from radar. Russians not trust Chinese. Chinese not trust Russians. If spotted, Russians think we Chinese aircraft. Send MiG fighter plane to shoot down. Many winds make flight bumpy. Must hold on."

"How much longer to Mongolia?"

"We fly over corner of Russia through mountains, and then Mongolia. Flight maybe another hour to border."

"Advise me when we've crossed into Russian airspace, and then Mongolian airspace."

"We tell you."

CHAPTER 40

The White House
Washington, D.C.

Friday, 11:30 a.m. (EST)

Shannon was in awe as they were motioned through the side gate of the White House lawn, just off 17th Street. If only her teammates from the Boston College field hockey team could see her now.

"Your identification cards, please?" A dashing marine captain stood at the gate. Zack and Shannon complied. "And now if you would follow me."

The marine led Zack and Shannon to a small, high-tech security booth on the perimeter of the South Lawn. After they walked through an X-ray booth, two uniformed Secret Service agents nodded their heads. The marine motioned for them to step out of the security shack and back onto the lawn.

"Commander, if you and Agent McGillvery would follow me, please." The marine captain, resplendent in dress blues, was trim and buff. His voice sounded almost robotic.

"By all means, Captain," Zack said. They walked across the corner of the green lawn and into an inconspicuous-looking small door near the hedgerows on the west side of the White House. There they were met by a tall, slim navy captain with an abundance of heavy gold cording hanging over his shoulder.

"Sir!" Zack shot a salute of warm recognition. "You're still here."

"Good to see you again, Zack." The pleasant-looking captain wore a name tag identifying him as Hancock. "When the president wants you to stay, you stay."

"Sir, I'd like you to meet Special Agent Shannon McGillvery, NCIS."

"I'm Captain Jay Hancock, naval attaché to the president."

"A pleasure, Captain."

"I'll take it from here, Captain," Hancock said, dismissing the marine.

"Aye, sir." The marine captain clicked his heels, pivoted 180 degrees, and marched away.

"What's our itinerary, Captain?" Zack asked.

"If you'll follow me, I'll explain as we walk to the Oval Office."

The Oval Office.

"After you, sir," Zack said.

The naval attaché motioned, and Shannon and Zack followed him through an interior corridor, then along a covered walkway adjacent to the West Wing.

"As usual," the attaché began as they walked down the passageway, "the president is running a tight schedule. But he wants to see both of you. The secretary of defense is in the Oval Office also. I believe you met him when you were here before." A couple of more paces.

"Right on time." Hancock checked his watch as the trio approached a reception area. A well-dressed blonde woman in her forties sat behind a desk. Four well-sculpted men with shifting eyes and icy looks stood, hands clasped, in a row behind her. The men wore dark business suits, sported closely cropped haircuts, and had small earpieces in their right ears with wires dangling into their suits. Two of the men stood guard to the left of an ornate door just behind the woman. The other two stood to the right.

"Hello, Zack." The woman's eyes twinkled. "It's good to see you!" She rose from behind her desk and gave Zack a broad smile. "I'm so glad the president was able to work this out!"

"I appreciate this more than you know—and I haven't forgotten that lunch."

"You'd better not."

Shannon cleared her throat.

"Excuse me," Zack said. "Gale, meet Special Agent Shannon McGillvery of the NCIS."

"I've heard such good things about you." She extended her hand for a friendly shake. "I'm Gale Staff, the president's appointments secretary."

Gale turned back to Zack. "I see you've been on television again. Everything okay?"

"Pretty scary day yesterday. We're fine now. Thanks, Gale."

"Anyway, you're right on time, and if you'll wait a moment, I'll see if he's ready."

Gale Staff picked up her telephone. "Sir, Commander Brewer and Special Agent McGillvery are here." A brief pause. "Yes, sir." She looked at the attaché. "Captain, the president is ready."

Shannon's heart jumped. *I'm not really here.*

"Follow me, please." Hancock stepped to the ornate white door with a large gold doorknob, opened it, and announced, "Mr. President, I present Lieutenant Commander Brewer and Special Agent McGillvery."

Shannon followed Zack into the Oval Office as the tanned, silver-haired man she had seen on television a thousand times rose from behind his magnificent mahogany desk.

"Please come in." A smiling President Mack Williams, wearing a dark pinstripe suit and a red tie, walked across the room to meet them just inside the doorway.

As the president shook Zack's hand, Shannon noticed two more men, also dressed in dark suits, hands clasped, flanking the inside door of the office.

"And you must be Special Agent McGillvery," the president said, smiling.

"Yes, Mr. President." His handshake was firm, yet incredible warmth radiated from the man.

"Let me thank you for the work that you did on the *Quasay* case. Your country owes a debt of gratitude to you. Thank you for coming."

"It's an honor, Mr. President."

"Zack, you remember Secretary of Defense Erwin Lopez." The president gestured to a medium-built, middle-aged Hispanic man standing a few feet to his left. "Mr. Secretary." Zack nodded.

"Commander. Special Agent McGillvery."

"Everyone, please have a seat." The president pointed the officers to four chairs positioned in a semicircle in front of his desk. The quartet sat down.

"Listen, Zack, I want you to know that I've been briefed on everything that we've gotten from this Catholic priest. We've checked him out and he's legitimate.

"And, Shannon?"

"Yes, sir?"

"Not only have I been briefed on it, but I've read every word of your report. This is excellent work. If I'm reelected, you're going to be on my short list for director of NCIS."

"Really, sir?"

"Yes, ma'am. It's a two-year appointment, and when Jones's term is up, I'll be putting together a list. Can't promise anything, but your name will be there."

"Even if I'm a registered Democrat, sir?"

"Nobody's perfect." The president smiled and winked. "First we'll put you on the White House prayer list." That brought obligatory laughter from everyone in the room. "Besides, a lot of great Republicans used to be Democrats first. Case in point—Ronald Reagan."

"Yes, sir. Commander Brewer keeps reminding me of that example."

"Good work, Commander." The president reached over and slapped Zack on the knee. Then he looked at Shannon again. "Seriously, I don't care about your registration. Not for this job anyway. Keep up the good work, and you'll be on my list."

"That's an honor, Mr. President."

"Well, your work has merited it. But let's get down to business. For the record, I'm also of the opinion that Diane may be alive."

Shannon felt goose bumps crawling up her spine. *Vindicated by the commander in chief.*

"Did you know I'm an ex-Navy JAG officer myself?"

"Yes, sir," Shannon said. "I'm aware of that."

"I met Diane Colcernian and felt like I knew her. And I'd never leave Diane or any member of our armed services out there, stranded or captured, if I could help it."

He looked at Zack. "I'd send a carrier task force for her, no matter what the consequences, if I could pinpoint her location."

"Thank you, sir."

"Now what we've done is this. We've positioned two extra satellites in orbit over the Gobi Desert and have been shooting pictures, but so far, nothing. I know you've heard this before, but this is like looking for a needle in a haystack."

"Yes, Mr. President."

"Now if we find this camp—and we may not because of cloud cover or because they may be moving it or whatever—but if we do, I'm willing to take action. What action, I don't know. But you have my word on that, Zack."

"Thank you, sir."

"Now the problem is that Mongolia is landlocked by Russia and China. Relations have turned hostile with those countries since the attack on the Dome of the Rock. And even if we find Diane, that could get dicey. They've both got nukes, and I can't just send the 82nd Airborne in across Russian or Chinese airspace to physically walk across Mongolia for a sweep by foot. However, I've instructed the secretary of defense here to draft an operational plan to send in a team of Navy SEALs in case we locate this camp."

The secretary of defense nodded his head.

"Details of the plan are still in the making," the president continued, "and I can't share those details right now anyway. But I want you to know that we are making concrete plans." The president chopped his hand in the air. "If we can find that camp, and if—and this is a big *if*—we are reasonably assured that Lieutenant Commander Colcernian is there, we'll go get her. Zack, do you understand me?"

"Yes, sir, I do, Mr. President. Thank you, sir."

"How about you, Shannon?"

"Yes, sir. Thank you, sir."

"But what I want both of you to understand is that your work has not been in vain. This matter has not been swept under the rug, and it has my attention.

"Now then. I understand that Captain Hancock would like for us all to step into the Rose Garden for a photo op. And after that, I understand a certain JAG officer has a lunch date with my appointments secretary."

"Guilty as charged, sir."

"I've got a better idea," the president said. "Zack, why don't you and Shannon join me and the first lady for lunch upstairs in the presidential dining room. I'll invite Gale up too, and the two of you can catch up. That okay with you guys?"

"It would be an honor, Mr. President," Zack said.

"What do you say, Shannon?"

"Yes, sir, Mr. President."

Shannon's heart was about to explode. Lunch with the president and first lady. It was almost enough to make her want to switch parties. No wonder this man was the president of the United States.

"Good! Then it's a date!" The president smiled. "Let's go take some photos and then grab some chow."

CHAPTER 41

Jackson had just gotten off the telephone with the director of the California Democratic Party when his cell phone chirped. It was Eleanor.

"Yes, Senator."

"Jackson, I need you in the conference room. We've gotta talk. Now!" She hung up the phone. *Oh Lord, there's no other explanation. I've been discovered.*

He would have removed the blasted bug by now, but the timing had never been right. Either Eleanor or Mary-Latham or someone else was already around. He couldn't risk running his hand under the wooden table and pulling out the quarter-sized microphone without raising a question. His stomach dropped into his intestines as he entered the staff elevator. This was it. He knew it.

Could he talk to someone? Was there still a chance to survive? Maybe he could call Professor Gansky. But could he trust the professor?

Dear God, help me. The elevator reached the fifth floor. He'd done it again. He'd prayed to a God whom Yale claimed was nonexistent. What was making him do this? Or *who* was making him do it? It was as if a yearning within him was urging him to pray.

A moment later the elevator doors slid open. He flashed his identification badge to the Secret Service agents manning the entryway, then marched into the conference room.

They were all there. Eleanor, Ray Everton, Mary-Latham, and half a dozen others. Their angry eyes bore into him.

"What's up, guys?" were the only words he could blurt out.

"*This* is what's up," Eleanor snapped, shoving a paper across the table to a spot in front of the only unoccupied chair.

A detective's report showing fingerprints on the plastic, suction-cupped microphone. *His* fingerprints. And there was nothing his Yale degree could do about it.

"It's already all over the Internet," Eleanor roared. "Look at it." *Dear God, don't let me become a public spectacle.* "Pick it up!" the senator ordered.

And there was nowhere to run. Nothing to say. He had to face this like a man. Oh, that sounded so sexist!

He picked up the paper.

"Turn it over and look," Eleanor ordered.

He did, and the photograph deflated his fear like a pin stuck in a beach ball. Thank God. He gazed at the photograph off Yahoo News showing Zack Brewer, Shannon McGillvery, and the president of the United States smiling and shaking hands in the Rose Garden.

Under the photo, a byline with today's date chronicled the event.

Washington — (AP) President Williams met with Navy JAG officer LCDR Zack Brewer and NCIS Special Agent Shannon McGillvery this afternoon in the Oval Office. The president, who hand-selected Brewer to prosecute the two most famous courts-martial in U.S. military history, the cases of *U.S. v. Quasay* and *U.S. v. Olajuwon*, got to know Brewer during those cases and has remained friends with the JAG officer since. While speculation swirled that Brewer spoke with the president about the highly publicized ongoing court-martial against gay naval officer Ensign Wofford Eckberg, the White House declined to discuss the subject of the brief meeting, describing the topic as "private" and "personal."

"A meeting today," Eleanor snorted. "And these pictures are already spread all over the Internet. How dare he!"

"His pollsters ain't stupid, Eleanor," Ray Everton quipped. "They read the same polls I read." A tone of admiration crept into his voice. "And they're good." He paused. A slight smile crept across his face. "Dadgum good. If I were them, I'd do the exact same thing."

"And tomorrow morning," Eleanor fumed, "these pictures will be on the front page of every newspaper in the South!"

"Yep," Ray said. "That sums it up. I'm telling you, Eleanor, if we don't keep Brewer out of the headlines, he's gonna cost us on Super Tuesday." He swigged his coffee. "Big time."

Eleanor stood, stomped across the floor, crossed her arms, then stomped back to the head of the table.

"I won't lose the presidency because of some punk, right-wing, ego-centric naval officer. It *just* is not going to happen." She slammed her fist on the table. She stood there, her eyes blazing, almost as if they were aflame. Then she lowered her voice, speaking with an eerie raspiness. "Mary-Latham, prep a statement that it is inappropriate for the president of the United States to discuss an ongoing military court-martial with the prosecutor. Just don't use Brewer's name. Point out that this highly inappropriate meeting underscores this president's determination to perpetuate discrimination in the military, and that when I am elected, I will put a stop to it."

"You sure you want to do that, Eleanor?" Everton asked. "You might draw more attention to the photographs."

"Yes, I'm sure," she said, fuming. "Confine the releases to the press in California, Massachusetts, New York, and New Hampshire. But send the first press releases to the *San Francisco Chronicle* and the *Los Angeles Times*."

"I advise against it, Eleanor. You can't contain a press release like that. The national media will be all over it. But that's your call," Everton said.

"One other thing, Mary-Latham."

"Yes, Senator?"

"Call Mohammed. Tell him I want to see him in my suite in thirty minutes."

Dear God, no. She's going to put a contract out on somebody. Either me or Brewer.

"Sure, Eleanor."

"This meeting is adjourned."

Gobi Desert
Southeast of Ulaanbaatar, Mongolia

The rusty blade ripped through the upper walls of her stomach. Four ice picks were jabbed through her abdomen. The excruciating flashpoints compounded the broad swath of deep, dull pain radiating from cuts made by the rusty knife.

She twisted and turned and twisted again, and finally twisted herself awake.

Her elbows pushed her shriveling body into an upright position. She squinted, and like radar, her eyes swept back and forth, searching the dim images inside the dark tent that had been her prison all these months.

Sleeplessness brought about by the pain was, in an oxymoronic sense, a relief of sorts. Returning to her conscious state proved that Jeffrey Dahmer was not literally carving her stomach out. Nor was Jack the Ripper stabbing her with ice picks.

Eighteen days had passed since they brought the tasteless, floury gruel that clung to the inner walls of her stomach for an hour at best. The gruel never arrested the acute hunger pangs that worsened each day. She'd eaten nothing since.

She wiped the cold sweat from her forehead. Her body shook from the cold.

Quick death, she had decided, was preferable to torture from starvation and freezing temperatures. She had prayed for a fast, merciful death, but to no avail. Barring a miracle from God, she was resigned to the probability that her death would come slowly.

CHAPTER 42

Gobi Desert
Near the village of Choyr, Mongolia
Approximately 100 miles southeast of Ulaanbaatar

Saturday, 8:00 a.m.

As the snowfall thickened from a few scattered flakes to a blinding flurry, Willie tapped the brakes of the jeep provided by the International Mission Board. The vehicle slid, then regained traction. Even with a four-wheel-drive vehicle, travel through Mongolia's Gobi Desert was treacherous.

Thank the Lord, Pam hadn't come along. In their short ministry of three months here, several members of their congregation had ventured into the Gobi, never to come back.

Aside from the great Trans-Mongolian Railroad, which connected Ulaanbaatar with Jining, China, only a single, sparsely traveled, two-lane road snaked three hundred miles southeast to the Chinese border.

The first leg of the trip stretched from Ulaanbaatar about a hundred miles through the nomadic village of Choyr. Beyond Choyr, it was another 110 miles to the village of Sainted, and from there, about another hundred miles to the Chinese border.

When Willie Mangum was asked by his interviewers at the Southern Baptist International Mission Board if he would serve in a foreign land in a desert, he had readily accepted. Service to the Lord in a hot, sand-swept land, probably the Sahara, probably to nomadic peoples, would be an honor. Pam, too, had agreed in the interview that this was a sacrifice they were willing to make. And there was one bonus that the

Lord appeared ready to provide in return. They both hated cold weather. At least they wouldn't need to bring extra sleeping bags.

Then they learned of a place on earth—of a desert—that did not fit the sun-parched Arabian stereotype. The great rocky desert of Asia, the Gobi, which stretched across Southern Mongolia, was indeed home to sparsely populated nomadic tribes and fierce sandstorms, but that is where any similarity to the Sahara ended.

Rocks, boulders, steppes, freezing temperatures, and snowstorms. All of these climatic conditions dominated the barren landscape of the Gobi. Camels and gers were the only evidence of civilization out here.

Out in the desert somewhere, between thirty to fifty miles east of Sainted, was the alleged camp holding the mysterious redheaded woman. The plan was to drive to Sainted in the jeep, then travel through the barren, jagged terrain by camel.

With Willie driving the jeep and Jagtai in the passenger's seat, they were approaching the first village of Choyr, about a hundred miles southeast of Ulaanbaatar, when the light snow that had been falling turned treacherous.

"Watch the speed, Willie," Jagtai said. Willie glanced down and saw that they were traveling at forty-five miles per hour. "This road's turning to a sheet of ice."

"Got it." Willie eased up on the gas, but the snow only worsened. "How far to Choyr?"

"Ten miles."

Willie sent up a prayer, but within seconds blinding snow blanketed the windshield and all the windows. He gripped the wheel and tapped the brakes again. A ferocious wind blew snow and ice from left to right across the road. The jeep slid to the left, and they slammed into a snowdrift.

Willie hit the gas. The wheels spun on the ice.

"Try reverse," Jagtai said.

Willie shifted gears. The spinning tires dug the rear of the jeep deeper in the snow.

"Hmph," Willie grunted.

"How's our gas?" Jagtai asked.

"Quarter of a tank."

"Well, we can cut the engine and save gas, and run the risk of our battery dying under this ice and snow, or we can run the engine, stay warm, and risk carbon monoxide poisoning," Jagtai said. "Or we can get out and walk."

"Heavenly Father," Willie prayed, closing his eyes, "please clear these weather conditions soon. Keep us safe, guide us, and direct us. In Jesus' name. Amen."

He opened his eyes and turned off the engine.

Gobi Desert
Southeast of Ulaanbaatar, Mongolia

The flash of light and blast of cold air brought her eyes open.

She stared up, only up, focusing on the drab ceiling of the tent, determined to ignore them.

"Hungry, my pretty?"

The delectable aroma of cooked meat wafted from the direction of the voice. She looked over toward them. The outline of two silhouettes blocked the bright daylight from outside.

She lurched forward, in their direction. Hunger pangs intensified as the warm, juicy smell saturated the tent. Saliva streamed from her mouth.

"We have fresh roasted lamb," one of the scruffy-faced captors said. "And vegetables, fresh from the market in a nearby town."

They paraded the feast on a silver platter just by her cot. She fought the urge to leap at the steaming lamb, to cram it in her mouth and swallow before they took it away. Her stomach growled with fury.

"So," said the captor holding an AK-47 assault rifle, "you never answered my question." His associate, holding the feast on the platter, plastered a cheesy grin on his face.

"Your question." She eyed them both. "I guess I could eat something."

The rifle bearer reached down, grabbed his knee, and bellowed out a sinister laugh.

"Iqbal!" the rifle bearer cackled. "Come."

A third silhouette crossed the threshold into the ger. He had a portable video camera.

"Now then, my pretty." The rifle bearer aimed the AK-47 at her head. "I am sure you will agree that anyone must earn his right to eat."

She sat motionless.

"Because there is no such thing, as you Americans call it, as a free meal."

He seemed even more pleased with himself, eliciting laughter from the server and the camera bearer. Still she did not respond.

"All right. Read this for the camera, and then ... lunch is served!" He laughed again.

He handed her the sheet of paper.

"*I denounce the United States of America, which has engaged in a pro-Zionist policy that embraces the fascist dictatorship of Israel while murdering thousands of innocent Arab and Palestinian women and children. I have seen the true light. The blood of these women and children is on President Williams' hands.*

"*I ask forgiveness from the families of the three Islamic chaplains who were murdered by the United States Navy. May Allah have mercy on my soul for my part in this atrocity. May Allah have mercy on us all.*"

"So easy. Is it not? Read and you will never be hungry again."

Her eyes fixed on the lamb. Her stomach shifted gears like the transmission of a stock car jumping into high speed. Excruciating pangs of hunger tore into her stomach.

CHAPTER 43

Claxton campaign
Sheerwater Restaurant
Hotel del Coronado
1500 Orange Avenue
Coronado, California

Thursday, 1:30 p.m. (PST)

They sat on the veranda outside the Del's oceanfront restaurant, where Jackson stirred his salad with his fork. The croutons needed rearranging, then rearranging again.

"You've not eaten anything," chided Mary-Latham, who had joined him for lunch.

Jackson checked his watch. "Watching my figure."

"Jackson, you're skinny as a rail."

"Okay. Trying to stay skinny as a rail."

Mary-Latham smiled, sipping a spoonful of clam chowder. "So what's your schedule this afternoon?"

Jackson checked his watch. "In one hour I'm due across the Coronado Bay Bridge for a fundraising speech to the San Diego County Democratic Party. And after that, an interview with the local NBC affiliate, KNSD-TV. Then I make the rounds at KFMB and KGTV, the local CBS and ABC affiliates." He abandoned his salad and grabbed his glass of water. "How about you?"

"Same old stuff." She sipped her coffee. "Press releases. More pieces ripping the navy for allowing hate crimes against Eckberg. Prepping statements for Web Wallace to read about Ekberg's broken collarbone at a presser we've scheduled for this afternoon. And then that thing about congratulating the NCIS and SDPD for apprehending Jacoby's shooter was a bit of a challenge to get just right."

Their eyes met, and her left eyebrow rose. "Jackson, did you find that a bit odd?"

Of course I found it odd. Especially since that police detective told me that Reynolds bought the gun in Vegas after Jacoby was shot. Should I talk to Mary-Latham about this? Can I trust her?

"You never know. Politics is a strange game."

"I've gotten a few inquiries about Chris Reynolds being Jacoby's killer, but most of the press seems to be buying off on it."

"Mindless sheep," Jackson grunted.

"And fortunately for us, liberal mindless sheep ready to be manipulated to suit our campaign's agenda."

"No kidding," he said. "So where's Eleanor?"

"With Mohammed. Took me awhile to track him down. They were supposed to meet at one o'clock."

"So where was he?" Jackson downed the glass of water and motioned for the waiteress to bring the check.

"Who knows with him?"

"Right."

"Don't you find their relationship a bit odd?" A curious look crossed Mary-Latham's face. Maybe he *could* open up with her. They'd been together off and on for more than ten years, since their time at Yale.

"Maybe a bit." He paused. "He's different. He seems to have the senator's ear."

"Yeah. All alone when nobody else is around. I wonder what they're talking about."

Tell her. You've gotta tell her.

"Who knows?" He checked his watch. "Anyway, I've got to get rolling."

"Yeah, me too."

Jackson checked the bill. He handed the waitress two twenties. "Keep the change."

"Oh, thank you, sir," the blonde waitress gushed.

He looked at Mary-Latham. "I'm going up to my room, then across the bridge."

"Raise a lot of money for the party." She winked and walked him to the elevator.

Five minutes later, he was in his personal suite. He looked around to make sure that no one else was there, then walked to the closet in his bedroom. The receiver and recording device were hidden in a suitcase under some underwear. He threw the suitcase on the bed and tossed the underwear out of the suitcase.

The blinking light meant that somebody in Eleanor Claxton's suite had said something in the last hour, which, according to Mary-Latham, would have been the time the senator was with Mohammad.

Shrill, Mickey-Mouse-like squeaking pierced the air as he rewound the tape. He punched the play button.

"Mary-Latham said you wanted to see me?"

"I just wanted to tell you that this is your lucky day."

"How's that, Senator?"

"The press seems to think that that lunatic stalker, Chris Reynolds, knocked off Jacoby. Seems like he was intent on killing all the military lawyers involved in the Eckberg court-martial."

"Hmm. Maybe they're onto something."

"Yeah, maybe."

"So is that why you called me up here? To tell me that the press has solved the mystery of the Jacoby murder?"

"Listen, Mohammed. We've got a real problem with Zack Brewer."

Silence occurred at this point. Fifteen seconds later, Mohammed's voice resurfaced on the tape.

"What kind of a problem, Senator?"

"A real problem."

"A Karen Jacoby–like problem?"

"Let's put it this way: if Brewer stays in the limelight, it could cost me the election. That can't happen."

"Let me ask again, Senator. Is this a Karen Jacoby–like problem?"

"Think about it, Mohammed!" Her angry voice pounded Jackson's eardrum. *"He could cost me the presidency! Read between the lines!"*

"Okay! Okay, Eleanor! I'm two steps ahead of you. I've already started surveillance on the guy. The navy was hiding him over at North Island—at least until they flew him to Washington—and NCIS has been hauling him around in a white panel truck. I'm going to—"

"I don't want to hear details. Okay?"

"Okay. Sorry."

"I just want to make sure that we're on the same page."

"We're on the same page, Eleanor."

"Good. Then get out of here and get to work."

Jackson's lungs pumped out of control. *Dear God, what is going on?* He felt as though hand grenades were exploding inside his chest and as though bullets were ricocheting in his throat. He jumped up from the bed, tripped, and fell. He scrambled to his feet, tossed the underwear back on top of the recording device, zipped the suitcase closed, and put it back in the closet.

He needed a cold shower. Fast. Even if he was late for his speech.

He saw a Bible, published by the Gideons, on the table beside his bed. In three days, he hadn't noticed it. Maybe the maid had put it there. Something pushed his hands toward it. The book fell open to a passage in Exodus.

"Thou shalt not kill."

His eyes were drawn to a passage a few verses above that.

"Thou shalt have no other gods before me ... For I the LORD thy God am a jealous God."

Why were these words striking his soul at this very moment? Why did they feel almost like medicine in the midst of turmoil?

Of course killing was wrong. Everyone knew that. But it seemed to him that the Bible was speaking to him about the circumstances that were tearing him apart right now. But there was no God. His professors had ridiculed the ignorant, emotional Christian right.

But if there was no God, then why was he here? Why was this information being revealed to him? Could it be coincidence?

His professors were wrong. There was a true God. His god had been politics. His god had led him to this moment, to the one true God above all, who had placed him here for a purpose.

And if there was a true God, then he—Jackson Kennedy Gallopoulous—had put the god of politics before the one true God.

"God, if you are there, reveal yourself. Help me! Somehow, some way. Help me do what's right!"

Gobi Desert
Southeast of Ulaanbaatar, Mongolia

The hunger demanded that she just read it.

She could always retract it later.

Plus, if she read it, maybe someone would see it and know that she was still alive.

Maybe her country would come rescue her. Certainly Zack would come if he saw her on television. Wouldn't he?

Maybe reading it was her only hope of survival. No one would actually believe she meant it. It was understood that hostages are forced to do such things under tortuous conditions. She looked at the script once more, and then the officer's oath that she had taken so many years ago flooded her mind.

"I will support and defend the Constitution of the United States against all enemies, foreign and domestic."

"You no want to eat?" The startling sound of chinking steel reverberated through the tent. The man had cocked his rifle and pointed it straight at her head. "Read!" The gunner nodded at the cameraman, and a red light on the camera flashed on. "Or I blow your head off!"

Her body shook. She could not stop it. She prayed silently. Someone took charge of her lips.

"Man does not live by bread alone, but by every word that proceeds from the mouth of God."

"Read, foolish woman!"

Her body calmed. The shaking stopped. The words that had rolled off her lips had calmed her. She felt supernatural boldness. "Rather than betray my country, I will eat your bullets!"

The rifle butt swung around like a baseball bat, crashing into her jaw. She saw stars, then blackness.

CHAPTER 44

U.S. Navy C-9
Final approach to Naval Air Station North Island
Friday, 5:00 p.m. (PST)

The U.S. Navy C-9 carrying Zack and Shannon crossed Mount McGill and then, descending to fifteen hundred feet, passed over the buildings of downtown San Diego, their magnificent glass reflecting the orange glow of the sun making its downward trek toward the Pacific.

Soon they were over the ocean, where the pilot, a navy lieutenant, made a wide, arching loop, bringing the plane back toward the southeast. Shannon felt the plane nose down toward Naval Air Station North Island, located at the tip of the long peninsula that separated San Diego Bay and downtown San Diego from the Pacific Ocean.

She looked across the aisle and saw the only other passenger in the cabin. She wondered how he could have slept so much on the return flight, after having spent the morning with the president of the United States.

Oh well. Just another day in the life of Zack Brewer, I suppose.

"Zack!" No response. "Zack!" She reached over and shook his shoulder.

"Yeah?" He yawned and rubbed his eyes.

"We're landing. Strap in."

"Thanks." He yawned again and fastened his seat belt.

A moment later she felt a bump as the plane's tires touched the concrete runway.

"Commander, Special Agent McGillvery, welcome home," boomed the navy pilot's voice over the loudspeaker. "We'll be taxiing over to the hangar, and the ground crew will bring a boarding ladder over to get you on the ground. Should be a couple more minutes."

The pilot's voice over the loudspeaker seemed to draw Zack out of his sleepy state. His eyes widened and he sat up a bit. "What time is it?"

"Little after 1700 hours local," she said.

"Quick flight."

"You slept the whole way."

"Need my beauty sleep."

A petty officer, a member of the flight crew, opened the door of the plane. Fading daylight and the cool San Diego breeze rushed into the cabin. "Boarding ladder's ready, Commander." His comments were directed to Zack. "Anytime you're ready to deplane."

Zack stood up and held out his hand, motioning for Shannon to stand. "Ladies first."

She stood, walked out ahead of him, and then stepped onto the platform at the top of the boarding ladder. Her boss, Barry MacGregor, and Zack's commanding officer, Captain Glen Rudy, were waiting at the base of the ladder. Both stood with their arms crossed and their necks craned up, staring at the exit ladder. Looks of consternation crossed their faces. Perhaps they were angry that she and Zack had jumped the chain of command. And boy, had they ever jumped the chain.

"Uh-oh." Zack stepped out onto the platform just behind her. "They don't look too happy."

"No kidding."

"Well, let's go face the music."

They stepped down about fifteen steps. Barry spoke first. "Shannon, we need to talk to the two of you."

"Barry, we had just run out of options—"

He held his hand up. "Forget that. I understand why you did what you did."

"You do?"

"Shannon, Chris Reynolds died about an hour ago."

The news hit her like a stun gun. Her lips froze. She had known that her job might one day require her to kill. But to come to grips with it . . . She looked at Zack, who put his arm around her shoulder and lowered his head.

"Oh dear God, please help me," she could only whisper. Her vocal cords constricted. "What have I done? I've killed a man."

Zack put his other arm around her and drew her close. "Shannon, what you did is your duty. You're my bodyguard. You saved my life, and who knows how many more."

Babcock & Story Bar
Hotel del Coronado
1500 Orange Avenue
Coronado, California

Friday, 9:00 p.m. (PST)

Sitting alone at the corner of the bar, Jackson sipped on a beer as he waited for Mary-Latham to arrive. There was no way she could be in on this, even if his worst fears were true. Eleanor had always made sure that she was one-on-one with Mohammed, and the tapes made no mention of Mary-Latham. The only remote connection he had observed was that Eleanor always seemed to ask Mary-Latham to make the contact with Mohammed.

They'd dated on and off at Yale, and at an academic powerhouse where the coed selection was not particularly choice, Mary-Latham was a flower on the frozen tundra. He would never tell her that he thought of her in that manner. She would punch him and call him a sexist.

That thought brought a smile to his face. He lifted the bottle of Corona to his lips.

Jackson had to reckon with his feelings. He'd harbored a long-standing soft spot for her, and as his doubts about Eleanor had grown, so had his longing for Mary-Latham.

No, he was certain, there was no way she was in on it. And the raised eyebrows from earlier today ... the question about Eleanor's odd relationship with Mohammed ... Perhaps Mary-Latham was having second thoughts too.

He finished the beer and ordered a second. Frankly, if he could sweep her off to a tropical island somewhere, he would do it in a heartbeat. Forget the lure of the White House. Forget liberal idealism. He could trust her. He knew he could.

"How'd your day go?"

He looked up in the direction of the velvet voice. She had ditched the pantsuit for a black skirt and sleeveless top. *Wow.*

"Have a seat." He stood and gently helped her onto a bar stool. "Want a drink?"

"Margarita." She smiled. He ordered.

"You look great tonight."

Her smile melted him. "You don't look half bad yourself, if you know what I mean."

A server brought her margarita and his beer. "Part of my day went great, to answer your question." She held out her glass, as if inviting him to toast. He clanked his bottle against her glass. "To Roosevelt, Kennedy, Clinton, and Truman," she said.

"I'll drink to that quartet of Democratic giants."

They sipped their drinks. "And what part of your day went so great?"

"I raised a lot of money for your Democratic Party," he said.

"Hmm." She sipped her drink. "You handsome, money-grubbing devil, you." There was another toast. "And what about the rest of your day?"

"Mary-Latham." He reached across the table for her hand. She extended her palm and rubbed her thumb gently against his lifelines. "There's something I need to talk to you about, but I need to know that it remains confidential."

"How confidential?"

"Absolutely. From everyone. And especially everyone we work with and for."

"I understand." She gave him another heart-melting smile and sipped her margarita with the hand that was not caressing his. "Jackson, whatever you say stays with me. I don't know if you realize how much you mean to me."

She leaned over and kissed him on the cheek.

And then their lips met.

Russian twin-engine aircraft
Altitude 6,000 feet
Over Sainted, Mongolia
260 miles southeast of Ulaanbaatar

Saturday, 2:30 p.m. (local time)

The plane turned and shook and rocked through the sky.

"Aaah! Aaah!" the woman shrieked.

"Shut up!" Fadil grabbed the back of the seat in front of him and yelled at Jeanette L'Enfant, whose sedatives had worn off.

"Dieu m'aide! Dieu m'aide! Dieu m'aide!" she screamed.

"Hang on!" Sergey said. "Pilots say heavy cross-winds! We try land again!"

The engines revved. The plane nosed down, and the rocky horizon was up, then down, then up again.

"Hang on!" Sergey yelled again.

"Je veux morir!"

"You want to die? You may get your chance," Fadil snapped back.

The ground came up, there was a violent bump, and the plane bounced like a soccer ball. A large gust of wind caught under the wing, and Fadil felt it start to flip. "In the name of Allah!" The pilots pushed on the throttle. The twin engines responded, pulling the plane back into the sky. Now the wings were waving up and down like a seesaw.

"Pilot say hang on! We try land again. Must land soon! Low on fuel!"

The plane swung around, trying to line up with the dirt runway. It was dropping like a rock, it seemed. The wings dipped sharply to the left. The nose went up. And they plummeted.

The left wing dipped into the runway, spraying a cloud of dirt. Then the wheels touched. They lifted off. The plane slammed into the ground, then bounced up. Then down again. Bumping up and down. Up and down. The plane slowed. Finally, they came to a rest.

On the ground, the howling wind threatened to blow them back into the air.

Fadil looked out the window. The dirt airstrip was surrounded by rocky terrain. Three Arab men were leading camels toward the plane.

He turned around and looked back. The woman, whose hands were cuffed, was sitting between Ghazi Jawad and Salah Abdul-Alim. "Looks like you won't get to die yet," he said in French.

She shot him a silent, angry glare through streaming tears.

"At least you've stopped your maniacal screaming."

She squirmed and continued to stare at him.

He sneered, then turned to Sergey, handing him an envelope. "Give this to your pilot friends. Five thousand for their services, plus the last thousand we owe you and your men. This brings us to the end of our road together. Best wishes finding your way back to Russia."

"Spaceeba," Sergey said, thanking Fadil in Russian.

Fadil turned back to the woman. "Look on the bright side, my beautiful. At least you will have an infidel friend to keep you company soon." That thought brought a laugh from Ghazi Jawad. "And her hair is even the same color as yours!" More laughing from the Islamic trio.

The door to the plane opened. A cold blast of air rushed in. "My brother!" A smiling, scruffy-faced Arab-looking man stuck his face inside the plane. "Welcome to Mongolia. We are ready for you now!"

"Let's go!" Fadil ordered.

Ghazi and Salah shoved the woman up, then out the door. Fadil followed them out into the cold.

This was it.

The last leg of his journey to glory.

Gobi Desert
Near the village of Choyr, Mongolia
Approximately 100 miles southeast of Ulaanbaatar

Saturday, 3:00 p.m. (local time)

The snow had stopped over four hours ago, yielding way to the Mongolian sunshine. Even still, the heavy snowbank had made their escape impossible. So far, anyway. They had started the engine every hour, running it for fifteen minutes to keep heat in the cabin. They would need to find gasoline if and when they made it as far as Choyr.

"It's a funny thing," Jagtai said. "Where we are headed, one hundred miles south of here, it is probably dry and warm."

Willie shivered under one of the quilts they had brought along. "Yeah, right. You native Mongolians think thirty-two degrees is warm."

Jagtai laughed. "Looks like it's melted some more. Want to try again?"

"What have we got to lose?" Willie quipped. "Just let fifty-below-zero air temperature in here when we open the door. That's all."

"Okay. I'll push. You crank the engine."

Willie turned the key and prayed. The starter whined, then whined some more. "Please, Lord, make it start." More whining, and then contact. "Thank you, Lord."

Jagtai got out and tromped around to the back of the jeep. "Ready?"

"Here goes!" Willie pressed on the gas. There was traction, and the jeep crawled out of the snowbank and back onto the road. "Thank you, Lord!" Willie yelled. "And thank you, Jagtai!"

Jagtai climbed back into the jeep, and they high-fived each other. Warm air now blew from the heater. Willie put his icy fingers in front of one of the vents.

"Let's go find a terrorist camp!" Jagtai was rubbing the palms of his hands together.

"I'm with you, brother!" Willie kicked the jeep back in gear, and they rolled out to the southeast.

CHAPTER 45

Special Agent Shannon McGillvery's residence
5800 Urban Drive
La Mesa, California

Friday, 11:30 p.m. (PST)

After making sure that Zack was tucked safely away in his quarters in the Navy Lodge, Shannon had arrived at the home she was renting in La Mesa. She had been home about thirty minutes when she sat down in her den and booted up her computer. The Quasay file had long since been closed. Now she created a related file: "In the matter of LCDR Diane J. Colcernian." Her investigation was now officially reopened.

She tried hard to focus on the file. But Diane was not the woman whose image kept appearing in her head. Surely Chris Reynolds had a mother. Somewhere. What was she feeling right now?

The idea that Reynolds, no matter how sick or deranged he was, would never see the light of day again haunted her. Surely there were good, decent things he did in life. Innocent walks in the park? Maybe a simple cup of coffee? Not even the simple things of life would ever be enjoyed by him again. All because of her.

The events of the last forty-eight hours had left her unable to sleep. Yet she still sipped on black coffee, perhaps out of nervousness more than anything. To shoot a man in the course of duty, then to fly to Washington for a meeting with the president, then to have lunch with the president and the first lady, and then to fly home and discover that the man she had shot was dead—all of it was a churning, surrealistic blur.

She was in love with Zack, and Zack was in love with Diane. And now if she could deliver her to him, what sort of ironic gift would that be? Maybe, maybe in some way it could assuage the wrong she had committed by killing a man.

Focus, Shannon. Focus on your job.

She studied the map in the file.

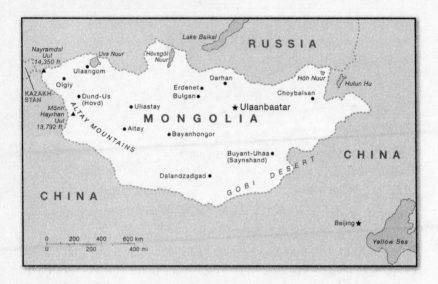

Where?

Where could they be hiding her? There was less than one week until execution of Plan 547. That is, assuming she was counting correctly. There could be less time than that.

"From this map, the Gobi Desert appears to stretch along the Chinese border for hundreds of miles. There has to be a way to pin this down!"

Her cell phone broke her concentration. The number was restricted. "McGillvery."

"Special Agent McGillvery?"

"Yes?"

"This is Jackson Gallopoulous."

"Who?"

"From the Claxton campaign."

"Oh, yeah." *Is this a hoax?* "How'd you get my number?"

"When you work for the senator, you have access to information."

A pause. "What can I do for you, Mr. Gallopoulous?"

"I need to talk to you."

"About what?"

"Commander Brewer."

"What about him?"

"Look, I can't go into it over the phone. Can you meet me?"

"When?"

"Now."

"Now?"

"It's urgent."

"Where?"

"Cabrillo National Monument. Point Loma."

"It's nearly midnight. Cabrillo's closed."

"That's why I want to meet you there. You can go under the gate. We need total privacy."

"How do I know you're who you say you are?"

"I can't prove that before we meet. Trust your instincts. Let me put it this way: I don't think Karen Jacoby was killed by Chris Reynolds."

That stopped her cold. "I'll see you in thirty minutes."

"I'll be there."

Cabrillo National Monument
Point Loma
San Diego, California

Saturday, 12:15 a.m. (PST)

The midnight moon flooded the tombstones as Shannon's car crept along Cabrillo Memorial Drive, right through the middle of Fort Rosecrans National Cemetery. The entrance to the monument area was about two hundred yards ahead, so she cut her lights, edging forward at no more than five miles per hour.

She stopped in front of the steel gate that swung across the entrance to the monument area. She cut the engine, then picked up her nine-millimeter. No other cars were around. She worked the bolt action and turned off the safety, then got out of the car.

Gripping the gun, she walked around the steel gate and down the solitary road toward the monument, which was probably a quarter mile ahead and not yet visible.

There were no signs of life, and as she rounded the small bend in the deserted road, she saw the statue of Juan Rodriguez Cabrillo standing sentry several hundred feet over the entrance to San Diego Bay.

She followed the brick pathway leading to the statue, which was located on a large circular brick patio on the cliff at the point above the great waterways of the city. The Pacific was off to the right, carpeted with the rich glow of the three-quarter moon. Straight ahead, across the entrance of the bay and down at sea level, Naval Air Station North Island jutted out at the end of the Coronado Peninsula. Off to the left, the lights of downtown San Diego and the 32nd Street Naval Station sparkled in the most vibrant naval city in the world.

"Agent McGillvery."

She whirled and pointed her gun in the direction of the voice. She could see the silhouette of a man in the shadows.

"It's me, Jackson Gallopoulous."

"Forgive me for my caution, Mr. Gallopoulous, but please raise your hands and approach slowly, and stop when I tell you."

"By all means." The figure raised his hands over his head and took one step. Then another. Three steps later, he was close enough.

"Stop right there."

The figure complied.

She pulled a flashlight from her jeans with her left hand and spotted his face. The subject squinted. As his eyes adjusted to the light, she recognized the face of the man she had seen on television. She killed the flashlight.

"Okay. I recognize you, Mr. Gallopoulous. Come on over."

"Can I put my hands down?"

"Sure."

He approached slowly. His boyish face was now visible in the moonlight.

"There's something I want to show you."

"About Brewer?"

"Indirectly. I think so."

"Okay."

He pulled a manila envelope from under his shirt. "Take a look at this."

She opened the envelope, shined the flashlight on the documents inside, and quickly read through them.

"These are websites suggesting the former vice president and your boss may be involved in the deaths of their subordinates?"

"Yes, I know."

"This is bizarre, Mr. Gallopoulous. Why show me this?"

"I think Zack Brewer may be in danger."

"What? You think your boss is going to bump off Zack or something?"

No answer.

"These rumors have swirled in the public domain for several years now. Weren't you aware of them?"

"I never gave them credence," he said.

"And now you do?"

Still no answer.

"If you believe any of this, then why work for her?"

"Look, I don't know if we have a lot of time here or not. All of this is happening so fast. Let's say I've come across some information that has me deeply concerned."

She studied his face in the moonlight. Why would a man of his stature be telling her this? Unless ... maybe...

"Look, Mr. Gallopoulous, we're already protecting Zack. In case you haven't heard, I killed a man this week who tried to shoot him."

"Yes, I heard."

"So what do you want me to do?"

Their eyes met. "Get Zack Brewer out of town, out of the country, to a place where Eleanor Claxton or anybody who works for her can't get to him."

"Like where?"

"I can't say."

"Mr. Gallopoulous, I appreciate all this, but you haven't given me much. With all due respect, I'd heard these rumors, and I could have done that Internet search myself."

"I understand. You'll have a package delivered to your house first thing in the morning."

"Is there anything you want to tell me?"

"Get Zack out of here."

"It's been interesting, Mr. Gallopoulous."

"Hear me. I'm pleading with you. Get him out of here."

He turned and disappeared into the dark.

Special Agent Shannon McGillvery's residence
5800 Urban Drive
La Mesa, California

Saturday, 8:30 a.m. (PST)

She had been up since seven o'clock, going through the Colcernian file, and now, after setting it aside for a moment, she studied the dossier of alleged deaths that Jackson Gallopoulous had provided her.

Zack was a potential political liability to the Claxton campaign. Especially if he wound up beating Web Wallace in court—which he likely would do. Maybe Gallopoulous had been sent by the senator as a ploy to get Zack off the case so that Wallace could get Eckberg off the hook. But how did that explain the websites?

Her front doorbell rang. She opened the door. "Package for a Miss McGillvery," the UPS man said.

"That's me."

"Sign here."

The package contained two cassette tapes. There was no return address. She walked into the kitchen and popped the first cassette into a tape player.

"You think radical Islam is dirty? You haven't seen anything. What goes on out of the public's eye makes 9/11 look like a picnic in the park. Get my drift? This was a dirty business before you came along, and if there are any more surprises, you are gone."

"Why, Senator, if I didn't know better, I would think you are threatening me."

"Let me put it this way, Mohammed. You aren't the first individual to work for me or my husband and carry out the duties that you do. Now, some of those people are still around. Some aren't. The ones who aren't deviated from the script. Some decided to take inside information from our campaigns and use it for political or monetary gain. Some tried blackmailing by threatening to go to the authorities or the press.

"But now they are gone, Mohammed. Every one of them.

Shannon finished listening to the first cassette, then popped in the second.

"Listen, Mohammed. We've got a real problem with Zack Brewer."

"What kind of a problem, Senator?"

"A real problem."

"A Karen Jacoby – like problem?"

"Let's put it this way: if Brewer stays in the limelight, it could cost me the election. That can't happen."

"Let me ask again, Senator. Is this a Karen Jacoby – like problem?"

"Think about it, Mohammed! He could cost me the presidency! Read between the lines!"

"Okay! Okay, Eleanor! I'm two steps ahead of you. I've already started surveillance on the guy. The navy was hiding him over at North Island—at least until they flew him to Washington—and NCIS has been hauling him around in a white panel truck. I'm going to—"

"I don't want to hear details. Okay?"

"Okay. Sorry."

Shannon put the tapes in her briefcase, grabbed her keys, and rushed out the door. What to do? If these tapes were authentic, no wonder Jackson Gallopoulous reacted the way he did. But were they authentic? The female voice sure sounded like Eleanor Claxton.

She *had* to get to Naval Air Station North Island. She *had* to check on Zack.

She raced down Urban Avenue and in a matter of minutes was on westbound Interstate 8. Something told her to punch on the radio.

"This just in from Coronado. In a stunning development, Jackson Gallopoulous, the campaign manager for the campaign of U.S. Senator Eleanor Claxton, is dead. Gallopoulous's body was spotted floating in San Diego Bay this morning next to the Star of India. Police retrieved the body from the water and discovered a gunshot wound to the head.

"An autopsy is scheduled to be performed later today, but according to preliminary reports, police speculate that Gallopoulous's death was a suicide.

"According to sources close to the campaign, Gallopoulous had become very depressed and was seeking treatment for the depression.

"Senator Claxton released a statement through a spokesperson describing Jackson Gallopoulous as a personal friend and a patriotic American whose passionate desire was to serve his country. According to the senator, he will be sorely missed.

"Stay tuned to KSDO for more information on this breaking story."
Chills shot down her spine. What sort of a powder keg was she sitting on? The radio report convinced her that she would need to make an extra stop before going to Zack's. She picked up her cell phone and scrolled down the list of stored numbers. She punched the talk button, and a moment later the commanding officer of the Navy Trial Command was on the line.

"Captain Rudy? Shannon McGillvery here. Sorry to disturb you on a Saturday, but I need to see you immediately ... Your home at Coronado? ... Yes, sir. I'll be there in about thirty minutes, sir."

8 East Fourth Avenue
Coronado Island
Coronado, California

Saturday, 9:30 a.m. (PST)

The morning sun was already glistening off the palm trees towering over the white stucco cottage on San Diego County's posh Coronado

Island when Shannon pulled up. She opened the door and stepped out. The warm morning breeze from the Pacific caressed her face. She grabbed the envelope and her briefcase and walked past the black Ford Expedition with the blue-and-white eagle sticker on the windshield, signifying that an officer holding the rank of O-6 in the U.S. military was the driver of the car.

She rang the doorbell, and Captain Glen Rudy, in a gold-and-blue U.S. Navy sweatshirt and blue jeans, opened the door.

"Sorry to bother you this morning, Captain."

"It's okay, Shannon. Come in."

He directed her to a sofa in his living room. "Have you heard the news this morning about Jackson Gallopoulous?"

"Claxton's campaign manager?" Rudy nodded his head. "Yeah, I heard. Don't agree with his politics, but that's a shame."

"Well, sir, I may have been one of the last people to see him alive."

"What?" A puzzled look crossed his face.

"He called me at home last night before midnight. Wanted me to meet him at Cabrillo National Monument at Point Loma. He said Zack's life was in danger and wanted me to get Zack out of town. He gave me this."

She handed him the Internet reports. He studied them. "Yeah, I've heard rumors about this stuff. I suppose Gallopoulous's suicide will add to all this."

"If that's what it was."

He looked at her over his reading glasses.

"If it was a suicide, sir."

"What are you saying?"

"The last thing Gallopoulous told me was that I'd be getting a package this morning." She looked at him. "I did get a package, sir. Two audio tapes. I'd like you to listen."

Rudy nodded his head. Shannon popped the tapes in.

Ten minutes later, Shannon asked, "What do you make of it, sir?"

Rudy scratched his chin. "Disturbing." He seemed to be deep in thought.

"Captain, we've got to get Zack out of here."

Rudy walked across the living room and looked out the window. "That could be problematic. He's in the middle of this court-martial, and—"

"Captain, please. Someone murdered Jacoby. Then I have this bizarre meeting with Gallopoulous last night and this morning he's floating in San Diego Bay with a gunshot wound to his head. Something's going on, Captain. I can't put my finger on it. Yet. But my instinct tells me Zack may be in danger. If there's anything at all, Captain, any connections you have in Washington, I ask you now to pull those strings." She paused, then added, "Sir."

Their eyes met.

"Please, Captain Rudy."

He stood with his arms crossed. "Listen, Shannon, why don't you drive over to the air station and check on Zack. I need to make a couple of phone calls."

"Yes, sir."

CHAPTER 46

Room 207, Navy Lodge
Rogers Road
Naval Air Station North Island
Coronado, California

Saturday, 10:00 a.m. (PST)

Shannon banged on the wooden door, then banged some more. "Dear Jesus, let him be okay." Panic set in as she fumbled for her cell phone. The naval air station was more secure than Zack's La Mesa home, and the Navy Lodge was located two miles inside the gate. But still, if somebody wanted to get to him ... She hit speed dial.

"Where *are* you?"

"Can't a guy have some breakfast?"

"You didn't answer my question. Where *are* you?"

"At the O-Club having a veggie omelet. Come over and I'll order you something."

"Don't go anywhere. Please."

"Okay, okay. What do you want?"

"Anything. I don't care. I'll be right there."

Officer's Club
L Road
Naval Air Station North Island
Coronado, California

The white linen tablecloth was adorned with a small vase of yellow mums, which, along with the silver water pitcher and the half-eaten veggie omelet, provided an idyllic foreground to the panoramic view of the sandy white beach and rolling blue Pacific. Indeed, the navy controlled some of the most beautiful and most expensive beachfront real estate in the world, which was one of the reasons he'd chosen the sea service over the army.

"More coffee, Commander?"

"Thanks, Sam."

Zack sipped the hot, freshly ground Folgers coffee, then forked his omelet. Somewhere across the Pacific, beyond Hawaii, beyond the Philippines, beyond Japan and Korea and China, was Mongolia. If only she were alive. If only she could sit here with him now, in this safe, beautiful place.

Lord, somehow ... some way ...

"Zack!"

He turned and saw Shannon, out of breath and wearing a navy warm-up suit, standing over his shoulder. She looked good in warm-ups, but it was a wonder they let her in the O-Club without the proper attire. She probably flashed her NCIS badge and walked on past the host.

"I've been so worried about you, Zack."

"Worried about me? You get paid to worry, Shannon. That's why you're so good at what you do. Have a seat. I ordered you an omelet."

Shannon sat down across from him just as his phone rang.

"It's Captain Rudy. I'd better take it." He put the phone to his ear. "Yes, sir. Yes, she's here with me right now. Here she is." He gave the phone to Shannon. "He wants to speak with you."

"Yes, sir ... Yes, sir ... Thank you, Captain." She smiled. "He wants to speak to you again." She handed the phone back.

"Really, sir? ... In one hour? ... What about the *Eckberg* case? ... I don't have time to pack? ... Very well, sir ... Aye, aye, sir." Zack closed his cell phone. "Can you believe that? They want me on a PC3 Orion for Kaneohe Bay MCAF in one hour."

"Hawaii! What's it all about?"

"He said I'd be briefed on the plane. Probably some mobile JAG trial team where they've got to do a quick court-martial or something."

Hangar 3
Naval Air Station North Island

10:45 a.m. (PST)

That looks like our bird," Zack said as they drove up into the parking area of Hangar 3. The large PC3 Orion, the navy's only land-based anti-submarine type aircraft, already had its four propeller engines running.

On the side was the emblem of the face of an eagle, set within a black circle, along with the words *Patrol Squadron 47* painted in gold.

They exited the car. The warm blast from the Orion's massive propellers blew in their faces.

A black Ford Expedition drove up with Zack's commanding officer at the wheel. Special Agent Alan Raynor was with him.

Captain Rudy, a stocky, ruddy-faced Texan, stepped out of the Expedition. He was in his working khaki uniform. Raynor, who had a gym bag draped over his shoulder, walked around the Expedition and joined Rudy.

Zack saluted his commanding officer. Rudy returned the salute.

"Just wanted to come out and wish you a safe flight." A smiling Rudy extended his hand.

"It was nice of you to come out, Skipper, but I hate that whatever they have me doing interrupted your Saturday."

"No interruption," Rudy said. "I live here on the island, less than a couple of miles away. Anyway, how'd you like some company on the flight?"

"Love to have you, Skipper."

"Well, I'd love to go, Zack. After thirty years in the navy, I'm still a sucker for Hawaii. But Agent Raynor has never been there. Mind if he rides along?"

Zack met Shannon's eyes. "Sure. Why not? The more the merrier."

A master chief, wearing an olive-drab flight suit, was walking from the direction of the Orion. He shot salutes at Captain Rudy and Zack. "Captain, Commander, I'm Master Chief O'Connor. Welcome to VP-47. Ready to go to paradise?"

"I believe the commander here and Special Agent Raynor are your passengers today, Master Chief," Captain Rudy said.

"Gentlemen, we're ready when you are."

"Zack," Shannon said, reaching for his shoulder, "take care of yourself." She gave him a soft smile.

He touched her shoulder. "See you soon. Okay?"

"You can count on it." She pecked him on the cheek.

"Let's go, Alan," Zack said, then followed the master chief up the boarding ladder and into the Orion.

Fifteen minutes later, with Raynor beside him in the aisle seat, Zack looked down as the Orion lifted off into the Pacific breeze. Why did he have a feeling that it would be a long time before he returned?

A few minutes later, he could see nothing below except the blue waters of the Pacific.

"Okay, Alan, what's the scoop?"

"What do you mean, Zack?"

"I mean, what's going on? What's the real reason that I'm on this plane, and why are you here with me?"

"You want to know now?"

"Now's as good a time as any."

"Hang on." Raynor reached down into his gym bag and retrieved an envelope. He handed it to Zack. "I'm supposed to stay with you until you are safely at your destination. Then you're on your own."

Zack opened the envelope and scanned the memo inside.

From: Commander Naval Personnel Command (NPC)
To: LCDR Zachary Brewer, JAGC, USN
Via: Commanding Officer, Navy Trial Command Southwest
            Commanding Officer, USS *Ronald Reagan* (CVN 76)
Subj: Permanent Change of Station Orders

Effective immediately upon receipt of these orders, you are to detach from your current duty station, Naval Trial Service San Diego.

You will report within seven days to your new assignment as Staff Judge Advocate to the Commanding Officer, USS *Ronald Reagan* (CVN 76).

Transportation is authorized by flight on any U.S. Navy aircraft on space available basis to Kaneohe Bay MCAF, and from there to USS *Ronald Reagan* (CVN 76), currently operating in the Western Pacific Theater.

Upon presentation of these orders, all naval aviation commanders are ordered to assist and cooperate with you by making transportation available to USS *Ronald Reagan* (CVN 76).

Thank you for your service to the U.S. Navy, and best wishes as you begin your duties at your new command.

Zack folded the orders. "Well, I'll be a monkey's uncle."

"What was that, sir?"

"Sorry, Raynor. Just a saying back home in Washington County, North Carolina." Zack looked out at the vastness of the Pacific. "Do you know how long I've been dying to get back to sea?" He looked back at Raynor. "Ever since Colcernian disappeared, that's all I've wanted. To go to sea. To get away from it all. All this media junk about me being such a great lawyer. It gets old. I'm a naval officer first." He looked at Raynor, who stared at him with a blank expression. "A naval officer."

Those three words rolling off his tongue brought him back to his roots, igniting a patriotic fire that traveled up and down his spine. He relished for a moment the thought of returning to sea. "But what about the *Eckberg* trial?"

"Captain Rudy said to tell you not to worry — that Lieutenant Commander Poole will finish the case, sir."

"Ah, Wendy." He felt himself smile. "She'll chew up Web Wallace and spit him out before breakfast."

"Yes, sir. I'm sure she will."

Zack closed his eyes, prayed silently for Diane, then fell asleep.

CHAPTER 47

Gobi Desert
Northeast of Sainted, Mongolia

Three days later

Grassy patches were sporadic in this section of the Gobi. And so when the terrain offered a slight opportunity for their camels to munch down some lunch, Willie led them down a hill to an area near a very narrow stream.

Camels could go days without food and water. Willie and Jagtai could not. Already, three days trekking through rocks, across hills, and through sand, out in the middle of a cold nowhere, had taken their toll. They had only a few days' worth of food left, and their water supply was low. The stream was an answer to prayer.

The camels ripped the grass out of the banks beside the stream, then lapped up water as Willie submerged a canteen in the cool, pristine water and thanked the Lord for his providence.

They had headed in the general direction of the alleged camp, at least according to the reports. But maybe those reports, or the directions, were wrong. Willie worried that their opportunity for finding whoever it was they were looking for was dwindling with every second. Soon they would have to turn back, returning over the terrain from which they had come. They could alter their course slightly, but unless they had missed something, their journey could have been for nothing.

Not really for nothing. At least he was obeying what he felt the Lord was calling him to do.

"Lord, you've called us out here for a reason. Maybe that reason was to get closer to you. If so, then so be it. But if there's anyone or anything you want us to find, then make it happen soon. Otherwise, I'll take it as a sign that our mission is over."

His prayer was interrupted by the sound of running feet. He turned and saw Jagtai jogging down the hill, a look of excitement on his face. With one hand he was giving Willie the *shush* signal, his index finger over his lips. With the other he was waving for Willie to follow him.

"What about the camels?" Willie asked in a loud whisper.

"Leave them. They aren't going anywhere," Jagtai whispered back. "You must see this!"

Willie followed his friend up a hill, up to a rock formation about twenty feet above them.

"Look! Down below!"

It was maybe a quarter mile down in a depression between several rock formations. Willie counted eight gers pitched in a circle, almost like an Indian camp from the old westerns he used to watch. But these gers looked more like geodesic domes than teepees. They were camouflaged the color of the landscape, obviously making their presence difficult to spot by aerial surveillance. A barbed-wire fence surrounded the gers.

Two men emerged from two of the gers. Willie brought the binoculars to his eyes. They had olive skin, black hair, and scruffy black beards.

"Jagtai, get the camera. Make sure the telescopic lens is in."

"Be right back."

Before Jagtai returned, someone else emerged from one of the gers. The reddish hair was the first thing he noticed. Willie adjusted the focus ring on the binoculars. *Dear Lord, this is a woman!*

"Jagtai, hurry!" he whispered.

"Coming."

The woman disappeared behind one of the gers as Jagtai handed Willie the camera. Willie adjusted the telephoto lens. The adrenaline in his body caused him to overfocus. Then underfocus. The gers and the two men came into clear view, their hands flailing in the air. They appeared to be arguing. The redhead was still out of sight. "Come on, baby. Come on back around into view." Willie snapped a couple of pictures.

"Come on ... Yes!"

The redhead reemerged into view. The camera's motor kept advancing the film, and Willie kept shooting.

The woman went back inside the tent.

"Let's go," Willie said.

"Where to?"

"Ulaanbaatar."

U.S. Navy E/A-6B Prowler
Electronic Attack Squadron One Three Nine (VAQ 139)
Altitude 1,500 feet over the North Pacific Ocean
200 nautical miles northeast of Japan

If you look down and way out to your right, you can see your new home, Commander." The pilot's voice could be heard through the headset of the flight helmet Zack was wearing.

Zack turned and looked out the right side of the cockpit. All he could see were the glistening ripples of the vast ocean.

"You've got better eyes than I do, Lieutenant."

"Look out at four o'clock, downrange twenty degrees."

Zack strained again. Then he saw it. A dark gray yardstick, way out in the ocean, churning white water in its wake. Several smaller yardsticks, each about one-third the size of the big one, surrounded her in a perimeter of about five miles, also churning white water. The USS *Ronald Reagan* and her battle group.

"Ever landed on a carrier, Commander?"

"Not as many times as you have, I'm sure, Lieutenant. But the answer to your question is yes. Sorry about that." Zack snickered.

"Sorry about what, sir?" the pilot asked.

"I know how you flyboys like to try to get a suspected landlubber to throw up on the first pass over the carrier."

The pilot chuckled. "Got me, Commander. But that's more the fighter guys who like to try that stuff. Anyway, the seas are pretty calm out there today. If I can get his right, hopefully we won't wind up in the drink."

"Roger that," Zack said as the Prowler started making a circle to line up behind the *Reagan* for its final approach.

"Commander, I'm getting ready to switch to our LSO frequency for landing. You're welcome to listen in if you'd like."

He wants me to listen to his conversations with the landing safety officer. He's still trying to spook me. "Sounds like fun."

"Very well, sir. Switching to LSO frequency now."

Passing by the stern of the USS *Ronald Reagan* at an altitude of 800 feet, the pilot banked the multimillion-dollar jet fighter away from the sun and pressed his microphone.

"Flight control, Prowler leader on final approach, requesting permission to land."

"Prowler leader, flight control." This was the carrier air traffic controller. "We've got you on visual now. Request for landing is granted. Proceed at your discretion."

"Roger that, flight control. Proceeding at discretion."

Completing the wide aerial loop behind the stern of the nuclear carrier, the pilot pointed the E/A-6B Prowler at the carrier's stern.

This would be like any other landing at any other airport in the world, Zack knew, except for the fact that the runway of this floating airstrip rolled slightly in the six-foot swells splitting around the carrier's hull. And except for the fact that the landing area on the rocking runway was only about five hundred feet in length, less than a quarter of the length of a normal runway. And also except for the fact that if the tail hook trailing underneath the fuselage missed one of the four steel cords in the aft of the deck, they could wind up with a cockpit full of cold, dark, North Pacific salt water and a free trip to the bottom of the "drink."

There was more chatter over the radio, though Zack was having trouble distinguishing the voices.

"Landing gear down."

"Tail hook down."

"Prowler One. LSO. Call the ball!" the LSO squawked, referring to the amber light on the stern of the carrier used for visual guidance for landing.

"Roger ball!" the pilot called back, indicating visual contact with the flashing light on the back of the carrier.

"Ten seconds to touchdown. No more radio contact, Commander," the pilot said. All landing signals would now be governed by a system of lights on the stern of the carrier run by the LSO.

Green light on.

Good.

"Three hundred feet."

"Two hundred feet."

The Prowler rushed at the carrier's stern. The ship was now a floating steel wall growing exponentially by the second, rushing head-on at the cockpit.

"Up! Up! Up!"

"Five seconds."

"Three seconds."

"Cut throttle."

A violent, jolting thump as forty tons of aircraft slammed against the steel deck.

Zack lunged forward under furious g-forces, his shoulder harness digging into his chest.

"Full throttle!"

The aircraft shook violently, its afterburners fighting the resistance of the powerful steel cable stretched across the floating runway and "trapped" by the plane's tail hook. Shuddering under the thrust of full power, the plane came to a restrained stop halfway down the carrier's deck.

"Cut power!"

The pilot pulled back on the forward throttles and switched off the engines.

"Nice job, Lieutenant," Zack said.

"Welcome to the *Gipper*, Commander," the pilot said, referring to the affectionate nickname that crew members called the *Reagan*.

Zack exhaled deeply. "It's good to be home."

CHAPTER 48

Embassy of the United States of America
Big Ring Road
11th Micro-district
Ulaanbaatar, Mongolia

Even in his short three months in Mongolia, Willie Mangum had enough experience with the United States Embassy to know that the consul's office was open to serve U.S. citizens living in Mongolia from 1:00 to 3:00 p.m.

Depending on which foreign service officer was working the desk, sometimes the service was excellent, and sometimes it was ... well ... Mongolian. In this case, Willie had brought Jagtai with him as a witness to what he was about to describe.

A smiling brunette, an American with a pixie haircut who would've been attractive had she ditched the thick, black, plastic-rimmed glasses, sat at the action officer's desk. "May I help you, sir?"

"I'm Willie Mangum with the International Mission Board." Willie handed her his passport. "This is my friend Jagtai."

"Hello." The desk officer studied Willie's passport, not looking up. "What can I do for you, Mr. Mangum?"

"I need to see Ambassador Amos. This is an emergency."

That brought eye contact from the young foreign service officer. "Ambassador Amos is busy. She doesn't see citizens without an appointment. You say this is an emergency?"

"Yes. We believe that a Western woman, maybe an American, is being held hostage out in the Gobi."

"Hmm." She studied both Willie and Jagtai. "That's quite an allegation you're making there, Mr. Mangum."

Typical smarter-than-thou State Department bureaucrat. More intelligent than the common riffraff. "Look. We went out and took photos three days ago." He pulled the eight-by-ten color photos out of the folder and laid them on the bureaucrat's desk.

She took them and sifted through them slowly. "Very interesting." Her voice sounded almost like that of Sergeant Shultz of *Hogan's Heroes*. "How do you know this is an American?"

"I don't know that for sure, but we've heard rumors to that effect. Let's put it this way—how many redheaded Mongolians have you ever seen?"

"Rumors." She studied the photos some more. "Hmph."

"Please, Miss—"

"Kerry. And you know unless we can prove this person is a U.S. citizen, I doubt there's anything we can do."

"I understand, Miss Kerry, but I'd still like to see Ambassador Amos."

Kerry eyed Willie and Jagtai a moment longer. "I'll call up to the ambassador's appointments secretary and explain the situation, but as I say, the ambassador doesn't see people off the streets. I'm sure you'll have to wait."

"Thank you," Willie said.

As the bureaucrat telephoned the appointments secretary, Willie prayed silently. *Lord, grant us favor with the ambassador. Let us see her as soon as possible.*

"Well, Mr. Mangum, I just got off the telephone with the ambassador, and she has asked me to deliver a message to you."

"Really?"

"Yes." The bureaucrat spoke with a tinge of contempt in her voice. "I've been instructed to tell you, and these are her words, that the ambassador"—she cleared her throat—"grew up as a Southern Baptist and would be happy to see you."

"Really? When?"

"This is highly unusual, Mr. Mangum, but Ambassador Amos has agreed to see you right now."

"Really?"

"Yes." She cleared her throat. "Really."

Thank you, Lord. "Thank you!"

"If you would follow me, please."

CHAPTER 49

Situation room
The White House
Washington, D.C.

This is dangerous, Mr. President, inexcusably dangerous!" The secretary of state, Robert Mauney, was reacting to the contingency plan that had been drawn up by the Joint Chiefs of Staff for a possible military operation in Mongolia.

The president sat at the end of a long mahogany table, around which members of his National Security Council also sat after being summoned to an emergency meeting.

"Don't get too upset at the Joint Chiefs, Mr. Secretary. I haven't ordered anything yet. But I did ask them to develop a contingency plan so our forces would be ready just in case."

"But, Mr. President, I urge you to remember the parameters you've set forth, sir. First, we would have to *find the camp*, and then we would have to be assured that Lieutenant Commander Colcernian is there. And frankly, sir, I'm skeptical. We can't tell from these photos that this is Colcernian.

"From our interview with Father Robert, the church colored L'Enfant's hair a red color. This photo could be L'Enfant, and that would make this a French problem, sir.

"Not only that, Mr. President, but as you know, our satellites have been shooting pictures of this area and we can't pinpoint the location. Not even with the sketchy information this missionary has given us.

"And besides, sir, even if—and this is still a long shot—these photos are of Colcernian, is it worth risking nuclear war with Russia or

China by crossing their airspace? Our relations with both of those countries have been icy since the Dome of the Rock. We can't reach Mongolia without crossing Russia or China. Sir, is one officer's life worth risking World War III?"

The president let that thought resonate for a moment. He looked at his security council. Vice President Surber was there. So was Cynthia Hewitt, his national security advisor. So were all five members of the Joint Chiefs of Staff, along with their boss, Secretary of Defense Erwin Lopez. All eyes were on him.

Lord, give me wisdom.

"Secretary Lopez."

"Yes, Mr. President."

"I've asked the Pentagon to draft a contingency plan just in case."

"Yes, sir, and we have, sir."

"Who will be presenting?"

"The chairman of the Joint Chiefs, sir."

"Very well," the president said. "Admiral Ayers?"

Admiral John F. Ayers Jr., the chairman of the Joint Chiefs of Staff, rose. "Thank you, Mr. President." In his service dress blue uniform, Ayers walked to the head of the table, to a position just beside the president. Several charts were positioned on an easel and covered with a cloth.

"Mr. President, Mr. Vice President, distinguished members of the National Security Council, at the president's direction, the Joint Chiefs have developed a plan for a military operation in Mongolia, which would involve the use of a carrier task force, from which a SEAL team would be launched off the Russian coast. This would involve violation of both Russian and Chinese airspace, so as the secretary of state has pointed out, it is not without risk.

"We've given this operation the code name Operation Genghis Kahn, named after the legendary Mongolian leader of the thirteenth century.

"Commander, Seventh Fleet has forward-deployed the USS *Ronald Reagan* to a position about two hundred nautical miles northeast of Japan, anticipating that any aerial incursion into landlocked Mongolia would be launched from either the Yellow Sea, the Sea of Japan, or the Sea of Okhostk."

Ayers sipped a glass of water, then tapped the Yellow Sea with his pointer.

"Now the problem with the Yellow Sea is that you have Communist North Korea on the peninsula to the right, it's very small, and we've got problems with flying over Chinese population centers."

OPERATION GENGHIS KAHN
Chart 1
Theater of Operations

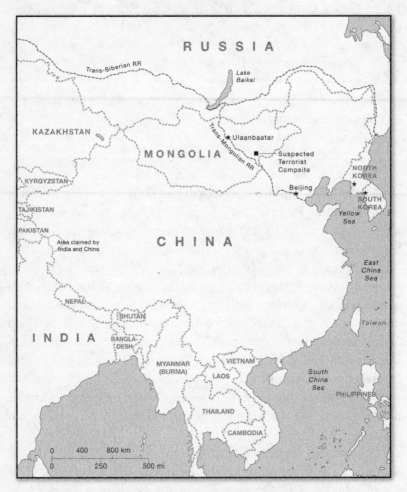

1. Yellow Sea 2. Ulaanbaatar 3. Trans-Mongolian RR
4. Suspected location of terrorist campsite

"Ladies and gentlemen, two things I want you to consider on this map. First, we have the location of the Yellow Sea." He tapped the

Yellow Sea. "The second is the location of the Mongolian capital city, Ulaanbaatar.

"Now if you start at Ulaanbaatar, you'll notice this line running down from Russia, through Ulaanbaatar, down to the Chinese border. This, ladies and gentlemen, is the great Trans-Mongolian Railroad, slicing through Mongolia and connecting Russia to China.

"Parallel to the railway is a sparsely traveled two-lane road that connects Ulaanbaatar to the Chinese border.

"Now if you look at the point at which the Trans-Mongolian Railroad enters China, we believe that the terrorist camp is in this vicinity. In fact"—the admiral sipped some water—"we think the camp is somewhere in this area." He tapped on the map again. "This is approximately fifty miles or so northeast of the spot where the Trans-Mongolian Railroad enters China. Located at point four on the map."

"Here's the problem. The Yellow Sea is surrounded by hostile nuclear powers, including North Korea to the right here, and China to the left. We move a carrier battle group in here, and it will be noticed. Plus, the shortest route would take us over the Beijing area, which is the most heavily populated area of China.

"We have the same problem with the Sea of Japan. A launch from here would involve flying over North Korea and, again, the heavily populated Beijing area." He turned to his aide. "Commander, would you pour me a little more water, please?"

"Yes, sir, Admiral."

The aide complied. "Now then, if you'll look at the east coast of North Korea and follow it all the way up the coast, about three-quarters of the way up the map, you'll see the Russian port city of Vladivostok." Another tap. "Now, gentlemen, the Russian navy ain't what she used to be, but we still must be concerned with them. And Vladivostok is the major Russian naval facility in the Pacific and is the headquarters of their Pacific fleet."

"Please go on," the president said.

"Yes, sir. Having grave concerns about launches from the Yellow Sea and the Sea of Japan, there is a third option. It would require a much greater strain on our ships, our planes, and our SEALS. But option three would be our best option for avoiding radar detection. It would also be the most dangerous to our fleet.

Ayers flipped to a second chart.

OPERATION GENGHIS KAHN
Chart 2
Sea of Okhostk

1. Initial flight path (projected) 2. USS *Ronald Reagan* launch position
3. USS *Ronald Reagan* current position

"This, gentlemen, is the Sea of Okhotsk. Now if you look at the bottom center of the map, at the intersection of 40 degrees north latitude and 150 degrees east longitude, this"—*tap-tap*—"is the current location of USS *Ronald Reagan*.

"Now, if the president orders this option, *Reagan* will sail a course slightly west of due north, following a course along the 150th longitude, entering the Sea of Okhotsk about sundown through the sparsely inhabited Kuril Islands.

"Once she clears the Kurils, she would maintain a course due north to the 50th latitude, and from there, turn northwest. Now if you look at the 140th longitudinal line, you will see that it forms the hypotenuse of a triangle with the Russian coastline.

"We would launch our choppers somewhere just a few miles west of the 140th longitudinal line, about the 55th latitudinal line, right about … here." *Tap-tap*. "Right in the middle of the water."

"From that point, our choppers, launched with no lights and flying just above the waves, would fly due west, crossing the Russian coast and praying they aren't detected. When they reach the coast—and by the way, this is a very thinly populated area—they would fly at treetop level, again to avoid Russian radar.

"Of course, this area is mountainous, which helps us duck under radar but also makes for deadly flying conditions. Our choppers would fly due west until they reached the Russian landmass, then turn southwest for a direct flight through these mountains and into Mongolia."

Ayers flipped to the final chart.

OPERATION GENGHIS KAHN
Chart 3
Mongolia

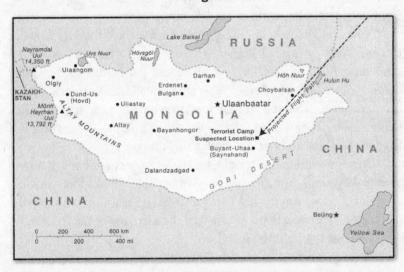

1. Suspected location of terrorist camp 2. Flight path (projected)

"This is a little closer map of Mongolia. Our choppers, if we make it this far, would fly a line from the northeastern corner of the map, just past this village of Choybalsan, down to a point just northeast of Sayshand, where we believe the terrorist camp is located. We hope that we would achieve optimal surprise under the cover of darkness and that our SEALs would rescue Lieutenant Commander Colcernian. We would fly back out along roughly the same path we took on the way in, rendezvousing with the *Reagan* the next morning just after sunrise."

Ayers took a sip of water. "Questions?"

The Director of the Central Intelligence Agency raised his hand. "Admiral, you mentioned that launching from the Sea of Okhotsk would pose the greatest danger for our men and equipment."

"That is correct, Director."

"Could you elaborate?"

"As I mentioned a moment ago, the distance from the Yellow Sea is about six to seven hundred miles one way. That alone would be a strain on even our longest-range choppers currently active on our carrier task forces. In contrast, a launch from the Sea of Okhotsk is going to be almost twice that distance. We estimate 1,300 miles from the launch point.

"There are no choppers in the U.S. military that can fly that far without refueling. For example, the SH-60F Seahawks aboard the *Reagan* have a tactical range of about 420 miles.

"Now, the chopper we'll use for this mission is the MH-53E Sea Dragon. We'll fly the Sea Dragons in from Japan. The Sea Dragon has a range of 1,050 miles. That will just about get us to the Mongolian border." Ayers took another sip of water, then added, "One way." He set his glass down. "That means we'll need to send choppers in to drop fuel tanks at several points along the way — on the ground — so that the Sea Dragons can land and refuel — both going and coming.

"This is mountainous terrain, and this whole operation is going to be very dangerous, but there's just no other way to make this work."

"But don't we run the risk that someone on the ground will spot the fuel tanks?" This question was asked by the secretary of the treasury.

"Yes, that is a risk, Mr. Secretary."

The secretary of state spoke up. "Set the fuel down where?"

"Two places, Mr. Secretary. The first is about six hundred miles from the launch point, just before we reach the Chinese border, near the Russian village of Blagoveshchernick.

"Then there would be a second drop point just inside the Mongolian border. Under the plan, we will not set down in China, obviously because of the dense population there."

"Excuse me, Admiral."

"Yes, Mr. Vice President."

"How would the choppers that bring in the fuel get back to the ship?"

"They would not, sir. Navy SEALs would remain on the ground and destroy those choppers. Obviously we don't want these choppers to fall into the hands of the Russians.

"All the choppers designated for this mission have been painted jet black, and all insignia visibly identifying them as U.S. Navy aircraft have been removed.

"After the SEALs have destroyed the fuel choppers, then the rescue chopper, on its way back from the Gobi, will pick those SEALs up when it refuels. There won't be enough fuel to go around. Ladies and gentlemen, this mission will cost us two or possibly three helicopters that will be used in the refueling part of this operation."

"Once we have identified the location of this camp, execution of this plan calls for launching a tomahawk cruise missile into the area, designed to coincide with the SEALs' arrival at the base to support the attack. Any tomahawk attack will be designed to disrupt and distract the terrorists, creating confusion while our SEALs go in and rescue the detainee. Now, the *Virginia* class nuclear submarine USS *North Carolina* is already on patrol in the Sea of Okhotsk ready to support this operation."

There was a collective moment of silence around the table.

The secretary of state spoke up again. "Admiral, as I understand this, we haven't pinpointed the location of this camp. Is that correct?"

"Not yet, sir."

"Doesn't it bother you that if this place exists, our satellites haven't been able to find it?"

"Mr. Secretary, I'd like to have an aerial photo of the precise spot, but frankly, I'm not surprised that we don't yet."

That comment triggered whispers around the table.

"Would you care to elaborate on that?" the president asked.

"Yes, Mr. President. The Gobi is a huge land mass. Our satellites only get two passes a day over the area, and unless we point them exactly in the right place, it may take us awhile. It could take weeks."

"Then why the hurry?" the secretary of state asked.

"Because of this Plan 547 that has come into play. If it's legitimate, it means Lieutenant Commander Colcernian could be executed in less than three days, sir. We just don't have the luxury of time."

"And we don't have the luxury of starting World War III, either." The secretary of state angrily waved his hands in the air.

"Admiral." This was the voice of Cynthia Hewitt, the president's national security advisor. "Without satellites to pinpoint the exact target area, and with fuel as a potential problem, how will you find the target area?"

"Excellent question. We've been in touch with the International Mission Board of the Southern Baptist Church, and this missionary, Mr. Mangum, is headed back out to the area. He will be accompanied by Special Agent McGillvery, who, as you know, is the NCIS agent who broke open this case. Their job will be to plant high frequency homing devices in the area around the camp. Our satellites will acquire the signal and then relay targeting information to the choppers, to the USS *Reagan*, and to the USS *North Carolina*.

"So the success of this mission," the secretary of state grunted, "depends on a Southern Baptist missionary."

"With respect, Mr. Secretary," Admiral Ayers responded, "the success or failure of this mission will depend on a lot of brave Americans— the crew of the *Reagan*, the *North Carolina*, the chopper pilots who have volunteered to fly this mission and are thereby risking their lives, and the Navy SEAL team that will be going in. And yes, the missionary who found the camp will be a key player in leading us back there, but I would point out that Special Agent McGillvery will be in charge on the ground until the SEALs arrive."

"If they arrive," Secretary of State Mauney corrected.

"Yes, sir," the admiral said.

"Thank you for the briefing," President Williams said. "Okay, any final discussions on this before I make my decision?"

"Mr. President," the secretary of state spoke up, "I urge you not to do this, sir. The evidence is just too sketchy. All we have, really, is the unconfirmed account from the Southern Baptist missionary and sketchy pictures of someone we can't identify. Remember, we know from Father Robert that Jeanette L'Enfant's hair was dyed red as a disguise before her capture. We know she is missing.

"Give diplomacy a chance, sir. Let us bring the French in on this. This may be their hostage, not ours. Together, maybe we can work with the French and come up with a diplomatic solution. The French have close ties with the Arabs, the Chinese, and the Russians.

"And even if we could know for sure that this is Lieutenant Commander Colcernian, Mr. President, we're talking about a possible military exchange with the two most powerful nuclear nations on earth next to us. It's an act of war to send military aircraft into Chinese and Russian airspace uninvited.

"What if, Mr. President, the entire Russian Air Force is unleashed against the *Ronald Reagan*? I know we have the best navy in the world, but those numbers are overwhelming. That's five thousand dead Americans in one swoop. Or worse, what if this triggers a North Korean invasion of the South, or a Chinese invasion of Taiwan? Or what if a trigger-happy Russian sub commander retaliates by launching a missile across American airspace?

"Please, Mr. President. I will support you either way. But please consider the grave consequences of your actions."

"Thank you, Secretary Mauney." The president turned to his defense secretary. "Secretary Lopez, what do you say?"

"Mr. President, Secretary Mauney is right that this is a dangerous mission, but we can do this. Despite the great global sentiment against us, our forces are the best in the world. We can carry out this plan, and we can do it at night. We can fly through the dangerous mountain ranges in China and Russia, and if Lieutenant Commander Colcernian is there, we can bring her home.

"Mr. President, an American naval officer has been taken hostage. With due respect to the secretary of state, this evidence is not sketchy. All of the pieces add together. The report brought by Father Robert. The confirmation of this Plan 547 by McGillvery's interrogation of Quasay. Now the photographs of a woman in the Gobi Desert roughly matching Colcernian's description.

"Mr. President, this is about principle. It's about an American officer whose life will end if we don't act. Think if we do nothing and then see a public execution on television. Think of the damage that would do to the prestige of America.

"Mr. President, like Lieutenant Commander Colcernian, you were once a Navy JAG officer. And you have said to the terrorists, 'You can run, but you can't hide.' Those were your words.

"They are banking on us thinking just like the secretary of state has suggested we think. Not that there's anything wrong with Secretary Mauney's reasoning, but if we do nothing and they execute Colcernian, they win.

"I remember 1942, Mr. President. Japan struck Pearl Harbor. Franklin Roosevelt sent Jimmy Doolittle and a brave group of American pilots on an incredibly dangerous mission to prick the heart of Japan—right in the middle of Tokyo.

"Let us do our jobs, Mr. President. We won't just prick the heart of terrorism with this mission. We'll knock them over the head with a sledgehammer.

"That's all, sir."

Only the sound of the ticking grandfather clock could be heard. The collective eyes of the National Security Council rested on Mack Williams, President of the United States.

Deep down, Mack believed Diane Colcernian was alive, and in Mongolia. But the secretary of state had a point. Saving her life could cause nuclear war. But the secretary of defense was right too. Pull this off, and America would demonstrate to terrorists that they can't hide anywhere in the world.

What to do?

Lord, you say in the book of James that if anyone lacks wisdom, all he has to do is ask. Well, I'm asking you now.

The words he had spoken to Zack Brewer came back to him. *"If we can find that camp and if—and this is a big if—we are reasonably assured that Lieutenant Commander Colcernian is there, we'll go get her. Zack, do you understand me?"*

"Secretary Lopez?"

"Yes, Mr. President?"

"Order execution of Operation Genghis Kahn."

"Yes, sir, Mr. President!"

"All military commands under your authority are to provide full cooperation to the U.S. Navy and its subordinate commands in the prosecution of this action. This National Security Council will reconvene in six hours and every six hours thereafter until prosecution of this action is complete, or at such other time as ordered by me."

"Yes, Mr. President!"

"This meeting is adjourned."

CHAPTER 50

Council of Ishmael temporary headquarters
Rub al-Khali Desert
250 miles southeast of Riyadh, Saudi Arabia

Adbur Rahman stood outside his leader's office and looked through the cracked door. The simple sign, a white cloth, its message written in Arabic and stenciled in green, hung on the wall behind the leader's desk.

God the merciful, God the compassionate.

On the wall on each side were paintings of the former Iraqi president, Saddam Hussein, and the man al-Akhma called "the greatest Muslim to walk the earth since the prophet Mohammed himself," the glorious hero of 9/11, Osama bin Laden.

Rahman knocked.

"Enter," Hussein al-Akhma said from the large chair behind his desk. The leader of the Council of Ishmael was dressed in white Arabic garb and spoke in his native tongue.

"Un hum del Allah" — Praise be to God — Rahman said as he stepped into al-Akhma's office.

"Un hum del Allah," Hussein al-Akhma responded without looking up. "What is it, Abdur?"

"A report on our camp in Mongolia, Leader. Jeanette L'Enfant is now in our possession, just as you ordered, sir."

That brought a smile and a scratch of al-Akhma's scruffy goatee. "Praise be to Allah. What was the fellow's name responsible ...?"

"Fadil, sir."

"Yes, well, give him some sort of prize. And how is Colcernian?"

"Three days until execution of Plan 547, if that is still what you want, Leader."

Al-Akhma took a drag from his Camel cigarette. "Of course that is what I want."

"Do you want us to arrange for publicity before or after the execution?"

"Here is what I have decided. We will shoot both Colcernian and L'Enfant by firing squad at midnight on day 547. The next day we will decapitate them. We will videotape the decapitation of their dead bodies and give the videotape and the photos of their heads on a platter to Al Jazeer!" Al-Akhma rolled back and folded his hands over his stomach. "And then we will mail their heads to Mack Williams at the White House!"

Abdur laughed and nodded, mimicking his leader.

"That should get us maximum publicity. Don't you think so, Abdur?"

"But of course, Leader."

"But I have decided that before that, you and I deserve a treat, Abdur."

"I do not understand."

"My friend, you and I are going to Mongolia to witness the festivities. But before we shoot these pagan maidens, perhaps you and I shall take turns with them in their tents." His laughter was coarse and loud.

Again, Abdur mimicked his leader's laugh.

"How does that sound, Abdur?"

"Like paradise on earth, before we even reach paradise, Leader. You are a genius!"

"I thought you would see it that way. Now come, we must begin our journey!"

CHAPTER 51

Buyant Ukha International Airport
Ulaanbaatar, Mongolia
Three days before execution of Plan 547

Shannon stepped into the baggage area, where two men waited for her. One was an average-built American-looking fellow in his midforties. The other was an average-built Mongolian who could have been almost any age between twenty and fifty. She recognized the American from the picture she had seen in her briefings.

"You must be Willie."

"I'm Willie, and this is Jagtai."

Shannon shook both of their hands. "It's a pleasure to meet you both."

"You too," Willie said.

"So did you get a package from the embassy?" She was referring to the homing devices, which had been delivered to the embassy under the cover of diplomatic immunity. Flying them in commercially would have created problems at various customs checkpoints.

"We've got 'em. They're in the car."

"Okay, what's the plan?"

Willie spoke up. "We've chartered a private plane to fly us south to Sainted. The plane is owned by a local believer from our church."

"When?"

"As soon as you get your bags."

"Let's rock 'n' roll."

Thirty minutes later, Shannon was airborne again, looking down on a landscape that could have passed for the surface of the moon.

Stateroom of the Commanding Officer
USS Ronald Reagan
Course 001 degrees
45 degrees N latitude, 150 degrees E longitude
Near the entrance to the Kuril Islands
North Pacific Ocean

Three days before execution of Plan 547

On board a U.S. Naval warship, a personal invitation to dinner with the commanding officer in his stateroom is accepted with a degree of formality, especially on a large ship like the *Ronald Reagan*, the navy's newest and last-to-be built *Nimitz* class supercarrier. In keeping with the customs and traditions of the naval service, Zack had changed from his khakis into his service dress blue uniform for his rendezvous with Captain Steven Long, USN, CO of the *Ronald Reagan*.

Zack knocked on the door of his new Skipper's wardroom. A mess steward, in a white jacket and black dinner pants, opened the hatch leading to the captain's personal living quarters aboard the ship.

"Ah, Commander Brewer." The steward gave him a friendly smile. "Captain Long is ready for you, sir."

"Very well," Zack said. The steward led him into the captain's private dining room. The table had been set with a linen tablecloth and silverware.

"Zack, thanks for coming," the tall, lanky captain said.

"Thanks for the invitation, sir. It's an honor."

"Care for a drink?"

"Water is fine."

Long chuckled. "I'd heard that the navy's most famous JAG officer stayed away from the spirits. And I won't try to tempt you otherwise."

"Thank you, Skipper."

"Anyway, have a seat." He motioned for Zack to sit down opposite him at the table, then turned to the steward. "George, water for the commander and a cabernet for me."

"Aye, sir."

"You know, Zack," said the salt-and-pepper haired captain, looking across the table, "I'm sorry it's taken a couple of days for me to invite you up. I like to have a new staff member up the first day he's aboard."

"Think nothing of it, sir."

"But the *Reagan* is about to be called into action."

Their eyes met.

"I'd heard some rumblings to that effect," Zack said.

"There will be a briefing of my staff in the morning, Zack. But I wanted to talk to you first, because I understand you may have a personal interest in what we're about to attempt."

That could mean only one thing. It had to. Zack felt his heart jump. "If I may be so bold as to guess, Captain, could this have something to do with the nation of Mongolia?"

A broad smile stretched across the skipper's face. "Zack, let me tell you about something the navy is calling Operation Genghis Kahn."

Flight deck, USS Ronald Reagan
Course 001 degrees
47 degrees 30 minutes N latitude
147 degrees 30 minutes E longitude
400 miles northeast of Sapporo, Japan
Sea of Okhotsk

Two days before execution of Plan 547

USS *Ronald Reagan*, the flagship of Carrier Strike Group Seven, was ordinarily accompanied by a small flotilla of warships, including cruisers, destroyers, and submarines, all of which carried out a single purpose — to protect the carrier from enemy attack.

The immediate battle group included three guided missile destroyers, a guided missile frigate, the heavy guided missile cruiser USS *Champlain*, the replenishment ship USS *Ranier*, and the nuclear submarine USS *Tucson*.

All of these ships would provide a formidable defensive perimeter around the *Reagan* should she ever come under attack from the air or from submarines underwater. With the exception of the submarine, every surface ship in the battle group had turned and sailed east just as the *Reagan* slipped through the Kuril Islands.

While all this made the carrier less likely to be spotted, it also left her far more vulnerable.

Zack had been ordered down to the flight deck by Captain Long to serve as a welcoming committee for the five helicopters that were now visible on the southeastern horizon.

As the choppers closed in on the great ship's fantail, flight deck personnel scurried about on the runway. The first chopper, painted black without any insignia, hovered over the aft section of the ship. Its powerful rotors blew a gust of wind across the deck, and the sound of its engines echoed off the steel runway. Deck personnel in yellow jerseys and yellow helmets directed the chopper as it nosed forward and feathered down on the front section of the runway, near the bow. The other four choppers followed, landing one behind the other.

The lead chopper cut its engines, and Zack followed close behind the flight deck personnel as they rushed to the MH–53E and opened its side door. They shot salutes to the emerging navy captain wearing the dark blue "Gestapo" uniform with silver eagles on each collar and the insignia of a Navy SEAL on his chest.

Zack met the captain's eyes and shot him a smart salute. "Welcome aboard, Captain Noble."

"Zack!" Captain Buck Noble saluted back and then gave Zack a bear hug. "We miss you already on the *Eckberg* case!"

"Sir, there's another job I'd like to volunteer for."

"Zack, you know our command master chief, Master Chief Cantor?"

"Sir," the master chief said with a salute.

"Master Chief." Zack returned the salute, then looked back at Captain Noble. "As I was saying, sir, there's another job I'd like to volunteer for."

"Forget it, Zack. I know what you're thinking. You're way too valuable to the navy for me to risk that sort of thing."

"But, sir—"

"Zack," Captain Noble interrupted, "if she's there, we'll bring her out." He slapped Zack on the back. "You bailed this command out a bunch of times when we needed you. And I owe you one. I know how you feel about her."

"God bless you, Captain. But don't think I won't spend the next thirty-six hours trying to change your mind." He paused, then added, "Sir."

"I wouldn't think you'd do anything other than pester the heck out of me about that, Zack."

"Your seabag, sir." An enlisted SEAL handed Noble his bag.

"Thanks, Petty Officer," Noble said. "Sure is cold out here. This is colder than Japan was."

"Come with me, sir," Zack said. "I'll take you to Captain Long's stateroom. He's got fresh coffee."

"Great idea," Noble said. "Lead the way, sailor."

CHAPTER 52

Gobi Desert
Southeast of Ulaanbaatar, Mongolia
Sometime at night

At least they were providing heat in the place now, Diane thought, as the bearded Arab brought more wood in and dumped a log in the stove in the middle of the tent. And the starvation techniques, at least since they had struck her with the butt of the rifle, had subsided. Now she was getting thin gruel once a day in the morning. They had to keep her alive so they could keep playing mind games with her, she supposed.

The flame in the stove responded to the fresh wood. The interior of the ger warmed.

She lay back on her cot, closed her eyes, and began to drift.

His face. The image of it. The dimple in his chin. His smile and wit. The way he fit so nicely in his white uniform. *Lord, please ... One day ... Somehow, some way ...*

"*Non! Non! S'il vous plâit! S'il vous plâit!*"

What? Diane sat up.

"*Arrêtez-vous! Laissez-moi la paix!*"

The sound of a woman's voice! Screaming in French! They had taken another prisoner. Her instincts took over. She got up and charged out of the ger and into the cold.

The commotion came from a ger across the way. She ran outside. Several men converged on her position.

An Arab man came out of the tent. He was dressed in a white shirt and white pants. As he opened the flap, the sounds of screaming and sobbing permeated the cold, moonlit Mongolian sky.

"Ah, Lieutenant Commander Colcernian!" The man spoke in perfect English as three others restrained her. "Did you know that your navy has promoted you?"

"Who are you?"

"Posthumously, I might add?" He leered at her. "You did not know you had company, did you?"

"Whoever it is, leave her alone, you animal."

"We have had her here several days. She is under medication."

"Leave her alone," she growled and raised her hand to strike him. The men with him restrained her.

"Tell me," he said, lighting a Camel cigarette, "do powerful men turn you on, Commander?"

She did not dignify the question with an answer.

"I am Hussein al-Akhma, the most powerful Arab man in the world."

"Here's what I think of you, Mr. al-Akhma." She spit in his face.

A hard punch sent her reeling. Before she could recover, al-Akhma bent over her, grabbed her in an ironlike grasp, and tried to kiss her.

"No!" She kicked him in the groin.

He doubled over, cursing. "How dare you strike the great Hussein al-Akhma!" One of his assistants hit her with the back of his hand. She fell to the ground.

Al-Akhma said, "Send her back to her ger. She will get hers soon enough."

Thirty minutes later, the woman was shoved through the flap of Diane's ger. Her head thumped against the wooden floor. She balled into a human clump. She heaved, as if hyperventilating, punctuating her desperate gasps for air with moaning sobs.

Diane looked at the flap. The captors were gone. For now. Or so it appeared.

She jumped to the floor and put her arms around the woman.

"It will be okay. Be strong. I'm here."

The woman buried her head in Diane's shoulder. "Here," Diane said, "drink this." She brought the half cup of water she had saved from that morning to the woman's lips.

The woman responded, bringing the cup to her lips. The staccato-like heaving slowed ever so slightly. It was then that Diane noticed the color of the woman's hair. It was auburn, very similar to her own. How odd, Diane thought, that she and the woman bore a striking resemblance in age, facial features, hair color, and body shape.

The woman finished the cup of water. Diane wiped a stray tendril of hair off her forehead. "Are you okay?"

"I think." The woman trembled and held on to Diane.

"Did they touch you?"

More deep, rapid breathing. "They did not rape me, if that is what you mean. They threatened. That leader, al-Akhma. He exposed himself—his assistant too. They tried to kiss me. I fought and scratched their eyes. At first they laughed. Then they got mad and left me alone."

"Thank God," Diane said quietly. "Here. Take my bed." She pointed to her cot. "Try to get some rest. I'll be here. They'll have to get to me to get to you, and I won't let them."

"You are sweet."

Diane helped her guest onto the only cot in the primitive tent. She pulled the blanket over her shoulders and adjusted her head on the small lumpy pillow.

The woman had been curled under the blanket, shaking, her eyes closed, for the better part of two hours. Diane was sitting on the floor near the woodstove when the woman's eyes came wide open, reflecting the flicker of the solitary candle burning beside the stove. The woman looked over at Diane and forced a half smile onto her face.

"What is your name?"

"My name is Jeanette." She spoke through glistening tears. "I am from France."

"It's nice to meet you. Jeanette. My name is—"

"You are Diane."

"Yes." The interruption stunned her. "How did you know that?"

"You are the world's most famous missing person. How could I not know?"

"People still remember?"

"Yes, of course people remember. Especially a person named Lieutenant Commander Zack Brewer."

Diane felt like hyperventilating. The sound of his name alone was enough.

"You still love him, do you not?"

"Do you know Zack?"

"I am a lawyer. I tried a case against him. It was a case of great international importance. But you would have no reason to know about it. It was tried after your disappearance."

"I'm stunned."

"Zack's performance in court was stunning. He soundly defeated me and my partner, Jean-Claude la Trec, who was the greatest avocat in all of Europe."

That comment brought a surge of pride to Diane.

"As you feel for Zack, I felt for Jean-Claude."

"Felt?"

"These Islamic radicals. This Council of Ishmael. They murdered him and kidnapped me."

"I am sorry."

"But I am happy to see that you are alive, even if I am the only person in the Western world besides Zack who believes it."

He believes! Praise God. He hasn't given up.

Diane lightly caressed Jeanette's shoulders and looked straight into her eyes. "Jeanette, before today, I had lost all hope. But I promise you this. I will do everything in my power to protect you. And with God's help, somehow, someday, we will get out of here. I don't know how it will happen. But now I feel it. It will happen.

"Before today, there was only faith. But now faith has been joined by hope."

They embraced, and Diane's eyes flooded with tears.

Bridge, USS Ronald Reagan
Course 001 degrees
57 degrees 30 minutes N latitude
140 degrees 30 minutes E longitude
80 miles west of Ayan, Russia
Sea of Okhotsk

Day 547, 1800 hours

It had been dark for three hours by the time the *Ronald Reagan* moved into launch position. Captain Long had invited Zack to the bridge to watch the launch of SEAL Team 3. All five helicopters were on deck, and the SEALs could be seen stowing their gear and weapons.

The excited voice of the combat information control officer suddenly boomed over the loudspeaker.

"Bridge! CIC! We've got two inbound bogies! Bearing zero-one-five degrees. Range three hundred miles. Look like Russian MiGs, Skipper. They're headed our direction."

Captain Long cursed under his breath. "Probably out of Vladivostok." He looked over at Captain Bill Cameron, the air wing commander who was on the bridge with him.

"Flight deck, Bridge. Belay launch of choppers. I repeat, belay launch of choppers! Launch F-18s for intercept of Russian MiGs. I repeat, Launch F-18s for intercept of Russian MiGs. All hands to general quarters!"

"General quarters! General quarters! General quarters!" Loudspeakers blared. Bells rang all over the ship. "General quarters! General quarters! General quarters!"

Even though the *Reagan* had launched no planes since she had been in the Sea of Okhotsk, two F/A-18E Super Hornets had remained in launch position on the catapults, ready to be shot into the air at a moment's notice.

"CIC, Bridge. Position of those bogies?"

"Bearing zero-one-five degrees. Range 250 miles, Skipper."

"Launch Super Hornets."

There was a flurry of activity on the flight deck as the pilot of the Super Hornet hit maximum throttle and the powerful steam-driven catapult slung the sleek aircraft off the bow. Fire from the twin engines blazed as the pilot hit the afterburners, climbing the fighter into the moonlit sky.

"Launch second fighter!" There was more furious scrambling below, the roar of jet engines, then a mighty shaking. The twin afterburners of the second jet pushed it to the heavens.

"CIC, Bridge. Position of those bogies?"

"Bearing zero-one-five degrees. Range 200 miles, Skipper."

"Are they still over land?"

"Bridge, CIC. Roger that."

"This is why you're getting paid the big bucks, Commander," Long said to Zack. "Talk to me about international rules of engagement."

"Sir, right now we've got a right to be where we are—in international waters. But if we shoot them down over their own country, we may start a war. But if they keep bearing down on our position, that could be construed as an act of hostile aggression, justifying the use of force."

"My problem is that once they're over water, they're less than a hundred miles out. I've got no destroyer screens out there, and they have a point-blank shot at me."

"Unless our planes nail 'em first," Zack said.

"What's your advice, Commander?"

"This is a deadly game of brinksmanship, but I'd protect U.S. assets and lives, sir, even if that means splashing the MiGs." Their eyes met. "You have the president's authority to do that."

The captain radioed the lead fighter. "Viper leader, *Reagan*."

"*Reagan*, Viper."

"Lieutenant, this is the captain speaking. As long as those MiGs are over land, hold fire. But when they cross the coastline, I want you to splash 'em. Understood?"

"*Reagan*, Viper. Roger that. Understand instructions to hold fire until MiGs cross coastline, then attack."

The tension on the bridge of the *Reagan* was thicker than the smoke in a Texas saloon. Seconds seemed like minutes. Minutes like hours.

"Bogies bearing zero-one-five degrees. Range 175 miles. Three minutes to coastline, Skipper."

"Viper leader, *Reagan*. Prepare to fire."

"*Reagan*, Viper leader. Arming missiles."

"Come on, baby," Captain Long said under his breath.

"Bridge, CIC. Be advised bogies have turned back! Repeat, be advised bogies have turned back!"

Applause broke out on the bridge.

"Viper leader, *Reagan*. Break off intercept! Do not fire! I repeat, do not fire!"

"*Reagan*, Viper leader. Roger that. I saw 'em turning, sir. Looks like they're headed back to Vladivostok. We're breaking off intercept and heading home."

"Flight deck! Launch SEAL team. Now!"

Three minutes later the first of the five giant black helicopters took off from the flight deck. Three minutes after that, all five had disappeared into the dark eastern sky.

Zack walked away from the captain and removed his officer's cover. Bringing the hat against his heart and looking out over the moon-draped waters of the black sea, he spoke softly. "Lord, grant them safety, grant them protection, and by the divine providence of your almighty hand, bring them back again, alive, with those who may be alive on the ground. Let her be alive, Lord. I ask for a miracle. Let her be alive."

CHAPTER 53

Gobi Desert
Northeast of Sainted, Mongolia

Three hours before midnight

Locating the ridge was a little more difficult in the dark, but when Willie looked out and saw the campfires in the middle of the camp under the moonlit sky, he knew the Lord had led them back to just where they were supposed to be.

"This is it, Shannon."

"Good work, Willie." Wearing a heavy parka, she crawled up between Willie and Jagtai and spied the area with her binoculars. "Okay." Her voice turned businesslike. "We've got work to do. Jagtai. Bring me the homing devices, please."

"Yes, Shannon."

"What can I do to help?" Willie asked.

"Pass me your flashlight."

He passed her the flashlight, and she turned it on as Jagtai returned with the box containing the homing devices.

The devices were about the size and shape of a laptop computer, Willie noted. *Dear Lord, please let them work.*

"Okay," Shannon said. "This is the one for the cruise missile targeting. Let's hope this baby fires up."

She punched a few buttons. In a few seconds, a host of green and yellow lights flashed across the top of the box.

"Great!" Shannon exclaimed. "Okay, if we don't move this baby, we're going to have a Tomahawk cruise missile for a midnight snack, right here on this ridge. I need one of you guys to circle all the way around to the other side of the camp down there and plant this baby about three hundred yards or so on the other side."

"I'll go," Jagtai said.

"Here." Shannon gave him one of the three M1 Garand rifles they had brought along. "Use this if you need it."

"Got it, Shannon."

Jagtai disappeared into the night.

"Okay, Willie, let's get this one fired up." Their eyes met. "You always pray, Willie?"

"That's my job. And even if it wasn't my job, the answer would still be yes."

"I'm getting more and more that way myself." She punched a few buttons on the homing device.

Nothing.

"Come on." She punched the buttons again. Yellow and green lights danced up and down the box.

"Thank you, Lord," Willie said.

"Thank you, Lord," Shannon parroted. "Now we just wait."

Control room
Nuclear attack submarine USS North Carolina *(SSN 777)*
Depth 100 feet
Forty miles east of USS Ronald Reagan
Sea of Okhotsk

Captain Don Hoover sat at the helm in the control room, sipping coffee and marveling at all of the high-tech gadgetry at the controls of his brand-new nuclear submarine, when the highest enlisted man on his sub, the chief of the boat, approached with paperwork in his hand.

"Captain, we've received targeting info for cruise missile launch in support of Operation Genghis Kahn, sir."

"Very well. Read targeting information, Chief of the Boat."

The chief of the boat complied. "Message is authentic, sir."

"XO?"

"I concur, sir."

"Weps?"

"I concur, sir."

"Very well. Load targeting information into computers for Tomahawk launch on my command."

"Aye, Captain," the weapons officer said.

"Captain, targeting information is loaded. Missiles ready for launch."

"Chief of the Boat, make depth for missile launch."

"Missile launch depth. Aye, sir."

"XO, take the boat to general quarters. Advise the crew to prepare for Tomahawk launch in T-minus 10 minutes."

"Aye, aye, sir."

The XO took the microphone. "General quarters! General quarters! General quarters! This is the XO. By order of the captain, all hands prepare for Tomahawk missile launch in T-minus ten minutes. Repeat, all hands prepare for Tomahawk missile launch in T-minus ten minutes. By order of the captain, this is the XO."

"Very well," Captain Hoover said, his voice deliberately calm. He sipped more coffee. "Chief of the Boat. Status?"

"Approaching missile launch depth in T-minus two minutes, sir. Stand by."

Captain Hoover watched the clock mounted on the bridge. The second hand made one complete sweep around the circumference. Then another.

"Missile launch depth, Captain."

"Very well. Launch Tomahawks."

"Launch Tomahawks. Aye, sir," the weapons officer said.

Then came a rushing sound and the whine of rockets. The *North Carolina* shook and vibrated as if it were about to fall apart in the water. Then a whooshing sound. Then another.

"Missiles away!" The weapons officer's voice exuded excitement. "Two Tomahawks airborne, bearing course two-two-zero degrees. Range eight miles. Altitude fifty feet above sea level, sir."

"Very well," the captain said. "We've done our jobs. Chief of the Boat, make depth two hundred feet."

"Make depth two hundred feet. Aye, Captain."

Hoover took a satisfying last gulp of his battery-acid coffee. "We'll hang out around here with *Ronald Reagan* till the party's over, then get the heck out of Dodge."

Gobi Desert
Northeast of Sainted, Mongolia

Day 547, fifteen minutes before midnight

Shannon looked into the moonlit sky. There were plenty of stars, but no helicopters. No sign of anything up there.

"Come on, guys. Where the heck are you?"

"Shannon, look!" Willie pointed toward the camp, where several of the men were gesturing wildly, as if they were arguing about something. One man stepped into one of the tents. A woman emerged at gunpoint. Her red hair glistened in the campfire and the moonlight. Her hands were tied behind her back.

"That's got to be Colcernian," Shannon said.

"No, maybe *that's* Colcernian!" Willie pointed to another tent, where more angry Arabs were leading another redheaded woman outside at gunpoint.

"Or maybe L'Enfant."

They pushed both women, guns trained at their heads, out toward two posts that had been sunk in the ground. The women tried to get away, but their captors now wound rope around them, securing each to a separate post.

"Come on, SEALs!" Shannon said, her voice soft but urgent. "Or I'm going to shoot these animals myself."

One of the men was now yelling at the others, and they lined up in a row. Two men started bringing rifles out of the tents, handing a rifle to each man in line.

"Dear Lord, they're forming a firing squad."

"Yes, they are," Shannon said. She worked the bolt action on her rifle. "Get your weapon ready, Willie."

Willie complied. "Who would have thought missionary work would lead to this?"

"You too, Jagtai."

"Done."

"Now if these SEALs don't get here, we're opening fire. I see five animals in the firing squad. There are three of us. I'll take the one on the left. Willie you take the middle. Jagtai, the right. Then fire on whoever is left standing. Got it?"

"Got it."

The leader screamed something in Arabic. Shannon brought a bead on the rifleman to the left. The firing squad brought their rifles to their shoulders.

"Non. S'il vous plâit!" The shrieking voice of a woman echoed through the night.

Where were the SEALs? There was no time to wait.

"Ready, gentlemen. On my mark. Fire!"

Rifle fire cracked the air in the midst of a huge, blinding explosion that rocked the earth. Then another of even greater magnitude. Thick, billowing smoke and blinding fire blocked their view of the terrorist camp, but shrieking and yelling in Arabic echoed through the hills. Then came the deafening noise of rotor blades from behind their heads.

Shannon looked up and saw the huge black silhouettes of two helicopters passing close over their heads.

"Yeah, baby! The cavalry has arrived! Let's go!"

CHAPTER 54

Bridge, USS Ronald Reagan
Course 001 degrees
57 degrees 30 minutes N latitude
140 degrees 30 minutes E longitude
80 miles west of Ayan, Russia
Sea of Okhotsk

Day 548, 11:00 a.m.

Zack hadn't slept at all during the night. Instead, he had spent the night in long, desperate prayer. He showered at six, and by eight o'clock he was in the ship's JAG office, going over paperwork with his assistant, Lieutenant Meredith, and the ship's senior chief legalman.

Nine o'clock came and went. Nothing. Then ten o'clock. By eleven o'clock, he headed up to the bridge for his morning meeting with Captain Long.

"Morning, Zack." Captain Long was in his chair, looking out at the cold gray sea, sipping coffee.

"Anything, sir?"

"Nothing, Zack. But remember, the choppers are under a radio blackout, and if they do show up, we probably won't hear anything till they're right on top of us. We're just eighty miles off the Russian coast, so as soon as they break out over sea, they'll be here in less than thirty minutes."

"Understood, sir."

"You look sharp today. Why the service dress blues?"

"Just in case ... You never know."

"Coffee?"

"Yes, sir."

"Petty Officer, fetch the commander a cup."

"Aye, sir."

"By the way, we did get a message in from the States for you. You seen it?"

"No, sir."

"From your old skipper. Here. I've got a copy in my clipboard." Captain Long handed Zack the document.

From: Commanding Officer, Navy Trial Command Southwest
To: Staff Judge Advocate, USS *Ronald Reagan* (CVN 76)
        Commanding Officer, SEAL Team 3
Via: Commanding Officer, USS *Ronald Reagan* (CVN 76)
Subj: General Court-Martial Results *U.S. v. Ensign Wofford Eckberg, USN*

Please be advised that general court-martial verdict in subject case is as follows: Guilty on all charges and specifications. Dishonorable discharge from naval service. Three years' confinement at navy brig. Three SEAL members involved in retaliatory assault awarded nonjudical punishment with thirty days' restriction and reduction in rank one enlisted grade.

Trial counsel LCDR Poole sends best regards.

Zack folded the orders. "Well, there's some great news. Way to go, Wendy!"

"Bridge, CIC. E-C2 Hawkeye reporting two inbound choppers bearing zero-nine-zero degrees. Choppers have just cleared Russian coast! Report inbound choppers are MH-53E Sea Dragon class, Captain!"

"Yes! Those are our birds!"

"CIC, Bridge. ETA?"

"Fifteen minutes, Skipper."

"Bridge, CIC. Hawkeye reporting choppers request emergency medical personnel on standby. Request body bags and master-at-arms personnel to take high-profile prisoner into custody. Also have intel on standby for interrogations."

"Any other news?"

"Negative, Captain."

Zack's heart sank.

"XO, contact ship's master-at-arms and medical. Also, I want an armed marine squadron to back up the master-at-arms."

"Aye, Captain," the XO said.

"Come on, Zack. Let's get to the flight deck!"

When Zack and Captain Long stepped from the carrier's towering steel structure known as the "island" onto the flight deck, deck crews in various colored jackets were already pointing to the two inbound black helicopters that appeared to be about a half mile off the carrier's stern.

Flight crewmen were signaling the choppers in for a landing toward the back of the runway.

The medical crew, consisting of corpsmen, doctors, and nurses, rushed stretchers, wheelchairs, and surgical kits to the landing area.

The U.S. Marine detachment on board, wearing fatigues and carrying M16s, trotted in closely behind the medical personnel. The marines set a roped perimeter to keep deck crews back away from the choppers' landing areas.

Zack had tried cases against the best lawyers in the world, and beaten them, and appeared on national and international television, but nothing he had ever done had struck such fear and excitement in him as he felt now. He wished he could slow his heart down to at least 120 beats per minute. Even that would help some. But his heartbeat quickened.

Rumors swirled on the flight deck that the SEALs had bagged one or more high-profile terrorists. Who could it be? And why the body bags? Someone was dead.

The rumble of helicopter rotors drowned out everything except a voice on the ship's loudspeaker saying, "Stand back! Make room for the choppers to land. Stand back!"

Chopper number one floated to the deck. Chopper two sat down beside it. Both cut their engines.

The choppers sat for what seemed an eternity as gusts of wind from the sea blew across the flight deck. Then Zack saw the medical teams sprinting to chopper one. The master-at-arms and marines rushed to chopper two. The doors on chopper one slid back. Stretchers and gurneys were lifted into the chopper. A few minutes passed.

Corpsmen lifted a mobile stretcher out of the first chopper, pushing an injured SEAL across the deck.

Then another.

Four stretchers altogether rolled out of the helicopter. Corpsmen worked out on the deck to insert IVs into several of the SEALs.

Then another stretcher was lifted out of the chopper. A zipped-up silver body bag lay on the stretcher. Zack's heart pounded with apprehension at the sight of the body bag. It was followed by two more.

When the injured had been removed from chopper one, the marines closed in on chopper two. The large bay door in the rear of the chopper swung open. A Navy SEAL stepped out. Zack recognized Master Chief Matthew Cantor.

The master chief turned and reached his hand into the chopper. A feminine hand reached out from the dark. Zack's heart skipped. A woman's red hair came into view. Then Zack saw the woman's face.

Navy SEALs had rescued Jeanette L'Enfant.

Crushing disappointment left Zack frozen behind the rope that separated the onlookers from the medical, aviation, and military police personnel surrounding the choppers.

Was Diane in one of the three zipped body bags? Had they even found her?

Zack fought tears as a U.S. Navy SEAL captain stepped out of the darkness into the light. Captain Noble's stern face was all business. He turned, reached his bulging biceps into the chopper, and yanked on an arm. Out stumbled an Arab man in a white shirt and white pants.

When the man looked up at the semicircle of naval personnel surrounding him, pandemonium erupted on the flight deck.

Hussein al-Akhma! In the flesh!

Cheers, whistles, and catcalls erupted at the realization that the SEALs had bagged the most notorious terrorist in the world. U.S. Marines surrounded the squirming terrorist, and the flight crew burst into chants of "NAAA-VEEE! NAAA-VEEE! NAAA-VEEE!" then changed to "USA! USA! USA!"

Like adoring fans cheering Hollywood celebrities exiting their limousines at the Oscars, the deck crew cheered wildly as each member of SEAL Team 3 stepped out onto the deck of the *Reagan*, waving and smiling.

The last of the SEALs exited the chopper. When no on else appeared at the door, the deck crew of the *Reagan*, a mighty choir of three hundred, spontaneously broke out into the song that was the all-time favorite of the man for whom their ship was named.

"God bless America . . .

"Land that I love . . ."

Zack stared at the empty helicopter, unable to sing.

"*Stand beside her, and guide her, through the night with the light from above ...*"

There was a stirring inside the chopper.

"*From the mountains ...*"

A familiar face with strawberry-blonde hair.

"*To the prairies...*"

Shannon McGillvery stepped onto the flight deck.

"*To the oceans ... white with foam ...*"

Shannon turned, reached into the chopper. A feminine hand grasped Shannon's, and then a woman with red hair and green eyes stepped onto the deck of the USS *Ronald Reagan*.

Zack jumped over the rope, sprinted past the marines, rushed like a blitzing linebacker attacking a quarterback, and threw his arms around her.

"Thank God!" Those were the only words he could muster.

He looked in Diane's face. He couldn't take his eyes off her. She was painfully thin, almost skeletal, and her body felt feather-light in his arms. But she had never looked more beautiful, especially when her lips curved into a shaky smile. And as they always had, her green eyes held a soul-deep glow as bright as the rising sun cresting the eastern horizon.

She hugged him as tightly as her trembling arms would allow, and smiling through tears, she whispered with him the words of the chorus swelling from the flight deck:

"*God bless America,*

"*My home sweet home.*

"*God bless America.*

"*My home sweet home.*"

"Promise me you'll never, ever leave me again." He drew her closer, and she buried her face in his chest. Locked in time. Transfixed in a sur-realistic moment of joy. A miracle from God.

"Never, ever again," she cried. "I never thought I'd see this day."

"God is good," he whispered.

He felt a hand on his back. Through his tears, he saw Shannon standing next to them, wiping her eyes and smiling.

"Thank you," he tried to say, but his voice was gone.

Shannon stepped closer and wrapped her arms around them both. "Welcome home, Commander. Welcome home."

EPILOGUE

Navy Exchange
Naval Air Station North Island
Coronado, California

Twenty-four hours later

Captain Glen Rudy picked up the copy of the *San Diego Union-Tribune* and beamed with pride. "That's my boy," he said as he read the good news.

NAVY SEALS CAPTURE AL-AKHMA!
RESCUE COLCERNIAN!
From Staff and Wire Reports

Washington—In a stunning development that has rocked the world, President Mack Williams announced today that U.S. Navy SEALs launched a top-secret daring rescue raid that hauled into custody the world's number one terrorist, Hussein al-Akhma.

And in an equally stunning development, the SEALs rescued Navy JAG officer LCDR Diane Colcernian in the same raid.

The president gave special thanks to NCIS Agent Shannon McGillvery for her assistance in gathering the intelligence that helped in solving the case. The president also thanked LCDR Zack Brewer for his assistance.

For national security purposes, the president declined to give information on the location of the raid but did confirm that it involved the men and crew of the San Diego–based aircraft carrier USS *Ronald Reagan* and the Pearl Harbor–based attack submarine USS *North Carolina*.

Four terrorists died in the operation, the president said. There were several American injuries but no fatalities.

In a message to terrorists worldwide, the president said, "You know who you are. You know where we came and got your leader. And now you know that no matter where you go, Uncle Sam is right around the corner, waiting for you with the steel, clenched fist of the United States Navy.

"I suggest that you buy a spaceship and fly to the moon, because on this earth, when you mess around with the United States of America, you can run, but you can't hide."